Thay

Don't you see?

We thought we lost the war.

But in truth, it's still going on.

And if we stop Szass Tam from getting what he wants . . .

Then we win.

The battle is lost, but
the war has just begun.

THE HAUNTED LANDS

Book I
Unclean

Book II
Undead

Book III
Unholy

Anthology
Realms of the Dead
January 2010

Also by Richard Lee Byers

R.A. Salvatore's War of the Spider Queen
Book I
Dissolution

The Year of Rogue Dragons

Book I
The Rage

Book II
The Rite

Book III
The Ruin

Sembia: Gateway to the Realms

The Halls of Stormweather

Shattered Mask

The Priests

Queen of the Depths

The Rogues

The Black Bouquet

FORGOTTEN REALMS

The Haunted Lands | Book III

unholy

Richard Lee Byers

Wizards
OF THE COAST
®

The Haunted Lands, Book III

UNHOLY

©2009 Wizards of the Coast, Inc.

Cover art by Greg Ruth
Map by Rob Lazzaretti
First Printing: February 2009

9 8 7 6 5 4 3 2 1

ISBN: 978-0-7869-5021-8
620-21909740-001-EN

U.S., CANADA,
ASIA, PACIFIC, & LATIN AMERICA
Wizards of the Coast, Inc.
P.O. Box 707
Renton, WA 98057-0707
+1-800-324-6496

EUROPEAN HEADQUARTERS
Hasbro UK Ltd
Caswell Way
Newport, Gwent NP9 0YH
GREAT BRITAIN
Save this address for your records.

Visit our web site at www.wizards.com

For Nigel

Acknowledgments

Thanks to Susan Morris and Phil Athans
for all their help and support.

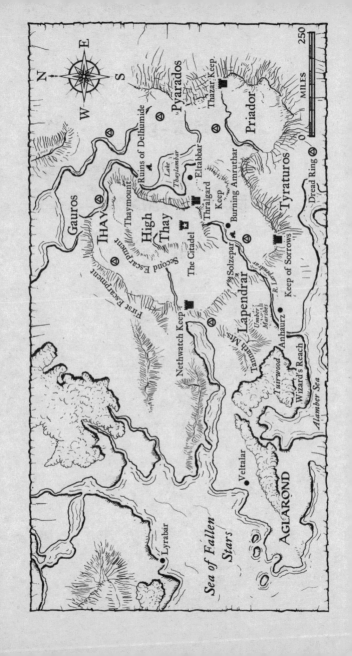

prologue

12–13 Ches, The Year of the Dark Circle (1478 DR)

Khouryn Skulldark patrolled the study. He picked up chairs and returned them to their proper places. Straightened sheaves of papers and arrangements of knickknacks. Shelved books. Checked surfaces for dust and brushed away a spiderweb in a corner of the ceiling. Since he was a dwarf tidying a room sized for humans, many of the tasks required him to climb up on the stool he'd brought along.

As he peered around seeking the spider that had spun the web—he'd catch it and carry it outside if he could—someone chuckled. Khouryn pivoted atop the stool without any fear of falling. Decades of martial training and warfare made him sure of his balance.

But he didn't turn quickly enough to catch the person who'd laughed at him. The doorway was empty.

He scowled. He was a thick-built warrior with a bristling black beard, who never went anywhere without his urgrosh—a weapon combining the deadlier features of a war axe and a spear—strapped across his shoulders. Some folk found it comical to see such a grim-looking fellow fuss over the minutia of housekeeping. But that was because they didn't understand that on campaign, order was everything.

No one lost and mislaid articles like an army on the march, and that included items that could mean the difference between victory and defeat. The only way to guard against such a calamity was through order and organization. And the only way to make sure that one would maintain such habits amid the myriad distractions of the field was to practice them even when the Brotherhood of the Griffon was billeted in pleasant cities like Veltalar.

The night doorkeeper, one of the servants who came with the house, appeared in the entrance to the study. The stooped old fellow looked shaky and ill at ease, and Khouryn wondered for a moment if he was the one who'd snickered. But no, with his hangdog countenance, he scarcely seemed the type.

"Someone outside?" Khouryn asked.

The doorkeeper swallowed. "Yes, sir. Asking for the master."

"Anybody we know?"

"No, sir."

"Well, it's too late for strangers to come calling, and the captain's not here anyway. Tell the whoreson to make an appointment like everybody else."

The doorkeeper swallowed again. "I tried."

"What do you mean, you 'tried'?"

"I wanted to send him away. He wouldn't go. I . . . I don't think I can try again."

"Why in the Hells not?"

"I don't know! I just . . . Please, sir, will you see him?"

Khouryn wondered if the doorkeeper had been tippling. It might explain his strange manner and why he suddenly seemed incapable of doing his job, mindlessly simple though it was.

"All right, show him in," Khouryn growled. Because somebody had to get rid of the intruder. After that, he'd sort the doorkeeper out.

"Thank you!" the elderly human said, almost as though Khouryn had just saved him from a dreadful fate. "Thank you! I'll fetch him at once!" He turned and scurried away. More perplexed than ever, the dwarf climbed off the stool.

The caller strode in a few moments later. Tall and gaunt, with a fair complexion and a mane of wheat blond hair, he had a face his fellow humans might have found handsome if it weren't so haggard and stern. He wore the brigandine and bastard sword of a warrior but also carried a small harp slung across his back.

Khouryn realized the stranger was alone. "Where's the doorman?"

"After he pointed out the proper room," the swordsman said, "I dismissed him." His baritone voice was as rich and expressive as his features were cold and forbidding.

"*You* dismissed a servant of this house."

"Yes. I need to speak to Aoth Fezim immediately. Do you know where he is?"

"Back up a step. Who in the Silverbeard's name are you?"

"Bareris Anskuld. Once upon a time, Aoth and I were comrades."

Khouryn shrugged. "I've never heard of you."

"Is Brightwing here? She'll know me."

Khouryn eyed the human quizzically. "I have heard of Brightwing. Many of the griffons we ride today are from her bloodline. But she's been dead for forty years."

Something altered in Bareris's implacable expression. Some emotion revealed itself. But it disappeared before Khouryn could make out what it was.

"I had hoped," Bareris said, "she had attained longevity in the same way as her rider. But since she isn't here to vouch for me, you'll just have to take my word for it that I am what I say."

Khouryn snorted. "I don't have to do a damn thing except follow my orders. Which say nothing about helping you."

"Please. I've traveled a long way, and my business is urgent."

"Everybody's business is urgent. Get out of here now, and I might let you in to see the captain another time."

Bareris started to chant blaring, rhyming words that pierced the ear like the brassy notes of a glaur horn. That got inside a listener's head and echoed and echoed there.

Khouryn finally understood what ailed the doorkeeper. Bareris had cast a spell on him to addle him and make him compliant, and now the bard or warlock or whatever was trying the same trick again.

But Khouryn was a dwarf, not a weak-willed human. With one fast, smooth motion, he pulled the urgrosh from behind his back, sprang, and cut.

Still chanting, Bareris leaped backward, and the stroke fell short. Khouryn instantly renewed the attack, this time stabbing with the spearhead at the end of his weapon's haft.

Bareris sidestepped, grabbed the urgrosh by the handle, and he and Khouryn struggled for possession of it. Khouryn felt it start to pull free of his opponent's grip. Then Bareris let go with one hand to grab him by the throat.

The human's fingers were icy cold, and the chill spread through Khouryn's body. Meanwhile, Bareris's chant kept reverberating in his head, louder and louder, paining him and shaking his thoughts to pieces.

The combination was too much. Khouryn's legs buckled and dumped him onto the floor. Bareris crouched over him, maintaining his frigid grip on his neck, and stared into his eyes.

"Where's Aoth?" the human demanded, and though he wasn't declaiming words of power anymore, something of the bright, pitiless essence of the chant still infused his voice.

Khouryn still didn't want to tell, but he couldn't help himself. The words just spilled out. "Spending the night with Lady Quamara."

"Who lives where?"

"A mansion on Archer's Parade."

"All right." Bareris straightened up. "Rest now."

Khouryn didn't want to rest, either. He wanted to jump up and attack. But with magic leeching his strength and resolve, it really was easier just to lie still and let his eyelids droop.

As Bareris reached the doorway, a new voice asked, "Was that truly necessary? He's one of Aoth's men."

"We're either in a hurry or we're not."

·· ·· ·· ·· ·· ·· ·· ·· ·· ·· ·· ·· ·· ··

The golden glow of dozens of lilac-scented candles revealed a chamber ideally suited for pleasure. Roast pheasant and beef, white and yellow cheeses, cherries, apricots, ginger cakes, and other viands along with a row of wine and liquor bottles, covered a tabletop. Somewhere—close enough to be heard but not to see or be seen—a trio of musicians played. An open casement admitted fresh air and provided a view of the stars. Mirrors gleamed around a bed heaped with pillows and covered with silks and furs.

It occurred to Aoth that the only discordant note was his own reflection, captured in one of the glasses. For with its squat, swarthy, extensively tattooed frame, coarse features, and weirdly luminous blue eyes, it scarcely looked as if it belonged in the middle of all this luxury.

But he did, curse it. These days, he did. He'd climbed to the top of his chosen profession, and if it was his renown and importance rather than any notable comeliness or grace that made a lovely, sophisticated, half-elf aristocrat like Quamara invite him into her arms, well, who but an idiot would care?

"Is everything all right?" asked the slim, auburn-haired servant, pretty in her own right, who'd conducted him into the room.

Aoth realized he was frowning and put on a smile instead. "Fine."

"My mistress will be with you shortly. May I pour you a drink while you wait?"

"A brandy would be good." He flopped down on a plush velvet chair, and she brought him a golden goblet a moment later.

He lifted the cup, but stopped short of bringing it to his lips. The dark liquid inside was bubbling and fuming. And while he realized it wasn't really happening, he also knew the vision was a warning.

More than ninety years ago, he'd suffered the touch of blue fire, one manifestation of the universal disaster called the Spellplague. Generally, the azure flames killed those they burned. Others, they warped into monstrosities.

Occasionally, however, someone actually benefited from their excruciating embrace, and Aoth belonged to that small and fortunate band. The fire had either entirely stopped him from aging or had slowed the process to a crawl. It had also seared its way inside his eyes and sharpened his vision. He could see in the dark and perceive the invisible. Sometimes he even glimpsed symbolic representations of other people's hidden thoughts and desires or portents of things to come.

The hallucination ended. He lifted his eyes from the poisoned cup to look at the servant. His altered sight didn't provide any supernatural insights into her motives or character, but he did belatedly realize that, even though he'd been calling at this house for nearly a month, he'd never seen her before. Neither her nor any of the other servants he'd glimpsed this evening.

Which meant impostors had usurped the places of the

originals, quite possibly murdering them and Quamara, too, all to set a trap for him.

Something in his expression alerted the servant that he was on to her. Her eyes widened in dismay. She whirled and bolted for the door.

Aoth rattled off an incantation and stretched out his arms. A fan-shaped flare of yellow flame leaped from his fingertips to catch the servant at knee level. She cried out and fell, then floundered around and slapped at the patches of fire leaping on her skirt.

Aoth jumped out of his chair and strode toward her. It would be prudent to get out of the mansion before his enemies made a second attempt to kill him, but maybe he had time for a few questions first.

Or maybe not. A hideous figure heaved itself through the door. Tufts of coarse fur bristled from a body clothed in rolls of rotting flesh, and a pair of horns jutted from the sides of its head. It wheezed and gurgled as it breathed, and it gave off a nauseating stench. It tramped right over the servant as it advanced on Aoth, and the slime dripping from its myriad sores burned and blistered her like his blaze of conjured fire.

The thing was a vaporighu, a kind of demon. Nasty, but Aoth wouldn't have feared it—well, not too much—had the spear that served him as both soldier's weapon and warmage's talisman been ready to hand. But unfortunately, he'd witlessly given it to one of the false servants downstairs, and without it, his magic was weaker than it ought to be.

But at least he'd fought vaporighus before and knew what to expect. As it sucked in a deep breath, he recited words of power, and, when the creature spewed its murky, toxic exhalation, thrust out his hand. Wind blasted the poison back in the brute's simian face.

Alas, it wasn't susceptible to its own venom, but the conjured gale did slam it reeling backward. That bought him time to assail it with darts of emerald light.

Bellowing, snot flying from its mouth, it rushed Aoth, pawlike hands flailing. He dodged out of the way and began another spell as it lumbered past. When it lurched back around to face him, he pierced its torso with a brilliant, crackling bolt of lightning.

Though the attack charred and blackened a patch of gangrenous, blubbery flesh, the vaporighu still didn't falter. It charged again. Aoth dodged and ran for the open casement. It seemed the quickest way to his spear.

A second demon swung itself into the opening. This one was as emaciated as the vaporighu was bloated, and a corona of flame played around its dark blue body and the sword in its right hand. Pale, stunted wings protruded from its shoulder blades.

A vaporighu *and* a palrethee. Wonderful.

But the latter was still taking stock of the situation in the room as it clambered through the window. Aoth pivoted back around toward the vaporighu, bellowed a war cry, and raised his balled fists, just as if he were crazy enough to try fighting such a horror with his bare hands. The vaporighu rushed him, and he flung himself out of the way. It slammed into the palrethee and, tangled, they both toppled out the casement.

Aoth whirled and sprinted the other way.

As he raced down the broad, curving staircase, he heard motion above him and glanced around. Two of the false servants were aiming crossbows at him from the top of the risers. He vaulted the railing, and the weapons clacked.

He landed hard on the floor below the steps, but the quarrels missed him. The assassins tried to reload their weapons, but failed to do it as fast as he could jabber a spell. A booming explosion of fire tore them apart.

Nice to see that his magic could still kill *something*.

Praying his spear was still in the false porter's closet, he raced on through spacious rooms paneled and furnished in gleaming wood harvested from Aglarond's many forests. Then a pair of blood red lions, their fangs and claws longer than those of their terrestrial counterparts, bounded through the doorway ahead of him.

Jarliths. The coursing beasts of the princes of the Abyss. Aoth didn't know whether to laugh or cry. Considering how quickly jarliths could charge and spring, he doubted he'd have time to do either.

But the lions of the Abyss didn't attack. Rather, they glared and growled, and the room darkened as though the flames in the lamps were guttering out. The creatures imagined they could blind him.

Their mistake gave him time to bring his powers to bear. He surrounded himself with a circle of floating blades spinning like the spokes of a wheel.

Evidently hoping to clear the obstacle, a jarlith ran at him and sprang. He leaped backward, and the defense moved with him. The whirling blades tore into the cat's forelegs, stopping it before its claws could reach him. It screamed, recoiled, and the other jarlith charged him. He caught both of them in a rain of conjured hailstones that hammered them to the floor.

But, bloodied though they were, they got up again, and the next moment, the vaporighu and palrethee stalked into the room. It looked as though, tangled together, each had inflicted ugly burns on the other. Still, like the jarliths, they showed no signs of being on the brink of incapacitation.

Despair welled up inside of Aoth, and he struggled to push it down. He raised his hands to cast another spell, quite possibly his last. Then a song, a pounding battle anthem, rang out from somewhere behind the vaporighu and palrethee. The fierce sound of it washed away Aoth's fear and sent fresh vitality tingling through his limbs even as it made the demons falter and peer around in confusion.

Aoth laughed. Though he hadn't heard that voice in nearly a century, he recognized it nonetheless. And he was suddenly confident that he was going to survive this nightmare after all.

Whisked through space by the arcane power of bardic music, Bareris Anskuld appeared near Aoth—but just out of reach of the wheel of swords—with the warmage's spear in his hand. As he tossed the long, heavy spear to his former ally, the semblance of life departed from him like a cloak he'd discarded so it wouldn't hamper the action of his sword arm. Undeath had bleached his skin and hair white as bone and had turned his eyes to ink black pits.

Aoth caught the spear and felt whole again. "Thank you."

Bareris didn't answer. He just kept singing, pivoted toward the enemy, and came on guard. The vaporighu lumbered at him, and one note of his melody banged loud as a thunderclap. The noise ripped chunks of rotten flesh away from the demon's bones.

The palrethee sprang forward, then lost its balance and pitched forward. When it did, Aoth could make out the vague smoky figure who had just plunged his sword into its back. At first, the spectral swordsman resembled a smeared charcoal sketch of Bareris. Then he flowed into a murky semblance of the demon he'd just attacked.

The phantom could only be Mirror. Somehow he too had survived.

The astonishment of it all might have slowed a less-seasoned combatant, but the roar of one of the jarliths recalled Aoth to the business at hand. Time enough to marvel at this unexpected reunion when he and his friends were out of danger.

He leveled the spear, rattled off a tercet, and power groaned through the air. Seven rays of light, each a different color, blazed from the spear like a whip made of rainbows to lash the jarliths.

One jarlith turned to gray, unmoving stone. The other froze and jerked in spasms as arcs of lightning danced across its body. But when the sizzling, popping effect blinked out of existence, it charged.

Aoth braced the butt of the spear against the floor and impaled the cat as it sprang. The impact jolted him but failed to knock him over. The jarlith's razor-sharp talons slashed the air in front of his face, falling short by the length of his little finger. Meanwhile the wheel of blades sliced into its guts again and again and again, and he sent destructive power stored in the spear burning up the shaft and point and into the creature's body.

The jarlith screamed and then went limp. Aoth dumped the carcass on the floor, yanked the spear out of it, and turned to see which of his comrades needed help.

Neither of them.

Mirror and the palrethee were fighting sword against sword. The ghost had changed again, into something approximating the form he'd worn in life, or so his friends believed: the appearance of a thin warrior with a drooping mustache and a melancholy countenance, armored in a hauberk and carrying a targe on his arm. Sometimes he shifted the shield to catch the strokes of the blazing sword. At other moments, the demon's weapon seemed to whiz harmlessly through his insubstantial body.

Meanwhile, he landed cut after cut on the demon, his shadowy blade plunging deep into its starveling torso. Strangely, whenever he did, the palrethee jerked, but Mirror's form wavered, too, like a mirage threatening to flicker out of existence. It was as if he couldn't strike this creature shrouded in hellfire without hurting himself as well. But every time, his shape reasserted itself, reclaiming as much definition as it ever possessed.

Bareris was using his sword, too, but defensively, just to hold the vaporighu back while he attacked with his voice. Aoth could feel the fearful, disorienting power in the keening melody.

It was magic devised to rip a mind to pieces.

The vaporighu dropped to its knees, pawed at its head, and tore away pieces of its own decaying flesh. Bareris gripped his sword with both hands, stepped in, and decapitated the demon.

At virtually the same instant, Mirror plunged his sword into the palrethee's chest, and its halo of flame blinked out. Its already emaciated body shriveled still further, and then it pitched forward onto its face.

Bareris sang a final descending phrase that brought his battle anthem to a conclusion. Aoth took another look around for onrushing demons or slinking crossbowmen. He didn't see any, and his instincts told him the fight was over. All the demons were dead, and any surviving human assassins had fled the scene.

He realized how winded he was and drew a deep breath. "It's good to see the two of you. Better than good. But what are you doing here? Did you know someone was going to try to murder me?"

"No," Mirror said. "We came in search of you because we need your help. It's the mercy of the gods that we tracked you down just in time to aid you. Who wanted you dead, do you know?"

"Nevron, almost certainly." The Spellplague had changed everything, including magic itself. The specialized disciplines that formed the basis of the old Thayan Orders of Red Wizardry had largely passed from the scene. But Aoth was certain that the former zulkir of Conjuration still commanded a veritable army of demons and devils.

"We have to talk," Bareris rapped.

"We will," said Aoth, "of course. But I have to finish figuring out what happened here. There's at least a chance Lady Quamara and some of the servants are still alive."

•• •• •• •• •• •• •• •• •• •• •• •• •• ••

They weren't alive. Aoth and his comrades found the bloody corpses in the wine cellar.

Mirror recited a brief prayer for the fallen and swept his semitransparent hand through a semicircular ritual pass. Millennia ago, he'd been a knight pledged to the service of a beneficent deity, almost a priest, in fact, and he still practiced his devotions despite the seeming paradox of an undead spirit invoking the holy. When he finished, he said, "I'm sorry. Were the two of you in love?"

Aoth sighed. "No. I was her amusement, and she was mine. But she was a sweet lass. She certainly didn't deserve to end like this. Nor did these others, I suppose."

"Now can we talk?" Bareris asked.

"No!" Aoth had half forgotten how the bard's grim singlemindedness used to annoy him. "I have to tell Quamara's brother and the city authorities what happened, and it's probably best that I do it without involving you. I know the undead are accepted in Thay, but Aglarond's a different matter. I'll meet you at my own house as soon as possible."

•• •• •• •• •• •• •• •• •• •• •• •• ••

"As soon as possible" turned out to be dawn, but luckily, unlike many undead, both his rescuers could endure sunlight. He ushered them into his house and study and found Khouryn snoring on the floor with his urgrosh lying beside him.

"He's all right," said Mirror quickly. "He wouldn't tell us where you were, so Bareris forced him. At the time, I didn't approve, but since you were actually in danger, I'll concede that his instincts were on target."

"You're sure Khouryn's all right?" asked Aoth.

"Yes. I can rouse him if you like, but it might be better to let him wake naturally."

"That's what we'll do, then." After all, Mirror had a master healer's knowledge and discernment, even if his chill touch was poisonous except for those moments when he deliberately channeled the power of his unknown god. Aoth bent over, picked up Khouryn with a grunt—dwarf soldiers were damn heavy, considering their stature—and deposited him on a divan.

He then dropped into a chair. "Sit if you like," he said. And they did, although Mirror's shadowy, faceless form seemed to float in the general vicinity of the stool he'd chosen, as opposed to actually resting on it. His shape and the seat's even appeared to interpenetrate a little. "Now tell me what's going on."

Bareris smiled bitterly. "Perhaps the easiest way to explain is to tell a story."

chapter one

Midwinter, The Year of the Dark Circle (1478 DR)

His boots crunching in the snow, Bareris walked the tangled backstreets of Eltabbar and sang a spell under his breath. Over time, the enchantment altered his appearance. Filthy rags mended themselves and turned to shining silk and velvet. His hand-and-a-half sword became a short, slender blade with a jeweled hilt and scabbard, and his brigandine vanished altogether. All the hair on his head disappeared as well, his eyes displayed discernible whites and irises once more, and his canine teeth lengthened into fangs. But it all happened slowly enough that no passerby, glancing casually in his direction, would notice the transformation.

Not that there was anyone to see, no one but Mirror flowing along as an invisible sensation of hollowness and wrongness at his side. Once, no matter how cold the weather, the streets would have teemed with folk celebrating the Midwinter Festival. These days, ordinary people took care to conclude their revelry, or the open-air portion of it, anyway, before the sun went down. They feared to encounter their masters when the latter were in a playful mood.

Bareris and Mirror emerged from a twisting lane too narrow to accommodate a wagon onto a broader, straighter thoroughfare. On the far side of an arching bridge spanning a frozen canal, their destination glowed with silvery phosphorescence. Sleighs, coaches, and litters waited in line to deposit their passengers under the porte cochere of a stone house with turrets at the four corners of the peaked slate roof. A luminous, runic emblem inlaid above the door, its shape and color in constant flux, revealed that at one time, the mansion had belonged to the extinct Order of Transmutation.

"I don't much like this," Mirror murmured. It was the first time he'd spoken in three days. Evidently he was coming out of his latest bout of ghostly disorientation or whatever it was, just in time to fret.

"My disguise will hold up," Bareris said. "You just remain as near to imperceptible as you can get."

"Even if they don't recognize us, there are plenty of other things that can go wrong."

"I don't care. This Muthoth bastard is one of Sylora Salm's chief deputies. There's a fair chance she'll put in an appearance. And even if she doesn't, there'll be other people to kill." He strode toward the bridge and felt Mirror glide along in his wake.

As Bareris spoke to one of the slaves minding the entryway, he infused his voice with magic. The enchantment persuaded the lackey that he saw an invitation in the newcomer's empty hand, and he and a fellow servant swung open the tall, arched double doors.

On the other side was a high-ceilinged marble foyer with several doorways opening off it. Bareris assumed that newly arrived guests were supposed to pass through the one directly opposite the entrance, where an usher waited to thump his staff on the floor and announce them.

But, disguised though he was, Bareris didn't want all eyes drawn to him or to have his false name and fraudulent title shouted aloud to give every listener the opportunity to reflect that he'd never heard of such a person. He led Mirror into one of the other doorways. If this structure was like other Thayan mansions of his experience, a series of interconnecting rooms and passages should provide a less conspicuous means of access to Muthoth's great hall.

Some of the lesser chambers were occupied. In one, a withered husk of a creature robed in red, still the color reserved for the realm's most powerful wizards, sat talking with another malodorous corpse wearing the silver skull-and-crossed-swords badge of an order of undead knights. In another, the hulking, red-eyed undead called boneclaws, Muthoth's household guards of choice, gripped naked prisoners in their enormous, jointed talons. Several guests hovered around the captives, shouting in their ears, pinching them, or jabbing at their eyes with stiffened fingers. Bareris gathered that the object of the game was to make a victim flinch and gash himself against a boneclaw's razor-sharp fingers, and that this was a sport on which the players had decided to gamble.

One captive had already severed an artery, and his lifeless body sprawled discarded on the floor. The remaining ones wept and pleaded, with blood trickling down their torsos and legs. A lithe female vampire knelt, licked gore off a taut, quivering stomach, and won a silver coin thereby.

Bareris could feel Mirror's wrath building as if the air at his side were growing colder and colder. "No," he whispered. "We didn't come here to rescue anyone."

"Perhaps we should have."

"But we didn't, and without a plan, we'd surely fail. Look, we've both been spared all these years for a reason; isn't that what you keep telling me? So we can't throw ourselves away. We have to pick our battles and fight intelligently."

"Move on, then. I don't promise to hold back if I watch any more of this."

Another two dozen paces brought them to a doorway opening on the great hall. An orchestra on a dais along the far wall played a pavane, and Bareris felt the old familiar urge, still alive in him when so much else had withered, to immerse himself in the music. He shook it off and surveyed the company instead.

He spotted a reasonable number of living revelers, mostly clad in red, proof that even after a century, Szass Tam hadn't *completely* transfigured the aristocracy. But the majority of celebrants were undead, shadowy specters, vampires with alabaster skin and chatoyant eyes, crumbling corpses, fleshless skeletons, and things so misshapen and grotesque they bewildered the eye, perhaps experiments created in the laboratories of the necromancers but granted positions of authority even so.

Good host that he evidently was, Muthoth had provided refreshments for all his guests. Some of the trestle tables proffered food and drink fit for mortals, but prisoners lay chained spreadeagled across others for the undead to devour.

A specter slid his fingers into a boy's face. The child screamed loud enough to drown out the orchestra as he grew old and died in a matter of moments. An undead ogre, its rotting body armored or perhaps simply held together by a framework of black iron rings and bands, ripped off a woman's head, then reached up inside her neck to claw out meat and stuff it in his mouth. More thralls waited caged in the corner to replenish the buffet.

Bareris procured a goblet of blood and pretended to sip from it as he sauntered around, eavesdropping, hoping to hear something tonight that would enable him to strike a blow against Szass Tam's government tomorrow. He might as well. It wasn't time to start murdering people yet. That would come later, when the revel grew wilder, and excitement and overindulgence left the attendees vulnerable. When more of them wandered from the great hall to other portions of the mansion to pursue intimate pleasures in private, purge themselves, or pass out.

The usher at the primary doorway knocked the butt of his staff on the floor. "Sylora Salm, tharchion of Eltabbar!" Bareris turned and bowed like all the other gentlemen, then lifted his eyes to inspect this foe he'd never seen before.

His first thought was that she was very like Dmitra Flass, who'd held the same office one hundred years before, a perfect example of a great Thayan lady. She was tall and slender, without a trace of hair on her head, and wore a shimmering scarlet gown that was a triumph of the dressmaker's art. Her ivory complexion was flawless, her smile deceptively warm, and a quick intelligence shined in her bright green eyes.

Perhaps she reflected Szass Tam's ideal of womanhood. Maybe the lich was genuinely fond of her, as supposedly had been the case with Dmitra. Bareris hoped so. He wanted to believe Szass Tam might actually feel at least a little bereft when she died.

And it should be possible to kill her, her sorcery and bodyguards notwithstanding. The gossips said she possessed a lickerish nature and enjoyed the attentions of vampires. He was disguised as such a creature and could exploit his bardic skills to seduce and beguile. When the opportunity presented itself, he'd lure her away to some private spot, then strike her down before she realized anything was amiss.

Or so he thought until Muthoth hurried out of the crowd to greet the new arrival.

His skinny frame robed in crimson, Sylora's lieutenant had clearly become a vampire at some point during the past century, but it didn't matter. Bareris still recognized the sharp, arrogant features, a face made to sneer and spit, and even if he hadn't, there was no mistaking the maimed right hand with its missing fingers.

"Stop staring!" Mirror whispered.

The phantom was right. Bareris mustn't make himself conspicuous. With an effort, he turned away.

"What's wrong?" asked Mirror, barely visible as little more than a man-sized column of blur and ache.

"I told you," Bareris said, "about the necromancers who took Tammith to Xingax. How I caught up with them on the trail, but they wouldn't give her back to me."

"Yes."

"Well, this Muthoth is one of them. I never knew his name or that he was still around. But now that I do, he's going to pay."

"Killing Sylora Salm would better serve the cause."

"To the Abyss with 'the cause.' Muthoth is our target, and he alone."

Tammith Iltazyarra had been Bareris's first and only love. And if Muthoth and his pudgy, timid partner had just taken the princely bribe he'd offered and set her free, everything would have been different. Xingax never would have transformed her into a vampire, and Tsagoth wouldn't have destroyed her. She and Bareris would have shared a long, joyful mortal life together.

Bitter though it was, he'd resigned himself that he almost certainly would never slay Szass Tam, the overlord who controlled all his lesser enemies and was the ultimate source of all his sorrows. Despite decades of scheming, he'd never even managed to kill Tsagoth. But by every melody ever sung, every note ever played, he could take revenge on Muthoth, and he would.

But it wouldn't prove to be easy. As the revelers danced to song after song, and one by one, the prisoners shrieked, thrashed, and died, Muthoth remained at the heart of the festivities. He seemed to be enjoying the celebration too much, or to be too concerned with the obligations of hospitality, for even the persuasions of a bard to draw him away.

Finally the slaves stopped setting out fresh food, living or otherwise, and the weary musicians switched to tunes less suitable for dancing. Taking the hint, or simply sensing the imminence of sunrise, the guests began to depart.

"What now?" Mirror asked.

"We hide," Bareris answered.

They stalked back into the lesser rooms. Shredded corpses, the occasional dismembered limb, and pools and spatters of blood now defaced the gorgeous carpets and handsome furnishings, and in some spaces, slaves had already made a start at trying to clean up the mess.

But the cozy room in which the undead sorcerer and knight had sat and chatted was empty. Mirror faded until he was entirely invisible once more. Bareris sang a spell under his breath to achieve the same effect.

Then they waited for the rest of the revelers to leave and the house to settle down. Occasionally slaves trudged or boneclaws prowled past them, but without so much as a suspicious glance in their direction. Finally Bareris said, "It's time to move."

"Where?" Mirror asked.

"Whatever Muthoth sleeps in, it's a reasonable guess that he keeps it in a bedchamber upstairs."

Still invisible, they made their way to a marble staircase. As they climbed, Bareris felt feverish with eagerness.

At the top of the steps, archways led in three directions. From what he could see, it appeared to Bareris that Muthoth had furnished the rooms directly opposite the stairs with grander, more ostentatious pieces than those visible to the right and left. Which suggested that those chambers comprised his personal suite.

The intruders headed into the more luxurious area and soon entered a large, square room. Bareris just had time to notice that it was strangely empty compared to the two they'd just traversed when the air flared fiery yellow. His head throbbed, reacting to the sudden release of arcane energy.

Looking like a reflection of himself cast in cloudy, rippling water, Mirror popped into view. Bareris looked down at his hands and saw that he was visible, too, and that the charm that had given him the appearance of a vampiric nobleman had dissolved.

Concealed doors flew open. Four boneclaws sprang from the closets in which they'd waited with the mindless patience of lesser undead for someone to come along and trigger this particular trap.

Bareris supposed he'd stepped on a rigged floorboard, an unseen rune, or something similar. He tried to tell Mirror to engage the two boneclaws on the right, but found he had no voice. The blaze of magic he'd unwittingly evoked had both deprived him of his invisibility and shrouded the room in an enchantment of silence.

As a defense, it made sense. Red Wizards had reason to fear rivals in their own hierarchy as much or more than any other foe, and quiet deprived a mage of the greater part of his magic.

As it divested a bard of every last bit of his. Bareris would have to rely on his sword.

Mirror, however, had other options. He raised his blade above his head, and it gave off a golden glow like sunlight. He'd summoned the divine light that was anathema to undead, anathema in theory even to Bareris and himself, but somehow he managed to wield it without annihilating himself or hurting his comrade.

One of the boneclaws on the right cringed, unable to continue its advance. The others kept charging forward. It was about as good a result as Mirror could expect, given that he was trying to evoke the sacred on the home ground of a vampiric necromancer.

Bareris lunged at the two boneclaws on the left. They snatched for him, and their already enormous talons shot out, stretching instantaneously to more than twice their normal length. They likely would have speared a less canny opponent, but he'd seen the trick before. He dived underneath the attack, plunged on between the two crimson-eyed creatures, whirled, and hacked at the back of a knee.

The boneclaw he'd cut pitched forward, but the other, startlingly quick for something so large, was already whirling around. It raked with both hands, talons elongating into blades like scythes, filling the space between itself and its foe.

Bareris leaped backward. It was the only way to avoid being sliced and impaled. He sensed the wall behind him and realized he wouldn't be able to retreat again.

The boneclaw scrambled after him, and he instantly sprang to meet it. The move surprised it, threw off its aim, and when it slashed downward, the attack arrived harmlessly behind him. He cut into its midsection and tore away chunks of wormy, desiccated muscle and gut.

The boneclaw toppled. Glimpsing motion from the corner of his eye, Bareris spun. The creature he'd merely crippled had come crawling after him. Its talons shot out at him, and he wrenched himself out of the way. Then Mirror, who currently resembled an undersized boneclaw himself, rushed in on the creature's flank and sheared into its neck. Its body jerked into rigidity, then collapsed.

Bareris glanced around, making certain the ghost had destroyed the other two boneclaws before coming to his aid. He had, but new foes appeared in the doorway leading deeper into the apartments: another pair of boneclaws and Muthoth himself, clad in a nightshirt but with a jet black staff clasped in his intact hand and several amulets dangling around his neck. Apparently Bareris had also activated an alarm that roused the vampire from his rest.

The fresh boneclaws advanced. Muthoth stayed behind them in the doorway and surveyed the situation. Then he swirled his maimed hand through a serpentine mystic pass, and the unnatural silence ended. Bareris could hear the slap of the boneclaws' feet on the floor, and the minute creak of their leathery sinews.

He realized Muthoth had scrutinized him, observed that

he looked like a warrior, not a mage, and drawn the erroneous conclusion that he couldn't work magic. The necromancer thought to dispel the unnatural quiet and so regain the use of his own spells.

If he didn't realize Bareris was a bard, that meant he didn't know him at all, didn't even recognize the man whose life he'd devastated. For some reason, the thought was maddening.

Muthoth chanted, and a carrion stench filled the air. Bareris stepped back, leaving Mirror to engage both boneclaws, and quickly sang his own charm of silence, each descending note softer than the one before. Muthoth's voice cut off abruptly, leaving his incantation unfinished and the spell wasted. The lustrous eyes in his pale face widened in surprise.

Bareris ran forward, trying to maneuver around the boneclaw on his left. Despite Mirror's efforts to hold its attention, it pivoted and slashed at him, and though he dodged, one of its talons sheared through his ribs. The stroke would have killed a living man, but he was undead and enraged and scarcely broke stride.

Muthoth retreated before him, back into the next room. As he did so, he thrust out his staff, no doubt a repository of magic he could employ even in the absence of sound. Shadows leaped and whirled, and suddenly Bareris felt numb and confused, his hatred dulled and meaningless.

Muthoth was trying to control his mind. Bareris forced himself to take another racing stride and another after that, clinging to anger and purpose, and the dazed, bewildered feeling fell away.

The vampire pressed his mutilated hand to an iron amulet, and a gray, vaporous thing with a lunatic's twitching face hurtled out of it. Bareris sidestepped the spirit's frenzied, scrabbling attack and cut through the middle of it. It broke into floating, vile-smelling wisps.

He closed the distance to Muthoth. Cut to the head. The vampire dropped under the stroke as his body reshaped itself, flowing from human form into the guise of a huge, black wolf.

Muthoth sprang. His forepaws hit Bareris in the chest and knocked him onto his back. Eyes blazing, icy foam flying from his muzzle, the vampire lunged to seize his adversary's throat in his fangs.

Bareris just managed to interpose his forearm, and Muthoth's jaws clamped shut on it instead. The lupine teeth cut deep, and Muthoth jerked his head back and forth. Bareris felt the jolting agony as the limb started to tear apart.

His sword was too long to use in such close quarters. He let go of it, drew up his leg, and groped for the secondary weapon he kept tucked in his boot. He drew forth the hawthorn stake and drove it into Muthoth's body.

The vampire flopped down on top of him and lay motionless. Evidently Bareris had pierced the heart.

He rolled Muthoth off him and clambered to his feet. He felt the hot itch as his wounds began to heal. Peering back the way he'd come, he saw that Mirror had already destroyed one boneclaw and, by the looks of it, was about to dispatch the other.

Bareris stooped, gripped Muthoth by the throat, and dragged him farther into the suite, until they passed beyond the magical silence. By that time, the vampire had reverted to human shape, give or take pointed ears positioned too high on his head and a few patches of fur.

Bareris knelt down, positioning his face in front of Muthoth's unblinking eyes. "Do you know me now?" he asked. "I'm Bareris Anskuld, the bard who overtook you on the way to Delhumide. And now I'm going to destroy you as you destroyed me."

He raised his sword and struck Muthoth's head off. Then he watched the two pieces of the necromancer's body rot and realized he didn't feel anything at all.

•• •• •• •• •• •• •• •• •• •• •• ••

Mirror found Bareris standing over Muthoth's crumbling, stinking remains. "Well done," he said.

Bareris frowned. "We fought this battle in silence. With luck, no one else knows it happened. Maybe we have time to look around a little."

"And carry away something useful," Mirror said. "Let's do it."

Bareris hung Muthoth's amulets around his own neck and picked up his black, gleaming staff. Then they prowled farther into the vampire's apartments.

They soon came to a portrait of a Red Wizard whose cool, crafty eyes and thin-lipped, resolute mouth seemed a mismatch with a rather weak chin. And when they saw the same face depicted again in a painting above the fireplace in a library, Bareris said, "I know where we are."

"What do you mean?" Mirror asked.

"A hundred years ago, this was more than a chapterhouse of the Order of Transmutation. It was the residence of Druxus Rhym himself, or one of them, anyway. I never knew the man, but when I was a boy, I saw him once or twice, riding in a procession, and that's him."

Mirror, of course, had never known Druxus Rhym. He'd been a broken, essentially mindless thing wandering the Sunrise Mountains when Druxus had been alive. But he'd heard his comrades speak of the zulkir whom Szass Tam had assassinated at the very start of the lich's long campaign to become sole ruler of Thay.

"If these books belonged to an archmage," he said, "there may be some powerful grimoires here."

"Let's hope I have the wit to recognize them," Bareris said. "You stand watch while I flip through them." He pulled a volume from a shelf.

And several books later, he whispered, "By the silver harp!"

chapter two

13 Ches, The Year of the Dark Circle (1478 DR)

Well?" demanded Aoth. "Don't stop now. What did you find?" Across the study, Khouryn mumbled and rolled over in his sleep.

"This," Bareris replied. He opened the pouch strapped to his belt and brought out a small volume bound in crimson. It didn't look old or in any way special, nor could Aoth feel any arcane power smoldering inside it.

"All right," said Aoth. "Do you expect me to sit and read the cursed thing, or are you going to tell me what's in it?"

"I'll tell you," Bareris said. "It's just . . . it's strange, crazy even, and I need you to understand and believe."

Aoth frowned in perplexity. Never before had he seen his old friend fumble for words. Even after despair and the lust for vengeance ruined him, Bareris had retained the facile tongue of a bard.

"Just spit it out. After all the weird and terrible things the three of us have survived together, of course I'll believe you."

"Very well. Do you remember the question Malark always used to ask?"

Aoth felt a pang of anger at the thought of the spymaster and false friend who'd betrayed the southern cause. "Why did Szass Tam murder Druxus Rhym, his own ally on the Council?"

"Yes. After reading this book, I finally know."

"That's nice, I suppose, but does it really matter at this late date, more than ninety years after the lich pushed us and the rest of his opponents out of Thay?"

"It matters. Do you also recall the story Quickstrike the grave-crawler told me?"

For a moment, Aoth had no idea what Bareris was talking about, and even when he did remember, the question seemed so bizarre that he wondered if decades of loneliness, anguish, and undeath had finally driven his friend completely mad.

"Dimly. Thousands of years ago, there was a kingdom in the Sunrise Mountains. Its greatest wizard and hero was a fellow named . . . something about digging . . ."

"Fastrin the Delver."

"Right. Somebody stole something from this Fastrin, and the loss deranged him. He slaughtered his own people and even mangled the psyches of their ghosts—Mirror here was one such victim—and when he'd destroyed the realm, he committed suicide."

"That's right," Mirror said, "and now I can add to the tale. Recent events have stimulated my memory, even though much is still lost to me.

"My friend Fastrin spent much of his time exploring ancient ruins," the ghost continued, "and his stolen treasure was an article he had unearthed on one such expedition: a book from the dawn of time. He claimed it contained 'the death of the world,' and after it disappeared, he was terrified the thief would unleash the power inside it. In his frenzy, he saw only one solution: kill everyone, just to be sure of getting anybody who'd learned the secret, and strip our spirits of reason and memory."

"It's a sad story," said Aoth, "and I don't mean to sound indifferent to your misfortune, but how can it possibly be relevant to anything that's going on today? You're not going to tell me that this volume you brought me is Fastrin's book? If that thing is thousands of years old, I'll eat it with pickle relish!"

"It isn't," Bareris said. "Two months ago, we stumbled across a collection of books that belonged to Druxus Rhym. This is one of them, written by Druxus himself. It's a series of scholarly notes and musings on a different volume, which, unfortunately, was missing."

Aoth shook his head. "Not the same book Fastrin found?"

"Yes," Bareris said, "with Fastrin's own notes appended to the back of it. Somehow it survived to the present day and fell into Druxus's hands. He doesn't say how, and we'll likely never know."

"What does he say?"

"The original book contains instructions for destroying everything. All life. The land, sea, and sky. The gods themselves."

Aoth snorted. "That sounds useful."

"It could be, because you wouldn't just obliterate them. You'd change them from essence to the pure potential that existed before anything else, even time and space. And then you—"

"I take it that the ritual contains a cheat that allows 'you' to survive unharmed amid all the annihilation."

"Yes, your soul, at least, if not your body. And then you could seize all that potential and build a new cosmos exactly to your liking, with yourself as master."

"Ah! And here I thought we were discussing something silly."

Bareris scowled. "Druxus saw the ritual as the greatest imaginable work of transmutation, and for that reason, it intrigued him.

But he also believed the practical difficulties were insurmountable, and that no wizard could ever perform the experiment even if he was crazy enough to want to try. He regarded the treatise as purely theoretical, an intellectual game, one that Szass Tam too might find interesting. And so, at the end, his notes indicate his intention to pass the book along to the necromancer."

"And you think Szass Tam read it and decided that he wanted to work the magic."

"Yes. It explains things that have always puzzled us. Why did Szass Tam finally strike for supreme authority in Thay after sharing power with his fellow zulkirs for centuries? Because he needed a completely free hand to make the realm over into a place where his 'Great Work' would be possible. Why did he kill Druxus? Because no one could know of his intent. Nobody would serve him knowing he plans to murder us all in the end."

"I suppose not. But still, this is all just speculation on your part."

"No. In his notes, Druxus tells us what the magic requires. It requires what Szass Tam has spent the last century creating. Hordes of undead and wizards mindbound to a single master so they can perform ritual tasks in concert even when miles apart. Huge circular monuments to raise the necessary power."

"You're talking about those new fortresses I've heard about."

"Yes. Dread Rings, the people call them. Mirror and I have seen a couple, and they look *exactly* like this." Bareris opened the book and held it out for Aoth to examine. On the exposed pages, Druxus had sketched a black, circular structure with spires rising above the walls in a jagged, asymmetrical pattern.

Aoth realized that at some point and for some reason, the discussion had stopped seeming as ludicrous as it should. He swallowed away a dryness in his throat. "But still, the fundamental idea . . . it's just not possible."

"Fastrin," Mirror said, "was as great a mage as any you have known. And he took this threat so seriously that it unhinged him and drove him to commit unspeakable crimes."

"I don't say the untried magic would achieve the promised result," Bareris said. "I have no way of knowing. Even if I got a look at Fastrin's book itself, I don't have the understanding of wizardry it would take to evaluate the contents. But based on what Druxus wrote and Szass Tam's manifest interest, I do believe the rite will do *something*. If it merely unleashes another cataclysm like the Spellplague, that's bad enough, wouldn't you say?"

"I guess," said Aoth. "But it's hard to believe that even Szass Tam would dare so reckless a gamble."

"Hard, perhaps, but impossible? You knew him, first as one of your masters and then as your enemy. You have experience of his limitless self-assurance, the grandiosity of his vision, and his ruthlessness. And I tell you again: *he's built the rings*. The last one was nearly finished when Mirror and I slipped out of Thay. It may be completed by now."

"All right. But why did you seek me out?"

Bareris frowned. "Surely it's obvious. The only way to stop Szass Tam is by force of arms, and you have an army. Even hiding in Thay, Mirror and I heard tales of your campaigns."

"What I have is a mercenary company, and I like to think it's the finest in the East. But do you think it could stop Szass Tam from doing anything he wants when all the council's legions failed before?"

Mirror said, "We have to try."

"No," Aoth said, "I don't. I won't lead the Brotherhood into certain ruin. I worked too hard to build it, and the men deserve better."

"If the whole world burns—"

"But you don't know that it will. All you have is a few jottings and a cartload of conjecture. Even if you're right about Szass Tam's intentions, maybe this mad scheme won't accomplish anything.

Or maybe somebody with a realistic hope of stopping it will intervene."

"Don't you see," Bareris said, "we thought we lost the war. But in truth, it's still going on, and if we stop Szass Tam from getting what he wants, then we win."

Meaning, you finally achieve a measure of revenge, thought Aoth. Whatever Szass Tam's planning, that's all you truly care about.

"I'm sorry," he said aloud. "The Brotherhood of the Griffon already has a contract for the coming season. Now, it goes without saying that you're welcome to stay here as long as you like . . ."

    •• •• •• •• •• •• •• •• •• •• •• •• ••

It took a while longer to bring the conversation to an end. But finally, by pleading fatigue and promising to continue arguing later, Aoth managed it. He installed Bareris and Mirror in a vacant room and then retired to his own bedchamber.

Only to find that, even though he truly was tired, sleep eluded him. After tossing and turning for a time, he rose, dressed, and tramped out to the stable behind the house in the hope that flying would relax him.

When he opened the door, Jet sprang down from the hayloft in which he'd taken up residence. The griffon's plumage and fur were both black as midnight. Even in the shadowy interior of the building, his scarlet eyes glittered in his aquiline head.

Jet screeched. "You fought a battle without me!"

Aoth didn't bother asking how his familiar knew. He could have smelled the scent of battle on his person or glimpsed a memory of the recent combat across the psychic link they shared.

"It wasn't by choice." He lifted Jet's saddle off its rack and slung it over his back. "Would you condescend to try a less violent form of exercise?"

Jet tossed his head. "Better than nothing, I suppose."

The morning sun was bright, but the air was cold. The seasons were just turning, and winter hadn't wholly surrendered its grip. Aoth activated the enchantment bound in one of his tattoos, and warmth flowed through his body. He then surveyed the clouds, looking, as was his unthinking habit, for signs of how and when the weather meant to change.

"I think we've seen the last of the snow," said Jet.

Aoth grunted.

"You're in a cheery mood."

"The zulkirs' assassins killed Quamara to clear a path to me."

"That's annoying."

"That's one word for it. Then two old friends turned up just in time to save my life. It turned out they'd come to ask for my help, and I said no."

Jet beat his sable wings and climbed higher. "I'm not surprised. You always say no to me."

"Because you always ask to eat horses that don't belong to us. But Bareris and Mirror—" His words caught in his throat as death appeared in the east.

He thought immediately of the curtains of blue fire the Spell-plague had sent sweeping through the land, but this was different and worse. This force was invisible, but he could tell from the swath of devastation that it stretched at least as far as the eye could see. And it left nothing but dust in its wake.

The brown, snow-capped peaks of the Tannath Mountains crumbled. The countless trees of the Yuirwood bowed as a great wind caught them and stripped them of their leaves, and then they dissolved. To the north, the advancing line of obliteration drank the waters of the Sea of Dlurg. The water that had yet to disappear surged as though eager to meet its end.

But strangely, all the annihilation happened quietly. The raging winds didn't tumble Jet across the sky, nor did Aoth choke on billowing dust. Because, he realized, this wasn't really happening. Not yet.

"What's the matter?" asked Jet.

"Take a look." Employing their mental link, Aoth allowed his mount to see what he was seeing.

Just in time to witness the destruction of Veltalar. The decaying slums of the old city, the wide boulevards and lofty towers of the new, and the green stone Palace of the Simbul itself broke apart with as little fuss as the mountains and forest had.

A second wave of destruction swept out of the east, cutting deeper into the ground that the first one had already scoured to bedrock. Aoth thought of concentric ripples spreading out from a pebble tossed in a pond, and then the vision ended as suddenly as it began.

"Wind and sky!" said Jet. It was the first time that Aoth had ever heard him sound shaken. "What was that?"

"The call to arms," said Aoth. "Damn it to the deepest Hell!"

•• •• •• •• •• •• •• •• •• •• •• •• •• •• ••

Some of the members of the Simbarch Council were human; some, slender elves with pointed ears, vivid green eyes, and a lack of facial hair; and some, mixtures of the two. All were proud aristocrats and accomplished spellcasters, which didn't keep them from eyeing a pair of undead strangers with a certain wariness. They tried to hide it, but every bard learned to size up an audience.

One of the elves, her long tresses shimmering black and her skin nearly as white as Bareris's own, gave Aoth a cool stare. "Captain, when you asked for a meeting, we didn't realize you intended to bring such . . . unconventional companions along with you."

"I know, Lady Seriadne," Aoth replied, "just as I know that

here in Aglarond, you mistrust the undead. To tell you the truth, my life has given me abundant reason to mistrust most of them myself. But Bareris Anskuld and Mirror are old comrades of mine. I vouch for them, and you need to hear them. They've come to warn us all of a terrible danger."

"All right," said a human with a neatly trimmed gray goatee, who wore mystic sigils subtly incorporated into the complex beadwork pattern adorning his doublet. "Let's hear it."

Peering up at the simbarchs seated along the two tiers of their gleaming oak dais, Bareris told his tale with all the eloquence he could muster; but even so, skepticism congealed in every face. He felt a desperate urge to use magic to sway his listeners, but he knew the attempt could only lead to disaster. It was inconceivable that fifteen strong-willed folk wise in the ways of sorcery would all succumb to his spell, and those who retained clear heads would likely realize what he'd tried to do.

Maybe, he thought, Aoth can convince them. He's a living man with a good reputation, and they evidently trust him. They wouldn't have hired him otherwise.

But in fact, the warmage's testimony didn't help. Indeed, when he described the vision that had overtaken him while he was flying above the city, it paradoxically seemed to reinforce the simbarchs' judgment that Bareris's story was nonsense. Bareris gathered that Aoth had never before told them about his augmented sight and, glowing eyes or no, it seemed suspicious that he claimed such a miraculous ability only now, when necessary to buttress his argument.

"So that's how it is," Aoth finished. The flat note in his voice revealed that he, too, realized they'd failed to convince. "Bareris and Mirror asked me to commit the Brotherhood of the Griffon to their cause, but we all know that one company of sellswords has no hope of stopping Szass Tam's scheme. The armed might of Aglarond, however, is a different matter."

The mage with the gray beard—whose name, Bareris gathered, was Ertrel—made a spitting sound. "When the lich made himself sole ruler of Thay, the East trembled. Everyone expected him to launch wars of conquest against his neighbors. But it never happened. Instead, he contented himself with making his own people's lives miserable and with building gigantic monuments to himself, and thank Sune for it. I can't think of anything stupider than provoking him now that he's finally lost interest in plaguing us."

"Lord Ertrel," said Bareris, "with respect, I explained: those 'monuments' are the structures Druxus Rhym sketched in the book."

"Yes," Ertrel said, "you did. But I fancy I'm a reasonably learned mage, and the ideas in your odd little book seem like so much gibberish to me."

Other simbarchs murmured in agreement.

"You just skimmed a few lines," Bareris said, "while you listened to me talk at the same time. Perhaps if you truly studied the volume, you'd feel differently."

Ertrel shrugged. "I doubt it."

"My lords," said Aoth, "I share your skepticism that any mortal, or any creature born mortal, could bring about the end of all things. It's a ridiculous notion on the face of it. But unlike you, I *know* Szass Tam—"

"Knew him a hundred years ago, you mean," another human simbarch interjected.

"—and I promise you, he's the one person in Faerûn arrogant and selfish enough to try, if he believed he'd emerge from the holocaust greater than the greatest god. And even if his experiment fails utterly, what will that matter to us if it kills us all in the process?"

"As you prophesy it will," Seriadne purred.

"Yes. I told you: I saw it happen."

"That must have been quite a spectacle."

Aoth took a deep breath. "You don't believe me?"

"Here's what I believe: The rivals Szass Tam drove out of Thay settled in the Wizard's Reach, territory that rightfully belongs to Aglarond. We of the council think it's time to reclaim it and have hired you to help us.

"But perhaps," the black-haired elf continued, "we should have looked elsewhere for additional swords and spears. Because you too are a Thayan in exile, aren't you, Captain? In fact, if the stories are true, the zulkirs would never even have reached their new home if you and Bareris Anskuld here hadn't played a crucial role in defeating the armada that pursued them over the sea."

"Our old loyalties," said Aoth, "have nothing to do with the current situation. We both left the service of the zulkirs a long time ago."

"But what if you're feeling nostalgic," Seriadne asked, "or the zulkirs simply promised you more gold than we did? Then you might concoct a tale to convince us to change our plans. If it worked, it would be an elegant solution. After we smashed our army to pieces against the rock that is Thay, we wouldn't be able to mount an invasion of the Reach for a good long while."

"I give you my word," said Aoth, "it's not like that."

"I hope not," Ertrel said. "As sellswords go—which isn't far in this regard—you have a reputation for honest dealing. Can we take it, then, that you still intend to abide by the pledge you gave us?"

Aoth hesitated, but only for a heartbeat. "Yes, my lord."

"You'll go where we send you and fight those we tell you to fight?"

"Yes, my lord."

"Then however you came by these absurd worries, put them aside. We simbarchs give you our word: no wizard could raise the kind of power you describe, and if Szass Tam truly imagines otherwise, we should all rejoice that the Terror of the East has gone senile."

chapter three

13 Ches–4 Tarsakh, The Year of the Dark Circle (1478 DR)

Bareris shrouded himself, Aoth, and Mirror in invisibility before they slipped from the house. Unfortunately, that didn't stop the watchers from shooting crossbows at them. Evidently, mindful of Aoth's considerable reputation as a warmage, the simbarchs had equipped their agents with charms that allowed them to see the invisible.

Aoth shifted his truesilver targe, and a quarrel glanced off it. Bareris sidestepped with preternatural quickness, and another bolt streaked past him. The bard drew breath, and Aoth saw the lethal intent in the set of his pallid features.

"Don't kill them!" said Aoth.

Bareris shrugged, then sang a melody soft and mild as any lullaby. The men in the shadows of the neighboring house collapsed. One snored.

Currently resembling a smeared caricature of Aoth wrought in glimmering smoke, Mirror bounded to the fallen spies. "One ran," he said and rose into the air, no doubt to hunt the man like a hawk seeking earthbound prey.

Bareris and Aoth trotted on toward the stable. "There was no need to kill them," said Aoth. "I knew you could stop them without it."

"If that is the way you prefer it, fine. But the fellow Mirror is running down won't be so lucky."

Smelling of feathers and fur, Jet waited beside his tack. "So I'm supposed to carry you and that, too," the griffon said.

"If you will," Bareris said. To Aoth's surprise, his friend's voice momentarily conveyed a hint of warmth or, conceivably, wistfulness. "I haven't flown on griffon-back in a long while."

Jet grunted. "Just make sure your touch doesn't poison me."

Aoth saddled his familiar with the unthinking deftness of long practice. He swung himself onto the griffon's back, Bareris mounted up behind him, and then Jet sprang forward, his aquiline forelegs and leonine hind ones thumping out the unique, uneven rhythm that every griffon rider knew. As soon as Jet cleared the doors, he leaped high, lashed his wings, and soared up over the rooftops toward the stars.

Mirror came flying to join them. Aoth didn't ask whether the ghost had actually needed to kill the fleeing crossbowman. He didn't particularly want to know.

Looking smaller astride a griffon than he did planted on his own two feet, Khouryn was the next to arrive. Then, one by one, the rest of Aoth's officers fell in behind their commander, forming a loose procession that stretched across the sky.

After his meeting with the Simbarch Council, Aoth had convened a meeting of his lieutenants in the back room of a seedy tavern in the heart of "old Velprintalar," the impoverished, decaying part of the city. In times past, the establishment sat on the harbor, as the dilapidated dock projecting out from it attested, but, thanks to the Spellplague, the retreating waters of the Sea of Dlurg had left it high and dry.

Goblets and tankards in hand, Aoth's lieutenants crowded into one side of the grubby room with its rickety chairs and smell of stale beer, puke, and piss and left the other half to the two undead strangers. That meant Aoth could see the embodiments of his present and those of his past arranged in two neat parcels. He felt a pang of resentment toward the latter and, knowing it was unfair, stifled it as best he could.

Lounging in a cloud of sweet cologne, one stocking orange and the other blue in the latest foppish style, auburn hair worn shoulder length, Gaedynn Ulraes took a sip of red wine, grimaced with exaggerated distaste, and set his cup aside. "Why does the emergency meeting spot always have to be somewhere disgusting?" he asked.

"I'm more interested in knowing why we're meeting," said Jhesrhi Coldcreek, her wizard's staff propped against her chair. The gold runes inlaid down its blackwood length complemented her tousled blonde curls, tawny skin, and amber eyes. "I thought the simbarchs liked us."

Aoth sighed. "They did, until I convinced them I'm not trustworthy."

Gaedynn arched an eyebrow his barber had sculpted into a fine line. "And how did you do that?"

Aided by Bareris, Aoth told the tale. His fellow sellswords reacted with astonishment but, to his relief, not overt disbelief. He supposed it was because they knew him better than the simbarchs did.

"In one respect," he concluded, "I guess I'm lucky. Our employers found my story so outrageous, it flummoxed them. Otherwise, they might have arrested me on the spot."

"Because," Jhesrhi said, "they think you intend to break our contract."

Aoth nodded. "And they're right."

Khouryn scowled. "You told me you never break a compact. That's what separates us from the scum. That's why I joined the Brotherhood of the Griffon in the first place."

Gaedynn grinned. "I thought it was to avoid having to stay home with that . . . remarkably *articulate* wife of yours." Jhesrhi shot him an irritated glance.

"I don't like it, either," said Aoth to the dwarf, "but I don't see a choice."

"Because these two dead men claim another dead man is going to lay waste to the whole world. Or our corner of it, anyway."

"I don't blame you if you can't believe it. You're all too young to have suffered through the Spellplague. But those of us who did know that at times, the world can be fragile as an eggshell. And I tell you again, I *saw* the devastation. In all our years together, have my visions ever turned out to be lies?"

"Not that I recall," Gaedynn said. "So it seems to me that, now that the Aglarondans have refused to heed your warning, the only sensible course of action is to flee west as fast as the wings of our steeds will carry us. But something tells me that's not what you have in mind."

"You're right," said Aoth. "With the simbarchs or without them, someone needs to try to stop Szass Tam."

"Possibly so," the foppish archer replied, "but even if it were feasible, I fight for coin, not noble causes."

"Would you fight for your life?" Jhesrhi asked. "Because that's what this is about. I'm having trouble wrapping my head around it, too, but there it is."

"For what it's worth," said Aoth, "I'll do my best to make sure we collect pay and plunder for our efforts. Still, I won't blame anyone who opts to leave the Brotherhood. Fighting Szass Tam was a daunting undertaking when Bareris, Mirror, and I did it before. Considering that he's had a century to consolidate his hold on Thay, it can only be harder now."

Everyone sat and thought about it for a moment. Then Khouryn said, "I can't claim I truly understand any of this craziness, or to be happy about abandoning a nice, profitable, winnable campaign to go risk our lives in the foulest Hell-pit in Faerûn. But you've always led us well, Captain. I'll stick with you and make sure the men who serve under me do the same."

"So will I," said Jhesrhi, and one by one, the other officers expressed the same resolve. Even Gaedynn, though he was last to commit. Aoth swallowed away a thickness in his throat and silently prayed to Kossuth that he wouldn't lead them all to their deaths.

"So what's the plan?" Gaedynn asked.

"The first step," said Aoth, "is to get away from here, before the simbarchs move to arrest me and detain the rest of you . . ."

Which was what they were attempting now.

The mercenaries had worked through the day and into the night, readying themselves for departure while trying to conceal their preparations from any outsider who might be watching. The next step was to reunite the men billeted in the city with the bulk of the company encamped outside, still without raising the alarm.

"I'm sorry," Bareris said abruptly.

"About what?" Aoth replied.

"I don't know how to behave like your friend anymore. Undeath withered that part of me."

Aoth sighed. "It started withering long before that, on the day you found out Xingax had turned Tammith into a vampire. If undeath changed who you are inside, it simply finished the job, and *I'm* sorry about that. Because I tried to help you grieve and move on, but I never found the right words or the right way."

"You hate being pulled back into this, don't you?"

"Yes. In Thay, my Rashemi looks made other Mulans view me with contempt. Out here in the rest of the world, they don't matter. In Thay, I was the servant of masters who cared nothing for my welfare. Here, I grovel to no one. In Thay, I lost my war, but I haven't lost one since, and my victories made me rich and respected.

"I think of all that," Aoth continued, "and I remember the horrors the necromancers sent to kill us, horrors that still trouble my sleep one night in three. You're damned right I don't want to go back."

"I hope you'll feel differently when we finally settle the score."

Aoth decided it would accomplish nothing to say that he never even thought in terms of there being "a score."

"Maybe so," Aoth said. "Now get ready. That's the west gate up ahead."

Veltalar wasn't a walled city, but it did have fortifications straddling the major roads into the city to control the flow of traffic. The west gate was one such barrier, perfectly positioned to keep an eye on the rows of tents comprising the Brotherhood's encampment.

It looked to Aoth as if there were extra sentries manning the battlements tonight, surely for that very purpose. He kindled silvery light in the point of his spear to make sure the other riders would know when Jet dived, then sent the griffon hurtling down at the gate.

Bareris sang, and though the magic wasn't aimed at him, Aoth's eyelids drooped and his limbs felt heavy. He gave his head a shake to rid himself of the lethargy, and some of the soldiers on top of the gate collapsed.

Jhesrhi swooped low, and her sleep spell picked off the warriors who'd resisted Bareris's enchantment. Still other men-at-arms ran from the base of the fortification, and Gaedynn and his mount plunged to earth to block their path. The archer shot an arrow imbued with a charm of slumber into the dirt at their feet, and they too dropped.

The other sellswords in the city, the ones who didn't have flying steeds, erupted from their hiding places and poured through the gate. The griffon riders flew over the portal, and they all rushed on to join their comrades in the camp.

Aoth was pleased to see the latter were ready to move. Everyone had his armor on, the griffons and horses were saddled, and the foot soldiers had their packs stuffed and ready to sling across their backs. Unfortunately, the company was leaving much of its baggage behind, but that couldn't be helped if they were to travel at maximum speed. In the paddock, a mule brayed as though protesting its abandonment.

Working in concert, Jhesrhi and Bareris cloaked the camp in illusion. For a time, the magic would make it look as if people were still moving around inside and would conceal the tracks the column left when it set forth.

Afterward, the master of griffons found a mount for Bareris, and he overcame its instinctual distrust of the undead by beguiling it with a song. Then the officers of the company convened for a final palaver.

"Are you sure," asked Aoth, "that you can lose a pursuing force in the Yuirwood?"

Gaedynn spread his hands as though amazed anyone would even ask. "Of course."

Jhesrhi scowled. "The Aglarondans will have elves to guide them."

Gaedynn was human. But he'd grown up among the elves of the Yuirwood, a hostage seized in a futile attempt to ensure his father's good behavior.

Gaedynn grinned. "That's fine, Buttercup. We'll play Foxes and Rabbits through the circles." He shifted his gaze back to Aoth. "Frankly, Captain, the person we ought to worry about is you. Are you sure you want to do this?"

"I'm sure I don't," said Aoth, "but it's the only thing *to* do. Get the men moving, and if Tymora smiles, I'll see you in a tenday or two."

Sensing that he was ready to go, Jet sprang back into the air. Bareris followed, and Mirror, a faceless blot of aching wrongness more felt than seen in the dark, brought up the rear.

•• •• •• •• •• •• •• •• •• •• •• •• ••

When Bareris had last seen Escalant, it had been a city in distress, crammed to overflowing with refugees and fearful that either Szass Tam or the Spellplague would destroy it. But as he surveyed the port from the air, it was plain the place had prospered in the intervening decades. Stevedores scurried to load or unload the dozens of merchant ships moored at the docks, while elsewhere, the sawmills, furniture manufactories, and slave markets were equally busy. It was no wonder the simbarchs wanted to add the town, along with the rest of the Wizard's Reach, to their own dominions.

He looked over at Aoth, flying on his left. "What now?" he asked.

The warmage smiled crookedly. "Look for the gaudiest, most ostentatious palace in town. It should be easy enough to spot."

With its high, gilded minarets and jeweled scarlet banners gleaming in the sunlight, it was. The travelers set down on the expanse of verdant lawn in front of the primary entrance. The high arched double doors were sheathed in gold as well. Unless they were gold through and through. Considering who lived here, anything was possible.

Bareris had given himself the appearance of life, and for a moment, the slaves who came to greet them didn't sense anything amiss. Then they noticed the shadow that was Mirror and faltered in alarm.

"It's all right," said Bareris, charging his voice with the power to calm and command. "We don't mean any harm. Simply tell your master that Aoth Fezim, Mirror, and Bareris Anskuld request an audience."

One of the servants scurried to deliver the message, and in time a dozen guards appeared to demand that the travelers surrender their weapons. They did, and the warriors escorted them into the presence of Samas Kul.

The archmage looked no older, but if possible was even more obese than Bareris remembered him, a heap of a man whose begemmed ornaments and gorgeous crimson robes failed utterly to render him any less repulsive. A small semicircular table sat just in front of his throne as if he were an infant or an invalid, while a bigger one farther away held enough food and drink to supply a banquet. Most likely, as in days of yore, he used magic to float viands from one surface to the other.

Statues—a dragon, a spider, a bear—wrought of various metals stood in alcoves along the walls: golems ready to spring to life if required. Despite these formidable protectors and the human guards who still surrounded Bareris, Aoth, and Mirror, Samas held a wand of congealed quicksilver in his pink, blubbery hand. Bareris supposed he could take the precaution as a sort of compliment.

The zulkir said, "You must be insane to come here."

"That," Aoth replied, "is a cold greeting for the legionnaires who saved your fleet and possibly even your life on the Alamber Sea."

Samas sneered. "You did render good service that night. But any gratitude you earned thereby, you forfeited when you deserted and took the whole of the Griffon Legion with you."

"Maybe that's fair. But when I discovered I was going to live a long time, I realized I didn't want to spend all those years bowing and scraping. And when I told the men of my intent, they agreed there was a better life to be had."

"A 'better life' that involved siding with the enemies of your own people!" Droplets of spittle flew from Samas's lips. "Of conspiring to overthrow all that remains of the Thay that was!"

"Yes, an offense for which you zulkirs tried to kill me. Nevertheless, here I stand before you, because none of that matters anymore. With your permission, we'll show you what does."

Bareris removed the red book from its pouch. "This belonged to Druxus Rhym. The simbarchs, for all their claims to arcane knowledge, considered it nonsense. But I trust that you, who presided over the Order of Transmutation, will see deeper."

Samas held out his hand. The book leaped out of Bareris's grasp and flew to the zulkir. Samas murmured a charm over it, perhaps checking to see if it was some sort of magical trap, then opened the cover.

•• •• •• •• •• •• •• •• •• •• •• •• •• ••

"Where," Lauzoril asked, "are Aoth Fezim and his companions now?"

Seated on the other side of the red maple table, a piece of roast duck in one hand, a cup of apple-flavored liqueur in the other, and his several chins gleaming with grease, Samas had to swallow before he could answer. "I locked them up, but I haven't punished them in any way. I would have liked to, but under the circumstances . . ." He shrugged, and his rolls of fat flapped in a way that made his fellow zulkir think of avalanches sliding down a mountain.

A shrewish glint in her eye, Lallara rasped, "Why did we need a dead bard and knight to stumble across this wretched book a hundred years after Druxus's death? You were his successor. Didn't you have the sense to take an inventory of his possessions?" She looked wizened and frail, but Laurozil knew the appearance was deceptive. Like all of them, she'd used magic both to extend her life and to ward off the genuine disabilities of old age.

Samas's round, sweaty, hairless face turned a deeper, mottled red. "If you recall, those were tempestuous times. Naturally, I made some effort to take stock of what he'd left behind—"

"But if it wasn't made of gold, ablaze with magic, or edible, you assumed it couldn't be important."

Inwardly, Lauzoril sighed. Once again, it was time to intervene. It made him miss Dmitra Flass, who, though he'd resented her pretensions to leadership, had likewise exerted her influence to keep their deliberations from descending into useless acrimony.

"We all wish we'd uncovered this information earlier," he said, "but what matters is that we have it now. We need to focus on what to do about it."

"I suppose so," Nevron said. Like the other male zulkirs, he'd maintained the appearance of relative youth and had strong, ugly features that sneered more often than not. Most of his tattoos were portraits of demons and devils bound to his service, and the scent of brimstone clung to him. "If we're agreed that the book is anything to worry about. Are we?"

"It's difficult to evaluate whether the ritual could actually destroy one world and allow the mage to mold a new one from the ashes," Samas said. "To say the least, it seems unlikely. But I see little reason to doubt that it would kill everything for hundreds of miles around."

Nevron scowled. "I think so too."

"As do I," Lallara said.

"Then it's unanimous," Lauzoril said. "Still, just because Szass Tam could attempt the rite, with dire consequences, doesn't mean he necessarily will."

"Our spies," Nevron said, "confirm Anskuld's report. The lich built his new castles in the same shape as Druxus's drawing."

"But perhaps," Lauzoril said, "he's found a way to raise this particular form of power and turn it to some less ambitious project. He wouldn't be the first wizard who simply"—*simply!*—"aspired to claim a place among the gods."

Lallara cackled. "The Szass Tam I remember already thought he was a god, or as good as."

"True enough," Nevron said, "and let's not forget that gods can subjugate one another and even die. I've lost count of how many did so in the past century. No, it makes perfect sense that Szass Tam, arrogant, merciless whoreson that he is, would seek to become something greater."

Lauzoril reflected that in different circumstances, he might have needed to suppress a smile at hearing Nevron refer to anyone else as "arrogant" or "merciless." But nothing seemed very funny at the moment.

Samas guzzled from his cup. "But I wonder if the actual gods wouldn't stop him."

"Like they stopped the Spellplague?" Lallara asked.

"She's right," Nevron said. "No mortal understands the ways of the gods, no mortal can command them, and that means you can't depend on them."

"Then you're saying Captain Fezim and his friends are right," Samas said. "Other people need to stop Szass Tam, and since we're the only ones who know of the threat and take it seriously, it will have to be us."

"How?" Lallara asked. "The necromancers already defeated us once, when we commanded far greater resources than we do now. I know we've always prattled about reconquering Thay, but we never actually set about organizing an invasion, did we? Because we knew we wouldn't stand a chance."

"Maybe we don't have to retake Thay," Samas said. "The so-called 'Dread Rings' define a mystic pattern with the Citadel, where Szass Tam will perform the conjuration, at the center. And we can assume that, gigantic though it is, it's like any pentacle.

Break any part of it, and the whole becomes useless. So all we need to do is seize a single fortress, neutralize its arcane properties with our own countermagic, and that will make the ritual impossible." He smiled smugly, and Lauzoril surmised that he'd enjoyed playing schoolmaster to the woman who so often mocked and fleered at him.

"Interesting," Lallara said. "I assume this is Captain Fezim's idea that you're passing along to us."

Samas glared.

"Wherever it originated," Lauzoril said, "it seems the most practical way—perhaps the only way—of addressing the problem."

"It does," Nevron said, "but it ignores one important point. The Aglarondans are coming to drive us out of the Wizard's Reach, and if we take most of our troops and wander off to Thay, they'll succeed."

"Given what's at stake," Lauzoril said, "perhaps even that doesn't matter."

Nevron scowled. "It matters to me. I'm a zulkir, a lord among men, and I intend to remain one so long as I walk the mortal plane. The East can burn, the whole world can crumble, if that's what it takes for me to keep my lands and titles until the end."

Her eyes flinty, Lallara nodded. Samas said, "The Reach is all we have left."

Lauzoril realized he agreed with them. Their perspective was a subtle kind of madness, perhaps, but whatever it was, he shared it. "All right. First we push back the simbarchs, then we deal with Szass Tam. Maybe the former will be good practice for the latter. As far as I can see, that just leaves one more minor matter to decide here and now. What shall we do with Captain Fezim and his comrades?"

"What do you generally do with deserters?" said Nevron. "Execute them."

"They are the people who warned us of Szass Tam's scheme," Samas said.

Nevron smiled. "Which is to say, they've served their purpose."

"Perhaps not their entire purpose," Lallara said. "Remember the old days. When we scored a victory against Szass Tam, these warriors played a part as often as not. And from what I understand, Captain Fezim's mercenary company—the army he built around our old Griffon Legion—is on its way here. They're coming to help us invade Thay, but they may have second thoughts if they arrive to learn we tortured their commander to death."

"I suppose we would be stupid to cast away such a weapon," Nevron said, "but it galls to me to think of that insolent Rashemi going unpunished."

Lauzoril fingered his chin. "Well, how about this? Someone will have to bear the brunt of it when Aglarond attacks. Let it be the Brotherhood of the Griffon. If Fezim and his company perish, that's his punishment. If they survive, they can serve as our vanguard in Thay. And if they make it through that, then we can always butcher the traitor when we come home again."

•• •• •• •• •• •• •• •• •• •• •• •• •• •• ••

As Aoth had anticipated, a substantial force of Aglarondans had chased the Brotherhood some distance into the Yuirwood before Gaedynn's maneuvering shook them off the trail. But even with elves and druids to aid their passage, the simbarchs had balked at the arduous task of bringing the whole of their armed might south through the dense forest with its dangerous patches of plagueland. Instead, they'd marched their forces east, to emerge from the fortified city of Glarondar onto the plains north of Escalant.

Aoth flew high above the field to inspect the Aglarondans in their battle array and the zulkirs' troops in their own formation. Bareris and Mirror accompanied him, but none of the other flyers. There was no reason to tire the griffons prematurely or to show the enemy just how many aerial cavalry there were, even though they'd had ample opportunity to learn before the Brotherhood switched sides.

Switched sides. Aoth tried to spit the unpalatable thought away.

He glanced over at Bareris, an uncanny ivory apparition astride his own griffon, its tawny wings gleaming in the afternoon sunlight. The bard's scowl suggested that his thoughts were bitterer than Aoth's.

"Cheer up," called Aoth. "The situation doesn't look all that bad."

"This is a waste of time," the bard replied. "We should already be in Thay." He nudged his mount with his knee and sent it winging to the left.

"It would be futile to go by ourselves," Aoth said, even though his fellow griffon rider was already out of earshot. "I'm doing the best I can, damn you."

Mirror floated closer. For Aoth, it was one of those moments when regarding the ghost actually was like peering into a warped and murky looking glass. "He knows that. But you have to admit, you would feel silly if, while we were busy fighting the simbarchs, Szass Tam performed his 'Great Work' and killed us all."

Aoth snorted. "Is that supposed to be funny? I don't think I've ever heard you try to joke before. You've come a long way."

"Some days are good, some, I'm as mad and empty as the day Bareris met me. But yes, I've emerged partway into the light, even as he's slipped farther and farther into darkness. At times I feel like some sort of vampire. As if I'm leeching his soul from him without even realizing it."

"I never knew you to fall prey to poetic fancies before, either." Aoth sent Jet swooping for a better look at some of the enemy's archers. "I'm sure your company has been as good for him as his has been for you. I suspect it's the thing that's kept him at least a little sane."

"I suppose it could be so." Mirror hesitated. "You were always a shrewd soldier. You do realize that, the way our side is formed up, a good many of the Aglarondans are going to end up hammering away at your Brotherhood. More than your fair share, I'd have to say."

Aoth snorted. "Nothing new about that. Lords don't pay good coin to sellswords only to hand the most dangerous jobs to their own vassals. And at least we are getting paid. I told the zulkirs the Brotherhood wouldn't fight otherwise."

Jet screeched. "It's starting."

.. ..

Arrows rose from ranks of Aglarondan archers like a dark cloud. Gaedynn scrutinized the arc of the shafts as they reached the apogee of their flight. The enemy bowmen were reasonably competent. Of course, one would expect as much, considering how many of them had some measure of elf blood flowing in their veins.

Strong hands grabbed him by the arm and jerked him onto his knees. "Down!" Khouryn snarled.

I was getting around to it, Gaedynn thought.

The sellswords equipped with tower shields or targes raised them to ward themselves and their more lightly armored comrades. The arrows whined as they fell, then clattered against the defensive barrier. Here and there, a man screamed where a missile found a gap.

Behind the foot soldiers and archers, wings snapped and rustled as the griffon riders took to the air. Gaedynn wouldn't have minded going with them, but Aoth had decided that in this particular combat, he'd be more useful directing the archers on the ground.

So he supposed he'd better get to it. "Archers!" he bellowed.

"Remember who you're supposed to kill, and shoot them!"

His bowmen stood upright. Some of them loosed at their counterparts on the other side of the battlefield. Jhesrhi, who had a particular knack for elemental magic, augmented their efforts with an explosion of flame that tore a dozen Aglarondans apart.

The remaining Brotherhood archers shot at enemy knights and officers, equestrian figures armored from head to toe, wherever they spotted them. Gaedynn took aim at a chestnut destrier and drove an arrow into its neck. It fell, catching its rider's leg between its bulk and the ground and, with any luck, crippling him. Not a chivalrous tactic, Gaedynn reflected, but then, he wasn't a chivalrous fellow.

•• •• •• •• •• •• •• •• •• •• •• •• ••

Nevron smiled, savoring the sight of thousands of warriors striving to spill one another's blood, the deafening racket of the bellowed war cries and the shrieks of agony. Unlike his fellow zulkirs, he relished the perilous tumult of the battlefield. Indeed, it was still his dream to abandon the dreary mortal plane and, unlike any living human being before him, conquer an empire in the higher worlds. Regrettably, the chaos of the past century, as magic and the very structure of the cosmos redefined themselves, had persuaded him to bide his time.

The demons and devils that accompanied him everywhere, caged in rings, amulets, or tattoos, shared his exhilaration. They roared and threatened, begged and wheedled, in voices only he could hear, urging him to unleash them to join the slaughter.

Although the zulkirs had arranged their formation with the Brotherhood of the Griffon at the center, the natural focus for the Aglarondans' greatest efforts, there were plenty of the enemy to go around, and they were making a creditable attempt to strike at every target within reach. Thunderclaps boomed in a ragged volley, and five flares of lightning leaped forth at the zulkirs' right wing, where Nevron stood amid a circle of lesser Red Wizards.

The thunderbolts winked out of existence short of their targets. Standing some distance away, Lallara gave a brusque, self-satisfied nod that flapped the loose flesh dangling under her chin. The old hag might be abrasive and disagreeable in every conceivable way, but Nevron had to concede that, despite the appearance of decrepitude she'd allowed to overtake her, her command of abjuration, the magic of protection, remained as formidable as ever.

Something similar might be said of Lauzoril. He looked like a priggish clerk or bloodless functionary someone had dressed in the scarlet robes of an archmage as a joke. But when he murmured a spell and swirled his hands, enchantment, the magic of the mind, plunged a cantering troop of enemy horse archers into terror, and they wheeled and galloped back the way they'd come.

Golden greatswords clasped in their fists, a dozen crimson-skinned angelic warriors abruptly appeared more or less in the same place from which the thunderbolts had stabbed. Nevron surmised that, invisible behind the spear-and-shield fighters assigned to protect them, the same wizards who'd evoked the lightning were trying a different tactic.

In so doing, they'd strayed into Nevron's area of expertise. He decided it was his turn to demonstrate that the wizardry of Aglarond, its vaunted elven secrets notwithstanding, was no match for the darker arts of Thay.

As the angels charged, he snapped his fingers. Three obese figures shimmered into material existence around him, each twice as tall as a man, with a pair of horns jutting from its head and anguished faces pressing out against the skin from inside its distended belly. Nevron heard the faces wailing even over the ambient din of the battlefield.

Careless of the humans they trampled or knocked aside, the solamiths lumbered forward to intercept the archons. The demons tore hunks of flesh from their own bodies and threw them. The missiles exploded when they struck the ground, engulfing the angels in blasts of dark, somehow filthy-looking flame.

•• •• •• •• •• •• •• •• •• •• •• •• •• ••

Aoth, Bareris, and Mirror waited for the rest of the griffon riders to join them in the air. Then Aoth swept his spear forward, signaling the attack.

His men shot arrows from the saddle. He rained down fire, lightning, hail, and acid, the spells of destruction that were a warmage's stock-in-trade. For an instant he remembered how, ashamed of breaking his pledge to the simbarchs, he'd done his best to sneak away from Veltalar without shedding Aglarondan blood. Well, the time for such squeamishness was past.

A long javelin-cast across the sky, Bareris rode singing, his long white fingers plucking the strings of a black harp. He was high enough above the ground that, were his music not infused with magic, no one below would even have heard him. But as it was, a company of enemy crossbowmen clutched at their ears, reeled, and fell. A couple tried to stab quarrels into their ears, while another drew his dagger and slashed his own throat.

Then Bareris oriented on a dead elf knight, a wealthy lord or mighty champion judging from the gore-stained magnificence of his trappings. The bard's song brought the corpse scrambling to its feet to drive its slender gleaming sword into another elf's back.

Meanwhile, the Aglarondans shot arrows and flares of magic at the foes harrying them from overhead. Trained to veer and dodge, the griffons avoided many such attacks, and their boiled-leather armor and natural hardiness protected them from others. When none of those defenses sufficed, a steed and its rider plummeted to smash against the ground.

Jet swerved suddenly. Aoth knew his familiar was evading and, since he himself hadn't detected an imminent threat, looked into the griffon's mind to find out where it was.

Above and to the right. He jerked around to see a trio of wasps as big as Jet himself diving at them, their wings a buzzing blur.

Jet couldn't wheel in time to bring his beak and talons to bear. It was up to Aoth. He burned one wasp to ash with a fan-shaped blaze of flame, but by then the other two were right on top of him. He drove his spear into one creature's midsection, channeled lethal force through the weapon, and the impaled wasp began to smoke and char. It clung to life, however, and jabbed its stinger at him repeatedly. He blocked the strokes with his mithral targe—each one slammed his shield arm back against his torso—but that left him with no hands or gear to ward off the third wasp hurtling at his head.

The third insect convulsed and, patches of its body withering and rotting, dropped. Still swinging his shadow-sword, Mirror chased the dying wasp toward the ground.

•• •• •• •• •• •• •• •• •• •• •• •• ••

Though she never would have admitted it to any of her fellow officers—particularly Gaedynn—Jhesrhi lacked the almost preternatural ability to predict the surge and ebb of combat that Aoth and certain others sometimes displayed. Thus, even though she and her allies were expecting a great charge, she had no idea it was about to begin until the enemy bellowed and all plunged forward at once. Their running footsteps and galloping hoofbeats shook the ground beneath her boots.

Up until now, although skirmisher had traded blows with skirmisher, and some eager warriors had forayed back and forth, it had mostly been archers, crossbowmen, and spellcasters fighting the battle. Throughout this preliminary phase, the zulkirs' forces had labored to degrade the Aglarondans' ability to attack at range, and to harass the knights and lords waiting idly on their mounts. The goal was to goad them into the charge they had just now launched.

From the enemy perspective, the move no doubt made sense. They outnumbered the zulkirs' troops by a comfortable margin, and they had considerably more horsemen. They should be able to smash the Thayan formation.

But they assumed that because they didn't know that Jhesrhi, fat Samas Kul, and some of his underlings had arrived at the field before them and prepared the ground. They didn't know what magic their foes intended to unleash.

Or else they do know, Jhesrhi thought wryly, and they think they have a trick that trumps ours. If she'd learned anything since Aoth delivered her from servitude and gave her a place in the Brotherhood, it was that in war, nothing was certain.

She peered through the gap between the shields two warriors held to protect her. When she judged that the enemy lancers, pounding along in advance of a horde of foot soldiers, had come far enough, she chanted words of power.

Elsewhere in the zulkirs' formation, Samas Kul and the Red Wizards he commanded did the same. She could tell because so much magic, discharged at the same time and to the same end, darkened the air and made it smell like swamps and rot. The golden runes on her staff blazed like little pieces of the sun, and nearby, one of Gaedynn's archers doubled over and puked.

Then patches of earth turned to soft, sucking muck beneath the charging Aglarondans' feet.

Warhorses tripped and fell, pitching their riders over their heads or crushing them beneath their bodies. Even when a steed managed to keep its footing, it broke stride, which meant that an animal running behind it was likely to slam right into it. Rushing spearmen and axemen sank in ooze to their knees or waists, as though they'd blundered into quicksand. A few dropped completely out of sight. In just a few moments, the fearsome momentum of the charge disintegrated into agony and confusion.

For an instant, Jhesrhi felt a pang of something that might almost have been pity, but you didn't pity the enemy. You couldn't afford to. She flourished her staff and rained acid on three of the nearest Aglarondans. The knights and their mired horses screamed and thrashed.

Red Wizards hammered the foe with their own attacks. "Down in front!" Gaedynn shouted to anyone who wasn't an archer, and as soon as they had a clear shot, his men loosed shaft after shaft. Wheeling and swooping above the Aglarondans like vultures keeping watch on a dying animal, the griffon riders also wielded their bows to deadly effect.

By rights, that should have been the end of the battle. But perhaps the simbarchs' wizards cast countermagic that kept the trap from being as effective as expected. Or maybe sheer heroic determination was to blame. Either way, muddy figures floundered out of the ooze and ran onward.

Of course, the snare had done some good. It had killed some of the enemy and deprived the charge of whatever order it originally possessed. But there were still a lot of Aglarondans, their features were still contorted with rage, and if they overran the zulkirs' formation, they could still carry the day.

•• •• •• •• •• •• •• •• •• •• •• •• •• ••

My turn at last, Khouryn thought. "Wall!" he bellowed. "Wall!"

His foot soldiers scrambled to form three ranks with himself in the center of the first. Everyone gripped a shield in one hand and a leveled spear in the other. The spears of the men in the back rows were longer than those of the fellows in front, so everyone could stab at once.

Khouryn had time to glance at the human faces to each side of him, and he felt satisfaction at what he saw: fear—that was natural—but not a hint of panic. They'd stand fast as he'd trained them to, as dwarves themselves would hold the line.

Howling, the first Aglarondans lunged into striking distance.

For a few heartbeats, the defense worked as theory said it should. Overlapping shields protected those who carried them and protected their neighbors, too. The bristling hedge of spears pierced foes reckless enough to come within reach, often before those warriors could even strike a blow.

But then, as so often happened, the work got harder. Aglarondans somehow sprang past the spear points, struck past the shields, and killed defenders, tearing gaps in the formation, even as the relentless pressure of their onslaught buckled the lines. Meanwhile, spears broke or stuck fast in corpses, and sellswords snatched frantically for their secondary weapons.

Khouryn was one of those whose spear stuck fast. He dropped it and his shield, too, and pulled his urgrosh off his back.

A white warhorse, its legs black with muck, cantered at him, turning so the half-elf on its back could cut down at him with his sword. Khouryn parried hard enough to knock the blade out of its owner's grip, then, with a single stroke, chopped the rider's leg in two and sheared into the destrier's flank. Rider and mount shrieked as one, and the steed recoiled.

Khouryn glanced around, making sure he was still more or less even with the soldiers to each side. To anyone but a seasoned warrior, it might have seemed that any semblance of order had dissolved into a chaos of slaughter, into the deafening racket of weapons smashing against shields and armor and the wails of the wounded and dying. But in fact, there was still a formation of sorts, and it was vital to preserve it.

He killed another Aglarondan, and more after that, until the gory urgrosh grew heavy in his hands, and his breath burned and rasped. The man on his left went down, and Gaedynn, who'd traded his bow for a sword and kite shield, darted forward to take his place.

Sometime after that, the enemy stopped coming. Peering out across the corpses heaped two and three deep in front of him, Khouryn saw the survivors fleeing north toward the safety of Glarondar. The Brotherhood's horsemen harried them along.

The last Khouryn knew, Aoth had been holding the cavalry in reserve. At some point, he must have ordered them forward, possibly to play a crucial role in foiling the Aglarondans' attack.

If so, Khouryn supposed he'd hear all about it later. For now, he was simply grateful for the chance to lower his weapon.

.. ..

Nevron studied the fleeing Aglarondans for a time, making sure they had no fight left in them. Then he drew a deep, steadying breath. He'd need a clear mind and a forceful will to compel his demons and devils back into their various prisons. They were having a jolly time of it hunting enemy stragglers, torturing and killing Aglarondan wounded, and devouring elf and human flesh.

He was just about to start when Samas floated up in the huge, padded throne that spared him the strain of having to waddle around on his own two feet. "Should we chase the Aglarondans and finish them off?" the transmuter asked.

"No," Nevron said. "A wounded bear can still bite, and we need to conserve our strength if we're going to Thay. The simbarchs won't try to take the Reach again for a while. That will have to do."

"But if we don't come back to protect it, they'll take it eventually."

Nevron spat. "I realize the name of Samas Kul is synonymous with greed. But if you're dead, I doubt that even you will care what becomes of your dominions."

chapter four

15–28 Tarsakh, The Year of the Dark Circle (1478 DR)

With his swarthy skin, the prisoner was evidently Rashemi, although if he'd ever been stocky, as his kind often was, hunger had whittled that quality away. He lay atop the torture rack with his arms pulled up behind him. To Malark Springhill, who fancied he might know more about how to destroy the human body than anyone else in Thay, its tradition of sophisticated cruelty notwithstanding, it was clear that the torture had already dislocated the prisoner's shoulders, and that his knee, hip, and elbow joints had also started to come apart.

Still, the Rashemi had yet to provide any answers. It was an impressive display of defiance.

Malark turned the winch another eighth of a rotation. The prisoner gave a strangled cry, and something in his lower body tore audibly. The sweaty, bare-chested torturer, speckled with little scars where embers had burned him, tried not to look as if he resented an amateur usurping his function.

Malark leaned over to look the prisoner in the face. "I want the names of your fellow rebels."

The Rashemi croaked an obscenity.

Malark twisted the windlass a little farther, eliciting a gasp. "I know you've had contact with Bareris Anskuld. Tell me how to find him."

Although it didn't really matter if he did. Over the course of the past ninety years, Bareris and Mirror had done more than any of the other malcontents left in the realm to hamper Szass Tam's government, but even so, their efforts hadn't amounted to much. Still, Malark had been Bareris's friend, and given the chance, he would gladly rescue the bard from the vileness that was undeath.

That final iota of stretching had evidently rendered the captive incapable of verbal defiance, but, panting, he shook his head and clenched his jaw shut. Closed his eyes too, as though blocking out the sight of his tormentors and the dank, shadowy, torchlit dungeon would make his situation less real.

Malark wondered if one of the spells he'd mastered under Szass Tam's tutelage would loosen the Rashemi's tongue, then decided he didn't care. It didn't really matter if he unmasked a few more impotent rebels, either. In truth, the success of such efforts had never mattered, only maintaining the appearance that the ruler of Thay was preoccupied with the same sort of trivia as the average tyrant, and with the Dread Rings completed, even that necessity had all but reached an end.

So why not let this hero perish with his spirit unbroken, his secrets preserved? Why not grant him that greatest of all treasures, a perfect death?

Malark turned the wheel. "Talk!" he snarled, meanwhile silently urging, Don't. You only have to hold out a little longer.

"Master—" the torturer began.

Malark turned the wheel. "Talk!" Up and down the length

of the rebel's body, joints cracked and popped as they pulled apart.

"Master!" the torturer persisted. "With all respect, you're giving him too much too fast!"

Doing his best to look as if the Rashemi's recalcitrance had angered him, Malark kept on twisting the winch. "Talk, curse you! Talk, talk, talk!"

The prisoner's spine snapped.

Malark rounded on the torturer. "What just happened?"

Once again, the fellow made a visible effort to cloak his irritation in subservience. "I'm sorry, Your Omnipotence, but his back broke. For what it's worth, he might live a little while longer, maybe even a day, and he won't enjoy it. But he can't talk anymore." He hesitated. "I *tried* to warn you."

"Damn it!" Still pretending to be furious, Malark ended the prisoner's ordeal by chopping his forehead with the blade of his hand. The blow broke the man's skull and drove scraps of bone into the brain within.

The torturer sighed. "And now he won't even suffer."

An impish urge took hold of Malark, and he glared at the other man. "This rebel possessed vital information, and now we'll never learn it. Szass Tam will hear of your incompetence!"

The torturer paled. Swallowed. "Master," he stammered, "I beg you, forgive my clumsiness. I'll do better next time."

Malark grinned and clapped him on the shoulder. "It's all right, my friend, I'm only joking." He made a gold coin appear between his thumb and forefinger, one of the petty tricks that had come to amuse him since he'd mastered sorcery, and pressed it into the torturer's hand. "Have a drink and a whore on me."

The torturer stared after him in relief and confusion as Malark climbed the stairs connecting the pocket hell of the dungeon with the guard station overhead.

Outside the small keep, under a gray sky fouled with smoke and ash from one of High Thay's volcanoes, the Citadel went about its business. Much of the kingdom was desolate now, particularly in the highlands, but Szass Tam's capital city still thrived. Masons slowly carted blocks of marble and granite through the streets, eliciting shouted imprecations from the traffic stuck behind them. Legions of vendors cried their wares, and beggars their afflictions. The naked thralls in the slave markets shivered in the cold mountain air.

People scurried out of Malark's way, then peered curiously after him. He supposed it was only natural. He was, after all, the only one of Szass Tam's zulkirs not Mulan nor even Thayan-born, the only one not undead, and the only one who customarily walked around without a retinue of lackeys and bodyguards.

He realized his station all but demanded the latter, but he just couldn't persuade himself to endure the inconvenience. Over the course of a long, long life, he'd discovered that clerks and their ilk rarely did anything for him that he couldn't do more efficiently and reliably for himself. And to say the least, a man who'd learned combat from the Monks of the Long Death scarcely needed soldiers to fend off footpads and assassins.

He turned a corner and the dark towers and battlements of the true Citadel, the fortress from which the surrounding city took its name, rose before him. Though Szass Tam had claimed it for his residence, he hadn't built it. The structure predated the founding of Thay itself and, according to rumor, was a haunted, uncanny place, with secrets still awaiting discovery in the caverns and catacombs beneath.

Malark had seen indications that rumor likely had it right, but it didn't much concern him. From his perspective, the important thing about the castle was that it was the focal point for the enormous circle of power defined by the Dread Rings, the place where a mage must position himself to perform the Great Work of Unmaking.

Pig-faced blood orcs, lanky gnolls with the muzzles and rank fur of hyenas, and stinking corpses with gleaming yellow eyes, soldiers all in Thay's Dread Legions, saluted Malark as he passed through the various gates and courtyards, and he acknowledged them all without breaking stride. He was eager to reach his quarters and resume his study of a certain grimoire Szass Tam had given him.

But when he saw the raven perched on his windowsill, a tiny scroll case tied to one of its claws, intuition told him the book would have to wait.

•• •• •• •• •• •• •• •• •• •• •• •• ••

The huge keep at the center of the Citadel had a round, flat roof. The wind flapping his scarlet robes, Szass Tam floated some distance above it. The elevation afforded him a good view of both the city spread out below him and the peaks of the Thaymount beyond. And, his sight sharpened by magic, he looked for the flaws in everything he beheld.

It was easiest to find them in people, ugly in body with their legs too long or too short, their wobbling, sagging flab, their moles, rotting teeth, and general lack of grace. Ugly in spirit, too, squabbling, cheating, every word and deed arising from petty lusts and resentments. And even the few who could lay some claim to comeliness of person and clarity of mind carried the seeds of disease and decrepitude, senescence and death.

The peoples' creations were simply their own failings writ large. Some of the buildings in the city were filthy hovels, and even the finer ones often offended against symmetry and proportion or, in their ostentation, betrayed the vanity and vulgarity of their owners. All would one day crumble just as surely as their makers.

It was perhaps a bit more challenging to perceive the imperfections in the mountains, snow capped except for the fuming cones with fire and lava at their cores. Indeed, another observer might have deemed them majestic. But Szass Tam took note of the gaping wounds that were gold mines, and the castles perched on one crag or another. Men had marred this piece of nature, and even had it been otherwise, what was nature, anyway? An arena of endless misery where animals starved, killed, and ate one another, and, if they overcame every other obstacle to their survival, grew old and died, just like humanity. As they always would, until the mountains too wore away to dust.

Szass Tam turned his regard on himself. Except for his withered hands, he might look like a living man, and, with his lean frame, keen, intellectual features, and neat black goatee, a reasonably handsome one at that. But he acknowledged the underlying reality of his fetid breath, silent heart, and cold, leathery flesh suffused with poison. The idiot priests were right about one thing: Undeath was an abomination. *He* was an abomination, or at least his physical form was. He could scarcely wait for the moment when he would replace it.

A compactly built man in maroon and scarlet clothing climbed the steps to the rooftop. He had light green eyes and a wine red birthmark on his chin. In his altered state of consciousness, Szass Tam needed a moment to perceive the newcomer as anything more than another bundle of loathsome inadequacies. Then he recognized Malark Springhill and drifted back down to stand before him.

Malark bowed. "Sorry to interrupt whatever you were doing."

"I was meditating," Szass Tam replied. "Preparing for the ritual. When the time comes, I have to be ready to let go of everything. If I feel even a flicker of attachment or regret, it could ruin the casting. So I'm cultivating the habit of viewing all things with scorn."

The outlander grinned. "I hope knowing me doesn't put you

off your game. I mean, since I'm indisputably such a marvelous fellow."

Szass Tam smiled. "You've been a true friend this past century, I'll give you that. And I tell you again, I can recreate you in the universe to come."

"Then I'll tell you again, that's the last thing I want. I just want to watch death devour the world I know, and fall into darkness along with it."

"All right." Even after a long association, Szass Tam didn't fully comprehend Malark's devotion to death, only that it had been the response of a mind ill-prepared to deal with the unique stresses of immortality. But he was willing to honor his wishes. "Did you come to consult me about something in particular?"

Malark's expression grew serious. "Yes. I've heard from my agent in Escalant. The zulkirs—the old ones in exile, I mean—intend to mount an invasion of Thay within the next few tendays."

Szass Tam blinked. "They can't possibly have amassed sufficient strength to have any hope at all of retaking the realm, or you would have learned about it before this. Wouldn't you?"

"I would, and they haven't. My man also reports that Aoth Fezim and his sellswords have hired on with Lauzoril and the others, and that Bareris Anskuld and Mirror slipped out of Thay to join the expedition."

Szass Tam shook his head at the perversity of fate. "If Anskuld and the ghost are there with Lallara and the rest, it can only mean one thing: they discovered what I'm about to do and rallied the rest of my old enemies to stop me."

Malark nodded. "That's my guess as well."

"I would very much like to know *how* they found out. Fastrin's book has been in my possession for a hundred years. Druxus never told anyone but me what was in it, and I never told anyone but you."

"Could the gods have played a part?"

"Except for Bane, they no longer have much reason to pay a great deal of attention to what goes on in Thay, and the Black Hand has given me a thousand years to do whatever I please. Still, who knows? I suppose at this point, the *how* of the situation is less important than what to do about it."

"Are you sure you need to do anything extraordinary? Thay is well protected, the Dread Legions stronger than any force your foes can field. The Dread Rings aren't just gigantic talismans; they're some of the mightiest fortresses in the East. The final preparations for the Unmaking will be ready in a matter of months or possibly even sooner. It seems to me that at this late date, it's impossible for anyone to stop you."

"I'd like to think so. Still, the zulkirs have powerful magic at their command, and in the old days, Anskuld, Fezim, and Mirror won victories that prolonged the war by years. So I want to crush this threat as expeditiously as possible, which means I want you to take an active part. It's the next best thing to doing it myself, and that isn't practical. I have to finish getting everything ready here."

To Szass Tam's surprise, Malark seemed to hesitate. It was even possible that a hint of distress showed through what was generally his impeccable poise.

Then the lich inferred the reason. "I swear to you," he said, "that when it's time to start conjuring, if you're still in the field, I'll fetch you. I told you you'll be at my side, and I keep my promises."

Malark inclined his head. "I know you do, Master. Please forgive me for imagining otherwise, even for an instant."

Szass Tam waved a dismissive hand. "It's all right. You've worked tirelessly for this one reward. In your place, if I suspected I might not receive it, I'd be upset too. Now, let's talk about how to make my old colleagues sorry they decided to revisit their homeland. How do you think they'll go about invading?"

A gust of cold wind tugged at Malark's sleeve, exposing a bit of the tattooing on his forearm. "They've held on to the Alaor since the end of the war," said the former monk, "presumably to facilitate an attack by sea, should they ever decide to make one."

"That's true, and just in case they ever did, we've built a formidable fleet. Do they have enough warships to contend with it?"

"Probably not."

"Then I predict they'll deploy their naval resources for what amounts to a feint. Meanwhile, the true invasion will come by land."

"If it does, it can't swing north through Aglarond. The simbarchs won't permit it. The zulkirs just fought a little war with them. That means they'll have to ford the River Lapendrar and come through Priador, almost within spitting distance of Murbant. That's good. We can harry them and slow their march to a crawl."

Szass Tam smiled. "There's another possibility. If I were the enemy, I'd come through the Umber Marshes."

Malark cocked his head, and his light green eyes narrowed. "Is it even possible to drag an entire army through there?"

"I've kept track of Captain Fezim's career, and he and his company have a reputation for traversing terrain that his foes, to their cost, believed impassable. Consider also that Samas Kul and the mages who serve him are capable of conjuring bridges out of thin air and turning ooze into dry, solid ground. Not every step of the way, of course—it's a big swamp—but they may be able to help the army over the most difficult passages."

"I suppose so," Malark said, "and if I were the enemy, I'd be thinking that Szass Tam might be reluctant to send one of his own armies into that pesthole of a swamp, and that it would have trouble locating my comrades and me even if he did. It would likewise occur to me that the marshes are big enough that it would be hard to predict exactly where we'd emerge. So with luck, we could at least make it into Thay proper without encountering heavy resistance."

"Exactly."

"So what do we do about it?"

"It might well be a waste of resources to send a conventional army into the fens, but I can send other things. If the zulkirs overcome that obstacle, they'll likely make for the Dread Ring in Lapendrar and lay siege to it. You'll be there to aid in the defense."

Malark nodded. "It should be easy enough, considering that we have to hold out for only a relatively short time. But I do have a suggestion. I take it that Tsagoth is still in charge of the Ring in Tyraturos?"

"I'm certain, my lord spymaster, that you would have known within the day if I'd reassigned him."

"Well, I'd like you to reassign him now. Give him to me to fight in Lapendrar."

•• •• •• •• •• •• •• •• •• •• •• •• ••

With reflexive caution, Malark took another glance around, making sure he was still alone. He was, of course. He was locked inside one of his personal conjuration chambers, with gold and silver pentacles inlaid in the red marble floor, racks of staves, cups, daggers, oils, and powders ready to hand, tapestries sewn with runes adorning the walls, and the scent of bitter incense hanging in the air.

He murmured words of power, pricked his fingertip with a lancet, and dripped blood onto the mass of virgin clay on the tabletop before him. Then, chanting, he kneaded those ingredients together with hairs, nail parings, and various bodily fluids. Magic accumulated, straining toward overt manifestation. It sent a prickling across his skin and made the shadows writhe.

As Szass Tam had taught him, he concentrated on what he was doing. Believed in the outcome. Willed it to happen. Yet even so, there was a small, unengaged part of him that reflected that while he *should* be able to perform this particular spell successfully, he'd never actually tried before, and it was supposed to be particularly dangerous.

Still, he didn't see a choice. He'd already had a plan of sorts, but it had been predicated on remaining in the Citadel awaiting an opportune moment to make his move. Now that the lich had ordered him forth, something more aggressive was required. And this scheme was the best he could devise.

He started shaping the clay into a crude doll. Suddenly, a pang of weakness shot through him, and his knees buckled. As he continued sculpting, the feeling of debility grew worse, as though his work was draining a measure of his life.

Was this supposed to happen? The grimoire hadn't warned of it.

Don't think about it! Focus on speaking the words with the proper clarity and cadence. On making the passes precisely and exactly when required.

A crazy titter sounded from thin air, the glee of some petty spirit drawn by the scent of magic. Malark raised his wand above his head and shouted the final words of his spell.

A flare of mystic power painted the room with frost. The doll swelled to life-size, becoming an exact duplicate of Malark right down to the wand, ritual chasuble, and the red and maroon garments beneath. The simulacrum drew up his legs and thrust them out again in a vicious double kick at his creator's ribs.

Malark only barely managed to spring back out of range. Grinning with mad joy, his twin rolled off the worktable, dropped into a fighting stance, and advanced.

"Stop!" Malark snapped. "I'm your maker and your master!"

The simulacrum whipped his ebony wand—a sturdy baton

designed to double as a cudgel—at Malark's head. Malark swayed out of the way, but once again, it was close. He needed the weakness and sluggishness to go away, because his twin certainly didn't seem to be laboring under the same handicap.

But he did seem wild with fury. Perhaps he could be tricked. Malark raised his foot a little as if preparing a kick, then lashed out with his own wand, beat his opponent's weapon, and knocked it out of his grasp. The cudgel clattered on the floor. It was far from the most effective attack he could have attempted, but he was also hindered by the fact that he didn't want to kill or cripple his other self.

The simulacrum laughed as though the loss of his club was inconsequential, and perhaps it was. Throwing one combination after another, he came at Malark like a whirlwind, and his creator had little choice but to retreat.

As Malark did, though, he watched. No one, not even a Monk of the Long Death, could make so many attacks in quick succession without faltering or otherwise leaving himself open eventually.

There! The simulacrum was leaning forward, ever so slightly off balance, and as he corrected, Malark dropped his own wand, pounced, and gripped the other combatant's neck in a stranglehold.

At once Malark felt his adversary moving to break free of the choke, but he didn't attempt any countermeasures. Now that he was staring straight into the simulacrum's eyes at short range, it was time to stop wrestling and try being a wizard once again. Imagining the indomitable force of his will, embodied in his glare, stabbing into his double's head, he snarled, "Stop!"

The simulacrum convulsed, then stopped struggling. The rage went out of his light green eyes, and he composed his features. "You can let go now," he croaked, his throat still constricted by Malark's grip.

Malark warily complied, then stepped backward. His twin remained calm. Rubbing one of the ruddy handprints on his neck, the simulacrum said, "I'm truly sorry. But being born is a painful, disorienting thing. All those babies would lash out too if they had the strength."

Malark smiled. "I'll have to take your word for it."

"And you have to admit, from a certain perspective, this is a setback. For centuries, my dearest wish has been that there be none of me. Instead, the number has doubled."

"Only temporarily, and in the best of causes."

"Oh, I know. I know everything you do, including your plan. I go west to foil the invasion while you stay here, hide, and set a trap."

•• •• •• •• •• •• •• •• •• •• •• •• •• •• ••

A patch of azure flame danced on the muddy, sluggishly flowing water, seemingly without having any fuel to burn. Evidently the Umber Marshes contained a tiny pocket or two of plagueland—territory where the residue of the Spellplague still festered—and Gaedynn had wandered into one of them.

He studied the blue fire with wary interest. Though he'd occasionally visited plagueland, he'd never actually seen the stuff before.

He would have been just as glad to skip the spectacle now. He fancied he'd feel at home in any true forest across the length and breadth of Faerûn, but this rust-colored swamp was a different matter. He hated the way the soft ground tried to suck the boots off his feet and especially hated the clouds of biting, blood-sucking insects. Back in the Yuirwood, the elves had taught him a cantrip to keep such vermin away, but it didn't seem to work on these mindlessly persistent pests.

Yes, if there ever was a patch of land that ought to be scouted on griffonback, this was it—except that the thick, tangled canopy of the trees made it impossible to survey the ground from on high. So somebody had to do it the hard way.

He skulked onward, glancing back at the azure flames periodically, making sure they were staying put. So far, so good, but in Aoth's stories they'd raced across the land in great curtains, destroying everything they engulfed.

Gaedynn faced forward again to see a troll charging him, its long, spindly legs with their knobby knees eating up the distance. The man-eating creature was half again as tall as a human being, with a nose like a spike and eyes that were round, black pits. It had clawed fingers and a mouth full of fangs, and its hide was a mottled red-brown instead of the usual green, possibly to help it blend in with the oddly colored foliage of the marshes.

Perhaps that was why Gaedynn hadn't detected it sooner, expert woodsman though he was. Or perhaps the distractions of the blue fire and stinging insects were to blame. Either way, it was a lapse that could easily cost him his life. He snatched an arrow from his quiver, laid it on his bow, and then the troll was right on top of him.

On top and then past. It ran by without paying him any heed, soon vanishing between two mossy oaks.

Gaedynn exhaled. From one perspective, he'd had a narrow escape, but he didn't feel lucky just yet, because it had certainly appeared that the troll was running away from something. If so, what had put such a fearsome brute to flight?

Whatever it was, it could easily pose a threat to Gaedynn and his fellow scouts as well. He whistled a birdcall. Somewhere off to the left, invisible among the trees and thickets, an archer answered in kind. On his right, however, sounded only the *tap-tap-tap* of a drilling woodpecker and the *plop* of something jumping or dropping in water. He whistled a second time and still couldn't raise a response.

As Gaedynn paused to consider how to proceed, the scout on his left yelped. Gaedynn waited a moment, then whistled the signal, but this time, nobody answered.

Keeping low, trying to move fast but stealthily too, Gaedynn headed in the direction of the yelp. Listening intently, eyes constantly moving, he promised himself that nothing else would surprise him.

And nothing did, but it was close. Scuttling beside one of the ubiquitous channels, he glimpsed motion from the corner of his eye, pivoted, and found a red mass rearing over him like a wave about to break. The thing was big as a cottage, but its shapeless, essentially liquid nature had enabled it to ooze along under the surface of the murky water undetected.

Gaedynn retreated and shot the arrow he'd initially intended for the troll. It stuck in the middle of his attacker—which gave off the coppery smell of blood——but didn't even slow it down. The creature heaved and flowed after him.

Some of the special shafts Jhesrhi grudgingly enchanted for him might hurt the thing more, but it seemed a poor idea to stand too close while he tried them. He sprinted away from it.

Something tall as the troll but broader, its inconstant shape vaguely human but composed of filthy water, made a splashing leap from an algae-covered pool on his left and half ran, half flowed to intercept him. It reached with enormous hands—the left one had the fingers fused together, as though it wore a mitten—and he felt the cold, poisonous wrongness festering inside them. It was the same sick sensation he sometimes had when obliged to spend time around Mirror, only more intense.

He could only recoil from the new threat, even though it took him back toward the pursuing blood-thing. Meanwhile, the mud and dark, stagnant water vomited up other horrors, each made of liquid or muck. Glancing around, he realized he was surrounded.

Regretting the necessity, he pulled his one arrow of sending from its place and used the bodkin point to prick the back of his own hand. The world seemed to shatter and reassemble itself in an instant, and he found himself some distance to the west, where a squad of Khouryn's spearmen flailed their hands at mosquitoes while slogging and slipping their way along.

.. ..

Sitting on a rotten stump, Aoth bit off a mouthful of biscuit. In truth, he was only a little hungry, but since the vanguard had to halt while its officers palavered, it made sense to eat. At least the bread was still relatively fresh. Like any veteran campaigner, he'd all too often been reduced to gnawing bread hard as stone and full of bugs.

"Can you guess," he asked, chewing, "exactly what you ran into?"

Gaedynn swallowed a mouthful of apple and tossed the core away. "Some of the creatures looked like water and earth elementals, but they had the feel of undead about them."

"They're both," Bareris said. Unlike his living comrades, he and Mirror hadn't bothered to sit or squat but rather stood just outside the circle. "In Thay, they call them necromentals. And the red thing was a blood amniote. It will drain your blood faster than a vampire, if it catches you."

Aoth snorted. "I see that even with Xingax slain and Szass Tam busy with greater matters, the necromancers are still making new toys."

"I'm afraid so," Mirror said. At the moment, he looked like a warped, dingy reflection of Khouryn. Aoth could tell it irritated the dwarf, though he was hiding his displeasure as best he could.

"Do you know how many there are?" asked Aoth.

Gaedynn shook his head. "I was a little too busy to make an accurate count."

"I thought you were supposed to be a scout," Jhesrhi said in one of her rare attempts at humor. She lacked the knack for it, and as usual, nobody laughed.

"I wonder," said Aoth, "if these creatures simply escaped from their keepers and wandered into the swamp. The Thay I remember was already infested with such horrors, and since then, the necromancers have had a century of peace and supremacy to perform any crazy experiment that came to mind." He scowled. "But no. In all honesty, I doubt this is pure bad luck. Somehow, Szass Tam knows we're coming and has sent some of his servants to slow our progress."

"I can see them doing a good job of it," Khouryn said. He slapped his neck and squashed the insect that had landed there, just above his hauberk. The blow smacked flesh and made the links of mail clink. "They can dog us while hiding in water or mud. Pop out, kill a man or two, and disappear again."

"Do we have to keep going in this direction?" Jhesrhi asked.

"Yes," Bareris said. "The rebels who smuggle arms into Thay taught me that, unpleasant as it seems, this is one of the few 'good' paths across the marshes. We'd have to backtrack a long way to pick up another."

He didn't have to explain any further. They all knew that even under the best of circumstances, it would be an onerous chore getting an army on the march to suddenly reverse direction. Here in the bogs, with the thick vegetation inhibiting communication and the soldiers all but walking single file along the narrow trails, it would be a nightmare.

"The delay," said Aoth, "might actually give Szass Tam time to place forces all along the edge of the swamp to catch us coming out. And who knows, if we did shift to a different route, we might find these necromentals and whatnot guarding it as well."

Gaedynn scratched at the bump of an old insect bite on his cheek. His nail tore the scab, and a drop of blood oozed out. "So you're saying, we fight."

"Yes," Aoth replied.

Khouryn frowned. "The men will have a difficult time of it on this ground."

"Or contending with elementals," said Aoth, "if they don't command any form of magic, or at the very least, carry enchanted weapons. In addition to which, it's not certain Szass Tam's creatures would show themselves to an entire company obviously formed up for battle. So I propose that we—those of us in this circle and a few others—go forward, let the brutes accost us, and kill them ourselves."

Gaedynn grinned. "Sounds like a nice, suicidal way to spend an afternoon."

•• •• •• •• •• •• •• •• •• •• •• •• ••

Jhesrhi Coldcreek lifted her staff high, murmured, and magic sent a colorless shimmer through the air. Then she cocked her head and squinted at the rust-colored poplars, mud, and channel of water before her. Bareris inferred that she'd cast a charm to sharpen her sight.

"See anything?" he asked.

"No." Judging from her clipped, cold response, she didn't much like it that, as the company proceeded forward, each member repeatedly swinging right or left to avoid water, mossy tree trunks, thick tangles of brush, and the more obvious patches of soft, treacherous ground, the two of them had ended up in proximity to one another.

"Neither do I," Bareris said. "Perhaps Aoth or one of the Burning Braziers can do better." The former could see all sorts of things with his spellscarred eyes, and the latter, successors to the warrior priests of Kossuth, god of fire, who'd accompanied the zulkirs into exile, knew spells specifically designed to reveal the presence of lurking undead.

Jhesrhi pushed a low-hanging branch out of her way. "I want you to know something. If this is all a trick, I'll destroy you."

Bareris frowned. "You mean, if Mirror and I are actually working for Szass Tam. If my mad tale about his wanting to end the world is really an elaborate ruse to lure his enemies back within his reach, because he feels the time has come to settle old scores."

The wizard's amber eyes narrowed. "You didn't have any trouble inferring the precise nature of my suspicions."

"Not because they're true; because they're obvious. I'd wonder the same thing in your place, particularly now that the necrementals have turned up on our route, almost as if someone told Szass Tam where to station them. But your captain vouches for Mirror and me. Trust his judgment, or, if you can't manage that, trust the vision that came to him while he was flying over Veltalar."

"I do trust Aoth Fezim. But I also know you're a bard. You can make people feel, think, and perhaps even see and remember whatever you want them to."

"I did do something like that to Aoth, once, a century ago." He remembered the guilt he'd subsequently felt for that betrayal, the pain of broken friendship, and his gratitude when the warmage eventually forgave him. "But it was a mistake, and I wouldn't do it again, even to strike a blow against Szass Tam. It's probably the only thing I wouldn't do."

She brushed gnats away from her face. "You don't have to convince me. I'm here. I'm following orders and doing my part. I just need for you to understand—"

"They're here!" called Aoth.

Bareris peered around and failed to spot whatever had alerted his friend. But a heartbeat later, the first of Szass Tam's creatures exploded up like geysers from muck and muddy water.

A Burning Brazier hurled a gout of holy fire at an undead earth elemental. It reeled backward, and Jet, who'd insisted on accompanying his master into battle, pounced on it. His aquiline talons and leonine claws tore away chunks of dirt as if he were a dog digging a hole. Aoth leveled his spear and pierced the necromental with darts of green light.

A second hulking creature made of mud swung an oversized fist at Mirror, who still resembled a shadowy parody of Khouryn. The ghost sidestepped and struck back with his weapon, which looked like Khouryn's urgrosh at the beginning of the stroke but turned into a sword before the end.

After that, Bareris couldn't watch any more, because what at first glance looked like a wall of dirty water erupted from a sluggish stream on his right and surged at him and Jhesrhi. He could make out the suggestion of heads and limbs amid the churning, surging liquid but couldn't tell just how many necromentals were actually rushing to attack, only that he and the wizard had drawn more than their fair share.

Infusing his voice with magic, he shouted. The sound blasted one necromental into a mist of sparkling droplets and blew away some of the liquid substance of another. Meanwhile, Jhesrhi chanted and pointed her staff. A flare of silvery power leaped from it and froze another pair of water creatures into ice. Off balance, one toppled forward onto its face.

Now that he and his ally had thinned the pack, Bareris saw there were two necromentals remaining, the one he'd wounded and another. And they were about to close the distance. He sprang forward to intercept them and keep them away from Jhesrhi, so she could cast her spells without interference.

He cut into a necromental's leg. It was hard to tell how badly he was hurting a creature made of water, but his blade, plundered from one of Szass Tam's fallen champions, bore potent enchantments, so it was presumably doing something. A huge open hand swung down at him. He dodged, and the extremity splashed apart against the ground. The droplets and spatters instantly leaped back together, reforming the hand.

Bareris dodged a blow from the other undead elemental, landed a second cut, and then something big and heavy—an attack he hadn't seen coming—smashed down on him, drenching him and slamming him to his knees. Water forced its way into his nostrils and mouth and down his throat like a worm boring into an apple.

The attack would have killed a living man. But while Bareris hated what his contact with the dream vestige had made of him, it had given him certain advantages. He was more resilient than a mortal warrior. Since he didn't need to breathe, he couldn't drown. And the poison touch of a fellow undead was innocuous to him.

He jumped back up, conceivably surprising the necromentals, and cut the one his shout had injured, distinguishable from the other because the magical assault had left it a head shorter. Retching water to relieve a painful pressure in his chest, and, more importantly, to recover the use of his voice, he whirled and dodged, thrust and cut.

The smaller necromental abruptly lost cohesion, its shattered form pouring to the ground like beer from an overturned tankard. That left him free to focus on the other.

As was Jhesrhi. She struck it with a blaze of fire that turned much of it into steam. Bareris snarled and commanded himself not to flinch or falter as the vapor scalded his face and hands. He supposed he should be glad that the mage had at least aimed high enough to avoid hitting him with the flame itself.

He whirled his sword in a horizontal cut through the necromental's belly. Jhesrhi chanted rhyming words with a sharp, fierce sound and rapid cadence. The undead water spirit started to boil, bubbles rising inside it. Bareris leaped back before the heat could burn him a second time.

The necromental stumbled around, pawing at itself, then broke apart like its fellow. Jhesrhi cried out.

For an instant, Bareris, still looking at the spot where the steaming remains of the necromental soaked the ground, imagined the wizard had crowed in triumph. Then he recognized the distress in her voice and pivoted.

Jhesrhi was reeling around in the midst of a dark, droning cloud, on first inspection no different from the swarms of mosquitoes that had tormented the living all the way through the swamp. But Bareris assumed the tiny creatures were actually another necromantic creation, capable of inflicting considerable harm.

It was a threat he couldn't dispatch with a sword, nor pulverize with a shout without battering the woman trapped in the midst of the cloud as well. As Jhesrhi fell to one knee, he coughed the last of the water out of his lungs and throat, sang a charm, and ran to her.

He'd cloaked himself in an enchantment designed to repel vermin, and as he'd learned over the years, it was never certain the magic would work on things the necromancers had made using bugs and the like for raw materials. This time, it did. Buzzing furiously, the mosquitoes flew away from him and Jhesrhi, and he shouted, a thunderous roar that obliterated the insects and blasted bark and dead branches from the oaks behind them.

He kneeled beside Jhesrhi. She seemed dazed though not unconscious, and she had little beads and smears of blood all over her body where the undead swarm had bitten her. He took her hand and sang a song of healing.

Her eyes shifted, focused on his face, and then she jerked her fingers out of his grasp. "Don't touch me!" she snarled.

"I don't need to anymore." He rose and lifted his sword. "You've done your part. Why don't you stay out of the rest of it?"

"No. I can fight." With the aid of her staff, moving like an arthritic old granny, she clambered to her feet, then peered around. "Oh, no!"

Bareris looked where she was looking, at Khouryn and Gaedynn. Apparently the two had fought in tandem, the dwarf wielding his urgrosh to engage any foe that ventured into range while the archer kept his distance and loosed arrows. Judging from the vaguely man-shaped piles of earth littering the ground around them, it had been an effective strategy. Until now.

Red, liquid tendrils rose from the soft earth beneath their boots like grass growing tall in a heartbeat. The blood amniote had flowed and burrowed through the mud to surround and cage them. The tendrils branched and connected, forming an even more secure prison, and the suggestion of mad, anguished faces formed and dissolved in the surfaces so created. The undead ooze extruded a huge tentacle, raised it high, and lashed it down at Gaedynn.

Confined as he was, the bowman couldn't dodge. The attack swatted him to the ground, and, as the tentacle lifted again, blood burst from his skin and flew upward to add itself to the substance of the amniote. Jhesrhi gasped.

"Hit it with everything you have!" Bareris said. "It doesn't matter if I'm in the way!" If his blistered hands and face were any indication, perhaps he hadn't needed to tell her that, but it still seemed like a good idea. Her slightest hesitation could cost Gaedynn and Khouryn their lives.

He charged the blood amniote, singing even as he sprinted as only a war bard could. It was harsh music, full of hate, designed to bleed the strength from an opponent, and the first sting of it made the gigantic ooze stop flailing at its captives. Bareris closed the distance, slashed at the creature's flowing, foul-smelling body, and then it started hammering at him.

He dodged, cut, and sang his spell of grinding, relentless destruction. More faces appeared in the crimson, latticed mass, and it seemed that a female one mouthed his name. Lightning crackled, thunder boomed, and blasts of fire roared, he felt sudden heat and glimpsed flashes at the periphery of his vision, but Jhesrhi managed to hit the huge undead without striking him. He thought they might actually have the situation under control. Then, instead of lashing at him with an arm, the amniote simply fell at him like an avalanche or a breaking wave.

He couldn't dodge that. The great, formless mass of it slammed him down on his back, then reared above him. Pain, different and worse than the shock of impact he'd suffered an instant before, wracked him.

His heart didn't beat, and he didn't bleed when a blade cut him. He'd assumed he didn't have any blood the amniote could steal. But now skin and muscle split, and the veins beneath them ruptured. Brown powder swirled up from the wounds.

The blood amniote faltered like a man who had taken a bite of food and found it unexpectedly foul. Its liquid bulk shifted toward Gaedynn and Khouryn.

His whole body throbbing with pain, Bareris scrambled to his feet and gritted out the next line of the song. He cut through a section of the amniote's body, and his blade left a trail of scarlet droplets behind it.

The ooze-thing oriented on him again, rearing above him. Then it broke apart, its liquid remains drumming the earth.

Bareris staggered to Gaedynn and Khouryn. Jhesrhi came running too, and flung herself down beside the scout. Neither he nor the dwarf had flesh torn in the same way as Bareris's—perhaps their blood had come out their pores—but they both looked as if someone had dyed them crimson.

"Help them!" Jhesrhi snapped.

Bareris saw they were both still breathing. "I can keep them alive, but they need a real healer. Fetch a priest."

By the time the healer, a young Burning Brazier with keen,

earnest features, finished his work, the battle was over, the nec-romentals and other horrors dispatched. The cleric eyed Bareris uncertainly, and the latter had a good idea what was going through his mind. On one hand, the priest's superiors had trained him to despise and destroy the undead. But on the other, Bareris was manifestly an ally and a warrior who'd been fighting Szass Tam, the great maker and master of zombies, vampires, and their ilk, for a hundred years.

"I can try to help you too, if you want," the young man said at length.

"Thank you, but your magic wouldn't work on me." Bareris remembered how another Burning Brazier had labored in vain to save Tammith after one of Xingax's creations bit her head off. Like every memory of his lost love, it brought a stab of pain. "Anyway, my wounds will close on their own in a little while."

After the Brazier took his leave, Jhesrhi approached. Looking down a little, avoiding eye contact, she said, "I snatched my hand away from you."

"I remember."

"I would have yanked it away no matter who was holding it."

And evidently that was as much of an apology or an expression of acceptance and trust as Bareris was going to get. Which was fine. He didn't need Aoth's troops to be his friends. He just needed them to fight.

chapter five

9 Mirtul, The Year of the Dark Circle (1478 DR)

Over the years, Aoth had grown used to spotting things from far away that other people failed to notice even at short range, and this was evidently such an occasion. On a ridge a half mile distant, men in mottled green, tan, and brown clothing lay motionless on their bellies, watching the great column that was the zulkirs' army marching north with its mercenary contingent still in the lead. Griffon riders soared almost directly above the necromancers' spies but evidently hadn't seen them.

Aoth blew his horn to snag the riders' attention, then pointed at the watchers with his spear. His aerial scouts took another look at the ridge, then readied their bows and swooped lower.

"You and I could have killed those men ourselves," Jet grumbled.

"I'm a commander now," Aoth replied. "I'm not supposed to slaughter with my own hands every enemy who wanders into view. It would look peculiar."

Still, he wouldn't have minded the exercise. It might have taken his mind off the sad spectacle of the land spread out before him.

It didn't surprise him, exactly. During the ten years of the zulkirs' war, he'd watched the conflict steadily ruin the land. Blue skies gave way to gray. Green fields withered or fell to weeds and tares as relentlessly as estates and towns fell to besiegers and marauders. Contaminated by the residue of malign sorcery, the soil and rivers spawned blight, disease, and monstrosities even when no wizard was trying to call them forth. And Aoth had heard that, after driving his rivals out, Szass Tam hadn't exerted himself unduly to repair the damage, for reasons that were finally apparent. The lich had been too busy building Dread Rings and otherwise preparing for the Unmaking.

As a result, much of Lapendrar remained a wasteland, either barren or given over to pale, twisted scrub the like of which Aoth had never seen before. No one was maintaining the roads— vegetation encroached everywhere, and at certain points, sinkholes had swallowed the roads, or rain had washed the highways away— evidence that the great merchant caravans no longer traveled the length and breadth of the kingdom. Crumbling ruins dotted the rolling plain, which rose gradually as it ran up to the towering cliffs called the First Escarpment.

Although the province wasn't all desolation. Periodically, Aoth sighted a plantation still growing normal food for those Thayans who still required it. But even there, it was zombies, not living slaves, who toiled mindlessly in the fields when their masters, in all likelihood, had already fled the invaders' approach.

He'd told Bareris the truth. He hadn't missed Thay, not after the first few years in exile, anyway. He'd lived a better life elsewhere than he ever had here. But even so, the realm had been home in a way that no other place would ever be again, and a land of contentment and prosperity for many even if its neighbors thought it wicked to the core. It was . . . unpleasant to see it so corrupted and diminished.

"What's wrong?" asked Jet, sensing his sour mood.

"I left my kingdom behind, and it turned into this."

"Did you have a choice?"

"Not really."

"Could you have done anything about it if you'd stayed?"

"Almost certainly not."

"Then you're rebuking yourself over nothing. Stop it!"

Aoth smiled. "Your grandmother would have told me exactly the same thing."

"That's because griffons are wise, and humans have a talent for stupidity. Look! Are those more enemy scouts?"

Aoth peered and decided, no, the four men and two women probably weren't, because they were gaunt, haggard, and ragged. Three were poorly armed, and the others carried no weapons at all. Most tellingly of all, they made no effort to conceal themselves as they advanced on the column with its trail of hanging dust.

Outriders trotted to intercept them. Bareris swooped down on his griffon, perhaps to vouch for the newcomers and make sure the horsemen did them no harm.

"Those are rebels," said Aoth.

Over time, more such folk came to join the column. Flying high above the army, Aoth observed them all, but even his spell-scarred eyes failed to recognize their feverish excitement until he and Jet set down on the ground again.

•• •• •• •• •• •• •• •• •• •• •• •• ••

Malark murmured the final words of the incantation, and magic whispered through the air. He considered casting the same spell yet again, then decided against it. It was important that no one stumble across the bare little room in which he'd stashed his supplies, but surely three layered charms of concealment were sufficient.

And if his refuge was secure, he might as well start hunting.

He drew on the scaly, yellow gauntlets with the barbed, black claws. He scarcely needed such weapons to kill in hand-to-hand combat, but some enchanter had flayed the hide from a demon's hands to make them, and the Abyssal taint still clinging to them should provide a different sort of obscurement.

His leather-and-crystal headband enabling him to see in the darkness, he skulked from the room into the maze of chambers and tunnels beyond, moving warily even though he doubted anyone else was around. Not here. Below him, so rumor said, lurked fearsome creatures, some that had dwelled there since the dawn of time and some that Szass Tam had placed, perhaps to contain the others. Above were storerooms, conjuration chambers, dungeons, and vaults, excavated by the long-vanished builders of the Citadel, that the current inhabitants had turned to their own purposes. But this level was a sort of empty borderland, deep enough that no one had bothered to exploit it yet but higher than the lairs of the monstrosities.

Malark found a staircase and climbed.

After a time, a faint, wavering, greenish gleam, the unmistakable light of perpetual torches, warned him he was nearing the deepest of the occupied levels. He left the stairs and stalked onward. Soft chanting led him into an ossuary, where hand bones arranged in intricate floral designs adorned the walls of one room, foot bones another, and vertebrae a third.

A necromancer stood with staff raised and eyes closed in the final chamber, the one decorated with grinning skulls. Perhaps the wizard admired Szass Tam, for like the lich, and in defiance of the usual Mulan preference for heads as hairless as any naked skull, he'd grown a goatish little chin beard.

"Hello," Malark said.

The necromancer's eyes popped open, and he faltered in his chanting. Malark felt something, some invisible entity the conjuring had held in its grasp, wriggle free like a fish escaping a net.

"Your Omnipotence," the bearded wizard said. He started to lower himself to his knees.

"Please," Malark said, "don't do that. You don't want to abase yourself before a man who means to kill you."

Straightening up, the necromancer peered at Malark as if he assumed his fellow Red Wizard was joking, but he wasn't quite sure enough to laugh. "Master?"

"I have to start murdering people down here, and I'd much rather begin with you than a menial. It's more sporting and will make a bigger impression."

The necromancer swallowed. "I don't understand."

"All you need to understand is this: I'm not going to use my own sorcery. If you start right now, you might have time to generate one effect before I cross the space between us." Malark sprang forward.

The necromancer snarled a word of command and thrust out his hand. Darkness leaped from his fingertips, swelled, and formed itself into an object shaped somewhat like a greatsword but made of sets of gnashing jaws lined with multiple rows of jagged fangs. Howling and gibbering in some infernal tongue, the fang-blade flew at Malark.

Who dived underneath its raking, slavering stroke, straightened up again, and tore away the necromancer's eyes and throat with two gory sweeps of the clawed gloves. The wizard fell backward, dropping his staff, which clattered on the floor.

Malark spun back around to defend himself from the fang-sword, then saw he wouldn't have to. Without the focused will of its creator to guide it, the weapon simply floated in the air.

Still, Malark thought it wise to silence its caterwauling. Screams of various sorts were by no means uncommon in these crypts, but even so, the noise might attract attention. He rattled off a charm of dismissal, and the blade disappeared.

Then he dipped a clawed finger in the necromancer's blood and daubed symbols emblematic of Shar, Cyric, and Gruumsh, deities whose worship Szass Tam had forbidden in order to honor his pact with Bane, on the brows of some of the omnipresent skulls. It was yet another form of obfuscation.

•• •• •• •• •• •• •• •• •• •• •• •• •• ••

Lallara gave Aoth a scowl. "What's the matter?" she snapped.

Actually, she supposed that from a certain perspective, it wasn't entirely bad that he'd insisted on a private palaver in the command tent with her, the other zulkirs, Bareris, and Mirror. Her back and thighs aching from another long day in the saddle, she'd rapidly grown sick of grubby, malodorous serfs and escaped slaves babbling praise and thanks and proffering shabby handicrafts and trinkets. It was a mark of just how far the world had fallen that such wretches even dared approach her.

But she didn't like having a man who'd once vowed to serve the Council of Zulkirs dictating to her, either.

Aoth answered her glower with one of his own. "The rebels obviously think you've come back to overthrow Szass Tam and restore the Thay that was. And you're encouraging them to think it."

"If their misapprehension inspires them to give us whatever help they can," said Samas Kul, "then why not take advantage of it?" He had a walnut pastry in one hand and a cup in the other, and as usual, he sprawled on his floating throne. The ungainly conveyance had snagged the edge of the tent door and nearly pulled down the shelter when he came in.

"Because as our allies," said Aoth, "they deserve to know the truth: that after we break the Dread Ring, we're going to leave."

Nevron sneered. "Allies."

"Yes," said Aoth, "allies. Not subjects. You can't claim to rule them when you fled this land before any of them were even born."

Lauzoril put his hands together, fingertip to opposing fingertip. "Whatever they believe, by aiding us, they'll be fighting for their only hope of survival. Isn't that what's truly important?"

"I suppose so," said Aoth. "And I think they're capable of understanding that if we explain it to them."

His pastry devoured, Samas sucked at the traces of sugar glaze on his fingers. "But where's the profit in risking it?"

Aoth took a deep breath. "Evidently I'm not making myself clear. I'm going to make sure they know the truth. I'm warning you so we can all speak it. That will be better for their morale than if they catch the mighty zulkirs in a lie."

"You'll do no such thing," Lauzoril said. "We forbid it."

Aoth said, "I don't care."

"But you took our coin!" said Samas.

"Yes," said the stocky warmage, his luminous azure eyes burning in the gloom. "You can well afford it, and my men deserve it. But this isn't our usual kind of war. We're fighting for our lives and perhaps the life of the world, not for pay, and you four wouldn't even know about the threat if not for Bareris, Mirror, and me. So I won't take your orders if I don't agree with them. In fact, you might as well consider me your equal for the duration."

Lallara felt a surge of wrath, and then, to her surprise, grudging amusement. The Rashemi bastard knew they needed him, and he was making the most of it. It wouldn't stop her or, certainly, any of the other zulkirs from punishing him in the end, but still, one could almost admire his boldness.

•• •• •• •• •• •• •• •• •• •• •• •• ••

When they had found out the rebels wanted to pay homage to them, the zulkirs had raised a section of ground to serve as a makeshift dais, then lit it with a sourceless crimson glow.

The archmages were gone now, and so were their chairs, but the mound and light remained, and the ragged, starveling insurgents, apprised that Bareris wished to address them, were assembling before it once again. Standing with Mirror and Aoth, he watched them congregate.

"The zulkirs had a point," he said. "These folk might well have fought better with hearts full of hope."

"Maybe so," said Aoth.

"So why did you insist on giving them the truth?"

Aoth shrugged. "Who knows? I suspected that returning to Thay would be bad for me. Maybe it's clouded my judgment. Or maybe *I* spent too many years as the council's ignorant pawn."

Mirror, at the moment less a visible presence than a mere sense of vague threat and incipient headache, said, "Telling them the truth is the right thing to do."

Aoth grinned. "Is that what the holy warrior thinks? How unexpected." He fixed his lambent blue eyes on Bareris. "I fully understand we need these people to scout and forage and find clean water. They know the country, and they've kept watch on the Dread Ring since the necromancers started building it. But even so, I don't fear to give them the truth, because I know you can inspire them to stay and fight. You're eloquent, and you fought alongside their grandfathers and fathers after the rest of Szass Tam's opponents ran away. You're a hero to them."

Bareris had heard such praise before, and as usual, it felt like mockery. "I'm no hero. I've bungled everything that ever truly counted. But I'll do my best to hold them." Judging that most if not all of the rebels had gathered, he climbed onto the mound and started to speak.

As he did, he was tempted to try to hypnotize his audience. But it was possible he wouldn't snare every mind or that some folk would shake off the enchantment in a day or so, and then, feeling ill-used, the rebels would surely depart. Besides, he found he just couldn't bring himself to manipulate them as egregiously as he'd once manipulated Aoth, not with the latter actually looking on.

So he infused his voice with magic to help him appear a wiser and more commanding figure than he might have otherwise. But he stopped short of enslavement.

First, he gave the assembly the truth Aoth insisted they hear and watched it crush the joy out of them. Then he reiterated that it was still vital that they fight. Because, while victory wouldn't bring down their oppressors, it would save their lives.

A man at the front of the crowd spat on the ground. At some point, a necromancer or necromancer's minion had sliced off his nose, and he wore a grimy kerchief tied around the lower portion of his face to hide his deformity. The cloth fluttered as his breath whistled in and out of the hole.

"My life isn't worth the trouble!" he called.

"I know that feeling," Bareris answered. "I've had it myself for a hundred years, so who am I to tell you you're wrong? But look around at your comrades who risked torture and execution to stand here with you tonight. Aren't their lives worth fighting for?

"And if they aren't reason enough," Bareris continued, "I'll give you another: revenge! When we take the Dread Ring, we'll butcher every necromancer, blood orc, and ghoul inside. I admit, we won't get Szass Tam himself, but we'll deprive him of his heart's desire, balk him, and gall him as no one ever has before.

"And one day, we rebels *will* drag him down off his throne and slay him. As it turns out, it won't be this year or the next, and the Council of Zulkirs may not be there to help us when we do, but it will happen. This siege is the beginning. Imagine what we can do with the arms and magic we'll plunder from the Dread Ring.

Imagine how word of our victory will draw new recruits to our ranks. We'll finally be a true army all by ourselves."

He looked out at the crowd and saw resolve returning in the set of their jaws and the way they stood straighter. He drew breath to continue on in the same vein, then froze when a hulking shape abruptly appeared at the back of the throng.

It was tall as an ogre and had four arms. Red eyes blazed from a head also possessed of a muzzle full of needle fangs. Bareris knew its scaly hide was actually dark purple like the duskiest of grapes, but it looked black in the night.

"I can see you're all brave little lambs," said Tsagoth, a sneer in his tone. "But this is your one warning: the Dread Ring is full of wolves."

He snatched up a young Rashemi woman and beheaded her with a single snap of his jaws. Blood gushed from the stump of her neck. He pivoted and disemboweled a man with a sweep of his claws. Short sword in hand, a third rebel charged the blood fiend from behind, and Tsagoth turned again and locked eyes with him. The swordsman jammed the point of his blade into his own neck.

Aoth ran into the crowd, while Mirror and Jet flew over it. Off to the side of it, Gaedynn, moving with almost preternatural speed, strung his bow and nocked an arrow. Meanwhile, Bareris drew his sword and sang. The world seemed to shatter and mend itself in an instant, and then, magically whisked across the intervening distance, Bareris was standing directly in front of Tsagoth.

The vampiric demon laughed down at him with gory jaws. "Too slow, singer," he said as he disappeared.

Bareris lunged. His blade encountered no resistance, proof that Tsagoth hadn't merely turned invisible. He'd employed his own innate ability to translate himself through space. Gaedynn's arrow streaked through the spot the creature's head had occupied an instant before.

Bareris stalked onward, pivoting, sword at the ready. He crooned a charm to give himself owl eyes.

A hand gripped his forearm. Startled, he wrenched himself around, trying both to break free and to bring his blade to bear before he saw that it was Aoth who'd taken hold of him.

"It's over for now," the sellsword captain said.

"You don't know that. Just because he ran, it doesn't mean he ran far."

"Of course it does. Think. No lone warrior, not even Tsagoth, would linger for long in the midst of an enemy army."

"Well, I'll make sure."

"No," said Aoth, his voice soft but steely, "you won't. You climbed up on that pile of dirt to motivate these folk, and it was working, but now Tsagoth's rattled them. You have to go back and talk some more. Otherwise, the blood drinker's undone your good work, and he wins. Is that what you want?"

Shaking, Bareris closed his eyes and struggled to dampen his hatred and rage at least a little. Tried to think of something besides Tammith crumbling in his embrace as the Alamber Sea dissolved her flesh like acid.

"I'll go back," he managed.

•• •• •• •• •• •• •• •• •• •• •• •• •• •• ••

Aoth posted more sentries and rousted Lallara and her subordinate wizards to cast additional defensive enchantments, just in case Tsagoth tried to sneak back. Then he returned to the center of the camp, where Bareris was still addressing the rebels and brandishing his naked sword for emphasis. The red light made the blade look bloody.

If Aoth was any judge—and after a century of commanding men, he'd better be—the bard's oration was having the desired effect. The rebels no longer regarded the blood fiend's incursion as a terrifying guarantee of horrors to come. Now it seemed an infuriating provocation.

Aoth made his way to Mirror's side. "Thank the gods for that golden tongue," he murmured from the corner of his mouth.

"It's bad that Tsagoth's here," replied the ghost. "We'll have to watch over our brother to make sure the old grudge doesn't goad him into folly."

"In case you didn't notice, I just promoted myself to acting zulkir a little while ago. I have this whole army to 'watch over.' Bareris knows what's at stake. I'm sure he'll be fine."

●● ●● ●● ●● ●● ●● ●● ●● ●● ●● ●●

Standing atop the battlements above the Dread Ring's primary gate, Malark—for it was easier to think of himself that way than as the original Malark's magically created surrogate, especially now that they were no longer in proximity—gazed south. The council's army was out there somewhere in the night, probably within a day's march of the fortress. The scouts and diviners had given him a good idea of its size and composition, but even so, he looked forward to seeing such a mighty host of killers for himself and to watching it and the castle's defenders slaughter one another.

A dark, looming form appeared before him. He reflexively shifted his feet just a little—though most observers wouldn't even notice, the change in his stance prepared him for combat—even as he perceived that the new arrival was Tsagoth, come to report as expected.

"How did it go?" Malark asked.

"Anskuld and many others saw me make the kills. One of my victims was a young, dark-haired Rashemi girl, pretty as you humans reckon such things."

"Excellent. Are you thirsty? Would you like me to conjure an imp for you to feast on?" Although, bound as he was into Szass

Tam's service, Tsagoth generally had to make do with the blood of mortals, he much preferred to prey on other creatures native to the higher worlds.

The blood fiend glared, his crimson eyes blazing. "I'm not a dog for you to reward with treats."

Malark decided not to observe that when Tsagoth, with his lupine muzzle, bared his fangs that way, there was a certain resemblance. "Of course not. You're my valued comrade, and I was trying to show you courtesy."

Tsagoth grunted.

"Why so touchy, if your errand went well?"

"When I arrived, the bard was addressing the rebels. He told them Szass Tam has some demented scheme to kill the entire world."

"Ah."

"Is it true?"

Malark considered denial but decided a lie was unlikely to allay the blood fiend's suspicions. "I wouldn't call it 'demented,' but otherwise, yes. Please tell no one else." Many of the Dread Ring's garrison wouldn't believe or understand Tsagoth even if he did tattle, and, like the undead demon himself, they bore enchantments that would oblige them to perform their functions no matter what they knew. Still, it would be pointlessly cruel to frighten them.

Tsagoth twitched as he felt Malark's mild-sounding request impose irresistible compulsion.

"Have I served well these past hundred years?" the blood fiend asked.

"I assume that's a rhetorical question. You're one of our master's greatest champions."

"I've done all I have in the hope that one day he would return me to my own plane. If you want my very best, one last time, promise me that after we preserve the Dread Ring, you'll send me home."

Malark sighed. "You think you'll be safe if you simply escape Faerûn, don't you? In all honesty, I have to tell you, you won't."

Tsagoth snorted. "I know Szass Tam is capable of making a great mess, but I doubt he'll even destroy this one squalid little excuse for a world. His magic surely won't reach into all the worlds there are."

"The Spellplague did."

"So people say, but I still like my chances."

"Have it your way, then. Once we eliminate the threat to the castle, I'll return you to the Abyss. Now, is it clear what I need from you next?"

"Yes. The zulkirs will camp on the lake or near it. When practical, I'm to seize Rashemi maidens and drown them, so they die in water like Tammith Iltazyarra did."

"Precisely."

"What I don't understand is why it's so important to nettle Bareris Anskuld and undermine his judgment. He's just one soldier in an army."

"In his way, he's as accomplished a champion as you are; I'm sure Aoth or the zulkirs will give him men to command, and in any case, this ploy is just one little element of my overall strategy. I'll give you tasks more worthy of your stature as the siege proceeds."

"All right. Whatever you want." Tsagoth hesitated. "Tell me one more thing."

"Surely."

"If you know what's coming, why do you serve Szass Tam so willingly?"

"The promise of perfect beauty and perfect peace."

"I don't understand."

Malark smiled. "No one does. It makes me feel lonely sometimes."

chapter six

10–14 Mirtul, The Year of the Dark Circle (1478 DR)

Long before he was old enough to enlist, Aoth had yearned to join the Griffon Legion of Pyarados, because he'd been certain he'd love flying. As he had. And more than a hundred years later, he still relished it just as much as ever.

But this was the sort of morning that took the joy right out of it. The cold rain chilled him despite the magical tattoo and minor charms intended to keep him warm and dry. Maybe he was sensing Jet's discomfort across their psychic link, for his familiar was certainly drenched as well as vexed at winds that consistently blew in exactly the wrong direction to help him go where he intended.

With the sky lumpy with storm clouds promising even heavier rain later on, it was shaping up to be a foul day. As such, it provided the perfect backdrop for Aoth's first look at the Dread Ring of Lapendrar.

The place was black and immense, and something about the

precise curve of its walls and shape of its fanglike towers screamed of arcane power, even though Aoth couldn't decipher the design. Maybe, as a warmage, his knowledge of wizardry was too specialized, or maybe no one could interpret it unless he'd first read Fastrin the Delver's book.

What Aoth *could* tell was that the walls were high and thick and laid out so that any attacking force would find itself shot at from at least two directions at once. And there were plenty of defenders to do the shooting. The battlements crawled with bellowing blood orcs, withered, yellow-eyed dread warriors, and red-robed necromancers all assembled to watch the besieging force march into view.

"Big castle," said Jet.

"Very," said Aoth.

"But I assume you've captured even bigger, over the course of your long and glorious career."

Aoth snorted. "Not so many as you might expect."

"Then we're doomed?"

"No. We have all the surviving members of the Council of Zulkirs on our side, whereas the Dread Ring doesn't have Szass Tam. He's in High Thay, getting ready for the Unmaking. That has to count for something."

Or at least he hoped so.

•• •• •• •• •• •• •• •• •• •• •• •• •• ••

Bareris looked around the council of war and saw fatigue in every lanternlit mortal face. The work of the last two days, necessary preparation for the struggle to come, had been taxing. The army had needed to pitch tents, build corrals for the animals, and make sure of its water supply. Raise earthworks and dig trenches and latrines. Enlarge and assemble the siege engines carried from the Wizard's Reach in shrunken form. The effort ultimately took its toll even on officers and Red Wizards, who for the most part left the manual labor to their subordinates.

But it hadn't tired Bareris—since becoming undead, he seldom knew exhaustion in the way that mortals did—and he didn't feel inclined to lounge in the command tent. He wanted to prowl the night and catch Tsagoth the next time the blood drinker came creeping to abduct and drown another girl.

But now that Aoth had appointed Bareris liaison to the rebel contingent of the army, it was his duty to be here, and even if it weren't, the meeting was important, its purpose to devise a strategy to capture the Dread Ring and so foil Szass Tam's designs. But it was hard to care about even that when the creature who'd killed Tammith with his own four hands was finally within reach.

Slouched in a folding camp chair, his enchanted spear and crestless, plumeless, no-nonsense helmet resting on the ground beside him, Aoth cleared his throat. "All right. We've all had a chance to take a look at the nut we have to crack. What are your thoughts?"

Gaedynn grinned. "Ordinarily, I'd scout a stronghold like this and say, you know, I'm not in any hurry. Let's just starve them out. But from what I understand, zombies and such don't need food, and on top of that, we may only have a few tendays before Szass Tam performs his death ritual. Actually, for all we know, he could be starting it this very moment or could start bright and early tomorrow morning, but we simply have to hope not."

"So why talk about the possibility?" Jhesrhi said. She inspected her grimy hand, then picked at one of her fingernails.

Samas Kul belched. He tossed away a chicken bone, and a candied pomegranate appeared to take its place. "If we could make contact with someone inside the castle—someone alive, I mean—perhaps we could bribe him to open one of the gates."

"I doubt it," Bareris said. "Szass Tam started shackling the minds of his agents at the beginning of the war. Given that the Dread Rings are crucial to his plans, it's unlikely that he'd station anyone there who was still in possession of his free will."

Lauzoril pursed his lips, an expression that made him look even more like a priggish clerk than usual. "Working together, Lallara and I *might* be able to break some of those shackles. Of course, then you'd still have to identify exactly whom it was. You'd have to find a way to communicate with him and convince him it was in his best interests to switch sides . . ."

"In other words," said Nevron, sneering, "the idea's too complicated, and we can't pin our hopes on it. We have to take the Ring by force of arms." He shifted his glare to Aoth. "Your avowed area of expertise, our 'equal for the duration.' "

"I've given the problem some thought," the warmage said, "and even with a company of griffon riders at our disposal, I doubt we can get enough men on top of a wall, or inside the walls, to open the place up for the rest of us. We need to break down a gate or a section of wall, and then we'll have a chance."

Lallara frowned. "Those fortifications are massive. Even if the builders hadn't reinforced them with enchantment—which they did—it would take too much time to batter them down with mangonels and such."

"That's true, Your Omnipotence. But every wall, no matter how strongly built, needs something solid to stand on."

"You're talking about mining."

"Yes."

"Wouldn't that take too much time as well?"

"If we did it in the usual way. But I hope we have an alternative. Jhesrhi?"

Her golden eyes catching the lamplight, the wizard said, "I'm well-versed in elemental magic, and I've studied the patch of ground on which the Ring stands. I know where the soil is softest and where an underground stream runs. I believe that if I spoke to the earth and water, I could conceivably topple a section of the east wall. But the job would be a lot more feasible if I had help. Master Nevron, I've heard that you and your disciples are as adept at commanding elementals as you are demons and devils, even if you don't see fit to call on them as often. Would you join me in this effort?"

Nevron's scowl deepened as if it vexed him to have someone who wasn't a zulkir speak to him as an equal. But he simply said, "I'll do it if someone can convince me the plan is practical. It will take more than I've heard so far. Let's say the wall falls."

"By all means, let's say that," Gaedynn interrupted. "The collapse breaks the magical pattern, and our work is done. Right?"

"Wrong," Nevron spat. "If we merely inflict physical damage and march away, they can restore the symbol. We need to take the Ring and then perform a ritual to render it harmless for all time. Now, as I was saying: The wall falls. Won't the army still have a great heap of rubble blocking the path into the fortress?"

"A heap of loose stones isn't the same thing as a solid wall," Jhesrhi said. "I'm confident that, with all the wizards in our army, we can clear it out of our way."

"Well, possibly so. But have you considered that when we strike to knock down the wall, the wizards inside the fortress will sense the attack and move to counter us? And no matter how skilled we are at elemental magic, inertia will be on their side."

Aoth scratched his chin. "Yes, that's the tricky part. We need to distract the bastards so thoroughly that they won't notice what you're up to."

"So we make what looks like a committed, furious assault," Bareris said.

"That's my thought," said Aoth.

Lauzoril put his hands together in front of his face, fingertip to fingertip, and peered into the space between his palms as if wisdom dwelled therein. "The feint will have to look convincing, which means it will give the enemy the opportunity to kill a good many of our troops. Breaching the wall won't help us if we end up too weak to exploit the opportunity."

"Well," said Aoth, "it would stop Szass Tam from using the castle as a giant talisman until his servants mend the hole. You're right, though: if the first battle cripples us, that delay won't save us in the long run. But I don't think the fight *has* to cripple us. We've been watching this place since we got here and have seen few flying warriors or steeds. Whereas we have griffon riders, so that's one advantage. Most if not all of their mages are necromancers, and they don't appear to have any priests at all. We have a greater diversity of magic at our command, so that's another."

"In fact," Khouryn said, "if I can get some ladders planted against the wall and a squad of my best men to the top of them, this 'feint' might just take the castle all by itself. Stranger things have happened."

Samas Kul shook his head. "I'm just not persuaded this ploy will work."

"Do you have a better idea?" Lallara waited a beat, as if to give the gluttonous transmuter a chance to respond. He didn't take it. "Because I don't, and we have to try *something*."

"I agree," Lauzoril said.

"As do I," Nevron said. He glowered at Jhesrhi. "But you'd better be as competent as you claim."

That seemed to settle it, for Samas pouted and held his peace thereafter. And, though no one said it outright, Bareris sensed that the zulkirs would expect the Brotherhood of the Griffon to do the hardest fighting and face the greatest peril, just as in the battle against the Aglarondans. He had a guilty sense that, as Aoth's friend, he ought to resent the unfairness, but he couldn't. Because if the sellswords were at the forefront and he was with them, it would maximize his chances of getting at Tsagoth.

Jet carried Aoth soaring over the warriors of the Brotherhood of the Griffon who didn't ride the steeds from which the company took its name—ranks of armored foot soldiers, lines of bowmen, lancers on restless, prancing horses, and artillerymen making final, fussy adjustments to their trebuchets and ballistae. Viewing them, he wished, as he often did at such moments, that he could be with every component of his army simultaneously to oversee everything it did.

"Well, you can't," said Jet. "So let's get on with it."

Not the most inspirational words that ever hurled fighting men into the jaws of death, but Aoth supposed they'd do. He looked across the gray sky, caught Bareris's eye, and dipped the head of his spear to signal. The bard nodded, raised a horn to his lips, and blew a call amplified by magic. Scores of griffon riders hurtled at the Dread Ring.

Blood orcs on the battlements bellowed to see them coming, while their undead comrades, rotting cadavers and naked skeletons, stood stolidly and waited with weapons in hand. Bareris struck up a song that stabbed terror and confusion into the minds of some of the swine-faced living warriors, and they bolted and plummeted from the wall-walk. Aoth pointed his spear and hurled a dazzling flare of lightning that blasted both live and lifeless defenders to smoking fragments. Gaedynn loosed one of his special arrows, and in a heartbeat, brambles sprouted where it struck, growing and twisting outward from the shaft to catch Szass Tam's minions like a spiderweb. Those griffon riders who lacked a means of magical attack shot shaft after shaft from their short but powerful compound bows, and hit a target more often than not.

The attackers focused their efforts on those portions of the south wall commanding the approach to the Ring's largest gate.

But since they were wheeling and swooping above the castle, the foes on every stretch of battlement could shoot back. Volleys of arrows and quarrels arced up at them. Necromancers in scarlet-and-black regalia conjured blasts of chilling darkness and barrages of shadow-splinters.

Pierced with half a dozen shafts, a griffon screeched and plummeted, carrying its rider with it. The warrior tossed his bow away, wrapped his arms around his mount's feathery neck, and they crashed to earth in one of the castle baileys. An instant later, another steed fell, both the griffon and the sellsword buckled in the saddle already slain and rotted by some necromantic curse.

It was a nasty situation, but it would have been far worse if not for the griffons' agility and the armoring enchantments Lallara and her subordinates had cast on them immediately prior to taking off. As it was, Aoth judged that he and his companions could continue as they were for a while, providing essential cover for their comrades on the ground.

A mental prompt sent Jet swinging to the right, toward three of the wizards who posed the greatest immediate threat. Aoth hammered them bloody with a downpour of conjured hail, then heard a vast muddled sound at his back that told him the charge had begun.

·· ·· ·· ·· ·· ·· ·· ·· ·· ·· ·· ·· ··

Khouryn had claimed that if Lady Luck favored them, a ferocious but more or less witless frontal assault might actually take the fortress. He'd judged that his bold assertion might help convince the zulkirs to endorse Aoth's plan. But he understood war far too well to believe what he was saying.

Still, he meant to attack as if he imagined he truly could get over the towering black wall and kill everything on the other side.

The feint had to look real, and if he balked, his men would too.

Besides, he'd told the truth about one thing: in battle, the unlikeliest things sometimes happened.

He kissed his truesilver ring through his steel-and-leather gauntlet. His wife had given it to him on their betrothal day. At the same time, he studied the battlements above the gate. When it seemed to him that there were fewer defenders up there and that a goodly portion of those who remained were busy loosing arrows at griffon riders, he drew a deep breath and bellowed a command. At once other officers and sergeants shouted, relaying his order. Bugles blew, transmitting it still farther.

Then he started to run, and the horde of men arrayed at his back pounded after him. He had no difficulty staying in the front rank. His legs might be shorter than human ones, but he fancied he carried the weight of armor more lightly than most.

Behind him, he knew, some men were carrying ladders or rolling the huge battering ram called Tempus's Boot along. Not part of the charge itself, acting more or less in concert with the griffon riders, archers and wizards sought to slay any creature that showed itself on the battlements. Squads of horsemen watched and waited to intercept any threat that might emerge from the fortress and try to drive in on the flanks of the running infantrymen.

No doubt it all helped, but none of it helped enough to make the charge anything but a desperate, dangerous endeavor. Arrows whined down from on high, slipped past the shields raised to catch them, and men fell. And even if the men weren't badly hurt when they hit the ground, sometimes their comrades trampled them.

Long, thick veins pulsing and bulging beneath their skins, bloated, hulking creatures heaved themselves over the parapet above the gate. The festering things looked like they might have been hill giants in life, before the necromancers got hold of them.

The drop from the lofty battlements didn't appear to harm them. They picked themselves up and lumbered toward the head of the charge. Khouryn aimed himself and his spear at the nearest.

.. ..

Jhesrhi, Nevron, and eleven of the latter's subordinates had prepared a patch of ground near the animal pens and baggage carts, close enough to the Dread Ring to monitor the progress of the attack but far enough away, they hoped, to make them inconspicuous.

Smelling of sulfur and sweat, Nevron scowled at the fight as he seemed to scowl at everything. "If the necromancers aren't distracted now, I doubt they ever will be. Let's get started."

Standing in a circle, reciting in unison, the wizards chanted words of power. At first, the only effect was to make Jhesrhi's entire body feel as numb as a foot that had fallen asleep. Then, abruptly, she seemed to float up through the top of her own head, to gaze down on the corporeal self she'd left behind. Her body was still speaking the incantation and would continue to do so until she took possession of it again, but it wasn't capable of doing anything else. That was why a squad of Nevron's guards was standing watch.

She looked around and found a single, silvery, translucent form floating beside her. Only Nevron, the infamous zulkir himself, had exited his body more quickly than she. She felt a twinge of satisfaction.

It took only a few moments for the rest of the assembly to rise like butterflies from cocoons. Then Nevron gestured, turned, and flew north, and everyone else followed.

They didn't go far before the zulkir dived and led them into the ground, where, attuned to the elements of earth and water, they could see as well as before. They beheld soil and rock but peered through them too, both at the same time.

That made it easy to swim like fish to their destination, the soft ground and subterranean stream they intended to command. Nevron and the other Red Wizards recited new spells, and elementals took on vaguely manlike forms, each in the midst of whatever substance was its essence. Whether they were merely revealing themselves or the magic was actually creating them was a question that had been debated since the dawn of time.

Either way, Jhesrhi had no need of such intermediaries. Not for this task. She whispered to the earth and moisture surrounding and interpenetrating her spirit form, and she felt them stir in response.

•• •• •• •• •• •• •• •• •• •• •• ••

Malark watched the battle unfold from the apex of one of the castle's fanglike towers. The elevation, coupled with the six arched windows placed at regular intervals around the minaret, provided a reasonably good view.

Which, though useful, had the unfortunate effect of feeding his frustration. The spectacle of so much slaughter made him itch to kill someone himself. But alas, there were times when a commander had to hold himself back from the fray to make sure he gave the proper orders at the proper time.

He tried to tell himself that, in fact, he *was* killing, that his were the guiding will and intelligence, and the Ring's garrison was simply his weapon. But that perspective only helped a little.

Suddenly, with a puff of displaced air, Tsagoth appeared beside him. The blood fiend's innate ability to translate himself through space made him an ideal choice to carry messages.

Tsagoth said, "Frikhesp reports that Nevron and his assistants are trying to undermine the wall."

"Good." Malark took another look out a window. "And the griffon riders are fully committed. Let's close the trap. Tell Frikhesp . . . no, wait." He strode to Tsagoth and gripped the scaly wrist of one of the demon's lower arms. "To the Abyss with commanding from the rear. Take me with you."

•• •• •• •• •• •• •• •• •• •• •• •• •• ••

Aoth glimpsed a flicker of motion below. He looked down. All around the inside of the Ring, doors—big ones, like the doors of a barn—were swinging open.

The first creatures to emerge looked like dozens of twisting, writhing scraps of parchment dancing in the hot air rising from a fire, but Aoth recognized them as skin kites. Behind them hopped gigantic eagles, their eyes milky or rotted away entirely, their flesh withered and decayed, skeletons in armor riding on their backs. The undead birds spread ragged, leprous wings.

Aoth realized that the master of the castle, whoever the whoreson was, had meant for the besieging force to believe he had no aerial cavalry to counter their own. To that end, he'd hidden his flyers in what must be extensive vaults underground. Living avians couldn't have tolerated such confinement, but undead could.

Aoth rained fire on the new additions to the battle, trying to destroy as many as possible while he and his comrades still had the advantage of height. He yelled to everyone within earshot to do likewise, and Gaedynn loosed an arrow that became a lightning-bolt in flight.

It wasn't going to be enough. The griffon riders' situation had abruptly become untenable, and they needed to disengage.

Assuming they could. Aoth needed Bareris to sound a retreat that everyone would hear even amid the howling chaos of combat, then wield his music to help hold the undead flyers back. He cast about for the bard, then cursed. Tsagoth was riding an especially large eagle, and Bareris was flying straight at him. Judging from the snarl contorting his face, Aoth doubted his friend was aware of anything else.

•• •• •• •• •• •• •• •• •• •• •• •• •• ••

Tempus's Boot, a massive, iron-capped, soth-wood log, swung back and forth in its cradle of rope, smashing at the crack where the two halves of the Ring's gate interlocked. Khouryn had somehow ended up in proximity to the ram without intending to but couldn't honestly say he was sorry, because the device had a roof of wood covered in wet hide. It shielded the operators from the stones and burning oil showering down from above.

Its relative immunity to those forms of attack made it a prime target for the undead monstrosities the enemy had sent over the wall. Creatures somewhat resembling the big goblin-kin called bugbears, but with gaunt bodies covered in oozing sores and a tentacle lashing beneath each arm, rushed toward the ram, leaped high, and bore some of the engine's defenders down beneath them. They wrapped the sellswords in their tentacles, plunged their jagged fangs into their bodies, and guzzled. The shrieking soldiers' bodies started to flatten as though their vampiric assailants were leeching bone instead of blood.

Khouryn charged, swung his urgrosh—his spear was long gone, stuck deep in the body of his first opponent—and struck off a bonedrinker's head before it even noticed the danger. But the next one wouldn't be so easy. It jumped up from its kill and sprang at him, tentacles whirling like whips and clawed hands poised to rake.

Khouryn ducked and sidestepped at the same time. He chopped, and the urgrosh's axe blade crunched through the bonedrinker's ribs and into the dry, leathery tissue beneath. The undead bugbear staggered a pace but didn't go down. Khouryn yanked his weapon free and sidestepped again, trying to get behind the brute—

Something that felt like a noose but could only be a tentacle wrapped tight around his ankle and jerked his leg out from under him. The bonedrinker whirled, pounced, and carried him down. It gripped and entangled him with all its various limbs, immobilizing his right arm and pulling him close enough to make it impossible to swing the urgrosh. It lowered its head and bit at his throat. The pressure was excruciating and nearly cut off his air, even though his assailant's fangs had yet to penetrate his dwarf-forged mail. He suspected they'd worry their way through in another heartbeat or so.

He took the urgrosh in his left hand, reversed his grip, and stabbed the spike into the side of the bonedrinker's head. Bone cracked, and the creature went limp.

Khouryn's impulse was to stay on the ground at least until he caught his breath, but impulse evidently didn't understand that it would be a bad idea to let another foe catch him supine. He crawled out from under the altered bugbear's corpse, clambered to his feet, cast about, and saw that other warriors had dispatched the rest of the bonedrinkers.

But now a dog the size of a house, its form made of mangled, rotting bodies fused together, was loping toward the Boot. Near it, a pale flash of wizardry froze in ice a ladder and the men struggling to climb it. After a moment, the trapped forms, whether made of wood or flesh and bone, broke apart under their own weight.

When is that damned wall going to fall? Khouryn wondered. We're getting massacred down here. He strove to control his breathing, took a fresh grip on his weapon, and moved to place himself in the path of the charnel hound.

•• •• •• •• •• •• •• •• •• •• •• •• •• ••

A shock of cold and carrion stink ran through the ground. It jolted Jhesrhi, and for an instant the packed soil around her became black, opaque, as if she still occupied her physical body and had been buried alive.

When vision returned, she kept on trying to make earth and water flow as she desired, but now she met resistance. The stuff crawled back at her, or, if not the matter itself, some hostile power infusing it did so. The chill and fetid reek intensified, nauseating her, making her dizzy. Meanwhile, the elementals turned and advanced on those who'd summoned them.

Jhesrhi realized the necromancers had expected an attack at this site and had set a trap. They'd tainted the soil with graveyard dirt, and the stream with water that had drowned men and in which their bodies had lain. The desecration had turned this whole buried area into a weapon they could use at will.

And unfortunately, mere comprehension was no defense, not when she felt so weak and sick. Frigid, slimy hands congealed and clutched at her, while at the periphery of her vision, an earth elemental—warped into a necromental now—grabbed a Red Wizard's astral form in three-fingered hands and ripped it in two, putting out its silvery light forever.

•• •• •• •• •• •• •• •• •• •• •• •• ••

A thought sufficed to send Jet hurtling after Bareris and his griffon. Maybe Aoth could persuade the bard to break off. Failing that, perhaps the two of them fighting in concert could kill Tsagoth quickly.

Aoth glimpsed motion at the corner of his vision and snapped his head around. Armored in black metal and mounted, like Tsagoth, on a particularly large eagle-thing, a huge, undead warrior was driving in on his flank. It wore no helm, perhaps because its gray, earless, hairless head, the eyelids and lips sewn shut with blue thread, often terrified its opponents. It held a javelin with a point carved from green crystal raised and ready to throw.

But first it gestured with its off hand. A sudden spasm made Aoth cry out and go rigid, while Jet's wings flailed out of time with one another. Then the deathbringer—as Aoth belatedly remembered the fearsome things were called—threw the javelin.

Still wracked with pain, Aoth could do nothing to protect himself. But Jet screeched, denying his own agony, and brought his convulsing body under control. He veered, and the javelin missed. The deathbringer immediately pulled two flails, one for each hand, from the tubular cases buckled to its saddle.

To the Abyss with that. Given a choice, Aoth knew better than to fight a deathbringer hand-to-hand even if he'd had the time. He drew a deep breath, chanted, and hurled fire from the head of his spear. The blast tore the eagle out from under its rider and ripped it into burning scraps.

Unless Aoth was lucky, neither the explosion nor the fall that came after would slay the deathbringer. But maybe he and the other griffon riders could get away before the undead champion procured another mount.

Aoth cast about, seeking Bareris again. His friend and Tsagoth were wheeling around one another in the usual manner of seasoned aerial combatants, each seeking the high air or some comparable advantage. Meanwhile, one of the bizarre creatures called skirrs, things like gigantic, mummified bats right down to the decayed wrappings, had climbed higher still for a plunge at the pallid target below. Blind with hate, Bareris evidently hadn't noticed it.

So Aoth and Jet had to dispose of the skirr as well. By the time they finished, half a dozen skeletal riders had flown to Tsagoth's aid. Having surrounded Bareris, they too were maneuvering, looking for a good opportunity to strike.

And Aoth hesitated. A warmage's most potent magic tended to produce big, messy flares of destructive power, and at first glance, he couldn't see how to scour Bareris's opponents out of the sky without hitting the bard and his steed, also.

Then Mirror, currently a murky parody of an orc, floated up into the midst of the fight, brandished his scimitar, and released a dazzling burst of his own sacred power. The undead eagles and their skeleton riders fell burning from the air. Tsagoth appeared unharmed, but, his mount destroyed, disappeared, translating himself through space to spare himself a fall.

The divine light, an expression of life and health, hadn't hurt Bareris's griffon, either, but the bard himself slumped on its back, part of his white mane charred away, his alabaster skin blistered and smoking. As Aoth flew closer, he wondered if the ghost couldn't have wielded his magic with more finesse and spared his friend, and then, abruptly, he understood. Mirror had deliberately included Bareris in the effect, willing to risk his existence if that was what it took to slap the crazy fury out of him.

Bareris straightened up and groggily peered about. Judging that he'd approached near enough to make himself heard, Aoth shouted, "Blow the retreat! Help me get our people out of here!"

Bareris shook his head, perhaps in negation, perhaps to clear it. "Tsagoth . . ."

"Gone! And if you stay to look for him, you'll just get yourself killed, and Tsagoth and Szass Tam will win! That's not any kind of revenge!"

Bareris peered about, jerked his head in a nod, and raised his horn to his lips.

•• •• •• •• •• •• •• •• •• •• •• ••

The wizard in scarlet and maroon—a lean man of middling height for a human, with a mark on his chin—brandished an unusually thick and sturdy-looking black wand. Shadowy tentacles burst from the ground under the feet of four of Khouryn's spearmen, whipped around them, and dragged them down.

Khouryn couldn't imagine what had possessed the fellow to descend from the relative safety of the battlements into the thick of the melee. To say the least, it was uncharacteristic behavior for a Red Wizard. But whatever he was thinking, his spells were doing considerable damage. Fortunately, Khouryn expected he could put a stop to it if he could only close with him. In his experience, it was a rare mage who could throw spells and dodge an urgrosh at the same time. In fact, it was a rare mage who could dodge an urgrosh at all.

A yellow-eyed dread warrior delayed him for a heartbeat. He had to chop its sword hand off and one leg out from under it, before he could get around it and advance. Then he heard a horn sounding the retreat, the high, blaring notes somehow cutting through the crashing, howling din of combat.

An instant later, the griffon riders winged away from the Dread Ring with other flyers in pursuit. The sight gave Khouryn a jolt of surprise. The castle wasn't supposed to have any aerial cavalry worth mentioning, and, caught up in the carnage in front of the gate, he hadn't noticed them until now.

Flying at the back of their company, Aoth, Bareris, and other spellcasters hurled great blasts of magic, seemingly expending every iota of their power to hold the undead back. The warmage painted a wall made of rainbows across the sky. The undead singer bellowed and shattered the bones of three cadaverous birds and the skeletal archers on their backs.

Khouryn wondered if Aoth was running because it was death to stay any longer, or because the east wall was down. But if Jhesrhi and Nevron had succeeded at the latter, surely Khouryn would have noticed some sign of *that*. He felt a sick near-certainty that this costly gambit had failed.

But now was not the time to think about it. If the griffon riders were fleeing, the infantry had to do the same, and it was up to him to make sure that as many as possible got away safely. He just prayed to the Lord of the Twin Axes that the run away from the fortress wouldn't prove as difficult as the charge up to it.

•• •• •• •• •• •• •• •• •• •• •• •• ••

At first, the grip of the phantom hands chilled and dulled Jhesrhi. Her mind seemed to soften and run, as if it were rotting away.

Then, however, revulsion stabbed through the crippling fog. Under the best of circumstances, she disliked being touched, and the poisonous clutch of the dead, here in solid, claustrophobic darkness, was unbearable.

Loathing threatened to explode into panic, and she strained for self-control. She had to think. Find the way out of this.

She couldn't call on earth or water for succor. The necromancers had corrupted them. Another power would have to liberate her. Air, itself emblematic of freedom. There was none here in this frigid quicksand snare, but she could will it here.

She shouted words of power. Dead men's hands tried to cover her mouth, but they were too slow. Wind screamed from elsewhere, forcing the poisonous earth back, making a bubble of pressure and emptiness in the midst of it. Jhesrhi floated at the center of the hollow.

It was a start, but she still needed a way out that wouldn't require swimming through tainted ground. She spoke to the wind, and, alternately whirling like a drill and pounding like a hammer, it cut a shaft to the surface. The circle of gray sky at the top seemed as beautiful as anything she'd ever seen.

It was only as she flew toward it that she remembered her colleagues and looked to see how they were faring. More of the luminous soul-forms had vanished, slain by the necromancers' curse. But some remained, and she wondered if she could do anything to help them.

Then new entities, grotesque as the necromentals but far more varied in shape, exploded into view. They roared and hurled themselves at the necromancers' servants, and their intervention allowed Nevron and his subordinates to break away. They fled into the vertical tunnel, and Jhesrhi led them up into the sky.

Afterward, they scurried back to their bodies as fast as they could. It only made sense. They'd failed in their mission, the enemy's assault had shaken them, and it was possible the necromancers had other tricks to play.

Jhesrhi plunged into her corporeal form in much the same way she'd exited it. For a moment, her flesh felt heavy as lead. As she halted her droning repetition of the ritual incantation, she caught a foul smell and peered around.

Six of her Red Wizard collaborators sprawled on the ground, their bodies so decayed that it looked as if they'd been dead for days.

The next instant, demons and devils appeared, their various blades and claws poised to strike. It was plain that their controller's will had snatched them out of combat unexpectedly, and, hideous as they were, their surprise might have seemed comical had the situation been less grim.

Or at least Jhesrhi found it droll, but, like most mages, she had some familiarity with such entities. Nevron's human bodyguards cried out and lifted their weapons, and the spirits, evidently happy they still had *something* to fight, rounded on them.

"Enough!" Nevron barked, and all his servants, mortal and infernal, froze.

The zulkir looked at the dead men on the ground and sneered as though their failure to survive made them contemptible. Then, his crimson robes flapping around his legs, he strode in the direction of the Dread Ring, no doubt to see how the rest of the battle was going. Jhesrhi followed.

It soon became apparent that the men who'd attacked the south face of the stronghold were retreating. When she saw how many of their number they were leaving behind, torn, tangled, and trampled on the ground, Jhesrhi felt sick all over again.

chapter seven

14–17 Mirtul, The Year of the Dark Circle (1478 DR)

Aoth, Bareris, and Mirror stood at the edge of camp, gazing at the approach to the Ring and the fortress itself. Mirror was invisible, a mere hovering intimation of wrongness, and hadn't spoken since the griffon riders had fled. Evidently his great evocation of holy power had addled and diminished him for a while.

Perceptible to Aoth's fire-infected eyes, even in the dark and even at such a distance, necromancers chanted on the battlements, the sound a counterpoint to the wailing of the wounded soldiers the retreat had abandoned. Responding to the magic, dead men lurched up from the ground to join the ranks of the castle's defenders.

That was unfortunate, but Aoth doubted it would be the worst thing to happen this cool, rainy spring night. He was sure the Ring had defenders he and his comrades hadn't even seen yet, vile things that couldn't bear daylight. They'd come out now and make quick strikes at the fringes of the camp, forcing men in dire need of rest to defend themselves instead, doing their best to undermine the besieging force's morale.

Or what was left of it.

"By the Flame," Aoth said, "this is why I balked at coming back. I like war—parts of it, anyway—but I hate fighting necromancers."

At first, neither of his companions answered, and he assumed that, as was so often the case, neither would. But at length Bareris said, "I know I should apologize."

Aoth shrugged. "I accept."

"When I saw Tsagoth, it drove me into a frenzy. Made me stupid. Everyone could have come to ruin if you and Mirror hadn't risked yourselves to save me."

"Maybe so, but what's important is that we did get away."

"So I know I *should* feel sorry and ashamed, but I don't. All I am is angry that Tsagoth got away."

Aoth didn't know what to say.

"It's all I have," Bareris continued. "Undeath has stripped other emotions away from me. Tammith told me it was like this. Told me how broken and empty she was. Told me that even when she seemed otherwise, it was just because she was *trying* to feel. But I didn't want to understand." He paused. "Sorry. I didn't mean to stray into that. This is my point: I at least remember how people are. I had to act the way they do, over the past ninety years, to make the rebels trust me. And I promise, I'll behave that way now. I won't let you down again."

Aoth sighed. "You still are 'people,' whether you believe it or not. Otherwise, you wouldn't have the urge to unburden yourself this way."

"No, that isn't it. I'm going to propose a plan when we confer with the zulkirs, and I want you to trust me enough to support it."

·· ·· ·· ·· ·· ·· ·· ·· ·· ·· ·· ·· ··

Malark crouched at the top of the stairs and studied the chamber below, particularly the arched doorway in the north wall. The hunting party would enter that way.

He didn't know exactly who or what the hunters were. He had yet to get a good look at them. But as he'd murdered the folk he surprised here in the depths, despoiled repositories of treasure, conjuration chambers, and the like, and done anything else he could think of to vex the other inhabitants of the Citadel, each team had been more formidable than the last, and this one would likely continue the trend.

The thought didn't dismay him and wouldn't have even if he'd feared to die. He'd shrouded both the stairs and himself in a spell of concealment. It likely wouldn't fool a Red Wizard for more than an instant, but that ought to be enough.

Intent as he was on the space below, there was still an unengaged part of his mind that wondered how his simulacrum was faring at the Dread Ring. Then, peering this way and that, the hunters stalked into view.

In the lead strode two walking corpses, not the usual zombies or dread warriors, but something deadlier. Even if Malark, favored with Szass Tam's tutelage in the dark arts, hadn't been capable of sensing the malign power inside them, the superior quality of their weapons and plate armor would have given it away. A greater danger, however, floated behind them, a vaguely manlike form made of red fog, with a pair of luminous eyes glaring from the head. And bringing up the rear were, most likely, the greatest threats of all: a trio of necromancers, their voluminous black-and-crimson robes cut and deliberately soiled to resemble cerecloths, glowing wands of human bone in their hands.

Malark decided to kill his fellow wizards first. Without their masters' spoken commands or force of will to prompt them, the undead might not even choose to fight.

Feet silent on the carved granite steps, he bounded downward.

One of the necromancers glanced in his direction, looked again, goggled, and yelped a warning.

It came too late, though. Malark reached the foot of the stairs, leaped high, and drove a thrust kick into one mage's neck, snapping it. He twisted even as he landed, reached out, and stabbed the claws of one scaly, yellow gauntlet into a second necromancer's heart.

Two wizards down, one to go, but the third was quick enough to interpose the crimson death, as the fog-things were called, between himself and Malark. The creature reached for him with a billowing, misshapen hand.

Malark ducked and raked the crimson death's extended arm. He didn't encounter any resistance but knew that the talons of the enchanted glove might have cut the entity even so. Or not, for that was the nature of ghostly things.

He felt danger behind him and lashed out with a back kick. Armor clanged when he connected, and rang again when one of the animated corpses fell backward onto the floor.

The other dead man rushed in on Malark's flank and thrust a sword at him. Malark pivoted, caught the blade in his hands—the demon-hide gauntlets made the trick somewhat easier—and twisted it out of the corpse's hand. He reversed the weapon and, bellowing a battle cry, rammed it through its owner's torso. The creature toppled.

Malark whirled, seeking the next imminent threat, but was a hair too slow. The crimson death's hands locked on his forearms and hoisted him into the air. Pain stabbed through him at the points of contact, and a deeper redness flowed from the entity's fingers into its wrists and on down its arms. It was leeching Malark's blood.

He poised himself to break free, and the surviving necromancer lunged and jabbed him in the ribs with the tip of his yellowed wand. Malark jerked at another jolt of pain, this one followed by a feeling of weakness. The touch had stolen much of his strength. He clawed and squirmed anyway, but it didn't extricate him from his captor's grip.

Merely inconvenienced, not damaged, the corpse he'd kicked to the floor clambered up again. It raised its sword to cleave him while he hung like a felon on a gibbet.

Malark would have preferred to finish the fight without using any more magic, but plainly, that approach wasn't going to work. He rattled off three words of power—a spell Szass Tam himself had invented, taught only to a few—and the crimson death dropped him. The corpse warrior faltered and didn't swing its blade.

The necromancer gaped when he realized he'd lost control of his servants, and then his eyes opened wider still when he belatedly recognized the man he was fighting. "Master?" he stammered.

"Kill me if you can," Malark answered. "You have a chance. I'm still weak from the touch of your wand." He charged.

The wizard extended his arcane weapon and started to scream a word of command. Malark knocked the length of bone out of line and silenced his foe by clawing out his throat.

Afterward, he dispatched the undead, who remained passive throughout the process. As always, it felt good to destroy the vile, unnatural things.

.. ..

Aoth looked around the command tent at the zulkirs and Bareris. "Let's get started," he said. "We'll be needed elsewhere soon, when the specters start coming."

Samas Kul frowned, disgruntled either that Aoth had possessed the audacity to call the assembly to order, or that he had, in effect, suggested that the lordly archmages perform sentry duty. "Can't the Burning Braziers keep the spooks away? I was hoping they were good for *something*."

"And I keep hoping the same about you," Lallara said. She turned her flinty gaze on Aoth. "We expended much of our power during the battle. We need time and rest to recover. But we understand that we must all do what we can."

Nevron glowered at her. A tattooed demon face on his neck appeared to mouth a silent obscenity, but perhaps that was a trick of the lamplight. "Do not," he said, "presume to speak for me." He took a breath. "But yes, Captain, I'll help, and so will my followers. What's left of them."

"I regret the loss of those who died," said Aoth.

"As well you should," Samas said. A cup appeared in fingers so fat the flab bulged around the edges of the several talismanic rings.

"We tried the best plan that any of us could think of," Lallara said.

"Well, I said from the start that it wouldn't work," Samas retorted.

"True. You did. I freely acknowledge that you've finally been right *once* in the hundred and fifty years we've known you. Now let's talk about something important."

"I think that's a sensible suggestion," Lauzoril said. It was Lallara who looked like a frail if shrewish old granny, but he was the one who'd bundled up to ward off the evening chill. "Captain, what's your assessment? After the beating we took today, is the army in any condition to continue the siege?"

"Well," said Aoth, "the real answer to that is that even if we six were the only ones left alive, we'd still have to continue, given what's at stake. But I know what you mean. Nasty as today was, more men than not made it back alive. I think our legions have at least one more good fight left in them." In fact, even the Brotherhood of the Griffon survived, although, battling at the forefront, its own aerial cavalry and Khouryn's spearmen had suffered a worse mauling than any of the zulkirs' household troops.

"But how do we continue the fight?" Lauzoril asked, fussily tugging his red velvet cloak tighter around him. "We need a new strategy. A better one."

"I think," Bareris said, "that when we conferred previously, His Omnipotence Samas Kul was right about at least *two* things. The only way to get a significant portion of our army into the Dread Ring is for someone who's already inside to open a gate."

"So we're back to trying to free some of the enemy from Szass Tam's psychic bonds?" Nevron growled. "I thought we all agreed that scheme was unwieldy."

"We did," Bareris said. "That's why I intend to go inside the Ring and open the gate."

"How?" Lallara asked. "Invisibly? Masked in the appearance of a zombie? I guarantee you the necromancers are prepared for such tricks."

"I'm sure they are. I expect them to spot me almost immediately. However . . ." In a few terse sentences, Bareris explained his plan.

When he finished, Lallara turned to Lauzoril. "Will it work?" she asked.

The other zulkir fingered his chin. "It might."

"I think so too," said Aoth, "but it's damn risky." Especially considering that the enemy commander had thus far anticipated his adversaries' every move. For all they knew, he might be expecting this as well.

"What concerns me," Nevron said, glaring at Bareris, "is your hatred of Tsagoth. I'm told it overwhelmed you today. What if it does so again once you're inside the fortress? What if you succumb to your obsession and forget all about your mission?"

"It won't," Bareris said. "I don't deny we have a history together, and when I saw him, I lost my head. But truly, it's Szass Tam I hate, and Tsagoth is just his instrument. You can trust me to remember that from now on. But suppose I don't.

Or suppose the scheme fails for some other reason. What have you lost? One warrior."

I'll have lost a friend, Aoth thought, but what he said was, "You can depend on Bareris, Your Omnipotences. When has he ever let you down?"

Lallara gave a brusque nod. "All right. How soon can the legions be ready?"

"A day or two," said Aoth. Somewhere to the north, someone shrieked. Inside the tent, everyone's head snapped around in the direction of the noise. "Assuming we can get them through the night." He picked up his spear, planted the butt of it on the ground, and heaved himself to his feet.

.. ..

Shrouded in invisibility, Bareris stalked toward the huge, black castle. Lallara had expressed doubt that such a defense would get him very far, but he hoped it would keep him from being noticed until he at least reached the top of the wall.

He made his approach shortly before the first gray insinuations of dawn could stain the black sky to the east. His timing might help him more than the magic. Undead entities and orcs could see in the dark, but not as far as a man could see by day. And creatures that couldn't abide the touch of the sun or, like the goblin-kin, were simply nocturnal by nature might already be retiring to their vaults and barracks.

He reached the foot of the west wall. If anyone had noticed him, there was no indication of it. He unclipped the coil of rope from his belt and sang a charm under his breath. The line warmed in his hands, then squirmed. He loosened his grip on it, permitting it to move freely, and one end writhed up and up until it reached the top of the black barrier before him. It looped around a merlon, tied itself off, and then he climbed it.

At the top, he peeked over the parapet. There were no guards in his immediate vicinity—no visible ones, anyway—so he swung himself onto the wall-walk and prowled onward, looking for a stairway to the courtyard below.

He was expecting to trigger some sort of enchantment, but also was tense enough that he still jumped when it happened. A mouth opened on the inner face of one of the merlons and cried, "Enemy! Enemy! Enemy!" A prickling chill danced over his body, and he didn't even bother to look down to verify that countermagic had ripped his veil of invisibility away.

He jumped off the wall-walk, sang a word of power, and fell slowly enough to avoid injury when he landed in the courtyard. Looking for a doorway, he ran. Other mouths opened one by one in the stonework to cry out his current location.

Blood orcs rushed out of the dark, then hesitated when they took in his ink black eyes and bone white skin. They wondered if a warrior so manifestly undead could truly be a foe, and under other circumstances, Bareris might have tried to bluff them. Now, however, he broke their bones and blasted them off their feet with a thunderous shout.

"Tsagoth!" he called in a voice augmented to carry throughout the fortress. "Show yourself!" He sprinted to a door at the base of one of the Ring's lesser towers and yanked it open.

No one was on the other side. Not in this little antechamber, anyway. He sang a spell to seal both the door he'd just entered and the one on the far side of the room, then took a better look around.

Even here, inside the fortress, the windows were mere arrow slits. He just had time to reflect that nothing solid and man-sized would have room to wriggle though when something else did, a flowing shadow with the murky, rippling suggestion of an anguished, silently wailing old man's face. It reached for Bareris, and he felt the chill poison that comprised its essence. The malignancy was nowhere near as dangerous to him as it would have been to a mortal, but no doubt the wraith could hurt him.

He sidestepped its scrabbling hands, drew his sword, and cut through the center of it. The phantom flickered, stumbled, then rounded on him. He cut down the middle of its head, and it disappeared.

Bareris pivoted back to the nearest arrow slit. He pressed his eye to it just in time to see a necromancer thrust out a wand made from a mummified human forearm. A spark leaped from the instrument's shriveled fingertips.

Bareris dived away from the opening and threw himself flat. The spark streaked through the arrow slit and, with an echoing boom, exploded into a yellow burst of flame.

Fortunately, only the fringe of the blast washed over Bareris. It stung and scorched him, but that was all. He scrambled back to the arrow slit, chanted a spell, and felt a throbbing in his eyes. He stared at the Red Wizard, and the necromancer cried out and doubled over, dropping the preserved forearm in the process. The blood orcs gathered around him gaped in consternation.

"I want Tsagoth!" Bareris howled. "Tsagoth! Bring him to me, or I'll curse you all!"

·· ·· ·· ·· ·· ·· ·· ·· ·· ·· ·· ·· ·· ··

Malark and Tsagoth stood on the wall-walk, high enough that Bareris couldn't possibly see them, listening to the intruder shout and watching more and more guards gather in front of the minor bastion in which he'd taken refuge.

Malark smiled. "Even after a century of undeath, even when he's raving at the top of his lungs, you can tell he still has that magnificent voice."

His breath smelling of blood, Tsagoth snorted. "'Raving' is the word for it. When you decided to drive him mad with hate for me, I never imagined it would work as well as this."

"Well, since their first assault failed, the zulkirs haven't dared make a move against us. In fact, there are signs they may even pack up and leave. If so, then sneaking into the Ring alone was Bareris's only hope of getting his revenge."

"But it's no hope at all. A sane man would have understood it couldn't possibly work."

Malark twirled his ebony wand in his fingers, a habit the Monks of the Long Death had taught him to promote manual dexterity. "Well, you've got me there. Are you going to go down and give him the duel he so desires?"

"If you tell me to. Otherwise, no. Obviously, I'm not afraid of him. Back aboard that roundship on the Alamber Sea, I held off him, his griffon, the ghost, and Tammith Iltazyarra, all attacking me together. But I don't reciprocate his hatred, either. How could I, when I can barely tell you human vermin apart? So let the dogs"—Tsagoth waved his lower right hand at the orcs, ghouls, and necromancers assembled below—"dig the badger out of his hole. It's what dogs are for, isn't it?"

"I suppose. It's just that Bareris is an old friend of mine, and I'd like to give him the gift of a fitting death. If he perished fighting you, that would do the trick. But I consider you a friend as well, and I won't compel you if you aren't so inclined."

Tsagoth laughed, though his mirth sounded more like a lupine snarl. "You're as crazy as he is."

"Perhaps. You're far from the first to tell me so."

"You know, I could *promise* him I'll meet him in single combat. Then the men could loose a few dozen arrows into him as soon as he comes through the door. That's a way to put him down before he kills any more of us."

Malark shook his head. "I won't do that."

"I figured as much."

"But I will let you lure him out, and then I'll duel him. After all, I betrayed him and the southern cause. He ought to hate me too, at least a little. If he meets his end fighting me, it's not as perfect as if it happened battling you, but it's still a death reflective of his fundamental nature."

•• •• •• •• •• •• •• •• •• •• •• •• •• ••

Peering through an arrow slit, Bareris saw a column of mist spill down from on high. When it reached the ground, it thickened and took on definition until it became a dark, four-armed figure half again as tall as a man, with glowing crimson eyes and a head part human and part wolf.

Bareris shuddered, and hatred like burning vomit welled up inside him. He closed his eyes to shut out the sight of the blood fiend. Struggled to remember his true purpose and his pledge to Aoth.

"I'm here, minstrel!" Tsagoth shouted, a hint of a lupine howl in his voice. "What is it you want?"

It seemed to Bareris that he had himself under control. He risked opening his eyes, and it was still all right. "Isn't it obvious? I want to face you in single combat!"

"Done. Come out and let's get started."

The quick acceptance of the challenge brought a fresh surge of fury. Made Bareris want to leap up this instant, rush outside—

He clamped down on the impulse. He needed to do more talking before permitting anything else to happen. "How do I know all your allies won't attack me the instant I appear?"

Tsagoth shrugged a peculiar-looking four-armed shrug. "You'll just have to trust me."

"I have a better idea. You come in here, and that will ensure it's just the two of us."

"The two of us and whatever snares you've prepared with your bardic tricks. I think not. Come out and take your chances, or all these soldiers and I will storm your pitiful little redoubt.

It should take about ten heartbeats."

"All right," Bareris answered, "I'll come out." He dissolved the locking charm he'd cast, opened the door, and, singing, stepped out into the open.

No quarrels or flares of freezing shadow leaped at him. Arranged in a crescent-moon arc some distance from the door, Szass Tam's servants were content to stand and stare, orcs and mages with malice and curiosity in their eyes, zombies with nothing at all in theirs. Tsagoth waited at the other end of the patch of clear ground, in reach at last after ninety years spent hunting him.

Bareris felt his anger deepen until its weight threatened to crush everything else inside him. He told himself that Tsagoth was merely Szass Tam's pawn and that sticking to his plan was the way to discomfit the lich. Reminded himself of every other consideration he'd counted on to help him maintain control. And at that moment, none of it mattered. How could it? He was a dead man, a ravening beast, capable of nothing but grief, self-loathing, and rage.

He switched to a different song, raised his blade high, and took an eager stride.

He closed half the distance, and then Tsagoth vanished. Bareris faltered, startled, anguished that the demonic vampire evidently intended to break his word. Then Malark, clad partly in crimson, a black wand or cudgel in his hand, floated down from the sky to stand where Tsagoth had been.

Bareris realized a measure of calm had returned to him. Consternation had blunted his frenzy. "My business is with Tsagoth," he said.

"But Tsagoth isn't as interested in you as you are in him," Malark replied.

"Has he turned coward?"

"Most assuredly not. But our mortal conventions of honor mean very little to him. Now, I have a proposition for you. You can't duel Tsagoth or retreat back into your bolt hole, either." The former spymaster pointed with his wand. Bareris glanced over his shoulder and saw that some of the enemy had shifted to block the way back into the tower. "But you can still have a measure of satisfaction. You can fight me."

"Why would you offer that?"

"For old times' sake. Call it an apology if you like. So, do you want to, or would you rather have all these Red Wizards, dread warriors, and whatnot assail you forthwith?"

"All right. I'll fight you. I'll kill you too."

"It's possible. Give me your best."

Malark dropped into a deep stance and started to circle. Grateful to stop talking and resume singing, Bareris poised his broadsword in a low guard and sidled in the opposite direction.

Malark suddenly sprang into the air and thrust-kicked at Bareris's head. Bareris ducked, retreated a half step, and extended his sword. The point should have caught Malark in the groin, but despite his forward momentum, the smaller man somehow contrived to snap his foot sideways into the threatening blade, knocking it out of line.

Malark touched down, pivoted, and slammed a back kick into Bareris's torso. Bareris felt a stab of pain as his ribs snapped. The attack sent him reeling backward, and Malark turned again and rushed him. Still singing, Bareris waited another moment, then planted his feet, regained his balance, and extended his sword a second time. Malark stopped short and once again avoided impaling himself, but not by much. Bareris's point was half a finger-length from his chest.

Bareris lunged, and Malark spun to the side. The sword missed his vitals but sliced a bloody gash in his forearm.

Malark grinned and inclined his head. "Good. Really good." He threatened with his black club, and then, when Bareris tried to parry, tossed the weapon into his other hand and spun it to bind his opponent's blade. Bareris sprang in closer, altering the relative positions of the blades so that he and not the spymaster was able to exert leverage. He heaved with all his inhuman strength and tore the club from Malark's grip.

At once he continued with a drawing cut to the knee. Malark hopped over it and hit him in the forehead with the heel of his palm. Bareris's skull crunched, and a bolt of agony blinded him. He hacked at the spot where instinct told him Malark must have gone, and evidently he guessed correctly. He didn't hit anything, but neither did any follow-up attack hit him, and when his vision cleared an instant later, the man in red was three paces away, where he must have leaped to dodge the cut. Malark whistled, and the black club flew up off the ground and into his hand like a dog obeying its master's call.

The duel went on that way for a while, each combatant hurting the other occasionally, but not badly enough to incapacitate. Bareris wondered how much longer he needed to stall. Because that was the problem with the spell he'd been weaving ever since making contact with the enemy, threading the incantation through his seemingly mundane speech and shouts as well as performing it in his song. The effect he hoped to create was subtle, so much so that he himself had no way of knowing whether he'd succeeded. Or at least, none that didn't require betting his existence on it.

He was still wondering when Malark took the decision out of his hands.

Bareris advanced, lunged, and made a head cut. Malark stepped into the attack and should have ended up with a cleft skull as a result. But as he moved, he swiveled his upper body ever so slightly to the side, and somehow, the stroke missed. He dropped his cudgel, grabbed Bareris's forearm, and twisted.

Bareris resisted, refusing to drop his sword or let his adversary tear apart his elbow. Whereupon Malark let go of his limb, and, straining when there was no longer any opposing force, Bareris lurched off balance. Only for an instant, but that was all the time his foe needed to snap a kick into his knee.

Bareris staggered, and the smaller man kicked his other knee. Neither leg would support Bareris now, and he fell prone in the dirt. He tried to roll over onto his back and raise his sword, but he was too slow. Something—a stamp kick, probably—smashed into the center of his spine, and then another cracked his neck. Pain blasted through him, and afterward, he couldn't move anymore. He tried to croak out the next syllable of his song, but even that had become impossible.

•• •• •• •• •• •• •• •• •• •• •• •• ••

Malark looked down at Bareris, who was squirming feebly and uselessly at his feet, and judged he hadn't done enough. The twice-broken spine would finish any mortal man, but given a little time, the undead bard might well recover even from that.

But he was unlikely to rise up if someone cut off his head, pulled the heart from his chest, and burned him. Malark plucked the sword from his hand to begin the process.

"Sleep in peace," Malark said. "I'm glad I was finally able to free you." He gripped the blade with both hands and raised it high.

A sort of groan sounded from the living members of the audience he'd nearly forgotten, particularly his fellow Red Wizards. They weren't protesting what a zulkir chose to do. None of them would dare. But plainly, they regretted it.

At first Malark couldn't imagine why. Then, abruptly, as if a key had unlocked a portion of his mind, he understood. Like himself, the other mages were necromancers. Their special art was to master the undead, and Bareris was a particularly powerful specimen. Thus, they deplored the waste implicit in destroying him when they could enslave him instead.

Malark realized he agreed with them. He tossed away the sword to clank on the ground, called his wand back into his grasp, swept it through a serpentine mystic pass, and recited the first words of a binding. He made an encouraging gesture with his free hand, and the other necromancers joined in.

When the spell was done, Tsagoth appeared beside him to inspect the pale figure still twitching and shuddering on the ground. "Did you enjoy that?" the blood fiend asked.

"For me," Malark said, "destroying the undead isn't sport. It's a sacrament. But yes, I did enjoy it."

"But you didn't destroy him."

For a heartbeat, Malark felt confused. Perhaps even uneasy. But then he frowned his formless misgivings away. "Well, no. At the last moment, I realized how useful he could be fighting on our side if the council attacks again. Imagine the effect on Aoth and the rebels' morale when their faithful friend rides out to slaughter them."

.. ..

Szass Tam snapped his shriveled fingers, and a rippling ran down from the top of the oval mirror. It looked like streaming water, and it washed the images of Malark, Tsagoth, and Bareris Anskuld away, so that the lich's own keen, intellectual face looked back at him once more.

It was good luck that he'd chosen to check on the Dread Ring in Lapendrar at this particular time, for he'd enjoyed watching Malark overcome the bard. Anskuld had never been more than a minor problem, but he'd been one for a hundred years, and after all the accumulated irritation, it was satisfying to see him neutralized at last.

Someone tapped on the door softly enough that it took sharp ears to hear it. Szass Tam turned in his chair and called, "Come in."

Ludicrously for such an exemplar of his brutish kind, bred for generations solely to kill whenever and whomever Red Wizards commanded, the blood-orc captain appeared to creep into the divination chamber as hesitantly as a timid child. Perhaps he didn't like the carrion stink and the litter of corpses and broken, filthy grave goods, for, insofar as he could without rendering the room incapable of its intended function, Szass Tam had filled it with such things. He'd done the same with many spaces reserved for his personal use. The ambience helped tune his mind for the Unmaking.

But he suspected the orc seemed uneasy because he had bad news to report, and the warrior confirmed as much as soon as his master told him to get up off his knees. "Your Omnipotence, we lost another hunting party. They found the demon—or it found them—outside the vault with the blue metal door, in the tunnels with all the faces carved on the walls. And it killed them."

I'm served by imbeciles, Szass Tam told himself and conscientiously tried to despise them for their inadequacies. "I'm sorry to hear it. Make sure we provide for the families of the fallen."

The officer swallowed. "There's more, Master. After the demon killed the hunters, it got the door to the vault open. It broke all the staves and wands you kept inside."

Szass Tam scowled. No stray predator from the Abyssal planes should have been capable of opening a door he'd sealed himself. And he'd spent the better part of four hundred years acquiring those rods across the length and breadth of Faerûn and even in lands beyond. To lose the entire collection, and not even to a thief—that at least would make sense—but to a creature who'd apparently destroyed it out of sheer random spite—

Szass Tam belatedly realized that if his disgust was appropriate, his sense of attachment and attendant loss was counterproductive, and he did his best to quash it. The staves and wands were flawed, contemptible trash, just like the rest of creation. They would have passed from existence within the next few tendays anyway, when the Great Work erased all the world. Thus, they didn't merit a second thought.

But he supposed he ought to provide a display of pique even though he no longer felt it. The orc would expect no less, and, mind-bound though they were, Szass Tam would rather his minions not question their master's sanity or true intentions. Ultimately, it didn't matter, but it had the potential to make this final phase of his preparations a bit more difficult than it needed to be.

So he scowled and snarled, "Kill the cursed thing! Take a whole legion into the crypts if you have to!"

"Yes, Master. We will. Only . . ."

"Only what?"

"Considering the cunning wizards and mighty creatures we've already lost, people are saying that maybe this demon's so nasty that only Szass Tam himself can slay it."

Szass Tam realized that if he still cared about the security of his fortress home and the safety of cherished possessions, as he wanted his retainers to believe, that was exactly what he'd do. And perhaps he could use a diversion, a break from the days and nights of near-constant meditation.

"All right," he said. "Forget about sending any more hunters. I'll go as soon as I get a chance."

•• •• •• •• •• •• •• •• •• •• •• •• •• ••

Throughout the night, some vague impulse prompted Bareris to peer up at the sky. Eventually he observed that dawn wasn't far distant, that it was, in fact, approximately the same time as when he'd invaded the Dread Ring. In the depths of his mind, something shifted.

Once the necromancers were certain they'd enslaved him, Malark had assigned him duties appropriate to a seasoned officer.

As the day dragged by, he'd performed them like a sleepwalker, feeling nothing except a dull, bitter anger he could no longer express or even comprehend.

He was still numb and incapable of contemplating his situation. But he slipped away from the band of ghouls Malark had placed under his command and stalked to a shadowy corner in an empty courtyard. No mouths opened in the stonework to proclaim his whereabouts; he belonged to the garrison now.

Once there, he sang softly. He couldn't have said exactly what he was doing or why, but he exerted his bardic skills anyway, striking precisely the right notes, rhythm, and phrasing to spark magic flickering in the air around him like a cloud of fireflies.

The spell picked at another power that, at this moment, seemed to cover his skin like a smothering coat of lacquer. The process stung, but the pain was a kind of relief, and by the time it ended, his mind was clear, his will, his own once more.

When he'd nudged Malark and the other necromancers to enslave rather than destroy him, he'd fully expected the binding to take. That was why, prior to sneaking into the castle, he, working with Lauzoril and Lallara, had imposed a different geas on himself. At the proper moment, he would find himself compelled to cast countermagic that would, if Tymora smiled, break the enemy's psychic shackles.

Keeping to the shadows but, he hoped, not so blatantly that he'd look like a skulking footpad if someone noticed him anyway, he headed toward a sally-port in the west wall. Still, no enchanted mouths opened to denounce him. The defense wasn't sophisticated enough to distinguish between the thrall he'd been a little while ago and the foe he was now. Some wizard had instructed it that he belonged in the stronghold, and as far as it was concerned, that was that.

The four guards currently standing watch on the battlements above the postern were gaunt dread warriors with smoldering amber eyes. Bareris couldn't muddle the minds of his fellow undead, and a thunderous shout or some other violent mystical attack was apt to draw unwanted attention.

But that was all right. He didn't mind doing things the hard way.

He climbed a set of stairs to the top of the towering wall and strode on toward the living corpses. They glanced at him once, then resumed their scrutiny of the rolling plain beyond the gate. Dread warriors were more sentient than ordinary zombies, but that didn't mean they were capable of casual curiosity.

The wall-walk was plenty wide enough for him to make his way past the first two. When he was in the middle of the group, their corrupt stink foul in his nostrils, he drew his sword, pivoted right, and struck.

The cut tumbled a dread warrior's head from its shoulders to drop into the bailey below. He swept its toppling body out of his way, rushed the one behind it, and split its skull before it could aim the spear in its gray, flaking hands.

He whirled and saw that slaying the guards on the right had given the ones on the left time to prepare themselves. The dead man in front held a scimitar in one hand and hurled its spear with the other.

Bareris crouched, and the spear flew over his head. He straightened up again and charged.

He cut a sizable chunk of the dread warrior's left profile away, exposing a section of black, slimy brain, but that didn't kill it. The corpse-thing tried to slash his leg out from under him, and steel rang when he parried. He shifted in close and hammered the heavy pommel of his sword into the breach in the dread warrior's skull. Brain splashed his hand, and his foe dropped.

He saw with a jolt of alarm that the last guard was raising a horn to its crumbling, oozing lips. He sprinted at it, slipped a cut from its scimitar, and struck the bugle from its grasp.

That frantic action left him open, and the dread warrior hacked at his flank. He parried, an instant too late, but though he failed to stop the attack from landing, his defensive action at least blunted the force of it and kept it from biting deep. He thrust up under the sentry's chin, and his sword punched all the way through the creature's head and crunched out the top of it. The guard fell.

Scowling at the burning pain in his side, Bareris freed his blade and cast about. As far as he could tell, no one had noticed anything amiss, and he meant to keep it that way.

He sang under his breath, and a shimmer curled like smoke through the air. First it hid the remains of the dread warriors, both the portions of them still on the wall-walk and those that had fallen to the ground. Then it painted semblances of them still standing at their posts.

Bareris was all too keenly aware that both wizards and undead were notoriously difficult to fool with this particular sleight. But he trusted his own abilities and dared to hope the phantasm would at least convince any foe who merely happened to glance in this direction.

Next he crooned a counterspell to obliterate any mouths that might otherwise have appeared and called out from the stone. When that was done, it was finally time to open the postern.

In this colossal stronghold, even the secondary gates were massive, designed to be operated by two or more soldiers at a time. But with his unnatural strength, Bareris managed. It was odd to feel the heavy bars slide and the valves swing apart when, beguiled by the mirage he himself had conjured, his eyes insisted that the sally-port was still sealed up tight.

chapter eight

17 Mirtul, The Year of the Dark Circle (1478 DR)

Invisible to hostile eyes—or so they hoped—Aoth, his fellow commanders, and a goodly portion of their army lay behind a shallow rise on the western approach to the Dread Ring. Blessed with the sharpest vision in the company, Aoth peered at the sally-port they'd selected before Bareris sneaked into the enemy stronghold. He *willed* it to open.

Crouching beside him, Jet grunted. "Yes. Wish for it. That'll make a difference."

"It can't hurt," said Aoth, and then, finally, the two leaves of the gate swung inward, first one and then the other. He could make out a fleck of white that must be Bareris pulling them open.

"By all the flames that burn in all the Hells," said Nevron, for once sounding impressed instead of contemptuous, "the singer did it."

"Or else the necromancers forced him to divulge his intentions and are exploiting our own scheme to set a snare for us," Lallara said, smiling maliciously. "Shall we go find out which it is?"

"Yes," said Aoth. "Let's." He drew himself up, the others followed suit, and for an instant, he thought again how odd it was to have zulkirs lying on their stomachs in the sparse grass at his direction. Even Samas Kul had grudgingly forsaken his floating throne, substituting a conjured armature of glowing white lines that wrapped around his bloated body and evidently enabled him to move without strain.

Only Aoth intended to march in the vanguard, so he had to wait while the archmages retreated to the center of the company and their bodyguards formed protective ranks around them. "Are you sure you want to walk in?" he asked Jet. "You could wait and fly with the rest of the griffons." He hadn't included aerial cavalry in the first wave lest it double the chances of being spotted.

Jet dismissed the suggestion with a toss of his black-feathered head. "I'll go when and how you go. Just don't think you can ride me in the same way you'd ride a damned horse."

"Perish the thought." Aoth glanced around and judged that they were ready. He pointed with his spear, strode forward, and the others followed.

As they advanced, Jhesrhi and other wizards whispered spells of concealment. Aoth could feel the power of them seething in the air, and, even with his fire-kissed eyes, he *didn't* see any foes lurking on the battlements waiting to spring a trap. Still, his throat was dry. He couldn't help imagining that when he and his comrades came close enough, flights of arrows and blasts of freezing, poisonous shadow would hammer down from the wall.

Fortunately, it never happened, and when, spear leveled, he warily stepped through the open gate, only Bareris was waiting to meet him. He grinned and gripped the bard by the shoulder. Mirror, on this occasion looking like the ghost of his own living self and not somebody else's, flitted in after him and saluted their friend with an elaborate flourish of his shadowy sword.

Bareris acknowledged them both with a curt nod.

Aoth looked around and found Khouryn already standing expectantly at his side. "Form ranks," he told the dwarf. "Quietly. We don't want the necromancers to know they have callers quite yet."

"I remember the plan," Khouryn said. He turned and waved a group of spearmen forward.

"Now where are the mages?" said Aoth.

"Here," said Jhesrhi, striding forward. The golden runes on her staff glowed. Silvery phosphorescence, the visible manifestation of some armoring enchantment, outlined her body. Her blonde tresses, cloak, and robe stirred as through brushed by a wind that wasn't blowing on anyone else. Several tattooed, shaven-headed Red Wizards trailed along behind her. "I assume it's time?"

"Yes," said Aoth. "Do it."

The wizards formed a circle and raised their instruments—two staves, four wands, and a clear crystal orb wrapped in a silvery web of filigree—above their heads. The mages chanted in unison, power warmed the air, and then a rattle ran from their immediate vicinity down the length of the fortress. It was the sound of doors banging shut in quick succession as they jumped and jerked in their frames.

The magic had sealed them. In some cases, those trapped inside the various towers and bastions would break them open again and rush out into the cool, moist dawn air. In others, the attackers would breach the doors themselves when they were ready, and pass through to kill whoever waited on the other side. Either way, the object was to fight the garrison a piece at a time instead of all at once.

"There's something you should know," Bareris said. "Malark's here, commanding the defense."

"I'm not entirely surprised. We knew we were up against someone clever."

"Be wary of him. He's spent the past ninety years learning sorcery from Szass Tam himself. He's even more dangerous than he was before."

"So are we." Aoth nodded to Khouryn, who relayed the command to the soldiers under his command. As the first hint of sunrise turned the sky above the postern gray, the spearmen stalked forward.

•• •• •• •• •• •• •• •• •• •• •• •• •• ••

Despite the howling, surging press of battle, the corpse moved in its own little bubble of clear space, as if even its allies were taking care not to come too close. It wore filthy bandages, but if someone had tried to mummify and so preserve it in the usual way, the process had failed. Putrescence leaked from between the loops of linen, and the thing smelled as foul as anything Bareris had encountered in a century of battling undead. As it shambled toward three of Aoth's sellswords, the miasma overwhelmed them. One actually doubled over and puked. The other two reeled.

It made them easy prey. The plague blight, as such horrors were called, grabbed the man who was vomiting and hoisted him off his feet. Streaks of gangrene ran through the man's flesh.

"Leave it to me!" Bareris shouted. Obnoxious though it was, the stink wasn't making him sick, and it was even possible his undead body was immune to the blight's corrupting touch, though he hoped to avoid putting it to the test. He ran up behind the creature and plunged his sword into its back.

It dropped the already lifeless body of its previous opponent and lurched around to face him. He slashed it twice more, then retreated and cut its hand when it pawed for him.

The plague blight kept coming as though its wounds were inconsequential. He shifted out of its path and shouted. The blast of sound smashed it into wisps of bandage, bone chips, and spatters of rot.

He pivoted, looking for whatever foe was rushing or creeping up on him now. None was, so he took a moment to try to take stock of the battle, difficult as that could be when a warrior was in the thick of it.

Aoth's plan to isolate the various components of the garrison had worked for a while. Long enough, one could hope, to give the attackers a significant edge. But then all the sealed doors opened virtually at once when some master wizard obliterated the locking enchantment. Now all of Szass Tam's minions could join the fight, and it became a desperate, chaotic affair.

The tide of battle carried Bareris to the main gate. Scores of his allies were fighting like madmen to gain control of it, so they could open it and bring the rest of the zulkirs' army streaming in. But enemy axemen and spearmen were struggling just as furiously to hold them back, while up on the battlements, archers loosed arrows and scarlet-robed necromancers hurled flares of fire and shadow. Confiscated after the besiegers abandoned it and animated by magic, Tempus's Boot rolled itself back and forth to bash at its former masters.

Hoping to see some griffon riders in the immediate vicinity, Bareris looked higher still. Aoth's aerial cavalry had entered the fight some time ago, and some of them ought to be here now, harrying the men on the wall-walk from the air. But they weren't. Evidently the enemy had them tied up elsewhere.

Bareris sang. The world seemed to blink, and then he was standing atop the wall in the middle of the necromancers.

Still singing—now a spell to leech the courage from his foes' hearts and the strength from their limbs—Bareris thrust his sword into one wizard's chest, yanked it free, and stepped past the toppling corpse to confront a second mage. That one brandished a wand capped with a miniature skull and rattled off words of power. Bareris felt coercion searing its way into his psyche like a branding iron. But this time, he wasn't sprawled crippled and helpless, and he cleaved the necromancer's skull before the binding was complete.

He killed the next mage. Dodged a hurtling, crackling ball of lightning. Slew another pair of wizards and saw they were the last spellcasters in that group.

He rounded on a squad of archers. A couple of the blood orcs recognized the danger, and they loosed their shafts at him. One arrow stabbed into his chest.

It hurt and rocked him back a step, but that was all. He knocked the bowmen off their feet with another bellow, and then something crashed into the back of his skull, pitching him onto his belly.

It wasn't like when the arrow pierced him; the pain and shock were almost overwhelming. But if he let them paralyze him, he was finished. He floundered over onto his back.

Tsagoth stood several paces away, a second round stone—originally intended as ammunition for one of the Ring's smaller catapults, probably—in his upper right hand. He tossed it into the left and threw it. Bareris rolled, and the missile smashed down beside him.

He scrambled to his feet, and the back of his head throbbed. He wondered just how badly his skull was cracked, and then Tsagoth made another throwing gesture, although now his hand was empty.

An explosion of multicolored light hammered Bareris. Tsagoth vanished.

The blood fiend shifted himself through space with perfect stealth, like the consummate predator he was. It was pure warrior's instinct that warned Bareris that his foe had appeared immediately behind him in hopes of rending him while he was still reeling from the blast. He spun and dropped low in the same movement, and Tsagoth's talons whipped harmlessly over his head. He thrust his sword deep into the vampiric demon's belly.

Tsagoth roared and convulsed but kept fighting. He leaned forward, actually imbedding the sword deeper to do so, and his four hands swept down.

Bareris couldn't free the blade in time to defend. He sang words of power instead, shielded himself with his free arm, and lowered his head in hopes of saving his eyes.

Tsagoth's claws tore his forearm and scalp, but Bareris didn't let the blows spoil the pitch and cadence of his magic. On the final note, force chimed through the air, and now he was the one who translated himself some distance backward.

He and the blood fiend regarded one another across the stretch of wall-walk and the gory corpses lying there. Tsagoth's stomach wound was already closing, faster than even Bareris could heal.

"So you decided to fight me after all," Bareris gritted.

Tsagoth laughed. "This time I have a reason. I'm ordered to defend the Dread Ring, and if I leave you running loose, those other worms on the ground yonder are likely to get the gate open. So come on. I'll give you what you truly want. I'll send you to join your woman."

Singing, Bareris advanced, but slowly. It gave the burning pain of his wounds time to ease and his enchantment time to tingle through his body.

He stepped into range, and Tsagoth clawed at him. Bareris wished himself a phantom. The attack raked harmlessly through him, and Tsagoth snarled and pivoted. Since he couldn't see Bareris anymore, he assumed the bard had tried the same trick he himself had employed, and shifted behind him.

But Bareris was using a different spell, and since he hadn't really changed position, he was behind Tsagoth now. He willed himself solid and visible again and cut into the blood fiend's back.

Tsagoth staggered and jerked back around, but not fast enough. Bareris had time to land two more cuts and still shift himself beyond the blood fiend's reach when the hulking creature lunged.

Of course, there was no such thing as a perfect defense; even his intermittently ethereal condition didn't qualify. If an attack surprised him, it would score, and Tsagoth was a cunning fighter. Once the undead demon realized what Bareris was doing, he used his ability to whisk himself through space to achieve a comparable effect. So, each trying to predict when and where the other would appear, the two combatants repeatedly materialized, struck, and vanished once again.

The difference was that Bareris guessed better. It was as though Shevarash, god of retribution, guided him. His strokes scored again and again, slicing a crosshatch of bloody gashes down the length of Tsagoth's body while he himself avoided further harm. And as his dance of vengeance continued, as the demon jerked in pain and Bareris's flying blade cast spatters of the creature's blood, a savage ecstasy swelled inside him.

Perhaps it made him careless.

He willed himself solid, made an overhand cut at Tsagoth's torso, then saw the blood fiend wasn't trying to defend himself. Instead, he hurled himself into the blow, willing to accept whatever harm it might do him if, at the same instant, he could drive his claws into Bareris's body.

The sword sheared into flesh, and so did Tsagoth's talons. Bareris stiffened at the shock of his new wounds, and then Tsagoth plowed into him and bore him down beneath him. The injured spot on the back of Bareris's head cracked against the stone, and a flare of pain made him convulse, insofar as that was possible with his huge opponent pinning him down.

Their claws still lodged in Bareris's body, Tsagoth's hands pulled in opposite directions. Agony ripped through the bard as his frame began to tear apart. The demonic vampire spread his jaws wide, then lowered them to Bareris's face.

Bareris told himself that this was the thing who'd destroyed Tammith, and rage lifted him above the crippling pain. Somehow he found the strength to concentrate and make himself a phantom once more. Tsagoth's fangs clashed shut in the same space his head occupied, but without harming him. The undead demon's body dropped through his and landed with a thump.

Bareris rolled clear, floundered upright, and made himself corporeal. Tsagoth snarled and started to rise. The last sword stroke must have hurt him, for he was floundering too. But he was still coming.

Shaking, his body ablaze with pain, Bareris gripped his sword with both hands, bellowed a war cry, and swung. The blow split Tsagoth's head from crown to neck.

Two more cuts chopped the head free of the body. Bareris reduced it to fragments, then turned his attention to the remainder of his foe's corpse. When he was certain that he'd demolished the blood fiend beyond any possibility of regeneration, all the strength spilled out of him, and he collapsed amid the carrion.

Where he tried to feel triumph. Or at least satisfaction. Something.

But he couldn't. For a few moments, as he had fought and gained the upper hand, he'd felt a teasing promise of joy, but there was nothing now but the torment of his wounds.

As Tammith had once tried to explain to him, this too was what it meant to belong to the living dead. You thirsted for something—blood, revenge, power, whatever—and the need was so hellish you'd do anything to ease it. But you couldn't, no matter what you tried.

As soon as he could, before his wounds had finished closing, he drew himself to his feet to hurl himself back into the roaring chaos of the battle. For after all, what else was there to do?

A griffon rider swooped past the arched window. Malark resisted the impulse to toss a javelin or darts of force at the sellsword and shrank back instead. If he didn't reveal his location, the enemy couldn't disturb him while he performed his next task.

And it was essential that he succeed. He'd helped the defense by unlocking all the magically sealed doors, but by itself, that wasn't going to be enough. The council's soldiers were pushing into every bailey. They'd taken possession of some of the towers and bastions already. By the looks of it, they were on the verge of seizing the fortress's primary gate to admit the rest of their army.

But Malark judged he could still turn the fight around—if he could blot the wan dawn light out of the sky. Then the specters and other entities lurking in the dungeons, the true night creatures to which the sun was poison, could emerge to join the fray.

Unfortunately, it wouldn't be easy. Ysval had been able to do it, but he'd been a nighthaunt. And then Xingax, but he'd grafted Ysval's severed hand onto his own wrist.

Malark would have to make do with pure sorcery. Encouraging himself with the reflection that at least he'd learned the craft from the greatest mage in the East, he raised his wand and started to chant.

•• •• •• •• •• •• •• •• •• •• •• •• ••

Jet beat his wings, flew above a skin kite, caught the membranous undead in his talons, and shredded it. Meanwhile, Aoth looked around the aerial portion of the battle for another foe and saw the sky was darkening.

With his fire-infected eyes, he'd noticed the process early. That gave him a chance to stop it if he could determine its source.

Unfortunately, no matter how he peered, he couldn't. The wizard responsible was hidden away somewhere.

He cast about for his own wizards and spotted the gleam of Jhesrhi's golden hair atop a captured bastion. She and some colleagues in red were hurling fire from the flat, square roof of the keep, while the soldiers standing with them shot arrows or dropped stones they'd pried loose from the parapet.

Aoth sent Jet diving toward the keep. Their haste nearly earned them a volley of arrows, but then the startled archers realized who was plunging down at their position and eased the tension on their bowstrings.

Jet spread his pinions wide and, despite his speed, touched down with scarcely a bump. "Jhesrhi!" said Aoth. "The sky's getting darker."

Jhesrhi looked up. "It is?"

"Yes, and that's bad. Can you find the person causing it?"

"Maybe. Darkness isn't an element per se, but air is, and the darkness is presumably flowing through the air. I'll speak to it."

She raised her staff over her head, closed her eyes, and murmured words of power. Aoth had a fair knowledge of elemental wizardry himself, for as a warmage, he relied on it extensively, but even so, he didn't recognize this particular spell. A cold wind kicked up, moaning, blowing one direction, then another, fluttering the hems of cloaks and robes.

Jhesrhi lowered her staff and used it to point at one of the taller towers. "It's just one man, and he's in the top of that."

"Thank you." Aoth dismounted, strode to the parapet, pointed his spear, and rattled off his own incantation. A bright, crackling lightning bolt leaped from the point of the spear, only to terminate just short of one of the windows of the minaret.

Aoth cursed and threw a pale blaze of cold. It too failed to reach the target. "The bastard's got wards in place."

One of the zulkirs' soldiers said, "Captain, we could do it the regular way. Break into the bottom of the tower and fight our way up from there."

Aoth shook his head and pointed to the sky. By now, surely everyone could see it was murkier than before. "We don't have time."

His glistening wand of congealed quicksilver in his hand, the harness of white energy still supporting his ponderous form, Samas Kul waddled forth from the circle of wizards with Lallara hobbling at his side. Aoth hadn't noticed his co-commanders before but wasn't surprised to find them here. The top of the keep was a relatively safe position from which to work their magic, and in his experience, his former masters didn't like facing unnecessary risks. That was the job of lesser creatures like legionnaires.

"I'll break open the tower," Samas said.

Lallara spat. "You couldn't breach the walls before."

"Then," Samas said, "we were outside the Dread Ring, which meant its defenses were at their strongest. Now, we're inside. Watch and learn." He raised his wand with a surprising daintiness that reminded Aoth of a conductor leading a band of musicians, then flicked it through an intricate series of passes.

A piece of minaret sparkled around its pointed window, and then the black stone turned to water. It cascaded down the side of the tower, leaving a ragged hole and revealing the man inside. It was Malark, clad in garments that were partly scarlet, denoting his status as a Red Wizard.

Aoth and Malark both aimed their weapons, but Szass Tam's aide was a hair quicker. Four points of yellow light shot from the tip of his wand.

"Get down!" Aoth yelled. Praying that the parapet would shield them at least to some degree, he threw himself flat, and his companions followed suit. Most of them, anyway. Lallara was moving too slowly. He grabbed her and jerked her down just as the sparks exploded into blasts of fire.

The heat seared him, and the booms nearly deafened him, but he wouldn't let them pound him into sluggishness. He raised his head and looked around.

Some of the warriors were badly burned, maybe dead. Thanks be to Kossuth, Jhesrhi and Jet looked dazed and a little scorched but essentially unharmed.

On the other side of the gap that separated the one high place from the other, violet phosphorescence seethed on top of the hole Samas had punched, patching it. Somehow, though he'd only had an instant, Malark had conjured a new defense. Now, protected by that shield, he was lifting the trapdoor that granted access to the lower levels of the tower.

He was still chanting and brandishing his ebony club too, and the sky was still blackening. Down in one of the western courtyards, a door flew open, and wolves with glowing crimson eyes—vampires, almost certainly——loped out.

Lallara snapped her fingers and floated back onto her feet as though invisible hands had lifted her. Samas heaved himself up in a way that reminded Aoth of a whale breaching. Jhesrhi rose, and the glowing runes on her staff pulsed brighter, first one and then another, a sign that she was angry.

Lallara glared at the minaret so intently that one could virtually feel her summoning every iota of her mystical might. Then she thrust her staff at it and screamed a word of power.

Samas seized Jhesrhi's blistered hand in his own meaty fingers. "I want your strength," he said, and though she stiffened like he'd jabbed her with a pin, she didn't pull away. He whipped the quicksilver wand through a complex figure.

Assailed by Lallara's spell of dissolution, the shield of violet light shattered like glass, the fragments winking out of existence when they fell free of the whole. As soon as the defense failed, Samas's power enfolded the minaret, and the entire top half of the black tower became a shapeless grayness that collapsed under its own weight and engulfed the nearly vanished Malark in the process. Portions of the stuff fell away from the central mass in globs and spatters. The rest flowed down what remained of the spire.

For an instant, Aoth couldn't tell what Samas had transmuted the stonework into. Then he heard the fresh screams rising from the base of the tower, looked down at the burned, battered, writhing men and orcs, and realized it was molten lead.

He rounded on the obese archmage, who was just letting go of Jhesrhi's hand. "Some of our own men were at the foot of that tower!"

"I killed Malark Springhill too," Samas answered, "and brought back the dawn light." Aoth saw that the sky was indeed lightening, and the vampire wolves were bursting into flame. "It's a fair trade, don't you think?"

Then, as if to save Aoth the trouble of framing an answer, the transmuter swayed and collapsed.

Lallara squinted at him. "Pity," she quavered, "he isn't dead. He simply swooned from his exertions." She turned to a soldier. "Guard him, and find a healer to tend him. And have food and drink ready when he wakes up. I guarantee the hog will want them."

Aoth scratched a patch of itching scorched skin on his cheek. Something was nagging at him, and after a moment, he realized what. He was finding it hard to believe that Malark was truly gone, charred, crushed, smothered in a heartbeat. It would have felt wrong even if the spymaster had simply been the supremely competent warrior of a century ago, and in the time since, he'd mastered a zulkir's skills on top of that.

Still, that was war for you. Even the greatest champion could die in an instant, as Aoth had observed time and again. And to say the least, it was doubtful that any human being could survive the magmalike inundation that Samas had dumped on Malark's head.

Anyway, the problem of the darkening sky was past, Aoth had a battle to oversee, and the best way to do it was on griffonback.

Sensing his intent, Jet bounded to his side. He swung himself back into the saddle, and the enchanted restraining straps buckled themselves to hold him there. The familiar leaped, lashed his black-feathered wings, and carried him aloft.

They climbed until they achieved a good view of the great southern gate. At the moment, he judged, it was the site of the most important struggle of all.

He sighed and sent a silent word of thanks to the Firelord when he saw that his side was winning. A lurching step at a time, paying a toll in blood for every miniscule advance but exacting even greater payment in their turn, the council's soldiers pushed, stabbed, and hacked their way toward the great valves, grinding the mass of defenders in front of them like grain beneath a miller's stone.

Meanwhile, Gaedynn and other griffon riders wheeled above the fight and shot arrows down at Szass Tam's minions. Singing, Bareris fought on the wall-walk, keeping it clear of enemy warriors when necessary and hammering the legionnaires, dread warriors, and orcs below him with his magic the rest of the time. Mirror battled beside him.

The defenders held out for a while longer, but finally the relentless assault proved too much for all but the stolid undead. Panicking, their human and orc counterparts cringed or turned and sought to run away.

But, hemmed in, they had nowhere to flee, and when they all but stopped fighting, the attacking infantry rolled over them like the tide.

At once, some of Aoth's sellswords scrambled to the mechanisms controlling the gates. The huge leaves cracked open, and a roar arose from the men waiting on the other side.

Aoth smiled. He was sure that he and his comrades would fight for the rest of the day and well into the night. But even so, he judged that in the truest sense, the castle had just fallen.

chapter nine

20 Mirtul, The Year of the Dark Circle (1478 DR)

Aoth found Bareris and Mirror atop the east wall. He himself wore a hooded cloak fastened all the way down the front to ward off the cold rain spitting down from the bulbous gray clouds, but the bard stood exposed and seemingly indifferent to the elements. Maybe, now that he was undead, they had no power to vex him.

Mirror was certainly beyond their reach. During the battle, some injury or malediction had knocked the personality and coherent thought out of him, and now he was less a visible presence than a sudden pang of vertigo when a person happened to look in his direction. If not for his spellscarred eyes, Aoth doubted he would have seen anything hovering there at all.

Bareris was gazing out across the rolling plains. Any other man would have done so with apprehension, but Aoth suspected that his friend did so longingly. Because what did Bareris have when he wasn't killing?

"See anything?" asked Aoth.

His long, white hair whipping in the breeze, Bareris smiled ever so slightly. "If something was out there, you wouldn't need me to point it out to you."

"Well, probably not," replied Aoth. "You know, you don't have to stand watch constantly. We have other sentries, and Jhesrhi has made friends with the winds hereabouts. They'll whisper in her ear if some threat appears."

"I don't mind. Since we finished cleaning out the dungeons, I have nothing better to do."

"You could sing and play your harp. Tell stories. The men—the wounded, especially—would be grateful for the entertainment."

"I'll be more useful up here."

Aoth sighed, and a drop of rain blew inside his hood to splat against his cheek. "Well, do what you think best, of course. Either way, you won't have to do it much longer. Lallara tells me the ritual's tonight."

Bareris finally turned to face him. "Is everything ready?"

"I think everyone understands it has to be. We can't dawdle here forever, even with the fortress to protect us. Another of Szass Tam's armies will come looking for us eventually, and we don't want to fight another battle like the last one. We've lost too many men." Aoth's mouth twisted. "The Brotherhood of the Griffon, especially."

Bareris hesitated, as though he had to search his memory for the response that would come naturally to any living man. But eventually he said, "I'm sorry about that."

Aoth shrugged. "It had to be done. Still, they were good comrades. I'll miss them. More to the point, I'll need to replace them, and it may be difficult. Until you dropped this mess in my lap, I had a reputation for keeping my word and for winning without taking many casualties—that last comes from choosing your causes and fights carefully. Now, it's all tarnished. I turned on the simbarchs and all but beat the Brotherhood to pieces against these black walls. So it remains to be seen whether warriors will flock to my banner as they did before."

"I'm sorry," Bareris repeated.

"Truly, I don't blame you." Aoth grinned. "At least, not too much. In fact, I want you and Mirror to stay with the company when this is over. We're a motley band of knaves and orphans as it is, and the others have gotten used to you. They'll make you welcome, and they won't care that you're undead."

"Thank you for that," Bareris said. "But it won't *be* over. Not for me."

"Don't be stupid! Of course it will! You killed Xingax and Tsagoth. We're about to wreck Szass Tam's great scheme. That's as much revenge as you'll ever get. The lich himself—his person, his existence—is beyond your reach."

"You heard the speech I made to the rebels. I more or less promised I'd continue to help them."

"And we keep our pledges," Mirror whispered, his sepulchral tone as chilling as the wind and rain. "The rule of our order requires it."

Aoth scowled. "For the hundredth time, neither Bareris nor I belong to your extinct fellowship, and we don't care about its code. In fact, he's just using obligation as an excuse to put me off." He shifted his gaze back to the bard. "But all right. I can see there's no swaying you. Just tell me one thing. What if, someday, by some miracle, you actually do manage to slay Szass Tam, and his destruction doesn't ease you any more than Tsagoth's did?"

"However I feel, I'll go into the dark as the dead are meant to do and hope Tammith is waiting for me there."

•• •• •• •• •• •• •• •• •• •• •• •• ••

The Dread Ring was an instrument built by an undead wizard to serve the unholiest of purposes, and to Jhesrhi's way of thinking, it would have made sense to try to break it in the purifying light of day. But Nevron had insisted they work at night, because the spirits he and his aides would invoke would be more powerful then.

He'd insisted on Jhesrhi's presence in the primary circle as well, perhaps because her escape from the trap under the wall had impressed him. Accordingly, she now stood with Aoth, Bareris, and the zulkirs on the same rooftop where Samas had melted the minaret.

She grasped the core idea of the ritual the zulkirs had devised, but not precisely how it worked. Fortunately, she didn't have to. During the initial phase, her job would be to raise power for others to direct. Still, though in most circumstances she was confident of her own abilities, she felt nervous as she waited to begin. What if, somehow, she spoiled the ceremony? Then Szass Tam would murder everyone in the East, everyone in all of Faerûn, conceivably, and it would be her fault!

Gaedynn was one of the spectators sitting on the parapet. He wasn't as much of a dandy on campaign as he was when idling in town, but with the siege won, he'd done his best to burnish his appearance. His new, jeweled rings and cloak pin, plunder seized in the wake of the castle's fall, helped considerably.

Perhaps he sensed that Jhesrhi was tense, for he gave her a wink and a grin. His attention evoked the usual awkward tangle of emotions. But on this occasion, gratitude predominated, and she managed a twitch of a smile in return.

In the courtyard below, yellow flame boomed into existence, at this moment of its birth leaping higher than the roof of the keep. The Burning Braziers had lit the bonfire that was key to their own ritual. Mirror, she knew, was down there with them. The ghost was no servant of Kossuth, but, paradoxical as it seemed, he evidently channeled some sort of divine power and believed he could be of more use standing with the priests of fire than among arcane practitioners.

The Braziers would use their magic to support the zulkirs' efforts. Scattered throughout the fortress, secondary circles of wizards would do the same. Every surviving spellcaster who'd marched from the Wizard's Reach was taking part in one fashion or another, and Jhesrhi told herself that all of them, working together, must surely have a reasonable hope of destroying the Ring, even if an infamous lich had built it.

However grudgingly, Lallara's fellow zulkirs had agreed that, as an expert in countermagic, she was best suited to lead the ritual. She thumped the butt of her staff on the rooftop and produced a bang like the slamming of a massive door. "All right," she said, "let's do this."

She chanted the first incantation, and one at a time, the other members of the circle joined in, either reciting in unison with her or offering contrapuntal responses. Down in the bailey, the Burning Braziers prayed, and the bonfire hissed and crackled, a hint of cadence and pattern, conceivably of language, in the noise. Farther away, the lesser wizards called out words of power until the whole gigantic fortress droned and echoed with the sounds of invocation.

Power gathered in the air, alternately caressing and scraping, searing and chilling, but whatever the sensation, it was never truly painful. To the contrary, a swell of exaltation swept Jhesrhi's lingering anxiety away.

Her consciousness expanded. Her thoughts brushed the cognition of those around her, and it was a touch she could bear without panic or loathing, an intimacy that verged on the seductive. She'd have to take care lest some other mind impress its shape on hers and compromise her identity.

She perceived the demons and devils Nevron had invoked,

but only vaguely, as shadows hovering at the borders of physical reality. The vast, ancient entities evidently didn't need to manifest fully to lend their aid to this particular endeavor, and that was just as well. Otherwise, their knowledge and commitment notwithstanding, some of the spellcasters might have fled in terror. Many of the common soldiers surely would.

Last but most clearly of all, she discerned the Dread Ring itself like a festering wound in the earth. Like a well of unnatural and inexhaustible power. Arcing away from it were lines of force linking it to other such talismans, defining an immense dark circle of death on the face of the land.

That was the Dread Ring that Jhesrhi and her allies had to destroy. Not the stone walls and bastions, although some of those might crack and crumble as an incidental effect of their assault, for battlements and towers could be rebuilt. They had to attack the *concept*, the *potential* of the Ring. If they could obliterate that, it would spoil the whole pattern, and none of the similar castles scattered across Thay would serve its intended purpose anymore.

Jhesrhi realized that since she now perceived the true, transcendent form of the Ring, it stood to reason that her partners in the circle must see it too. Lallara glanced around as though gauging whether everyone was ready, then raised her staff and rammed it down with all the strength in her deceptively frail-looking arms. Jhesrhi expected a louder bang than before, and perhaps that was exactly what happened, but if so, she didn't hear it.

That was because, as the rod plunged down, she felt the power they'd all raised plunge with it. The magic both stabbed a hole to a different level of reality and thrust her—or perhaps just her spirit— into it, as if she were an ant clinging to the flat of a blade.

She cast about. Previously, she'd seen the essence of the Dread Ring as a well. Now she and the rest of the circle seemed to float deep inside it. The curved walls weren't solid, though, but made up of crisscrossed bands of shadow. Beyond them lay nothing but a sort of twilight, extending as far as the eye could see.

Bareris was the first to attack. He shouted, and his thunderous voice chipped away blackness where one length of shadow overlapped another. Then Aoth hurled fire from his spear and burned away a little more.

Lauzoril spoke in a gentle voice like a father coaxing a child, and a section of well dissolved into dark vapor. Lallara snarled a spell, and a kite shield made of crimson light appeared in one portion of the cylindrical, weblike structure, withering the strands that occupied the same space. Nevron fingered an amulet dangling on his burly chest, and a huge winged devil with long, extravagantly curved horns appeared to stab at the black lattice with an iron trident. Samas brandished his baton, and a section of the construct turned to gold. Jhesrhi could feel that the transmutation compromised it as much as any of the other assaults.

She needed to start her own assault. She couldn't detect any fire, water, or earth ready to hand. If she wanted to use them, she'd have to produce them. But air was here, or at least the notion of it, for everyone could breathe and talk. She conjured a howling whirlwind that tore away chunks of blackness like a thousand raking claws.

She smiled at the thought that things were working out. Breaking the Ring would be a big, arduous job, but the important thing was that plainly, they *could* damage it. Now they just had to persevere.

Then their attack roused the defensive enchantments.

Ragged, flapping things like bats—or their shadows—erupted from the dark construct in a blinding cloud. They engulfed Jhesrhi in an instant, and pain danced across her body, although she couldn't tell precisely how her assailants were hurting her—biting, clawing, or doing something stranger.

In any case, they were touching her, and she flailed at the

vileness of it with her staff. Perhaps she hit one or two of the creatures, but that was of little use when she had dozens clinging to her and whirling all around her.

Fortunately, responding to her need, her conjured whirlwind struck to greater effect. It roared to her, snatched up the bat-things in its spin, and tore them into what resembled scraps of black paper.

Panting and trembling, she cast about and saw that her comrades too had managed to defend themselves. Lallara wore a corona of rosy light, and when the flying shadows touched it, they blinked out of existence, although each such contact dimmed it an iota. Hideous demons hovered around Nevron in a protective sphere. Samas flicked his quicksilver wand through a star-shaped pattern, and a dozen pieces of living darkness turned into mice, which, bereft of wings, plummeted down the well.

Still, Jhesrhi judged that her optimism had been premature, and events soon proved her right. No matter how many bat-things she and her allies destroyed, the well birthed more, and it was only during those precious moments when they'd cleared every immediate threat away that they were free to strike at the construct itself.

Then she noticed she was growing short-winded. Wheezing. Fighting for breath as if someone were holding a pillow over her face. Or as if the whirlwind she'd conjured to serve as her weapon were laying claim to *all* the air around her.

Something comparable was befalling her allies. Nevron plainly bore several wounds beneath his scarlet robes; blood soaked patches of silk and velvet above them and stained the cloth a darker red. He summoned another demon, a hairless, somewhat manlike creature with claws and feathered wings, and instead of simply appearing before him, the spirit burst forth from a tattoo on his wrist, taking the ink with it and leaving raw, shredded flesh behind.

Meanwhile, Bareris sang, and his bone white mouth and the tissue around it cracked and rotted. Samas brandished his wand, and pieces of his own corpulent form altered. Bumps of gold jutted from his skin like warts, and fishy scales encrusted the left side of his face. Lauzoril gripped a dagger in his fist, and as he recited his spells, flailed his arm repeatedly as though trying to cast the blade away. As though he feared that if he didn't get rid of it, he'd use the weapon to harm himself. But his fingers wouldn't open.

The attackers could all still use their magic. But every time they did, the well turned a portion of it against them.

Jhesrhi looked to Aoth, who was hovering a short distance above her. Bat-things flew at him; he pierced them with darts of azure light from the point of his spear, then jerked and grunted as though something had stabbed him as well.

"We're not going to make it," she whispered. There was no air left for anything louder. Not in her lungs, anyway.

But Aoth heard, and he glared with his lambent blue eyes. "Yes, we will! All of you, remember, we're not alone! Our comrades are still feeding us strength! Reach out and take it!"

Hard to focus on that when she was suffocating, with black spots swimming in her vision and raw animal desperation yammering in her mind. But she was a wizard, with a wizard's disciplined mind, and after a moment, she succeeded in shifting her perception to the Ring of stone and timber.

But she didn't see it as she would have if she'd reoccupied her corporeal form. Rather, she floated high above the stronghold and somehow perceived an abundance of information all at once. Though still chanting, she and the other members of the primary circle had fallen to their knees or onto their sides. Gaedynn and the other spectators watched them helplessly. Down in the courtyard, Burning Braziers whirled flaming chains and danced in and out of the bonfire. Sometimes they emerged with their clothing ablaze, but even then, they continued to whirl and leap. Glowing as if his body were made of sunlight, Mirror stood with his sword upraised. Elsewhere, Red Wizards recited rhyming spells and flourished their wands, orbs, and staves. Some bled from the eyes or nostrils, spat out teeth that had suddenly slipped from their gums, or collapsed thrashing and foaming in epileptic seizures. Szass Tam's wards were afflicting them as well.

Still, Aoth was right. Power floated above the castle in an opalescent haze. Jhesrhi immersed herself in it, drew it into her, and then she could breathe again. She lingered for another moment, bracing herself, refocusing her mind, then leaped back into the well.

From that point onward, it was a little easier, although the bats never stopped hurtling at her, and the well never stopped trying to steal her breath. Not until glowing red cracks sheared up and down the length of it, zigzagging through every section all at once. An instant later, the entire structure shattered into a million tumbling shards.

And a heartbeat after that, she was back inside her body on the rooftop. She prayed it was because the place her spirit had just visited no longer existed.

She was sore from head to toe but particularly in her chest. She was also soaked with clammy sweat, and when she tried to stand, she found she barely had the strength. Gaedynn started toward her, then stopped when he remembered she wouldn't want his help.

The other members of the circle floundered up as well. From the looks of it, they all felt as spent and achy as she did, but none displayed any of the bizarre injuries that had so disfigured their discarnate souls.

Nevron glowered at Lallara. "Did we really do it?" he demanded. "Can you tell?"

"Give me a moment," Lallara snapped. She closed her eyes, took several long, deep breaths, and murmured an incantation.

Then the first smile Jhesrhi had ever seen on that wrinkled, haglike countenance pulled the corners of the pale lips upward.

Jhesrhi felt her own lips stretch into a grin. Sensed the joy bursting forth across the rooftop as her companions observed Lallara's expression. In another moment, someone would let out a cheer.

Except that then, the crone's smile twisted into a scowl. "Wait," she said.

•• •• •• •• •• •• •• •• •• •• •• •• •• •• ••

"Wait," said Szass Tam, and the trio of vampiric knights he'd brought with him halted at the intersection of five tunnels. Narrowed eyes slightly luminous in the gloom, alert for any sign of their quarry, the blood-drinkers peered down the shadowy passages.

Szass Tam dropped to one knee and sketched a triangle on the floor with a withered fingertip. His digit left a trail of red phosphorescence behind. When completed, the glowing arrowhead spun around. And kept on spinning, endlessly, until its maker snorted in mingled annoyance and amusement and wiped it from existence.

"Did you pick up the demon's trail?" a vampire asked.

"No," said Szass Tam, rising. "Whatever it is, it knows enough sorcery to cover its tracks."

"Well, don't worry, Your Omnipotence, we'll find it."

In another time, the warrior's expression of loyalty and confidence might have elicited Szass Tam's favor. But now that he'd trained himself in scorn, he nearly sneered at the vampire's sycophancy. But there was no need to *show* his disdain and several good reasons not to, so he simply chose a corridor at random and headed down it. His bodyguards prowled along behind him.

After a while, they came to an alcove containing a shrine to a minor godling, a psychopomp and guardian of tombs, who'd died thousands of years before. Something had smashed the statue's avian head and the inscription on the pedestal beneath.

"Has anyone reported this?" Szass Tam asked.

"No, Master," the same vampire told him.

"It's recent damage, then." Which meant the demon might still be in this part of the subterranean complex. Perhaps where divination had failed, luck had succeeded.

Szass Tam touched the topaz set in one of his rings and wrapped himself in an almost invisible haze that would deflect a blow like plate armor. Then something jolted him and sent him staggering.

"Master!" said the talkative vampire. "Are you all right?"

Szass Tam regained his balance. "Yes." For an instant, he'd wondered if the demon had leaped out of nowhere and struck him, wondered, too, if an earthquake had rocked the Citadel and the mountain and catacombs beneath, but now he could tell that neither was the case. Rather, he'd experienced a purely psychic shock.

Unfortunately, that didn't make the situation any better. Indeed, it was nearly as bad as it could be.

He brandished his staff. "I have to leave you."

"Should we—," began the knights' spokesman. Then magic whined through the air, enfolded Szass Tam in its grip, and translated him to the apex of the keep.

Attuned as he was to the gigantic instrument he'd created, he'd felt it when one of the Dread Rings broke. Now that he was on the roof, at the very hub and linchpin of the dark circle, he could tell with certainty that, as he'd guessed, it was the fortress in Lapendrar that had surrendered its essential nature. Impossible as it seemed, his enemies must have prevailed against Malark, Tsagoth, and all the castle's other defenders. Now the symbol

Szass Tam had defined on the face of Thay was warping, collapsing like a spiderweb with a critical anchoring strand severed.

The terrible irony was that Szass Tam had elaborated on the pattern in Fastrin's book and had built more Dread Rings than its ancient author suggested. He'd judged that in an endeavor like the Unmaking, one couldn't have too much power. But now, the loss of one perhaps unnecessary castle threatened to render all the others useless.

At first, no matter how he strained, he couldn't think of a thing in the world to do about it. Finally he closed his eyes. Centered himself and fought for calm. He was Szass Tam, and he didn't panic. He wouldn't panic now.

When he felt ready, he considered the problem anew with all the cold objectivity he could muster. And saw something he hadn't realized before.

The sigil the Dread Rings defined could never exist again—not in the conventional, three-dimensional world. But there were many more dimensions than that, even if people couldn't ordinarily perceive them. Were it otherwise, the mortal plane and all the higher and lower worlds wouldn't be able to coexist.

He dropped his staff to clatter on the roof and summoned a different one, fashioned of clear crystal, into his hand. Once, it had belonged to Yaphyll, the greatest seer he'd ever known; he'd found it sealed in a secret vault in the Tower of Vision after the zulkirs had abandoned Bezantur. It was the best tool he possessed for what he had in mind, which was no guarantee that it was powerful enough.

He brandished the glittering staff and recited words of power, and an image of the realm's plains, plateaus, and mountains, the rivers, lakes, and seashore appeared floating in the air before him. Black dots designated the Dread Rings and the Citadel.

He spoke again, and the map shifted, although no one else would have seen it alter. That was because Szass Tam now viewed it in four dimensions, in a manner foreign to normal human perception.

And the experience was all but intolerable, like looking directly at the sun. As a necromancer, Szass Tam was used to contemplating the bizarre, the hideous, and the paradoxical, but even so, this view spiked pain through his eyes and deep into his head.

He forced himself to keep peering anyway, until he had the information to make his calculations. Which revealed that four dimensions were not enough.

So he called for five and let out an involuntary groan. Five were much worse than four, exponentially worse, perhaps. And five weren't sufficient, either.

So it was on to six, and then seven. Whimpering, shuddering, and jerking uncontrollably, he wondered if the mere act of observation could kill a man, even if the fellow was already dead. Given what he was suffering, he suspected it could, but even so, he refused to relent. He'd always known he was risking his existence by undertaking the Great Work, and if he perished now, so be it.

Eight dimensions. Then nine. And nine *were* enough. When he took the proper two-dimensional cross section of that curved and infinitely complex space, the surviving Dread Rings and his present location fell into the proper positions relative to one another.

He raised all his personal power and likewise tapped the reservoirs of mystic energy that were the Rings themselves. He wielded the magic like a scalpel, first cutting the tainted bonds that linked the healthy Rings to the ruined one. Then he destroyed the remaining ties.

The Dread Rings immediately threatened to fall out of harmony, to lose their fundamental relationship with one another. Szass Tam locked them in temporary correspondence through sheer force of will. Next, using his power as if it were an etcher's diamond-tipped stylus, he inscribed new paths between them, connections that ran through nine dimensions and the empty places between the worlds.

When he finished the new pattern, it demonstrated its viability by flaring to life, not with light but with pure power, perceptible as such to a mage's senses. Szass Tam immediately willed the nine-dimensional map to vanish, then, his strength spent, collapsed. His eyes and head blazed with agony, but he smiled anyway.

chapter ten

21–25 Mirtul, The Year of the Dark Circle (1478 DR)

It isn't possible," said Samas Kul. Disappointment hadn't robbed him of his appetites, as the buttered roll in his meaty hand and the crumbs scattered down the front of his gorgeous robes attested. But it seemed to Aoth that though the archmage ate and drank as ceaselessly as ever, there was a sullen quality to it instead of the usual gusto. "Break a pattern and you rob it of its arcane virtues. Every apprentice knows that."

"What a pity," Lallara drawled, "that Szass Tam isn't an apprentice."

Samas glared at her. "Do *you* understand how he did it?"

"No," Lallara said, "but the other Dread Rings are still functional, and so is the device they comprise. We've all verified it. So it's time to stop whining that 'it isn't possible' and figure out what to do next."

Aoth agreed with her. He just hoped there was something *to* do and that someone would have the cleverness and the will to propose it. He wouldn't have wanted to bet on it.

The Dread Ring of Lapendrar possessed all the amenities of any great castle, including a hall equipped with a round oak table and chairs where lords and officers could palaver. It was here, beneath hanging black-and-scarlet banners adorned with skulls and other necromantic emblems, that the zulkirs, Bareris, and Aoth had assembled for a council of war. And when the sell-sword captain looked around at his companions, it appeared to him that weariness and discouragement had set their stamps on every face.

Or rather, every one but the bard's. Bareris's expression was just as it had been for a hundred years, joyless and haggard but keen as a blade. Aoth had the odd and vaguely resentful thought that for his friend, it was a good thing their plan had failed. Now he had a better excuse to go on hating and fighting.

Everyone sat silently for several heartbeats. Then Samas's throne floated back from the table. "That's it, then. I have treasure to move out of Escalant. I assume the rest of you have your own arrangements to make."

Aoth didn't realize he was going to jump up out of his chair. It just happened, and the seat overturned to bang on the floor behind him. He leveled his spear and said, "You're not running. Not unless we all decide it's the only thing to do."

Samas's face turned a deeper red, and inside its yards of jeweled vestments, his gross body seemed to swell like a frog's. "Are you truly mad enough to try to dictate to *me?*"

Aoth smiled. "Why not? We're co-commanders, remember? Besides, our cause is too important, and too many of my men gave their lives to get us this far."

"This is on your own head, then." Samas's quicksilver wand writhed out of his sleeve and into his hand like a snake. "Which would you prefer: to turn to smoke or to live on as mindless worm?"

"Surprise me." Aoth roused the power in his spear, and the point glimmered.

"Don't," Lauzoril said, sounding no more forceful than a priggish tutor reproving unruly children. But his voice carried a charge of coercion that balked Aoth—and Samas, too, evidently—like a dash of ice-cold water in the face.

And a good thing, too, for in the aftermath, Aoth realized he didn't truly want to fight Samas, and not because he feared him. The past century had taught him more combat magic than the zulkirs likely comprehended even now. But no matter who won, the duel would accomplish nothing. It was just that Aoth was frustrated, and, selfish and arrogant as they were, the archmages made tempting targets at which to vent his feelings.

He set his spear on the tabletop and inclined his head in the implication of a bow. "Master Kul, I apologize. Obviously, it isn't my place to give you orders. But I ask you to stay at least until we all finish our talk. Surely you can afford that much time."

"Yes," Nevron said, "stay. We insist."

Samas looked around the table, and then his throne floated back to its original position, settling to the floor so gently as to be silent despite its grandiose size and the bulk of the man inside it. Aoth sat back down in his own chair.

Samas took a long drink from his silver goblet. "All right, then. Someone convince me we have something sensible to talk about. Can we seize control of a second Dread Ring?" He glowered at Aoth, and the other zulkirs turned to him as well.

Aoth sighed. "It's unlikely. We lost too much of our strength taking this one. To be honest, we might find it difficult even to reach another Ring. The only way to do it is to march deeper into Thay, and we're almost certain to encounter resistance along the way."

"Then there *isn't* anything to discuss, and this is just a waste of time."

"Not necessarily," Bareris said.

Aoth felt a flicker of hope. "Do you have an idea?"

"It's not a new one," Bareris said, "but it fits the situation. If we can't destroy the weapon, we have to destroy the creature who intends to wield it."

Nevron snorted. "Assassinate Szass Tam, you mean. You're certainly right that it's not an original notion. Over the decades, I've sent scores of demons and devils to do the job. The Church of Kossuth emptied out its monasteries dispatching Black Flame Zealots. And all to no avail."

"What," replied Bareris, "if all of you—or rather, all of us— were the assassins, and we took the lich by surprise? Wouldn't we have a reasonable chance of overwhelming him, and then finding the vessel where he stores his soul to keep him from rising again?"

"Yes," Lallara said, "and perhaps if we had a net with a long enough handle, and the strength to lift it, we'd have 'a reasonable chance' of scooping stars down from the sky too. But there's no way to take Szass Tam unawares, perhaps no way to get close to him at all. The Citadel is too well guarded, and you can't translate yourself into it."

"What," Bareris asked, "if you already had an ally inside, he had some ability to open portals in space, and he tried to help you come through? Do you think that the four of you, working in concert, could overcome the wards then?"

Lauzoril frowned and laced his fingers together. "Possibly."

"Do we have such an agent in place?" Samas asked.

"Not yet," Bareris said.

"Then what's the point of speculating?"

"Somehow, I'll get myself inside."

"Frankly," Lauzoril said, "that seems unlikely. I'm not sure you could penetrate the defenses even in times of peace, and surely, by now, Szass Tam and his lieutenants are aware of our presence in the realm. They're watching us in one fashion or another."

"I assume so," Bareris said. "That's why I want the army to head for another Dread Ring just as if we actually believed we could lay siege to it successfully. That should mask our true intentions and rivet the foe's attention on you. Meanwhile, Mirror and I will sneak into High Thay by ourselves."

"So," Samas said, "we zulkirs march deeper and deeper into enemy territory, fighting for every mile, lingering dangerously close to the site from which Szass Tam will ultimately send forth waves of death magic. All in the hope that you'll eventually contact us and tell us that somehow, against all rational expectation, you've figured out how to get us into striking distance of the lich."

Bareris smiled. "Pretty much."

"Preposterous."

"I don't particularly like it, either," said Aoth. Indeed, it pained him to imagine the punishment the Brotherhood of the Griffon would endure; only the vision of all-encompassing destruction he'd seen over Veltalar could have induced him to subject them to such an ordeal. "But so far, it's the only plan we've got."

"That isn't so," Samas said. "We zulkirs can be far from here in a heartbeat. You griffon riders also have a good chance of getting clear. If you're concerned about the rest of your troops, then find the coin to put them aboard fast ships, and even they may get away."

"But what if there isn't any such place as 'clear' or 'away'? What if Szass Tam truly can kill the whole world?"

Samas sneered. "If you understood magic as we do, you'd realize that's impossible."

"You all thought it was impossible for the lich to continue with one Ring destroyed too, and look how that worked out. Don't try to tell me you're certain of his limits."

The obese transmuter opened his mouth, then closed it again. In fact, it appeared that Aoth had succeeded in silencing all four zulkirs, for a moment anyway, and despite the circumstances, he found it rather satisfying.

Then Lauzoril said, "Still, if it's a choice between sitting peacefully in Waterdeep and gambling that the tide of death won't reach that far, or staying here fighting the worst the necromancers can throw at us, knowing that at any moment, the Unmaking could commence just a few hundred miles from our location . . . well, you see my point."

"I do," said Aoth. He reminded himself not to speak of all the innocent lives that would be lost if the zulkirs abandoned them to their fate, because he knew his former masters wouldn't care. Indeed, such an appeal was likely to stir their contempt. "But I thought you all decided that the Wizard's Reach is worth fighting for."

"We *did* fight for it," Samas said. "We did everything practical. Now it's time to regroup. Maybe the Reach will survive, for despite your pretensions to prophecy, Captain, we still don't actually *know* that Szass Tam's ritual will do anything at all. And if the Reach does perish, at least we'll still have our lives, much of our wealth, and our magic. In time, we'll acquire new dominions."

"Then run," said Aoth. "By all the Hells, you did it in Bezantur ninety years ago. I don't know why I expected any better of you this time around."

Nevron glared. "Be careful how you speak to us."

"To the Hells with that and with you," Aoth snapped. "Of course, we all see that this is a desperate situation, but you're supposed to be zulkirs of Thay. The greatest of wizards, and warlords on top of that. Bareris is offering you a chance, however dangerous, to take revenge on the creature who betrayed you and cast you down from your high estate, and to reclaim your mastery of the realm. But you're too cowardly to take it. You'd rather play it safe!"

Nevron scowled but found nothing to say in return. For a moment, neither did anyone else. Then Lallara looked to Bareris and asked, "Do you *truly* believe you can find a way inside the Citadel?"

"I've spent decades slipping in and out of places the necromancers believed impregnable," the bard replied. "So why not Szass Tam's own house?"

"Why not, indeed?" she answered. "All right, I'll go along with your scheme. It's idiotic, but I won't have it said of me that I ran like a rabbit whenever the lich waggled that stupid beard of his in my direction."

"I'll stay too," Nevron said, "because I *am* a warlord, Captain, with a destiny of conquest greater than you can comprehend. Maybe it's time I start acting the part."

"Then I too will stay for as long as I see a point to it." Lauzoril smiled tightly. "I know the rest of you see me as somewhat . . . bloodless. But I've hated Szass Tam for a long time. It's enticing to think I might finally get the chance to show him just how much."

Lallara gave Samas a nasty leer. "That leaves you, hog."

"Curse you all," the transmuter said, sweat beading his ruddy brow. "This is madness."

"Oh, probably. But what if you desert us, and then the mad plan works? I hope you don't think we'll tolerate you back in Thay or in the Wizard's Reach, either. By the Seven Shields, I'm not sure I could abide the thought of your continued existence anywhere."

"All right!" Samas snarled. "If you all insist, we can try it and see where we are in a few days."

Once they all had agreed, they had to elaborate on Bareris's basic idea, and that took most of the night. Selûne and her trail of glittering Tears had forsaken the sky by the time the council broke up.

Though tired, Aoth felt an impulse to mount the battlements and check for signs of trouble before he sought his bed. Pulling his cloak tight against the cold breeze whistling from the east, he started up the stairs that climbed to the top of the wall, and Bareris followed a step behind him.

"That went all right," said Aoth, "but when we were arguing about what to do, I was surprised you left me to do so much of the talking. After all, you're the eloquent one."

"Since they all came around," Bareris replied, "plainly, you were eloquent enough. Besides, I couldn't talk and hum at the same time."

Aoth stopped and looked around. "I didn't hear any humming."

"Because I did it very softly." Bareris's black eyes suddenly opened wider. "But I swear, you weren't the target!"

"I believe you. I trust you, and even if I didn't, my feelings didn't change. I was resolved to continue the fight before the council ever began. I'm just appalled because those four are zulkirs. More than that, Lauzoril is the master of enchantment, and Lallara, of defensive magic."

"I knew it was risky. Still, I hoped I could give them a little nudge and get away with it."

Aoth took a deep breath. "Well, I won't argue with success. Or claim to be outraged at the thought of manipulating them as callously as they've always exploited anyone under their sway."

"Good. I wouldn't want to part company with bad feelings between us."

"When will you and Mirror split off from the army?"

"As soon as the march is under way."

"I believe the griffon you were riding survived the battle unharmed."

"Thanks, but I don't need him. At this point, any sentry who spots a griffon rider will immediately think of Aoth Fezim and his sellswords. I'll do better to choose another steed from among the ones the enemy kept here in the Ring." A smile came and went on his pallid face. "It was . . . pleasant to ride a griffon one last time."

"After we destroy Szass Tam, you can ride them whenever you like."

"I think I'll visit the stables now." Bareris turned and headed back down the stairs.

•• •• •• •• •• •• •• •• •• •• •• •• •• ••

Malark felt a hostile presence lurking on his right. Employing the mental skills he'd learned as a Monk of the Long Death, he ignored it and kept his awareness focused on the silent stretch of tunnel ahead of him. That was where his quarry was likely to appear.

The Watcher, as generations of Red Wizards and their servants had called his invisible and unwanted companion, haunted a section of the catacombs decorated with dingy paintings of scenes from which all the people and animals seemed to have vanished—throne rooms without monarchs or courtiers, wedding feasts devoid of bride, groom, guests, and musicians, and forests uninhabited by birds or squirrels. The spirit never actually did anything to mortals who trespassed in its domain. Still, most people found the pressure of its hateful regard so nerve-wracking that they gave this part of the dungeons a wide berth.

To Malark, though, it was no great matter. He actually found himself more distracted by thoughts of his magical twin.

He'd sensed it when his counterpart had died, and he felt a wry sort of envy. He'd wooed death for centuries, to no avail. His twin had needed to exist for only a few days before the greatest of all powers had seen fit to extinguish him. And since the two Malarks had been exactly alike, it was difficult to perceive any sort of justice in the event.

But in light of the destiny he was pursuing, he didn't really mind—unless his double's demise indicated that the unique instrument Szass Tam had created was in jeopardy. At the moment, it must still exist, for Malark was sure he would have sensed its destruction, also. But was it safe? Despite the regent's tutelage, he wasn't a master diviner, and his magical inquiries on the subject yielded ambiguous results. And unfortunately, hiding here in the depths, he had no other way of obtaining information.

He took a breath, let it go, and sought to dismiss the problem from his mind just as he expelled air from his lungs. A warrior could fight only one fight at a time. He'd address other concerns after he won the current battle.

Thanks to his headband, he glimpsed motion at the very limit of his vision. The murky shapes passed quickly from left to right, proceeding north along a passage that intersected the one he was peering down.

Malark waited for another moment after they disappeared, then, making sure to move silently, jumped up and sprinted through the maze of tunnels. The Watcher kept pace with him. No doubt Szass Tam and the vampire knights felt its oppressive stare as keenly as he did, for its nature was such that it was capable of despising multiple intruders at the same time.

Malark came to a branching passage, halted, and listened. He heard nothing and wasn't surprised. The undead moved quietly too, especially when they were hunting.

If he'd needed to recite an incantation and time the final word with the stalkers' appearance in the gloom, that might have posed a problem, but he'd had the foresight to store the spell he required in a ring. When his pursuers, following the trail he'd laid for them, came into view, he extended his arm and breathed the trigger word. A spark erupted from the cabochon ruby set in the gold band and streaked at Szass Tam and his bodyguards.

When it reached the hunters, the spark flared and boomed into an explosion of yellow flame. Malark knew better than to suppose it would do much harm to Szass Tam. The lich was too powerful and too wrapped in protective enchantments. But with any luck, it would incinerate the vampires.

It certainly appeared to. It took Malark an instant to realize he'd glimpsed only two armored bodies breaking apart in the flash.

Which suggested he wasn't the only one capable of trickery. Szass Tam and two of the knights had stayed together in an effort to snare his attention while a third vampire prowled alone in the hope of creeping up on him.

Malark pivoted, and the creature was right behind him. The warrior was just completing the process of changing from wisps of mist to human form, but he already had his sword in his hand. He made a horizontal cut at Malark's torso.

Malark hopped back just far enough to evade the attack, then instantly lunged, cudgel shimmering with destructive power and poised to strike. The guard took a retreat and parried the blow.

As Malark would have expected of a warrior Szass Tam evidently trusted, the vampire was an expert combatant. Not so expert that Malark couldn't defeat him, but the problem was that he couldn't bide his time and wait for an opening. With luck, the fire magic had staggered the archmage, but he'd recover quickly and advance. And if Malark was still stuck here dueling the vampire when his liege lord arrived, Szass Tam would surely strike him down.

Malark murmured the opening words of an incantation and flicked the ebony wand through a star-shaped figure. Fangs bared, the vampire sprang in and made a head cut. The move was virtually a reflex for any seasoned warrior: If the wizard you're fighting starts reciting a spell, hit him before he can finish. Spoil the magic.

Malark shifted inside the arc of the cut, and the blade fell harmlessly behind him. Remembering that he mustn't shout—Szass Tam might well recognize his battle cry—he focused his strength, stiffened his fingers inside their clawed demon-hide glove, and drove them through the vampire's breastplate and ribs and into his chest. He gripped the creature's cold, motionless heart and ripped it out. The knight collapsed.

Malark dropped the heart, ran back the way he'd come, and held the hand with the ruby ring behind him. The gem dropped sparks as if they were caltrops, which then flowered into sheets of bright, crackling flame. The fires extended from wall to wall and might slow Szass Tam down a little. They might also keep him from getting a good look at his quarry and do so more reliably than any illusory disguise or charm of invisibility.

A wind howled down the passage, staggering Malark and blowing out his blazing barricades like candle flames. Recovering his balance, he dived into another branching passage a bare instant before a lightning bolt crackled down the one he'd just vacated.

When planning this chase, Malark had decided that if he were Szass Tam, this was the point at which he'd shift himself through space. Because if the lich had the layout of the catacombs memorized—and his protégé was certain he did—then he knew that the twisting passage his quarry had just ducked down was supposed to be a cul-de-sac. So he'd want to advance far enough to bottle up the supposed demon before the marauder realized it had nowhere to go.

But Malark actually did. Yesterday, he'd employed a tunneling spell to connect the dead-end passage with another. He scurried on unimpeded, ultimately to what looked like just another section of painted wall, this mural a murky underwater view of a sea divested of fish, shells, and coral.

He whispered words of release and touched the tip of his wand to the invisible sigils inscribed across the seascape, avoiding the one that only existed to spray a thief with freezing cold. The signs glowed like red-hot iron for a moment, each in its turn, and then the hidden door clicked as the latch released.

Malark swung it wide open and left it that way after he passed through. On the other side was a spacious, high-ceilinged chamber crammed with some of Szass Tam's greatest treasures. An axe with a diamond blade, still lodged in the skull of the colossal dragon it had slain at the conclusion of its final battle. Gold and silver vials, each containing the sole surviving dose of some exotic potion. Tapestries in which the figures moved if one watched long enough, and spoke if one listened hard enough, doorways to small artificial worlds created by a long-extinct order of mystic weavers. A plentitude of sarcophagi, canopic jars, and grave goods looted from the tombs of the Mulhorandi lords who had once ruled Thay.

Since he didn't want Szass Tam to hear breakage and come running prematurely, Malark had stamped flat a chalice crafted of some strange green metal and had snapped the head off an exquisite ivory carving of the goddess Nephthys on a previous visit. He grabbed the ruined items and set them outside in the passage as if they'd been tossed there, then crouched behind an enormous block of carnelian crawling with carved, spidery-looking symbols—some sort of drow altar, perhaps.

After that he had nothing to do but wait for Szass Tam to appear. Well, that and tolerate the spiteful scrutiny of the Watcher. He hoped the entity was enjoying the show.

He imagined Szass Tam creeping down the tunnel, proceeding warily since the constant bend kept him from seeing more than a pace or two ahead. He imagined the lich's annoyance when he discovered he didn't have his quarry cornered after all, and his further vexation when he beheld the secret door standing open and more of his treasures defiled.

What he would he do then? That was the question. Because, if one stopped to think about it, the view before him looked like it could be a baited trap, and he was more than wily enough to perceive it that way. He knew, moreover, that the contents of the vault were fated to perish in any case and had been training himself to regard them, like the rest of creation, with disdain.

So it was entirely possible that he'd seal the chamber up again, locking it so well that even his trusted apprentice couldn't breach the wards a second time, and fetch reinforcements.

But Malark hoped the archmage would make a different choice. Szass Tam likely had *some* lingering attachment to the precious things he'd collected, and even if he didn't, the "demon's" desecration of them was an affront to his dignity, just like the rest of Malark's escalating series of provocations.

And perhaps the chase, with its violence and frustrations, had roused Szass Tam's passions and left him eager to make the kill. If so, it seemed likely that he'd enter even if he did suspect a trap. For he was, after all, the greatest wizard in the East, capable of defeating virtually any foe under almost any circumstances.

Szass Tam wasn't in sight yet, but his dry, pleasant voice recited a spell outside the door. A wave of chill swept over Malark, and for a heartbeat, his body felt heavy as lead. He recognized the enchantment. The lich had just made it impossible for anything lurking in the vault to escape by shifting itself through space.

Then Szass Tam stepped into the doorway. A red halo of protective power outlined his thin frame, and a blade blacker than night hovered before him. Malark recognized that magic as well. The flying sword was a sort of mobile wound in space, and its slightest touch would rip him—or a big piece of him—out of the mortal world.

Szass Tam's gaze raked the room and failed to catch on Malark's hiding place. That was something, anyway.

"I take it," said the lich, "that I'm supposed to grope my way through the clutter and give you a chance to pounce out at me. Please forgive me if I take another approach." He leveled his staff, slowly swept it from left to right, and spoke the first line of a spell of reanimation.

Reciting as quickly as he could, Malark whispered his own spell. Darts of green light leaped from his outstretched fingertips.

Their trajectory would give away his location, so, staying low, he immediately scurried from behind the carnelian block for another piece of cover. He'd rely on his ears to tell him whether the attack had disrupted Szass Tam's incantation.

It didn't. The archmage continued to speak with flawless cadence and inflection. It was likely the darts hadn't even stung him through his armor of light.

He snapped out a final word like the crack of a whip, and for an instant, the darkness boiled. Stone scraped on stone, and then the lids of the sarcophagi crashed to the floor. Smelling of embalmer's spice and dry rot, wrapped in linen, the Mulhorandi dead stood.

The nearest mummy was within easy reach of Malark. It gave a croaking call and, without even bothering to step out of its coffin, made a sort of toppling lunge at him, its withered, bandaged hands outstretched to grab.

Its touch would rot living flesh, but Malark's gauntlets would protect him, or at least he hoped so. He sidestepped the mummy's attack, sank the talons of one gloved hand into its temple, and yanked its head off.

It had only taken an instant, but that was an instant too long. The undead creature's groan and the ensuing scuffle had surely revealed Malark's location. He ran, and a blaze of shadow seethed through the air. He dived, but the fringe of the attack grazed him anyway.

That was enough to make his back arch in agony and flood his mind with terror. He fought against both. Held in a scream and brought his spasmodic muscles back under control. Scuttled onward.

Another mummy groaned and lurched at him. He parried its flailing fist with his cudgel, then bashed its chest in, at that same instant sensing danger. He sprang to the side, and the black sword slashed through the space he'd just vacated. He scrambled behind a gigantic dragonfly preserved in an even bigger lump of amber, the whole mounted on a bronze pedestal.

Perhaps he was safe for a breath or two. No mummies were close enough to strike at him, and the shadow blade couldn't target what Szass Tam couldn't see. Maybe he had time for another spell. He flourished his baton and whispered the rhyming words.

Power prickled across his body, which was no guarantee that the charm would actually protect him, considering that Szass Tam himself had animated the mummies. Malark supposed he'd know in a moment.

He slowed his breathing and sought to suppress what remained of his pain. Then he scrambled out from behind the dragonfly, again staying low in the hope that it would keep Szass Tam from spotting him. It might. The lich had taken only a few steps into the vault, and a number of sizable artifacts lay between the two of them.

The same precaution wouldn't throw off the mummies converging on his last position. Yet they took no notice as he darted between a pair of them. Thanks to his magic, they now mistook him for one of their own kind. And while they were seeking him in the back of the chamber, and Szass Tam waited for them to reveal his position, Malark had a few precious moments to try to steer this confrontation to the desired conclusion.

First, he needed to maneuver Szass Tam to the proper spot. Kneeling behind what appeared to be a common alchemist's oven but was no doubt something infinitely more valuable, he murmured sibilant words of command.

Szass Tam peered this way and that, then stiffened when he felt the magic bite. He appeared to sneer the unpleasant sensation away.

Malark had been certain the elder wizard would shrug off the effects of the spell, but that wasn't the point. If he'd succeeded in annoying the lich before, then surely it was more irksome still for someone to try to use necromancy against him, the greatest practitioner of that dark science, as if he were no more than a common zombie or ghoul.

Malark rapped his cudgel against the side of the kiln, then ran. An instant later, jagged shadows spun around the device in a maelstrom of conjured fangs and claws.

Then Szass Tam drew the flying blade back to float in front of him. As he advanced on the kiln, the weapon leaped this way and that in an unpredictable pattern of defense. Meanwhile, Malark circled.

Szass Tam stepped around the oven and scowled to discover that it didn't have a mangled corpse sprawled behind it. He raised his staff and began another incantation.

This one would conjure a flying eye that he would no doubt send to the ceiling. There, it would survey the entire vault from above, allowing its maker to see it too. Then he wouldn't need the mummies or any other spotters to pinpoint the whereabouts of his quarry.

He'd likely cripple or kill Malark the instant after. In light of Malark's previous failure to hinder Szass Tam's spellcasting, the spymaster decided he needed to close *now,* even though the lich hadn't positioned himself precisely as he'd hoped.

He charged.

He had some semblance of cover part of the way, but none for the last few feet. As he burst out into the open, he hoped that astonishment might paralyze his opponent for a critical instant. After all, Malark Springhill had supposedly died in Lapendrar and was supposedly Szass Tam's faithful disciple as well.

He should have known better. The lich hadn't existed as long as he had and hadn't achieved supremacy in Thay by freezing in the midst of combat. The black blade leaped at Malark.

He hurled himself underneath the stroke, slid forward on the dusty floor, and sprang upright again. Now the flying sword was behind him, the worst place for it, but he ignored the peril to concentrate on pivoting and driving a thrust kick into Szass Tam's midsection.

As intended, the attack knocked the lich stumbling backward, but it also jolted Malark as if he'd kicked a granite column. For an instant, he feared he'd broken his leg.

When he set it down, it was plain he hadn't, but there was worse to come. His stomach turned over, and the room tilted and spun. Another effect of Szass Tam's armoring enchantments, perhaps, or simply the result of touching the undead creature's poisonous flesh.

Whatever it was, he couldn't let it slow him down. He was certain the shadow blade was making another attack. Instinct prompted him to fake left, then shift right, and the stroke missed.

But at the same time, Szass Tam snarled a rhyme and thrust out a shriveled hand. A splash of liquid appeared in midair, and, nauseated and dizzy as he was, Malark couldn't dodge it and the sword too. He flung up his arm and shielded his eyes, but the acid spattered the rest of him, burned him, and kept on burning.

He knew a spell to wash the vitriol away, and another to purge himself of sickness, but had no time for either. Now that he'd knocked Szass Tam backward to the proper spot, he had something else to do, something that neither the lich nor the philosopher-assassins of the Long Death had taught him.

Rather, he'd learned it as a boy growing up in a long-vanished city beside the Moonsea, before he'd betrayed his best friend for the elixir of perpetual youth, suffered the despair of endless life, or discovered the consolations of devoting himself to death. In that bygone age, he and the other children had played kickball in a field near the purplish waters, with a tree at each end to serve as a goal. He'd gotten pretty good at scoring points once he learned to take an instant to line up his shot.

And, ignoring his vertigo, churning guts, and the searing pain of the sizzling, smoking acid, twisting out of the path of a sword stroke that slashed close enough to catch his sleeve and make it disappear, that was what he did now. Then he launched himself into a flying kick.

chapter eleven

27 Mirtul–9 Kythorn, The Year of the Dark Circle (1478 DR)

When the scout arrived, the artisans were giving So-Kehur's everyday body a second pair of hands, human-looking except for being made of sculpted steel. He'd long since learned to manipulate four crablike claws, tentacles, or what have you at the same time. Now he wanted to see if he could make the precise gestures required for spellcasting with four hands simultaneously, and whether that would enhance the effect of the magic.

He waved the artisans away with the flick of a tentacle and, using his eight arachnoid legs, turned his cylindrical body in the scout's direction. He extended several of his eyes at the ends of their flexible antennae to view the newcomer from multiple angles at once.

Because he'd taken the trouble to do so, he saw the kneeling scout tremble ever so slightly. The creature was an undead soldier with a gray withered face and glazed, sunken eyes, but even so, he feared his lord. So-Kehur found it gratifying.

But it was detrimental to morale to terrorize underlings who'd done nothing to deserve it—he'd learned that observing Szass Tam—so he'd try to make the scout feel at ease. "Please, get up," he said. His voice was indistinguishable from that produced by a normal larynx and mouth, for that was necessary for his conjuring. "Would you like some refreshment?"

"No, thank you, Master," said the scout. His leather trappings creaked as he straightened up. "One of the grooms offered me a prisoner as I was climbing off my eagle."

"Good. Then tell me what you've seen."

"The invaders abandoned the Dread Ring and marched south again. I thought they'd go back into the Umber Marshes and on home to the Wizard's Reach, but they didn't make the turn."

So-Kehur felt a surge of excitement. If he'd still possessed a pulse, no doubt it would have quickened. "You mean they're heading toward Anhaurz."

"It looks that way."

"The lunatics must actually believe they can reach and destroy *another* Ring—the one in Tyraturos." So-Kehur had no idea why the archmages of the council were so fixated on the gigantic strongholds, but it seemed evident they were. "They mean to take the High Road up the First Escarpment. Of the three likely ascents, it's the only one without a fortress guarding the top. But to get to the High Road, they need to use the bridge here at Anhaurz to cross the Lapendrar."

The undead warrior inclined his head. "The autharch is wise."

"So this is where we'll stop them!"

In his youth, So-Kehur had been a coward, even if it never quite prevented him from doing his duty. But on the plain below Thralgard Keep, in the battle that broke the southern legions, he'd finally found his courage, and afterward, he'd vowed to make sure it never slipped away.

To that end, he'd started replacing parts of his body with grafts from the undead and, when even those began to seem insufficiently strong to protect him from any conceivable threat, with metal. He supposed that at some point afterward, he must have decided to dispense with an organic form entirely, to become a disembodied brain, charged with the energies of undeath to nourish and preserve it, encased in a steel shell, although oddly enough, he couldn't recall the exact moment when he'd made such a choice. Rather, when he looked back, it seemed to him as if the process had simply happened by degrees.

In any case, his transformation had mostly worked out all right. Much as he'd loved to eat, he no longer missed it, or the touch of a woman, either. The cravings faded after he divested himself of the organs with which a person gratified them. Strange abilities emerged to take their place, along with the desire to exert his newly developed strengths.

That last was the problem because the War of the Zulkirs was over, and afterward, Szass Tam proved unexpectedly reluctant to start any new ones. Instead, he devoted himself to erecting the Dread Rings, unnecessary defenses for a realm already impregnable, or, conceivably, monuments to overweening vanity. Either way, it left So-Kehur with no outlet for his aggression except hunting rebels, scarcely a challenge for the consummate killer he'd become.

Now, however, an enemy army was heading straight for Anhaurz, a slayer in its own right. Ninety years ago, the Spell-plague had destroyed the town, and when Szass Tam appointed him autharch and gave him the task of rebuilding it, So-Kehur'd done so in a way that expressed his yearning for battle. The new Anhaurz was a true fortress city, constructed and garrisoned to break any force that dared to assault it. Even one led by the likes of Nevron and Lauzoril.

"Fetch me my maps!" So-Kehur called. One of the artisans scurried to relay the order.

.. ..

The road south ran a few miles west of the towering cliffs the Thayans called the First Escarpment. Close, but not nearly close enough for anyone to menace the Brotherhood of the Griffon and the zulkirs' legions with missiles hurled from the top.

Or so Jhesrhi would have assumed, before the stones started showering down along with the cold drizzle from the overcast sky. They hammered the road with uncanny accuracy too.

It was plain that only folk who could fly had any hope of stopping the bombardment, so Aoth led griffon riders to the top of the crags, which appeared to be deserted. But the breeze whispered to Jhesrhi that her enemies were almost directly below her, shrouded in an invisibility that couldn't blind the tactile sight of the wind.

She drew breath to shout a warning, then saw that she needn't bother. The concealment hadn't fooled Aoth's spellscarred eyes, either. He pointed his spear, power glimmered around it, and a greenish cloud swirled into existence around the hidden men, revealing their forms to those who soared above them.

Some of the enemy doubled over, puking. Other, hardier crossbowmen shot a volley into the air, but the griffons veered, swooped, and dodged most of the quarrels. Their riders shot back, and Szass Tam's warriors fell.

With their bodyguards slain, the Red Wizards died almost as easily. Afterward, the griffon riders set down to loot and learn whatever they could.

The magical artillery used a scrying pool to provide a view of the highway. Beside the water was a flat piece of slate incised with a groove carved to mirror the slight curve of the road. One aimed and launched a barrage by placing a black pebble at a point along the depression. Then the rocks heaped on a slab of granite vanished to reappear above the designated spot.

Since Thay had been at peace for some time, it seemed likely the apparatus was relatively old. Jhesrhi wondered if someone had crafted it during the first War of the Zulkirs, and if so, which side the craftsman had been on.

"What do you think?" Gaedynn asked.

She turned to face him. As was so often the case, he seemed to be smirking at a joke that was opaque to everyone else, and his long red hair shined even on a gray, cheerless day.

"It's cleverly made," she said. "I've never seen anything exactly like it."

"It's good that you can appreciate such things," he said, "seeing as how we're likely to have them hurling death at us with some regularity."

She frowned. "You know we have no choice but to do what we're doing."

"Because two dead strangers and a funny old book said so, and then our captain suffered a hallucination."

"You know his visions come true."

"So far."

"Are you just babbling to hear yourself, the way you generally do, or are you actually thinking of running?"

He grinned. "If I did, honeycomb, would you go with me?"

"You know I owe Aoth everything."

"Whereas I don't. Honestly, I think he's lucky to have enjoyed the benefit of my services for as long as he has." Evidently glimpsing something from the corner of his eye, he turned. She looked where he was looking and saw Aoth straightening up from a red-robed corpse with a folded parchment in his hand. "Shall we go see what the old man's found?"

•• •• •• •• •• •• •• •• •• •• •• •• •• ••

"You should sing," said Mirror, striding, flickering a little, effortlessly keeping pace with Bareris's steed. The ghost was merely a shadow in the deepening twilight, his form too indistinct to resemble anyone in particular.

Bareris's mouth tightened. He truly wished his friend well. He wished Mirror's mind could be clear every instant of every day. But it was at those times that the phantom became talkative, and the chatter sometimes grated on Bareris's nerves.

"I don't want anyone to take me for a bard," he said. That was why he'd left his harp behind when he and Mirror had split off from the army.

"There's no one but me to hear you," Mirror said, and he was indisputably right. The tableland atop the First Escarpment was even more blighted than the plains below. A traveler encountered hamlets and cultivated fields less frequently and saw even more gnarled, pallid flora and deformed wildlife. High Thay was bleaker still, as if Szass Tam's actual residence was a fountainhead of poison that lost a bit of virulence as it seeped down from the Citadel.

"Still," Bareris said, "I don't see a point."

"We're finally going to try to kill the creature you hate above all others, with the fate of the East—at a minimum—hanging in the balance. You must have feelings about that. Don't you want to express them?"

"I always feel the same, and singing doesn't help it."

That answer seemed to irk or discourage Mirror, and they traveled in silence for a time, the cantering gait of Bareris's steel gray mount eating up the miles. As best he could judge, the burly, misshapen beast was a cross between a horse and some infernal creature and seemed not to require sleep or rest.

In time, a crescent moon rose to reveal the black, rectangular shape of a tax station. It was no surprise to see it. Such bastions lined the Eastern Way. But Bareris scowled to behold the roadblock, even though they too were common. The soldiers garrisoning tax stations threw them up for any number of reasons, including extortion and simple boredom.

"It figures," said Mirror. "We passed through Nethwatch Keep without any trouble only to get stopped out here in the middle of nowhere. Unless you want to go around."

"No," Bareris said. "They've already seen us. If we just play our roles, they'll pass us through."

He thought it would work. He was wearing the trappings of a Thayan knight, plundered, like his demon horse, from the Dread Ring, and if that proved insufficiently convincing, he'd bring his bardic powers of persuasion to bear.

But as he rode closer, he saw that the soldiers manning the barricade were yellow-eyed corpses, all but immune to the sort of songs that addled the minds of the living. And when one of them recognized the outlaws who'd bedeviled Szass Tam's servants for a century, Bareris and Mirror had no choice but to fight.

So they did, and when they had finished with the soldiers at the roadblock, they broke into the tax station and slaughtered every creature within. Because no one must survive to report who'd perpetrated the massacre. And for a precious time, the exigencies of combat drove all other thoughts from Bareris's head.

When the fight was done, Mirror—who had at some point taken on the appearance of a gaunt, withered ghoul complete with fangs and pointed ears—frowned. "The authorities will likely blame the local rebels for this. They'll make reprisals."

"Good," Bareris said, then caught himself. "I mean, good if they don't even suspect that we were the ones who passed by in the night. Not the reprisals part."

．．　．．　．．　．．　．．　．．　．．　．．　．．　．．　．．　．．　．．

Keeping low lest the moonlight glint on their armor or the saddles, tack, and packs slung over their shoulders, Toriak and three companions slunk toward the sleeping griffons. Fortunately, the winged creatures occupied a field somewhat removed from the rest of the camp. The zulkirs' soldiers were leery of the beasts, and well-trained though the griffons were, it would be stupid to keep them close to the horses whose meat they so relished. So, once Toriak and his companions crept clear of the smoky, crackling campfires and rows of tents, they didn't have to worry quite so much about being spotted.

Or so he imagined. But as he cast about for Dodger, his own beloved mount, a figure rose from behind the moundlike form of a different griffon. Gaedynn's long, coppery hair was gray in the dark, but his jeweled ornaments still gleamed a little. He nudged the beast before him with his toe, and it made an annoyed, rasping sound and stood up too.

"I don't remember ordering you lads to make a night patrol," Gaedynn said.

Toriak wondered if a lie would help, then decided it plainly wouldn't. He took a deep breath. "We're leaving."

"Remember the compact you signed when you joined the Brotherhood. You can leave between campaigns, not when we're in the field. Then it's desertion, and it's punished the same as in any other army."

"We already took plenty of loot from the Dread Ring," Toriak said. "It's stupid to hang around any longer."

A dark form reared up, and despite the gloom, he recognized its contours immediately. His voice had woken Dodger, and in all likelihood, the voices of his companions would rouse their particular griffons. He made a surreptitious gesture, hoping they'd understand he was encouraging them to talk.

"I take it," Gaedynn said, "that you don't credit the warning of impending universal doom."

Standing to Toriak's right, Ralivar snorted. "Things like that just don't happen. Not anymore. Maybe they never did, except in stories." His griffon raised its head.

"I'm skeptical myself." Casually, as though making some petty adjustment to his garments, Gaedynn laid an arrow on his bow. "But it would be embarrassing to bet that it isn't going to happen and then be proved mistaken."

"I'll risk it," Duma said. Maybe her griffon hadn't been asleep, or at least not soundly, for it rose to its feet at once. "It's better than fighting in the vanguard time after time."

"But that's what sellswords do," Gaedynn said. "More to the point, it's what we have to do in this situation. Because we're better than the council's troops, and only we can win the toughest fights."

"We don't care! Like Toriak said, we're leaving! Do you think you can stop us and four griffons too?" Sopsek half-shouted, making sure his mount would hear. Toriak winced at the loudness, but no answering cry of alarm sounded back in camp, and at least Sopsek's griffon did spring to its feet, cast about, and, like its fellows, come prowling across the field to stand with its rider. Sensing the tension between their masters and Gaedynn, the creatures glared at the latter, and the one steed crouched in front of him.

"I promise that at the very least, I'll stop a couple of you," Gaedynn said. He still hadn't bothered to draw his arrow back to his ear, much less aim it. "Would anyone like to volunteer to die first in the hope that his gallant sacrifice will aid his comrades-in-arms?"

To the Abyss with this, Toriak thought. He drew breath to order his mount to attack, shifted his grip on his saddle to use it as a shield against the officer's arrow, and then a huge shape emerged from the gloom at Gaedynn's back. Toriak hadn't noticed its approach because, unlike the other griffons, it was black as the night, except for eyes like lambent drops of blood.

Jet screeched, a cry like an eagle's scream with an undertone of leonine roar. The other griffons shrank back before the leader of their pride, then slunk away from their human masters.

"Now," said Gaedynn, "it appears to be two griffons and me against the four of you. Still like your chances? If not, I'd scurry back to camp before Aoth comes to find out what stirred up his familiar."

•• •• •• •• •• •• •• •• •• •• •• •• ••

Gaedynn watched the would-be deserters until he was sure they actually were returning to camp. Then he scratched Eider's feathery neck and told her she could go back to sleep. The griffon grunted, shook out her wings with a snap that would have knocked him staggering if he hadn't seen it coming and stepped back, then lay back down in the dewy grass.

Gaedynn turned to Jet. "Thanks for backing me up," he said.

"Glad to," the familiar rasped. "Do you think more men will try to leave?"

"I hope not. With luck, those four will warn other malcontents that we're alert to the possibility. And speaking of them, I need another favor. Please don't tell Aoth they sneaked out here tonight."

"You don't want them punished?"

"They're good soldiers. It's just that they know we're in a tough spot, and they had a little crisis of confidence, possibly exacerbated by strong drink plundered from the Dread Ring's cellars. They'll rediscover their nerve in the morning. Besides, I have my own reputation to consider."

Jet cocked his aquiline head. "Your reputation for not caring about anyone but yourself?"

Gaedynn grinned. "Unkindly put! But something like that."

•• •• •• •• •• •• •• •• •• •• •• •• ••

A chunk of rock and soil supporting a single pine tree floated just west of the Lapendrar, one of many such islets in the sky, raised by the Spellplague. It commanded a view of Anhaurz, so Khouryn and Aoth landed their griffons on top of it, dismounted, walked to the dropoff, and surveyed the city.

Khouryn reflected that despite the distance, Aoth's luminous sapphire eyes no doubt made out every detail with utter clarity. Squinting, Khouryn had a harder time of it but fancied he was seeing enough to draw conclusions.

After a time, Aoth said, "It didn't always look like that, but then, I remember hearing that the blue fire destroyed it. It's been completely rebuilt since then."

Khouryn dug his fingers into his beard to scratch an itch on his chin. "The question is, why? The civil war was over, and while this town commands the river crossing, it's also well inland from the edge of the realm. To say the least, the average lord wouldn't fortify it to the extent that this one—or his predecessor—has."

"Then I gather you wouldn't relish laying siege to the place."

Khouryn snorted. "You gather rightly. The bridge amounts to a castle by itself, and combined with the rest, it's as bad as the Dread Ring. Maybe worse." He grinned. "In other words, it's perfect!"

Aoth grinned back. "It's so strong that turning away from it won't call into question our resolve to reach the Ring in Tyraturos. We'll head southwest down the Lapendrar—for after all, the other direction would take us dangerously close to the Keep of Sorrows—looking for a place to ford."

"Which we won't find," Khouryn said, "because the spring thaw and the spring rains have swollen the river. Actually, we'll be headed toward the border even though it will look like we're still trying to march deeper into the country."

"Not bad, eh? We might actually make it out of Thay with a company left to lead."

"As long as the bard and the ghost succeed at their task, and then everything else works out. As long as we aren't still diddling around taking in our surroundings when Szass Tam sends forth his tides of death."

Aoth's smile turned wry and crooked. "You know, for a moment there, I actually felt my spirits lift."

•• •• •• •• •• •• •• •• •• •• •• •• •• ••

Even in Szass Tam's own city, where his undead minions were ubiquitous and the living scurried like mice to make way for them, there were rebels, and Arizima Nathandem was their leader. In her youth, the Red Wizards had taken her as an apprentice, until a training exercise gone awry left her with a persistent stammer and the inability to recite spells with the requisite precision. Then they'd cast her out as a useless cripple.

At first agreeing with that judgment, she'd fallen a long way, her Mulan blood notwithstanding. She'd landed in a festhall and still worked there today, though age had long since wrinkled her face, whitened her hair, and stained some of her teeth and outright stolen the rest. Now she managed the house, and it served the rebel cause admirably. No one questioned it when people of all stripes came and went at any hour of the day or night.

She conducted Bareris and Mirror into a sort of mock torture chamber, equipped with soft leather whips, switches, blindfolds, gags, and restraints, but no implements likely to inflict permanent harm. Just toys to amuse a Thayan noble bored with ordinary forms of sexual congress.

Arizima sat down stiffly on the bed. "It's b-been a . . . long time," she said.

"Your circle wasn't fighting," Bareris replied. "Our time was better spent elsewhere."

The old woman scowled. "We sp-spy. We can't do anything

more, not here at the heart of it all, or Szass . . . Tam's agents will swoop down on us like hawks!"

Mirror, who currently resembled a blood orc they'd passed in the street, inclined his head. "We understand that, Lady. My brother meant no offense."

Arizima cackled. "'Lady,' is it? You'd think the b-bard would be the one with the golden tongue."

"You lead a band of our comrades," the phantom replied. "That makes you a knight, or as good as, in my eyes."

"Thank you," she said. "That's kind. Now, why have you . . . returned, and how can we help you?"

"Help us find a way into the Citadel," said Bareris, "so we can destroy Szass Tam."

Arizima peered at him as though looking for some sign that he was joking.

"I mean it," Bareris said, and, as clearly and convincingly as he could, he explained the lich's scheme and what he and his comrades intended to do about it.

By the time he finished, the old woman was shaking her head. "Tear down this world and put up a new one with himself as the only god? That's madness!"

"I agree," Bareris answered, "but the trouble is that it truly does seem like Szass Tam's particular flavor of madness. And while the zulkirs of the council doubt the ritual will accomplish its goals, they do believe it may well devastate Thay and neighboring lands."

"So after all our years of hoping and praying and trying to nibble away at the necromancers' reign, it's now or never."

"Yes. But the good part is that if our plan works, we'll have four archmages popping out at the lich to attack him by surprise. That's never happened before. The zulkirs were never willing to bet everything on this sort of gamble."

"All right," Arizima said. "I under . . . st-stand, and I *want* to help. I just don't know if I can. We've watched the fortress for decades, but the more you look, the more discouraged you become."

"I assume that it's still impossible for a mage to translate himself inside."

"Yes. I've seen demons try. They appear in midair looking like they ran headfirst into a wall."

"But what if I were to disguise myself with magic?"

"It won't work. There are wards to strip away illusions and shrouds of invisibility."

"Then what if I just walk in as though I have legitimate business inside? I don't look all that different from many other undead. I have the proper uniform and that 'golden tongue' you spoke of. And after all, it is the regent's palace. There must be people coming and going all the time."

"All the d-d-doorkeepers are undead, so you'd have trouble making your blandishments work on them. And if you did persuade them, they'd assign an escort to take you where you c-claimed you wanted to go."

"Curse it." At the periphery of Bareris's vision stood an **X**-shaped wooden stand with shackles to hold a prisoner's wrists and ankles, and he had to resist a sudden urge to turn and give it a kick. Hoping it would calm him, he took a breath instead. "Very well, if neither magic nor pure brazenness will serve, that leaves skulking and climbing."

"Yes," Mirror said, "but not for you. Not yet."

Bareris frowned. "What are you talking about?"

"I can fly," said the ghost. The tusks and snout of the orc melted away, and his face became a murky semblance of the melancholy, mustachioed one he'd worn in life. "I have innate abilities to walk through walls and fade from view that Szass Tam's defenses may not affect, or at least, not as strongly as they'd cancel out a sorcerer's tricks. If things go wrong, I'll have a better chance of getting away. So let me try to slip inside by myself, and if I succeed, we'll both go in tomorrow night."

Bareris didn't like it. Now that they'd come this far, now that Szass Tam was only a mile away, the urge to press on burned like a fever inside him. But he couldn't deny that Mirror's idea made sense.

•• •• •• •• •• •• •• •• •• •• •• •• •• ••

In the dark, the Citadel loomed like a bizarre, multi-bladed weapon raised to gut the moon. Like any castle worthy of the name, it stood at the center of a patch of open ground and had sentries patrolling the battlements.

Peering from between two of the buildings nearest to the fortress, Mirror watched the guards and timed them as they made their circuits. When he understood the routine, he waited for a gaunt, yellow-eyed dread warrior to trudge by, then darted forward.

He didn't advance invisibly, because even if such a trick would work for him, it wouldn't for Bareris. So he sneaked as he had in life when creeping up on an enemy. He stayed low, kept to the deepest shadows, and reached the foot of the outermost wall without incident.

He inspected the huge granite blocks and the mortared chinks between them. He doubted that an ordinary climber could scale the vertical surface unless possessed of exceptional skill. Not quickly enough, at any rate. Bareris, however, was inhumanly strong, remarkably agile, and knew charms to make himself stronger and more nimble still. Mirror judged that his friend could make it.

That meant it was time for him to do the same, before the next guard came tramping along. Alternately checking to make sure the minimal hand- and toeholds didn't run out and watching the crenellated wall-walk overhead, he floated upward.

With his head at merlon-height, he took another wary look around. This section of the battlements was still clear and, according to his estimation, should remain so for a little while longer. He rose until his feet were at the level of the walkway, then stepped through a crenel onto the ledge.

It was conceivable that if Bareris made it only this far, he could help Aoth, Nevron, and the others translate themselves into the Citadel. But the bard doubted it, and based on all that the past hundred years had taught Mirror about Szass Tam's wiles, he was inclined to agree. They assumed they'd need to cross the courtyard below, get past the inner wall, traverse a second bailey, and slip inside the towering central keep itself to have any hope of success.

Onward, then. Mirror took a step toward the inner edge of the walkway—since Bareris knew a charm to drift down to the ground unharmed, the ghost didn't need to bother with finding stairs, either—and a sudden jolt of pain froze him in place. At the same instant, pale light shined from the stones beneath his feet.

From the corner of his eye, he could just make out the crimson glyph that had appeared on the wall-walk three paces to his left. For a moment, he had a childish feeling that what had befallen him was unfair, because he hadn't actually stepped on the then-invisible sigil and wouldn't have expected it to affect a non-corporeal entity in any case. But he supposed that his predicament too, was an example of Szass Tam's cunning.

He strained to move, but paralysis held him fast. He silently called out to the god whose name he had never remembered but whom he nonetheless adored, and tried again. He took a tiny, lurching step, then a bigger one, and then the clenched, locked feeling fell away.

But at the same instant, figures as shadowy and poisonous as himself surrounded him. Perhaps the necromancers kept the murks, as such undead were called, caged inside the wall, or maybe the flare of light had drawn them; focused on breaking free of his immobility, Mirror had missed the moment of their advent. Before he could come on guard, the spirits scrabbled at him with long, wispy fingers, their weightless essence raking through his.

The attacks caused no pain in the physical sense, but they did something worse. Confusion and fear surged through his mind and threatened to drown coherent thought. Every day he struggled for clarity and purpose, for identity itself, and now the murks were clawing them to shreds.

He called to his deity a second time, and for an instant, his shadow-sword blazed with golden radiance. The murks withered away to nothing. Since they and he were made of the same unnatural foulness, the glow could just as easily have slain him as well, but it didn't. He'd learned to direct it, or perhaps it was simply the god's grace that enabled him to do so.

Something stabbed him in the back. He turned to see a corpse at the top of the stairs he hadn't bothered to locate before. The gaunt thing wore a mage's robe, and its sunken eyes glowed. Tattooed runes covered the exposed portions of its gray, rotting skin.

Mirror's mind still seemed to grind like a damaged mechanism. It took him an instant to recognize the thing as a deathlock, an undead wizard less formidable than a lich but troublesome enough. And the spells inked into its body would give it additional power.

The deathlock extended its hand, and darts of ice hurtled from its long, jagged nails. Mirror tried to block them with his shield but moved too sluggishly. Fortunately, the attack, magical though it was, passed harmlessly though his spectral body.

He charged the undead sorcerer before it could try again. He cut it and cut it until it tumbled back down the stairs . . .

Where it collided into the foremost of the blood orcs who were rushing up. Other figures were hurrying along the battlements. Atop one of the lesser keeps, a horn blew.

Plainly, it would be suicide to continue forward. Willing himself as invisible and intangible as possible—as close to utter emptiness as he dared—Mirror whirled, leaped off the wall, and sprinted back the way he'd come.

He didn't know how to tell Bareris their scheme was impossible. For warriors of his forgotten brotherhood, it was shameful to say such things; it was an article of faith with them that righteousness would always find a way. But he didn't know what else to say.

chapter twelve

11–18 Kythorn, The Year of the Dark Circle (1478 DR)

Bareris reached for the handle of the tavern door, then faltered.

He scowled at his own foolishness. Why should he feel timid about a trifle like this when he'd spent the past hundred years battling the worst horrors the necromancers could create? But perhaps that was the point. He was accustomed to war and vileness, whereas he'd long since abandoned the practice of entertaining, and he had no idea whether time, sorrow, and the passage into undeath had left the knack intact.

But he had to try. In the wake of Mirror's failure to penetrate the Citadel, it was the only idea that either he or the phantom had left. And so, masked in the appearance of a dark-haired little Rashemi, wishing he'd sung when Aoth and then the ghost asked him to—it might have knocked some of the rust off—he entered the ramshackle wooden building with the four hawks painted on its sign.

The common room was crowded. He'd hoped it would be, but now the size of the audience ratcheted up his anxiety another notch. The yarting, a musical instrument that Arizima had procured for him, made his intentions plain, and the buzz of conversation faded as he carried the instrument to the little platform where, no doubt, other minstrels had performed before him.

Nervous though he was, he remembered to set his upturned cap on the floor to catch coins. He tuned the yarting's six silk strings, then started to sing "Down, Down to Northkeep."

To his own critical ear, he didn't sing or play it particularly well, and since he hadn't practiced it in a century, he supposed it was no wonder. But when he finished, his audience applauded, cheered, and called out requests. Somebody wanted "Barley and Grapes," a tune he'd often performed during his years abroad, so he gave them that one next. And thought it sounded a little better.

The third song was better still. The glib banter—joking with the men, flirting with the women—came back more slowly than the music, but eventually it started to flow as well.

He sang sad songs and funny ones. Ballads of love, war, ribaldry, and loss. Memories of a Thay of green fields and blue skies, of cheer and abundance. And as the music visibly touched his audience, he found to his surprise that it moved him too.

Not to happiness. He was done with that. But to an awareness of something besides the urge for vengeance, in the same way that being with Aoth or Mirror occasionally could. And in that awareness was the suggestion of ease, a tiny diminution of the pressure that drove him ever onward.

I could have had this all along, he thought. Why didn't I?

Because hatred was his sword, and he had to keep it sharp.

Besides, even a hint of solace felt like a betrayal of Tammith's memory.

Still, perhaps it wasn't entirely unforgivable to appreciate this interlude as he'd appreciated riding a griffon again, and for the same reason. Because it was almost certainly the last time.

Before he was done, he even gave them Tammith's favorite, the tale of the starfish who aspired to be a star. His eyes ached, but undeath had robbed him of the capacity for tears, and no one had cause to wonder why a comical ditty would make him cry.

When he judged it was time for a break—he didn't need one, but a live man surely would have—his cap was full of copper with a sprinkling of silver mixed in, and his appreciative listeners were happy to drink with him. It was the latter he'd hoped to accomplish.

He offered tales and rumors to prompt them to do the same without feeling he was interrogating them. Gradually he drew out all they'd heard about the dungeons beneath Szass Tam's castle and strange creatures roaming the slopes of the mountain on which their city sat.

•• •• •• •• •• •• •• •• •• •• •• •• •• ••

So-Kehur crawled on the outer face of the gate at the west end of the bridge. The structure was a barbican sufficiently high and massive to discourage any attacker, but that didn't necessarily mean every bit of stonework remained solid enough to withstand a pounding from the council's artillery and magic. So far, though, that did indeed appear to be the case.

It occurred to him that, clambering around the heights with various limbs extended to anchor him, he must look rather like a metal spider. It likewise crossed his mind that some folk might think it beneath the dignity of the autharch of Anhaurz to make this inspection.

But he fancied that any first-rate commander would understand his desire to see for himself. Aoth Fezim would understand.

And speaking of the sellsword captain, the troops he led, and the archmages they served, where in the name of the Black Hand were they? So-Kehur swiveled his various eyes to gaze at the highway running north. No one was there but the common sort of traveler, and, as was often the case in the bleak new Thay that Szass Tam had made, not many of those.

So-Kehur shivered in frustration. Patience, he told himself, patience. It was good that the enemy army was advancing slowly. It gave him that much more time to prepare for the siege to come.

A voice called from overhead: "Milord?"

He looked up at the battlements. His aquiline face tattooed with jagged black lightning bolts, Chumed Shapret, his seneschal, was standing there, along with a sweaty, tired-looking soldier in dusty leather armor.

So-Kehur felt a pang of excitement, because Chumed's companion was one of the scouts they'd sent forth to keep track of the council's army. Apparently, intent on his examination of the higher reaches of the gate, he'd missed seeing the fellow arrive below him. He climbed toward his minions as fast as he could, and they each shrank back an involuntary step. Maybe they were afraid that in his haste, he'd close a set of serrated pincers on one of them or sweep them from their perch with a flailing tentacle.

If so, they needn't have worried. He'd long since learned to handle a steel body better than he'd ever managed the form into which he'd been born. He swarmed over the parapet, retracted his various limbs to their shortest lengths, and the two soldiers dropped to their knees before him.

Though he generally enjoyed such deference, he was too eager to leave them that way for more than an instant. "Rise!" he said. "And tell me, when will the council arrive?"

The scout gave Chumed an uncertain look. "Tell him," the officer said.

The scout shifted his eyes back to So-Kehur. "I don't think they're going to, Master. Arrive, I mean."

"What are you talking about?" So-Kehur demanded.

"They swung around the city and headed south. They're looking for another way to cross the river."

So-Kehur told himself it couldn't be true, but obviously, it could. It made perfect sense that even zulkirs and one of the most respected captains in the East would hesitate to attack the stronghold he'd made of Anhaurz, especially considering how much of their strength they'd already expended taking the Dread Ring.

So-Kehur felt dizzy, and the tall towers rising from the sides of the gate and at intervals down the length of the bridge seemed to mock him. He'd labored long and hard to create an invincible weapon and had succeeded all too well. The result of all his work would be to deny him the slaughter he so craved.

But no. It didn't have to be that way. Not if he refused to allow it.

He turned his eyes on Chumed. "How soon can our troops be ready to march?"

Chumed blinked. "March, Milord?"

"Yes, march! We'll head west a little way, then hook around to pin the invaders against the river."

The seneschal hesitated. Then: "Master, naturally we would have defended the city had the enemy chosen to attack. That's our duty. But unless I'm mistaken, we haven't received any orders to go forth and engage the council elsewhere."

"No other force as large as ours is close enough to do it, and anyway, I'm in authority here. Do you think the regent would have given me my position if he didn't trust me—indeed, expect me—to show initiative?"

"Master, I'm sure Szass Tam has complete confidence in you. But in light of the powers the rogue zulkirs command, maybe it would still be prudent to consult him before you act. I mean, you're a Red Wizard and have other mages under your command. Surely someone knows a way to communicate with High Thay quickly."

Yes, surely. And if So-Kehur were to employ it, perhaps Szass Tam would opt to leave his old enemies unmolested in the hope they'd eventually leave Thay of their own volition. He never would have done so in the old days, but Szass Tam had changed since establishing the regency, and no one truly understood his priorities anymore.

Even if the lich did want the invaders pursued and destroyed, he might decide to dispatch a more seasoned general to command the effort, or even descend from the Thaymount to see to the task himself. So-Kehur could find himself consigned to a subordinate role or left behind to mind Anhaurz while the blood spilled elsewhere.

And all those possibilities were unacceptable.

He tried to frame an excuse to give Chumed, then suffered a spasm of irritation. He was thinking like the old So-Kehur, that plump, cringing, contemptible wretch. The new So-Kehur was a lord, and lords didn't have to justify their decisions to their subordinates. Rather, they disciplined them when they were insolent.

Drawing on one of the peculiar talents he'd developed after abandoning the external attributes of humanity, he lashed out with his thoughts. Chumed cried out, staggered, and nearly reeled off the wall-walk before collapsing onto his side, where he writhed and bled from his chewed tongue and his nostrils. Though not the target, the scout too caught a bit of the effect. Crouching, face contorted, he clutched his forehead in both hands.

For a moment, So-Kehur remembered his long association with Muthoth and how the other young necromancer had liked to bully him. He felt both squeamish and pleased to at last be the bully himself, but of the two emotions, pleasure was by far the stronger.

He delivered only a few restrained blows to Chumed's psyche; the seneschal was too useful a deputy to kill. Upon finishing, he said, "I trust we're done with questions and second-guessing."

Shaking, Chumed clambered to his knees. "Yes, Milord."

"Then get our army ready." Meanwhile, the artisans would transfer So-Kehur's brain into a body specifically intended for the battlefield.

.. ..

Mirror thought he heard something that might have been a footfall, the faint sound almost covered by the whistling of the cold mountain wind. Or perhaps he simply sensed the advent of trouble. Either way, he didn't doubt his instincts. They'd saved him too many times, even if they hadn't helped on the terrible day when Fastrin killed his body and dealt his soul the spiritual wounds that had never truly healed.

"Come on," he whispered. He started toward an extrusion of basalt large enough to serve as cover, then saw that Bareris wasn't following. The bard was still singing under his breath, still casting about with wide, black eyes and a dazed expression on his pallid face.

Even after centuries as a phantom, Mirror almost reached to grab his friend and drag him behind the rock before remembering that his hand would simply pass through Bareris's body. Instead, he planted himself right in front of the bard and said, "Brother, come with me *now*." Insofar as his sepulchral tone allowed, he infused his voice with all the force of command that had once made younger warriors jump to obey.

Bareris blinked. "Yes. All right." Mirror led him into the patch of shadow behind the basalt outcrop.

They scarcely had time to crouch before a dozen ghouls—hunched, withered, hairless things with mouths full of needle fangs—came loping down the trail. Szass Tam had plenty of patrols watching for signs of trouble, even this far down the mountain.

The creature in the lead—judging from the stomach-turning stench of it, it might be one of the especially nasty ghouls called ghasts—abruptly halted, raised its head, and sniffed, although how it could possibly smell anything but itself was a mystery. Mirror willed his sword into his hand. But then the ghast grunted and led its fellows on down the path.

Mirror waited for the patrol to trek farther away, then whispered, "It's a good thing neither of us sweats."

Bareris didn't answer. That wasn't unusual, but the reason was. Crooning to himself, he was already slipping back into his trance. He started to straighten up.

"Wait," Mirror said. "Give the ghouls another moment."

Bareris froze in a position that would have strained a living man.

"All right," continued the ghost, "that should be long enough."

Bareris finished rising and continued onward, straying from the trail as often as he walked on it, halting periodically to run his hand over a stone or a patch of earth. Prowling behind him, Mirror watched for danger and tried to believe this scheme might actually work.

He told himself he should believe. He had a century's worth of reasons to trust Bareris, and even were it otherwise, faith had been the foundation of his martial order and his life. Still, his friend's plan seemed like a long shot at best, partly because Mirror had never seen the bard do anything comparable before.

Rumor had it that the cellars of the Citadel connected to natural caverns below. Bareris reasoned that the caves might well let out somewhere on the mountainside, and Mirror agreed the notion was plausible.

It was his comrade's strategy for finding an opening that roused his skepticism. Bareris had collected stories concerning killings and uncanny happenings on the slopes. Some of those tales were surely false or had become confused as they passed from one teller to the next. Even the ones that were accurate didn't necessarily reflect the predations of creatures that emerged from the catacombs to hunt. The desolate peaks of the Thaymount were home to a great number of beasts likely to devour any lone hunter or prospector they happened across.

Still, Bareris had tossed all the dubious stories into his head like the ingredients of a stew. Somehow the mixture was supposed to cook down to a measure of truth, or perhaps a better word was inspiration. Then magic would lead the singer to the spot he needed to find.

Let it be so, Mirror silently prayed. I don't know how it can be, but let it be so.

Day gave way to night. Light flickered on the northern horizon as, somewhere in that direction, a volcano belched fire and lava. The ground rumbled and shivered, and loose pebbles clattered down the slopes.

Some time after, Bareris abruptly halted and sang the brief phrase necessary to give his song some semblance of a proper conclusion. "We're close." His voice and expression were keen, purged of the dreamy quality the trance had imparted.

Mirror cast about. "I don't see anything."

"I don't, either, but it's here." The slope above this narrow length of trail was steep enough that an ordinary man might well have hesitated to climb on it. But Bareris scuttled around on it quickly, with minimal concern for his own safety. Since a ghost couldn't fall, Mirror tried to examine the least accessible places and spare his comrade at least that much danger.

Neither found anything.

Mirror looked down at the bard. "Should we go higher?" he asked. "Or investigate the slope beneath the trail?"

"No," Bareris said. "It's here. It's right in front of us."

Or else, Mirror thought, you simply want it to be. But what he said was, "Good enough." They resumed picking over the same near-vertical stretch of escarpment they'd already checked.

Until Bareris said, "I found it."

He was standing—or clinging—beside what appeared to be just another basalt outcropping. Mirror floated down to hover directly in front of him and still couldn't see anything special about it. "You're certain?" he asked.

"Yes. Last year or the year before, this stone was higher up the mountain. Then a tremor shook it loose, and it tumbled down here to jam in the outlet like a cork in a bottle. For a moment, I could see it happening."

"Let's find out what I can see," Mirror said. He flew forward into the solid rock. For a phantom, it was like pushing through cobwebs.

Almost immediately, he emerged into empty air. A tunnel ran away before him, twisting into the heart of the mountain.

He turned, flowed back through the stone, and told Bareris he was right.

Bareris sang a charm. He vanished, then instantly reappeared. "Damn it," he growled. "Even this far under the castle, I can't shift myself inside."

"But I can go in," Mirror said. "I'll explore the caves and find a second outlet. Then I'll come back here and fetch you."

Bareris shook his head. "If the stories are true, there are things lurking in the tunnels that could hurt even you. Things you might not be able to handle by yourself. Besides, what if there isn't another opening, or we run out of time while you're looking for it?"

"What's the alternative?"

"Yank the stopper out of the jug."

"I know you're strong, but that stone is bigger than you are, and you don't have any good place to plant your feet."

That made it sound as if Mirror's only worry was that the boulder wouldn't pull free. In truth, he was equally concerned that it would, suddenly, and carry Bareris with it as it tumbled onward. The bard knew a spell to soften a fall, but it wouldn't keep the rock from crushing, grinding, and tearing him to pieces against the mountainside.

"I can do it," Bareris said, "or rather, we can. You'll help me with your prayers."

Mirror saw that, as usual, there was no dissuading him. So he nodded his assent, and while Bareris sang a song to augment his strength, Mirror asked his patron to favor the bard. For an instant, the god's response warmed the cold, aching emptiness that was his essence even as the response manifested as a shimmer of golden light.

Still singing, Bareris positioned his feet on a small, uneven, somewhat horizontal spot unworthy of the term "ledge." He twisted at the waist, found handholds on the boulder, gripped them, and started straining.

At first, nothing happened, and small wonder. Standing as he was, Bareris couldn't even exert the full measure of his strength. Then the stone made a tiny grating sound. Then a louder one.

Then it jerked free, so abruptly that it threw Bareris off balance. The stone and the bard plummeted together, just as Mirror had envisioned.

For the first moment of the stone's fall, Bareris was more or less on top of it. Its rotation would spin him underneath an instant later, but he didn't wait for that to happen. He snatched at the mountainside, and his left hand closed on a lump of rock. He clung to it, and the boulder rolled on without him, bouncing and crashing to the floor of the gorge far below.

Mirror floated down to the place where Bareris dangled. "Are you all right?"

"Fine." Bareris reached for another outcropping with his free hand, revealing the tattered inner surface of his leather gauntlet and the shredded skin and muscle beneath.

•• •• •• •• •• •• •• •• •• •• •• •• •• •• ••

The tunnels were lava tubes or splits in the stone, produced by earthquake and orogeny. Unlike limestone caverns, they had no stalactites or stalagmites to hinder Bareris's progress. But that was the only good thing about them. They were a maze of unpredictable twists and cul-de-sacs stretching on and on in the darkness, and, unsurprisingly, the stories that had enabled him to locate the entrance were of no use at all when it came to finding his way inside. He'd sung a song to locate worked stone—specifically, whatever archway was closest—and it gave him a sense that the nearest such feature lay to the northeast. But that didn't guarantee he'd be able to grope his way to it anytime soon.

Perhaps perceiving his impatience, Mirror said, "You could try to bring Aoth and the zulkirs to us now. They might know magic to guide us all through."

"I thought of that," Bareris replied. "But what if these caves don't actually link up with the dungeons?"

"Then perhaps they can blast a way through."

"Perhaps, but I imagine that would ruin any hope of taking Szass Tam by surprise."

"by surprise."

"by surprise."

Startled, Bareris turned to Mirror and saw that the ghost, who currently resembled a smeared reflection of himself, looked just as surprised. He knew he hadn't truly repeated himself nor spoken loud enough to raise echoes in the sizable cavern he and the phantom were traversing. Yet he had an eerie sense that something—or everything—*had* repeated, as if the world itself were stuttering.

He and Mirror had hiked a long way without encountering any of the long-buried perils for which these depths were infamous, but he suspected their luck had just run out. He drew his sword, and the ghost's shadow-blade oozed outward from his fist. Pivoting, they looked for a threat. It might be difficult to spot. Too many fallen boulders littered the cave floor. Too many alcoves and tunnel mouths opened on blackness.

"Do anything? You see," said Mirror, his voice rising at the end of the second word. "Bareris, I swear, I said that properly. Or at least, I didn't feel that I was jumbling the words."

"I believe you," Bareris said.

"What's happening to us?"

"*us.*"

"I don't know, but maybe . . ."

"*maybe*"

"*maybe*"

". . . we should keep moving."

"Way? Which."

Good question. More than one passage appeared to run northeast, and the magic pointing in the direction of the arch couldn't differentiate between them. Bareris chose at random.

"Let's try this one."

He took a stride, and the darkness deepened.

Only a supernatural manifestation could account for such a thing, because here in the heart of the mountain, the dark had already been absolute. The undead enjoyed a measure of vision even so, but now Bareris couldn't see as far as before, and even nearby objects looked hazy, as though he were viewing them through fog.

He sang the opening notes of a charm to conjure light. Perhaps it would reveal the location of the creature or creatures he suspected were hiding in the murk.

Something snatched him off his feet and hurled him ten paces backward into the cavern wall.

The shock of impact was enough to stun even him. He sensed rather than saw something looming over him, poised to attack again. He raised his sword, hoping the thing would impale itself when it struck. Though he doubted that would be enough to keep the blow from smashing home.

Light flared in the darkness. It stung Bareris, and he realized it was more than just a flash. It was the power of Mirror's god, invoked to smite an undead foe.

The radiance gave Bareris his first look at the thing. It was huge, a formless cloud of darkness with several ragged arms writhing and coiling from the central mass. Without turning—lacking a head, eyes, or an internal structure of bones and joints, it didn't need to—it shifted its tentacles away from Bareris to threaten the ghost on the other side of it. One arm struck at Mirror, and he caught the blow on his shield. But it still knocked him back, a sign that both he and the creature existed in the same non-corporeal state.

Mirror cut at the arm as it started to retract. "It's a vasuthant!" he shouted.

Unlike Mirror, evidently, Bareris had never encountered a vasuthant, but the undead horrors figured in a couple of the ancient tales he'd collected over the years. They were sentient wounds in the fabric of time itself, a condition that allowed them to play tricks with the march of the moments to destroy their prey.

If this entity truly was a vasuthant, even Mirror couldn't contend with it unaided. Bareris floundered to his feet, drew a deep breath, and shouted. The thunderous bellow shook the cave, brought stones showering from the ceiling, and blasted a bit of the vasuthant's blackness loose from the central body. The wisps instantly withered away to nothing.

The vasuthant turned its attention back to him, as the new tentacles squirming from its cloudy body attested. Gripping his sword with both hands, Bareris poised himself to dodge and cut.

With luck, his enchanted blade would hurt the creature, insubstantial though it was.

The vasuthant snatched for him. He sidestepped, swung at its arm, and slashed completely through it. He felt just a hint of resistance, as though the blade were severing gossamer threads. The end of the creature's limb boiled into nonexistence.

Time skipped backward.

The vasuthant snatched for him. He sidestepped, but it adjusted its aim, and the tentacle coiled around him anyway. It yanked tight as a noose encircling the neck of a man dropped through the trapdoor of a gallows, somehow exerting crushing pressure even though it had no solidity.

The vasuthant jerked Bareris into the center of its shifting darkness. Pain burned through him. The creature was trying to poison him with the energy of undeath. Since he was undead too, the effect wasn't as devastating as it would have been to a living man, but it might well prove lethal over time.

It was difficult even to see the arm gripping him now that the vasuthant had merged it with the central cloud. Bareris cut at the place where he judged it ought to be, but even if he was right this time, the stroke had no apparent effect. Another burst of agony jolted him, and the relentless constriction around his waist threatened to pinch him in two.

Just barely visible through the murk, Mirror called to his god and slashed his sword through a portion of the vasuthant's body. Its shadowy core seethed, and the ring of pressure around Bareris's torso loosened.

Bareris bellowed a war cry and swung his sword. The tentacle frayed from existence, dropping him to the cavern floor. Still inside the animate darkness, he cut at it repeatedly until it flowed away and uncovered him.

Without taking his eyes off the thing, Bareris asked, "Are we winning?"

"I don't . . ."

"don't"

". . . know," Mirror replied. "I only ever fought one vasuthant, and this one's bigger and more powerful."

So they really had precious little idea what they were facing. But Bareris surmised he needed some mystical defense in place to counter the creature's manifest ability to revisit a moment that hadn't worked out as it would have preferred. He sang, and eight more Barerises sprang into existence around him, each with a stance and facial expression identical to his own.

Just in time too, for an instant later the vasuthant surged forward like a towering black wave.

A tentacle flailed, and one of the illusory doubles burst like a soap bubble at its touch. Bareris stepped in and cut the vasuthant.

A tentacle flailed, and a different illusory double burst like a soap bubble at its touch. Bareris stepped in and cut the vasuthant.

He grinned a wolfish grin. Perhaps he'd hit on a winning tactic.

Then one of his duplicates vanished without the vasuthant snagging it with one of its limbs or making any other form of visible attack. It was a pointed reminder that the entity still possessed capabilities he didn't understand.

Still, he liked his and Mirror's chances better than he had before, partly because when the vasuthant obliterated all his illusory doubles, he could always sing up another batch.

He and his companion battled on, often with sword strokes, sometimes with their mystical abilities. Bareris chanted to leech the strength out of the vasuthant much as it had tried to do to him. Mirror hammered it with flares of celestial power. Meanwhile, time lurched and stuttered.

The latter effect was disorienting and obliged them to defend themselves from many of the vasuthant's most cunning attacks not once but twice. Still, they kept the living darkness from doing grievous harm to them, while their attacks withered bits of it.

Bareris could only hope they were cutting and burning away enough to matter. Since the thing was merely churning blackness floating in blackness, he still couldn't tell.

But it seemed a good sign when the creature abruptly flowed back beyond the reach of its opponents' swords. Bareris wondered if it had finally had enough, if it might ooze into some hole and let him and Mirror pass. Then he felt a frigid prickling on his skin. Power was accumulating in the air, as if an adept like Lallara or Lauzoril were working a particularly potent spell.

Mirror apparently felt it too, for he charged. Flanked by a pair of duplicates, the remnants of the third group he'd conjured, Bareris drew breath to shout.

Neither he nor the ghost managed to act in time to balk the vasuthant. Something exploded from it, a force neither visible, audible, nor tangible, but delivering a psychic shock so overwhelming that it froze both its adversaries in place.

Or perhaps it was simply the realization of what the vasuthant had wrought that paralyzed them. For Bareris once again had a beating heart in his chest and a glow of warmth in his flesh. He was once again the Mulan youth growing up in the slums of Bezantur.

Which meant Tammith was waiting for him there. He had yet to make the disastrous choice that led to her destruction.

He told himself it was nonsense. Though he sensed his transformation was more than mere deception, reason said it couldn't last or change the past even if it did. Still, he was slow to move, his two minds, his two realities, pulling him in opposite directions.

Beside him, Mirror, now a figure of solid flesh, looked just as stupefied. He had no guilt or anguish over an abused and murdered lover to transfix him, or if he did, he'd never told Bareris about her. But no doubt the sudden restoration of his maimed mind and memory and deliverance from the endless hollow ache of undeath were equally overpowering. That, or the excruciating comprehension that his resurrection was only temporary.

Churning and coiling, the vasuthant rushed forward. Retreating, Bareris sang to raise a curtain of fire, or at least a semblance of it, between his foe and himself.

He stumbled over the phrasing, perhaps because it was a powerful, difficult spell, and the boy whose form he now wore and whose intrusive thoughts were addling his own had yet to master it.

The vasuthant reached for him, and he felt a sick near-certainty that its power had diminished his martial skills as well, that he could no longer wield his sword well enough to fend it off. He was about to perish with Szass Tam unpunished and Tammith unavenged.

Then the vasuthant's arms whirled past him to reach for Mirror instead, and when Bareris followed the motion, he understood why. Mirror had already turned back into a ghost, which meant that at the moment, he posed a greater threat to their adversary.

Mirror rattled off an invocation, and his murky blade shined so brightly that Bareris had to squint to look at it. The phantom charged the vasuthant with the weapon extended like a lance.

Power groaned through the air. With a snapping sound, several jagged cracks opened in the section of cavern floor between Mirror and the vasuthant. Then shadow swirled around the ghost, almost obscuring his running form, dimming the light of his sword, and enclosing him in a sphere of gloom. Mirror froze midstride, immobile as a statue.

The vasuthant swung its tentacles back toward Bareris. He retreated, and the creature snatched and destroyed one of the remaining duplicates.

Then Bareris's heart stopped pounding, and for an instant, he felt horribly cold. He was undead once more and suffered an irrational pang of loss, even though he needed all his abilities to have any hope of survival. Without Mirror fighting beside him, that hope was slim enough as it was.

The last of his doubles vanished.

Power sizzled around him, and invisible needles jabbed across his body. Then an unseen agency threw him straight up into the air. Aping his every move, voluntary or otherwise, the last of his illusory duplicates hurtled up beside him.

Bareris just had time to fling up his arms to protect his head before he crashed into the cavern ceiling. The collision hurt but didn't cripple or stun him, and he sang the word that would slow his fall and spare him a second impact.

But unfortunately, the charm didn't allow him to control where he landed. The vasuthant flowed underneath him, and he dropped into its black, fuming core. At once pain stabbed him, and as the nearly invisible arms snaked at him from every side, wrapping around him, the torment intensified, even as it did him serious harm.

He spun, dodged, and struck. Each successful evasion or cut bought him another moment of existence but nothing more, because the vasuthant formed new arms as fast as he destroyed them. Meanwhile, the passing instants shuffled and repeated themselves until he thought the confusion of that alone might break his mind.

Standing in the center of the living darkness, he was also standing at the heart of the wound in time, and the more the creature exerted its powers, the more grievous that injury became. When he realized that, something—instinct, perhaps, certainly not a fully formed idea—prompted him to sing.

Since he couldn't call anything that could fight as well as he could with sword and magic, he generally had little use for summoning spells. Nor was he currently attempting any of the several such melodies in his arsenal. Rather, this song was an improvisation devised to take advantage of the vasuthant's own chaotic essence.

Just beyond the periphery of the creature's vaporous form, other Barerises—this time, by no means identical—wavered into being. One was the young man who'd adventured with the Black Badger Company, seeking wealth to buy Tammith and himself a life of ease. Another was the griffon rider who'd fought in the first War of the Zulkirs. The rest were versions of the undead fugitive who'd skulked about Thay in the ninety years after.

The pallid outlaws attacked. The youthful wanderer and the legionnaire faltered, and Bareris realized they couldn't see in the dark. He conjured light to reveal the cave and the creature it contained, and they too advanced on the entity with slashing blades.

The vasuthant couldn't form and direct enough arms to hold them all off at the same time, and, perhaps because Bareris and Mirror had already hurt it severely, or because it had already expended so much of its power, it quickly withered under the onslaught. It boiled, thrashed, then shattered into nothingness. Bareris felt a sort of intangible thump as the insult to time repaired itself.

With the breach closed, his counterparts couldn't remain. Most faded instantly, but for some reason, the youngest lingered another moment. He seemed to gaze at his older self with consternation, pity, or conceivably a mixture of the two.

It made Bareris want to say something. But he had no idea what, and his younger self dimmed to nothingness before anything came to mind.

Bareris felt inexplicably ashamed, strangely bereft, and scowled the emotions away. Surely his inner turmoil was just a transient and meaningless aberration, an aftereffect of the psychic punishment he'd endured.

He needed to focus his attention on Mirror. The vasuthant might be gone, but the bubble of gloom it had created remained, with the ghost still a motionless prisoner inside.

Bareris walked to the sphere, took a moment to center himself and regulate his breathing, than sang a song of liberation. The dark globe withstood the spell without so much as a quiver.

•• •• •• •• •• •• •• •• •• •• •• •• •• ••

"Are they sure?" asked Samas Kul. A stray crumb dropped from his ruddy lower lip.

Lallara sneered at him. "Do you actually think Captain Fezim's scouts could be mistaken about observing an entire army on the march?"

Nevron's attendant demons and devils didn't think so. They whispered, hissed, and snarled in voices only he could hear, begging him to take them into another battle.

The invaders had been working their way down the Lapendrar when a patrol led by Gaedynn returned mid-afternoon. Upon hearing the redheaded archer's report, Aoth immediately summoned the zulkirs to a council of war in the shade of a stand of gnarled, fungus-spotted oaks on the riverbank. Lallara conjured a dome of silence to keep anyone from eavesdropping, and as a result, the world had a strange, hushed quality. Nevron could no longer hear the cheeping birds in the branches overhead or the gurgle of the current.

"Gaedynn and the other griffon riders are certain of what they saw," said Aoth. Unlike Nevron, Lallara, and Lauzoril, he hadn't bothered to tell an underling to fetch a camp chair. He sat cross-legged on the ground, his back against one of the tree trunks and his spear on the ground beside him.

His immense floating throne ludicrous in the wan sunlight and open air, Samas made a sour face. "You said that if we avoided

Anhaurz, we wouldn't have to fight another battle."

"I said I hoped we wouldn't," Aoth replied. "But either Szass Tam ordered the autharch of the city to chase us, or else the bastard simply wants a fight. The rebels claim he's some sort of intelligent golem or living metal monstrosity, so Kossuth only knows what's in his mind. Anyway, he's maneuvering to come at us from the west and pin us against the river."

"Could we march faster and keep away from him?" Samas asked.

"Conceivably," said Aoth, "but it would destroy any illusion that we're serious about reaching the Dread Ring in Tyraturos."

Lauzoril laced his fingers together. "What if we actually did cross the Lapendrar? Then this metal man's army and ours would be on opposite sides of it. I understand that we couldn't ford without the aid of magic, but we have magic."

"That too might work," said Aoth, "but at the cost of putting us exactly where we don't want to be: deeper inside Thay, where the river that shielded us from Anhaurz's army might cut off our escape when an even bigger force descends on us later."

"So you recommend we stand and fight," Lallara said.

"Yes," said Aoth.

"I agree," the old woman said.

"As do I," said Lauzoril.

"And I," Nevron said. His familiars roared and cackled to hear it.

"Can we win?" Samas asked. "Even after the losses we sustained taking the first Ring?"

"The enemy is fresh, and there are a lot of them," said Aoth. "But the four of you are zulkirs. That should tip the scale in our direction."

•• •• •• •• •• •• •• •• •• •• •• •• ••

Heedless of the risk that it would draw Szass Tam's sentinels or other dangerous creatures, Bareris sang as loud as possible. He also sustained the final piercing note longer than anyone but an undead bard could, expelling every trace of breath from his lungs, pouring all the force of his trained will into the tone.

Mirror's prison weathered the assault just as it had resisted all of Bareris's previous attempts at countermagic.

In desperation, he drew his sword, grasped the hilt with both hands, and tried to smash the shadowy sphere as if it were an orb of cloudy glass. No matter how hard he struck, the blade glanced away without leaving a mark.

This was bad. He thought he understood what had befallen Mirror. The vasuthant had snared him in a petrified moment where the ghost could take no action, because *nothing* could happen without even a slight progression of time for it to happen in.

But unfortunately, inferring that much didn't enable Bareris to break the enchantment. The songs he ordinarily employed for such tasks hadn't done the job, and he no longer had any hope of improvising a new spell to manipulate time itself. The conditions that made that possible ceased when the vasuthant perished.

If he called to the zulkirs and they succeeded in translating themselves into the caverns, it was possible that one of them—Lallara, perhaps—could liberate Mirror. But as he'd explained to the ghost, he had his reasons for not wanting to summon the archmages prematurely. These particular caves might not connect to the Citadel's dungeons, and even if they did, the longer the zulkirs wandered around on Szass Tam's home ground, the likelier it was that the lich would detect such a concentration of arcane power and prepare a deadly reception for them. Better, therefore, to wait to call them until it looked as if they might be able to sneak up on their supreme foe relatively quickly.

Perhaps Bareris could wait until he found a way into the

dungeons, and then he could perform the summoning. Then he and his allies could backtrack to this cave—

But no. Even as he conceived the idea, he knew it wouldn't happen that way. The archmages would never spend precious time and brave additional perils just to rescue Mirror. It wasn't in their natures.

So that left two alternatives. Bareris could press on alone and trust that whatever danger arose from this point forward, he'd be able to contend with it unaided. Or he could stay here and continue to assail the bubble of frozen time with countermagic, resting when he exhausted his power and hoping that eventually, somehow, one of his spells would breach Mirror's prison. Knowing all the while that Szass Tam could start the Unmaking at any moment.

Bareris looked at Mirror, a shadow locked in shadow with a blade that glowed like moonlight in his hand. "With so many lives at stake," he said, "I have to go on. And I know you'd want me to."

That last part was plainly true. If he were able, Mirror would tell him to leave him behind. But Bareris suspected he'd just lied about his own motives—that in truth, it was the possibility of revenge compelling him onward, as it had once prompted him to break faith with Aoth—and it made him feel even more like a traitor.

Still, he'd made his decision. He turned his back on Mirror, chose one of the exits opening to the northeast, and strode toward it. Once he rounded the first bend in the tunnel on the other side, it was impossible to look back and see the ghost even had he wished to do so. Which he didn't. He needed to focus on whatever lay ahead.

He told himself that if he survived, he'd come back for Mirror. Told himself too, that it was absurd to imagine that one could truly save a man already dead. Mirror's existence was a cold, hollow mockery of life, misery without end, as a fellow undead knew only too well. The phantom was probably better off suspended as he was.

Bareris stopped and raked his fingers through his hair. Then he turned and retraced his steps.

"I know this isn't what you'd want," he said to Mirror. "It's not what I want, either. But apparently it's what I'm going to do."

He sang until no magic remained to him, and the dark bubble stayed intact. He waited until his power replenished itself, then began again.

He chanted one incantation, sang another, then started a third. And as the music hammered it, the bubble sheared apart and crumbled like a wasp's nest burning in an unseen flame. It was hard to say why, for he'd cast the identical spell several times before. Perhaps all his attempts at countermagic had exercised a cumulative effect, or maybe it was just that he'd finally gotten lucky.

Mirror bounded out of the disintegrating sphere, then stopped and cast wildly about when he perceived the vasuthant was no longer in front of him.

"It caught you in a kind of trap," Bareris said. "I killed it, then set you free."

"Thank you," Mirror said. Then, perhaps struck by something in his comrade's manner, he peered at him more closely. "How long did it take to free me?"

Bareris shrugged. "Buried in these tunnels, it's hard to know. But too long. We have to get moving."

chapter thirteen

19 Kythorn, The Year of the Dark Circle (1478 DR)

Other creatures emerged from the gloom to menace Bareris. But fortunately, none were as formidable as the vasuthant, and one by one, he and Mirror killed them or put them to flight. Until finally, a basket arch appeared at the end of a stretch of tunnel.

They'd been seeking it so long that, for an instant, an irrational part of Bareris's mind didn't trust it to be real. He had a sense that it would vanish like a mirage as soon as he took another step.

But it didn't, and on the other side was a passage plainly created by artisans, albeit probably not human ones. The faded murals on the walls depicted lizardfolk carrying on the business of a civilization that looked as complex and advanced as any extant today. For an instant, Bareris wondered what calamity had reduced the reptiles to the primitive brutes with which he was familiar.

Maybe, he thought, one of their wizards had attempted the Great Work.

Mirror grinned. "You did it, my brother. You found a way in."

"We haven't done anything yet," Bareris said. "Stand watch while I try the next part."

He extracted five small, sealed silver vials from his belt pouch. Each contained a drop of blood drawn from Aoth, Nevron, Lauzoril, Lallara, or Samas Kul. Clasping them in his left hand, he sang under his breath to send a message. To establish a connection over hundreds of miles.

After a time, he felt the link establish itself, a sensation like a rope pulling taut. He concluded the first song and began another, cobbled together from the same tones, rhythms, and words of power that enabled a bard to shift himself instantly from place to place. Objects appeared to ripple and ooze as he undermined the integrity of the space in which they existed. Violet sparks fell from the air like snowflakes.

•• •• •• •• •• •• •• •• •• •• •• •• •• ••

Aoth had found a battlefield to his liking. True, he and his allies would have the Lapendrar at their backs—no practical way of avoiding that—but a bend in the river would protect their right flank, and a patch of woods—and the archers Gaedynn would station there—should keep the enemy off the left. In addition, his side had claimed the high ground. True, it wasn't much higher than the surrounding grassland, but it might make a difference even so.

Once he was certain that Khouryn and the zulkirs' commanders were setting up the battle formation properly, he, Jet, and half a dozen of his fellow griffon riders flew out to take another look at the foe. As before, he found himself intrigued by the steel behemoth marching in the lead. So-Kehur, autharch of Anhaurz, looked like a scorpion with some additional limbs and a mask of a glaring human face attached, and he—if "he" was the right pronoun—was as huge as the undead octopus-things that had burrowed up out of the ground at the battle of the Keep of Sorrows.

His army looked nasty too. He had mounted lancers. Spearmen. Crossbowmen. Orcs, dread warriors, Red Wizards, and shuttered black wagons like coffins on wheels to carry entities unable to bear the sun. Their progress shrouded the marching columns in a haze of dust.

"Can we beat them?" asked Jet.

"Yes," said Aoth.

"Even though we're still torn up from the last fight?"

"Yes. Why the sudden doubts?"

"Because I get peeks at what's inside your head, O Mighty Captain."

Aoth snorted. "I'd be a fool if I *liked* the situation we're in. But that doesn't mean we can't handle it. I suspect this So-Kehur, who- and whatever he is, has no idea of the kind of power that four zulkirs—"

"Aoth . . ."

It was Bareris's voice crooning his name, and, startled, Aoth reflexively cast about to find the bard. For an instant, he saw him too, standing with Mirror in a corridor decorated with painted lizardfolk. Then the image melted away, exposing the mound of gray cumulus cloud behind it. A sense of connection, however, remained.

Aoth felt elated and disgusted at the same time, the former because Bareris had succeeded in his mission, the latter because the timing could scarcely have been worse. But there was nothing to be done about the when of it.

Responding to his master's unspoken desire, Jet wheeled and raced back toward the river. Aoth surveyed the battle lines on the rise, spotted four scarlet-robed figures—and the attendants who generally followed them around—toward the rear of the formation, and sent Jet plunging down to alight beside them.

"We have to go," said Samas Kul. Aoth observed that the transmuter had abandoned his floating throne. Once again, he wore a harness made of white light to help him carry his bulk around.

"I know," said Aoth, "but I need another moment." He dismounted, cast about, and found Khouryn already waiting to confer with him. The dwarf wore a leather arming cap but hadn't yet donned the steel helmet that went on top of it. "Bareris just called us."

"I figured that out," Khouryn said. "You're sure you need to go too?"

Aoth lowered his voice. "Someone should be there—someone besides Bareris and Mirror, I mean—who thinks that stopping the Unmaking is more important than saving his own skin."

Khouryn nodded. "I see that. Well, don't worry. The army could use all the magic you five are taking away with you, but we'll manage."

"I know you will."

"Now!" Nevron shouted.

Aoth turned. The zulkirs had moved apart to clear a space among them, and eight soldiers stood inside it. Aoth and Jet hurried to join them.

"Are you sure about this?" asked Aoth the griffon. "Stay here, and you can fight under the open sky."

Jet clacked his beak shut on empty air. It was one of several mannerisms the familiar used to expressed annoyance. "I already told you, I'm coming."

"Everyone, be silent!" Lallara snapped. She raised her staff, chanted words of power, and, one by one, the other archmages joined in.

The world shattered into chaotic points of brightness, and Aoth had a sudden vertiginous feeling of hurtling like an arrow shot from a bow. Translating oneself through space wasn't a part of his own specialized discipline, but other wizards had taken him on such journeys a time or two, so he was prepared for the sensation.

He wasn't ready for what happened next.

The travelers should have appeared before Bareris and Mirror as quickly as a hummingbird flicks its wings. Instead, they abruptly found themselves suspended in a gray void that, Aoth realized, was scarcely even a space in the truest sense but rather a condition of transition and indeterminacy.

He felt multiple pressures acting on him simultaneously. Something—the spell the zulkirs had cast, presumably—shoved him relentlessly forward. But he couldn't *go* forward, because something else—Szass Tam's wards against this form of intrusion—had him in its grip. Bareris and the archmages had weakened those defenses, but not enough, with the result that Aoth and his companions were like men trying to squeeze through a hole too small to accommodate them. The effect was painful and growing worse.

One of the soldiers screamed, and then, armor groaning and bones snapping, his body crumpled in on itself and disappeared. Perhaps, ejected back into the real world, the corpse had fallen to the ground somewhere outside the Citadel.

A second warrior's body compressed as if it were no weightier than a sponge. Blood gushed from his mouth and nostrils.

Lallara rattled off a spell of protection. The pressure holding Aoth in place abated, and he had a sensation of lurching forward. Then Szass Tam's defenses clamped down again, arresting him. Another bodyguard shrieked as magic crushed him like a grape in a press.

Lallara glared at Aoth. "Back at the Dread Ring," she said, "I saw you conjure a prismatic wall."

He didn't see how the spell could help them, but he was willing to follow her lead. The Firelord knew, he had no ideas of his own. "Where do you want it?"

"It doesn't matter! Just cast as many as you can."

The balance of pressures acting on Aoth's body was becoming more excruciating by the moment, but he managed to grit out the incantation with the necessary precision. Multicolored radiance flared from the point of his spear, but instead of forming the usual barrier, it arced over to Lallara and cloaked her decrepit-looking form in rainbows, which coruscated as she chanted words of command. Aoth inferred that since a prismatic wall was a defensive enchantment, she, with her mastery of that form of magic, could siphon its power to strengthen her own spells.

He cast another wall, then another, and she wrapped those around herself as well. Szass Tam's wards mashed three more soldiers to pulp. Then the gray space burst apart.

The surviving travelers materialized down the length of the corridor in which Bareris and Mirror awaited them. Aoth stumbled a step, then caught his balance. A warrior exclaimed at the sudden darkness, and, with a casual gesture, Lauzoril kindled a globe of floating silvery light.

Aoth grinned at Bareris. "Nice work."

"How do you figure that?" Samas demanded, shrill with displeasure. "We nearly died. Both my guards *did* die."

Nevron sneered. "You're a sad excuse for a zulkir if you need soldiers to protect you. But if you do, rest assured, we still have plenty." He made a sweeping gesture to indicate his own person with all its talismans and tattoos, and, by implication, the demons and devils caged inside them.

"We did experience an awkward moment," Lauzoril said, "but in my view, the scheme worked as well as we reasonably could have expected. All the important people made it through, and a few of our underlings as well. So I suggest we turn our attention to finding Szass Tam."

•• •• •• •• •• •• •• •• •• •• •• •• •• ••

Bareris had hoped that the zulkirs could cast a divination to pinpoint Szass Tam's location, and in fact, Samas Kul tried. But for some reason, the magic simply indicated that the lich was somewhere above them. Since that took in the entire fortress, it wasn't much help.

Bareris struggled to quell a pang of impatience, to take solace in the thought that surely the *lord* of the Citadel couldn't be hard to find. The castle must be crawling with servants who kept track of his whereabouts, the better to meet his needs.

Lauzoril shrouded the company in an enchantment akin to some of the spells in Bareris's arsenal. With luck, it would beguile anyone who happened to see them into believing they were famil-iar faces with legitimate business in the catacombs. Then they started looking for the way up.

At first the trek was uneventful, with only the occasional scuff of a footstep, creak of leather, or Samas's wheezing to break the silence. Rumor had it that the dungeons were as haunted and dangerous as the caverns below, but it took a while for one of its denizens to reveal its presence.

Eventually, though, the intruders climbed a staircase and found themselves at a spot where two passages diverged from a common origin, and a murky painting of a farm without farmers or animals, its fields infested with tares and weeds, adorned a nearby wall. And suddenly Bareris's hackles rose as he sensed a hostile scrutiny.

He cast about but couldn't find the source of the glare boring into him. "Aoth?" he said.

The warmage peered around with his luminous, azure eyes. "Sorry. Even I can't see it. Which may mean that somehow, there truly isn't anything to see."

"I think it's a ghost," Mirror said, pity in his tone, "but terribly old and faded. It's forgotten nearly everything."

It was what Mirror might have become, Bareris supposed, if the two of them hadn't encountered one another in the Sunrise Mountains.

"I can sic a demon on it," Nevron said.

"It hates us," Mirror said, his resemblance to Bareris gradually bleeding out of his shadowy features, "but I don't think it has the power to hurt us."

"Then ignore it, and move on," Lallara said.

That sounded good to Bareris. He took a stride and felt the phantom shift position. Which was contrary to common sense, since he hadn't pinned it down to a specific location before. Yet even so, he somehow perceived a surge of movement, and then, though he still couldn't see it, his instincts told him the spirit had planted itself squarely in front of the procession.

"Does it think it can bar our path?" Samas asked.

"Whatever it believes," Lauzoril said, "I daresay we can walk right through it, and I see no reason why we shouldn't."

"Wait," Mirror said, his face oozing into a wavering mockery of Nevron's brutal features. "I sense it's trying to do something. Nothing harmful, just . . . something."

Slowly, as if the process required extreme exertion or concentration, a horizontal line scraped itself into existence on the painting of the deserted farm. The spirit then scratched a crude little arrowhead on the left end.

"It's pointing for us to turn around and go in the other direction," Lallara said.

"Because the ghost hopes to send us into harm's way," Samas said. "You said we should ignore it, and for once I agree with you."

"Wait," Mirror repeated. "I have a feeling it isn't finished."

For several moments, it seemed he was mistaken. Then, even more slowly than it had drawn the arrow, the haunt scratched a pair of letters above it.

Bareris felt a pang of excitement. "'S. T.' Szass Tam?"

"How can it be?" Lauzoril replied. "The spirit has no way of knowing we're hunting the lich and no motive to help us even if it does."

"Unless it's trying to lead us into a trap," Samas said, "just as I warned you." His wand crawled out of his voluminous sleeve with its trimming of diamonds.

Bareris peered around and strained to listen as well. As far as he could tell, he and his fellow intruders were alone with the haunt. "I imagine Szass Tam could think of better ways to lure us if he wanted to. Ploys less likely to rouse our suspicions. And remember, we tried to enter the castle in a way that would keep him from noticing."

Samas snorted. "'Tried' being the operative word."

"Maybe," said Aoth, "the spook has a grudge against Szass Tam. It would hardly be the first undead that a necromancer had ordered around against its will. In any case, I think we should follow its lead, at least for a little way."

"Even if this is a trap," Samas said.

"We dared to come here," the warmage replied, "because together, we should be able to overcome the worst our enemies can throw at us. Besides, if we haven't been as sneaky as we hoped, and Szass Tam does know we're wandering around in his cellar, we'll have to fight him on ground of his choosing eventually."

"That makes a certain amount of sense," Lauzoril said. He wore a dagger on his belt, and now he loosened it in its sheath.

Lallara and Nevron concurred with Lauzoril, and Samas grudgingly assented to the will of the majority. The intruders stalked in the direction the arrow pointed, past more dingy murals addressing the theme of a world devoid of people or beasts, with their guide's malevolent scrutiny wearing at them every step of the way. Whenever they came to an intersection, the entity contracted from a general miasma of loathing to a localized node of it to lead them in the right direction.

They found a pair of bodies, burned by some conflagration to clumps of half-melted armor, scraps of blackened bone, and ash. Then came a mural of an underwater scene without any fish in it. The haunt positioned itself in front of the painting as if to indicate they'd reached their destination.

"I can see runes on the picture," said Aoth, "but I'm not familiar with them."

"Describe them," Lallara said, and he did so. "Hm. The 'hand with an eye in the palm' is only there to unleash some sort of unpleasantness. Point to the others as I call them out. The 'triangle inside another triangle.'"

Aoth indicated the proper spot, and she rapped it with the head of her staff. For a moment, the sign glowed red.

So did the others as she touched them in their turns, and when she'd tapped them all, a latch clicked. The door concealed within the mural cracked open.

"Let me," said Aoth. He swung the panel a little wider and peered through. "It looks like a vault full of treasure." Spear leveled, he crept through the opening, and Jet lunged forward to place himself at his master's side. Everyone else followed.

At first, Bareris saw nothing more than Aoth had indicated: a big, dark room full of old and no doubt precious articles, intriguing under other circumstances but irrelevant to the task at hand. Then Aoth rounded a gigantic dragon skull with an axe buried in the top of it, pointed his spear, and spoke a word of command. A bolt of lightning crackled from the spear to strike at the threat he'd evidently spotted.

Bareris scrambled forward until he could see what his friend had seen, and then a shock of amazement, elation, and rage froze him in place. *Szass Tam* sat before them on a high-backed stone chair with arms carved in the shape of dragons and feet in the form of talons gripping orbs. Around it glittered a transparent, nine-sided pyramid composed of arcane energy.

It didn't look as though Aoth's lightning had hurt the lich, but one way or another, Bareris meant to do better. He shouted a thunderous shout. It rattled the sarcophagi and statuary and brought grit drifting down from the ceiling but didn't even appear to jolt the lich. Bareris drew breath to sing a killing song.

Szass Tam chuckled and shook his head. "This is unexpected to say the least. I hoped the Watcher would fetch someone to rescue me, but I never dreamed it would be all of you. Well met."

"'Well met'?" Bareris repeated. "'Well met'?" His fingers clenched on the hilt of his sword, and he started toward the figure in the pyramid.

"Easy," said Lauzoril at his back. "We're in no danger, nor is there a need for precipitous action. I daresay our vengeance can be as protracted as we care to make it."

Szass Tam nodded. "I assumed the former zulkir of Enchantment would recognize Thakorsil's Seat. Perhaps if you expound on its properties, you'll set your companions' minds at ease. Then we can all enjoy a civil conversation."

Lauzoril hesitated as if it felt wrong to follow the suggestion of a hated enemy. But then he said, "The Seat is a prison originally designed to hold the archdevil Orlex, and the presence of the pyramid indicates that at least the first ward is active. Szass Tam can't leave the chair or do anything to hurt us."

"Then . . . it's over?" Samas asked, incredulity in his voice. "He's helpless, and we can reclaim our dominions?"

"Before you start planning the victory feast," said the lich, "you might want to ask yourselves how I came to be in this predicament. Listen, and I'll explain."

•• •• •• •• •• •• •• •• •• •• •• ••

When Szass Tam felt the backs of his calves slam against the hard stone edge, he realized that Malark's kick had hurled him staggering into the same artifact in which he himself had once imprisoned Yaphyll. He made a frantic, floundering effort to arrest his momentum and landed in Thakorsil's Seat anyway.

Instantly the nine-sided pyramid sprang into existence around him. It was still hazy; it looked as if it had been sculpted from fog instead of gleaming glass. It would hold a captive nonetheless but not for long. Not unless someone commenced the proper ritual.

Szass Tam had never taught Malark the magic or anything else about the Seat. But he suspected his lieutenant had somehow obtained all the necessary information anyway.

Malark murmured a charm to wash the acid from his body, then drank an elixir that partially healed his burns and blisters. Then he recited an incantation to send the mummies shambling back to their sarcophagi.

Meanwhile the force holding Szass Tam in place and in check attenuated. If Malark didn't start the ritual soon, he'd be able to act. And perhaps the spymaster wouldn't. He needed a mage pledged to the gods of light, and no such prisoner was in evidence. If Malark imagined he had time to scurry to another part of the catacombs to retrieve one—

But no. He didn't. Malark plucked a glass bead from the pouch on his belt and dashed it to powder against the floor. A skinny, naked young woman, gagged and with her hands tied behind her, appeared in a flash of ruddy light. The bead had held her shrunken and in stasis until Malark required her.

He thumped her on the back with the heel of his hand, paralyzing her, then lowered her to the floor. Employing his clawed yellow glove, he carved a pair of identical runes in her forehead, and the bloody symbols burst into flame. He chanted the opening words of the first of the rituals of twin burnings, and Szass Tam felt coercion clamp down hard. It would remain impossible for him to rise or cast a spell at the man before him.

He could still talk, so he shouted at Malark. Insults. Threats. Obscenities. Nonsense. Anything to shake his concentration. For if Malark made even the slightest error in either his incantations or his cutting, the rite would fail.

But that didn't work out, either. Szass Tam had trained his student too well, and when the former monk of the Long Death carved the last double sigil on the sacrificial victim's charred, torn corpse, and a rune briefly flared into visibility on one face of the pyramid, the lich knew the Seat could conceivably hold him forever.

"Perhaps I deserve this," he said, "for long ago, I resolved never to trust anyone, and I broke the vow with you. Still, I'd like to know *why* you've betrayed me."

"A moment," Malark croaked. The dozens of lengthy incantations had dried out his throat, and since he no longer required precise intonation, he was letting the rawness show in his voice. He unstoppered a leather waterskin and took several swallows. "There, that's better. Master, you do deserve an explanation. And I promise you, it's not that I've forsaken the dream we share."

"Then why?" Szass Tam asked.

"Well, for one thing . . ." Malark hesitated. "Your Omnipotence, ever since I joined your cause, you've been a generous friend and mentor to me. I've learned to admire your wisdom, courage, and vision. But you also embody the unnatural vileness of undeath. You're the last creature who should undertake the task of recreating the world."

"I intend," Szass Tam answered, "to make a universe unafflicted with suffering or death."

"I believe you." Malark closed his eyes for a moment, and some of the remaining burns on his body faded. He was using a technique he'd learned as a monk to speed the healing process. "But it wouldn't work out like that. It couldn't. The new world would reflect your fundamental nature and come out worse than this one. That's one of the reasons I'm going to perform the Unmaking in your place."

"That's absurd."

"Not really. You taught me most of your secrets—if you recall, you even let me read Fastrin's book. And I am a spy. With ninety years to poke around, I uncovered the rest of them.

"Which is to say, I've practiced the same preparatory meditations you have, and I can perform the ceremony. Confined to Thakorsil's Seat, you won't be able to interfere, and no one will turn up to release you. Not when you're sealed in a hidden vault in a part of the dungeons everyone shuns. Not when people don't even realize you've gone missing." Malark swept his hand from his shaven crown down the length of his torso, and his form became Szass Tam's, tall, gaunt frame, chin beard, shriveled fingers, and all.

"And so," Szass Tam said, "in preference to a lich, a traitor will shape the world to come."

"No," Malark said.

"What do you mean?"

"I told you you're unfit to ascend to godhood. It's true and justification enough to meddle in your plans. But there's a deeper reason. I worship Death, and I originally joined your cause because you told me your intent was to kill everything, including me. My desire for that perfect consummation hasn't changed.

"But I can't leave it to you to bring it about, because if I did, it wouldn't *be* perfect. One thing—you—would survive. I won't commit that blasphemy."

"If the master of the ritual dies with everything else, than there's no one left to spark a new creation."

Malark shrugged. "I only care about the moment of absolute and universal annihilation. Afterward, the void will either bring forth new forms or it won't. Either way, I won't be around to see, although truthfully, I rather hope it doesn't."

"I don't suppose I can dissuade you by pointing out that you're insane."

"That's like ice rebuking snow for being cold, don't you think? Now, I regret having to cut our conversation short, particularly since this is the last time we'll see one another—"

"You're mistaken about that."

"—but as you know better than anyone, I have matters to attend to. So I'll bid you farewell. I realize I haven't left you much of a vantage point, but I hope that even so, you'll be able to perceive a portion of the spectacle to come." Malark turned and walked away.

Szass Tam believed that one should never lose one's composure in the presence of an enemy, so he waited for the door to click shut and for another moment after that. Then he slammed his fist down on the arm of the Seat.

He'd always prided himself on his ability to read people. In the old days, he'd often gleaned the tenor of his fellow council members' unspoken thoughts, and they'd been as devious an assembly as the East had ever seen. How, then, had he been so disastrously wrong about Malark?

Well, in a very real sense, he hadn't been. He'd comprehended the essential nature of Malark's obsession. That was what enabled him to turn the spymaster and led him to believe he could trust him. He just hadn't realized how ambitious Malark would become in his efforts to serve the terrible object of his devotion.

In any case, it was useless to fret over the error now. Szass Tam had to find a way to free himself. After all, Yaphyll had done it. True, she'd had a lucky combination of circumstances to help her, but Szass Tam had his intellect. He assured himself that it would serve just as well.

First—as part of a methodical examination of all the

possibilities, not because he thought it might actually work—he gripped the stone arms of the chair and tried to stand.

The Seat stabbed forbiddance into his mind, sparking fear, jumbling his thoughts, and opposing the will to rise with the compulsion to remain as he was. Defying the psychic intrusion, he kept trying anyway, but it was as if something had fused his body to the stone surfaces behind and beneath it.

He then tried to shift himself through space, off the Seat and beyond the confines of the pyramid. The chair attempted to deprive him of the will and the focus to do that as well. Once again, the psychic assault failed to shake him, and once again, it didn't matter. He suffered a kind of mental jolt as his prison held him fast.

He tried to speak to one of his captains up in the castle. He felt the magic, intended to carry the words like leaves on the wind, wither when it reached the inner surface of the pyramid.

He attempted to summon a demon, but no such entity appeared.

He sought to call the mummies forth from their coffins. They didn't heed him, either.

He hurled fire and lightning at the gleaming construct around him and at the massive stone chair beneath him, without so much as scratching either one.

He'd sometimes flattered himself that fear was a weakness he'd left behind the day he discovered his gift for sorcery. But he realized he was afraid now. With a spasm of annoyance, he pushed the useless emotion out of his mind. There *must* be a way out of this. He simply had to think of it.

With all his attention focused inward, he pondered for some time before the spiteful regard of the Watcher recaptured his notice. Even then, it took a while longer before it occurred to him that the entity could be anything more than a distraction.

He'd verified repeatedly that even when he managed to overcome the Seat's psychic interference and cast a spell, the pyramid dissipated the magic when it tried to pass through. That was why he hadn't been able to wake the mummies or summon a demon.

But the Watcher was inside the pyramid with him, and outside too. That was its peculiar nature, to be omnipresent within the gloomy crypts and passages that constituted its domain.

He spoke a spell of binding. His swirling hands left trailing wisps of scarlet light as he made the necessary gestures.

Perhaps the influence of Thakorsil's Seat kept him from casting as powerful a spell as he would have under normal circumstances. Or maybe the Watcher's diffuse and ambiguous nature made it particularly difficult to compel. Either way, when he spoke the final word, he sensed that he'd failed to hook his fish.

No matter. He was the greatest necromancer in all Faerûn, and he would catch it. He took a breath and began again.

He soon lost count of how many times he repeated the spell. But at last, when even he had nearly depleted his powers, he felt the spell seize its prey and the ghost thrashing like a hare in the jaws of a fox.

"Enough," he said. "Whether you realize it or not, you crave oblivion, and I'm willing to give it to you. But only if you serve me to the best of your ability."

The spirit quieted. Its regard conveyed as much hatred as ever, yet even so, it had a different quality. Szass Tam sensed a sullen acquiescence.

The Watcher's submission allowed him to probe its essence and examine its qualities. In most respects, they were disappointing. The entity was incapable of leaving its haunts even under magical duress. It was too mindless ever to recover the power of speech, either to articulate the words that would dissolve the first rune or to communicate with someone who could.

But it still might be able to interact with the physical world to a limited degree. Szass Tam focused his will on it, reinvigorating the decayed capacity and reminding the ghost of its existence.

The process evidently hurt, for the spirit writhed. But he had it in his grip now, too firmly for it to escape.

"Now," he said, "you can make a mark." Leaning forward, he drew an arrow in the dust at his feet. "You can make this one to guide people here. Do you understand?"

He sensed that it did. Probably its people had used arrows to point directions when it was alive.

"If the arrow isn't enough to bring them, draw these." Szass Tam wrote his initials.

He assumed two letters were just about all the Watcher could manage. Even if the phantom had been literate during its mortal existence, it hadn't been in Mulhorandi, and it was unlikely that its tattered mind could retain as many unfamiliar symbols as would be required to spell out his entire name, let alone an even lengthier message.

He made the Watcher write the letters until it got them right about nine times out of ten. When further practice failed to improve on that, he told it, "All right. Use what I taught you, and fetch someone. Anyone."

The Watcher didn't leave. It was still glaring at him. But presumably its awareness also pervaded the rest of its environs and was ready to obey his commands.

Which left nothing for Szass Tam to do but try to believe that before time ran out, someone would come to this all-but-forsaken area and heed the promptings of an entity that knowledgeable visitors had long since learned to ignore.

•• •• •• •• •• •• •• •• •• •• •• •• ••

19 Kythorn, The Year of the Dark Circle (1478 DR)

"And my faith was not misplaced," the lich concluded, "for here you are."

Bareris laughed. It was the first time he'd done so in ninety years, and it hurt his chest. "Yes, here we are. But unfortunately for you, we're not as credulous as you hoped. Even if we were, we wouldn't believe your story, because some of us watched Malark die."

Unruffled by his foe's jeering attitude, the lich said, "I assume you mean during your siege of the Dread Ring in Lapendrar."

"Yes," Samas said, satisfaction in his tone. "I killed the wretch myself."

"Bravo," said Szass Tam dryly. "I'm not terribly surprised, for I ordered him to Lapendrar. But we all know of magic that allows a person to be in two places at the same time. As you likely recall, if I make the proper preparations, I can appear in several places simultaneously."

"Still," Bareris said, "your story's ridiculous. Malark's immortal and wants to murder the whole world, himself included, just because he loves Death and thinks it will bring him a moment of ultimate joy? I knew him for ten years and never saw a hint of any of that."

Aoth frowned. "But you know, I always sensed that he had his secrets, didn't you? And wild as it is, this story does explain why he would betray the southern cause, even though we were winning at the time."

"It would take someone as formidable as Malark to imprison the lich," Mirror said. At the moment, he was a shadow of the warrior he'd been in life. "And someone with a cunning mind and, most likely, a knowledge of sorcery to keep anyone from realizing Szass Tam was missing. Which his captor plainly has. Otherwise, we would have run into search parties."

Bareris clamped down on a surge of fury. Told himself that his friends weren't really betraying him, even though that was how it felt. "How can you believe a single word that comes from this liar's mouth? He'd say anything to persuade us to set him free."

"Of that," Lallara quavered, "I have no doubt. Still, Captain Fezim and Sir Mirror make a legitimate point. Preposterous as this tale may initially appear, it hangs together rather well."

Nevron threw up his hand in a gesture that, like nearly everything he said or did, conveyed contempt. Bareris caught a whiff of the brimstone smell that clung to the zulkir's person. "Fine. Let's say it's all true. Springhill isn't really dead. He's running around up in the Citadel wearing Szass Tam's face, and he intends to perform this 'Great Work' himself. That means we need to go kill him and make it stick this time."

The big man sneered at Szass Tam. "But it doesn't mean we need you. We came here prepared to butcher the master, so I'm sure we can handle the apprentice."

Szass Tam smiled. "You'd think so, wouldn't you? But ask yourselves this: Suppose you meant to perform a lengthy ritual that every entity in the cosmos would want to stop if it understood what you were attempting. What would you do to keep others from interfering in your work?"

Laurzoril narrowed his eyes and cocked his head. It made him look even more like a priggish scholar. "I'd do my conjuring in some hidden sanctuary with potent defenses to fend off anyone who found me despite the concealment."

"Exactly," the necromancer said. "Malark's on the roof of the Citadel, except not really. He's in an artificial worldlet, a Chaos realm, that I created. He's attuned himself to the place and is more or less its god, so my menagerie of guardians will obey him."

"Hang on," said Aoth. "You're telling us that Malark has *already gone* into this stronghold?"

"By my estimation—it's difficult to judge the passage of time when you're sitting alone in a crypt—he entered and started the Unmaking a couple of days ago. Luckily for us, the ritual takes considerable time. But I imagine the first wave of annihilation will race forth in the not-too-distant future."

"It's all nonsense," Bareris insisted.

"None of us," said Szass Tam, "is quite the diviner Yaphyll was. But if you exercise your mystical faculties, you may detect a profound disruption building."

The zulkirs exchanged glances. Then Lauzoril and Nevron murmured charms. Their eyes became unfocused and their features slack as they gazed at something beyond physical reality. Meanwhile, Mirror breathed a prayer, evidently asking his god to grant him a glimpse of the unseen.

Then the ghost cried out as he had never done even when some undead horror was clawing him to tatters of ectoplasm. His murky form smudged beyond recognition.

"What did you see?" asked Aoth.

"Something fouler than I've ever seen before," Mirror answered. "Something truly unholy. I understand now what drove Fastrin mad. Why he was willing to slaughter us all to keep that . . . force from ever coming into existence."

Szass Tam sighed. "I meant to create paradise. Perfection. But now that Malark's perverting the purpose of the magic, I won't dispute your assessment. Now there's nothing to do but stop him."

Lallara glowered at Szass Tam. "Go ahead and tell us how to free you," she said. "It will save time later if we actually decide to do it."

"No!" exploded Bareris. "He's manipulating you! Drawing you deeper with every word!"

"Of course he is," Lauzoril said, blinking. "But unfortunately, that doesn't mean there's no validity to what he says."

"Which is that you'll never reach Malark without my aid," Szass Tam said. "Not in time."

Aoth looked at the figure under the gleaming pyramid. "Tell us how to transport ourselves to this 'Chaos realm.' What to expect and the passwords that will get us past whatever guardians there are. Afterward, we'll take it into account that you helped us."

Szass Tam laughed. "Of course you will! We zulkirs were always known for leniency and forgiveness."

Aoth scowled. "I'm not a damn zulkir."

"And you're not capable of keeping four of them from dealing with me however they desire, not even with the ghost and the griffon to help you."

"Curse it, if the eastern lands die, you die with them."

"Is that all you think will happen? You're mistaken, but never mind. The only real way to settle the question is to let the experiment proceed, and we all agree we'd rather not. Yet even so, I won't surrender my secrets."

"Because if you're going to die, you don't care what happens to anyone else."

The lich shrugged his narrow shoulders. "Believe what you like. But the fact of the matter is, there's no point in telling you anything if you're going to leave me in the Seat. Because you'll still fail. You need my knowledge *and* my power."

Aoth turned to Lauzoril. "Can you make him talk?"

"No," the zulkir replied. "Only the first rune is in place. It binds him to Thakorsil's Seat, but it would take all nine to divest him of his free will. In addition to which—"

"If you tell me no," said Aoth, "then I believe it. So I say we free him."

"I agree," Lallara said.

"Much to my disgust," said Nevron, "so do I."

"And I," Samas said.

Bareris raised his sword. "I'll kill the first person who tries."

Nevron snorted. "This situation grows more farcical by the moment." He swept his left hand through the start of a mystic pass, and the sapphire ring on his middle finger glowed.

Aoth grabbed Nevron by the wrist and yanked his arm, spoiling the gesture before it could unleash the demon or devil that would otherwise have sprung forth to attack Bareris. Plainly astonished that his former underling would dare, the zulkir gaped at him.

"Just wait, curse it." Aoth let go of Nevron and came closer to Bareris. He lowered his voice when he spoke again: "You can't do this. They'll only kill you if you try."

"The dream vestige already killed me."

"Don't play word games."

Mirror came to stand beside Aoth. "I understand how you feel," the phantom said. "But thousands of lives are at stake. Maybe even the life of the whole world, just as Szass Tam says."

I don't care, Bareris thought. But something kept him from proclaiming it aloud.

"You know this won't be the end of it," said Aoth. "We'll fight the lich before we're through."

"You *don't* know that." said Bareris, "and you don't know how it will come out even if we do. Right now, he's helpless. Right now . . ."

He saw that nothing he could say would sway them. That, much as it would grieve them, they would even fight him if he forced the issue.

Fine. Better to slay them or to perish at their hands than to do anything to aid the monster responsible for Tammith's destruction or to stand idle while anyone else aided him. No matter what was at stake.

Yet he knew that if Tammith were here, alive and uncorrupted by vampirism, that wasn't what she'd say. Knew too that Aoth and Mirror had been his friends for a hundred years, even when bitterness and undeath denied him the capacity to respond in kind. He pictured the young Bareris he'd conjured up to fight the vasuthant, regarding him with a kind of reproach in his eyes, and something tipped inside his mind.

He lowered his sword and stepped from between Szass Tam and the zulkirs to signal that the latter could do as they saw fit.

"Thank you for seeing reason," said the lich, and the remark jabbed Bareris like a taunt. "Now, this is the incantation to erase the sigil . . ."

As Szass Tam instructed the other archmages, Bareris fantasized that as soon as the crystal pyramid blinked out of existence, he'd rush forward and strike so quickly that neither the lich nor anyone else would have time to react. His limbs quivered, and he could virtually feel his legs sprinting, his arm swinging his sword.

He also prayed that everything the regent had said was a lie, just as he himself had maintained. That Szass Tam would leap from the Seat, laugh at their gullibility, and lash out at them, and they'd have no choice but to fight him after all.

But when the construct of solidified energy faded, Bareris didn't spring forward. And when Szass Tam rose, he didn't summon any wraiths or hurl blasts of shadow at his liberators.

He simply stretched and said, "Thank you. Shall we be on our way?"

chapter fourteen

19 Kythorn, The Year of the Dark Circle (1478 DR)

Jhesrhi looked at the several dozen assembled mages, most of them robed in scarlet, then glanced down at Khouryn.

"Ready?" asked the dwarf.

No, she thought. She was confident of her ability to cast spells, but leadership was a different matter. Most people didn't even enjoy her company, let alone look to her for guidance. True, she managed to direct her assistants in the Brotherhood, but there were only a couple of them, and they'd joined the company knowing and accepting that she was in charge. The Red Wizards weren't part of the same chain of command. They were strangers, and notoriously arrogant strangers at that.

She shifted her grip on her staff. "Yes."

Khouryn evidently didn't like something he detected in her expression or tone, for he frowned through his bushy mustache and beard. "They're used to taking orders from the zulkirs. Now, whether they realize it or not, they're looking for somebody else to order them around, and who better than you?"

"Someone dressed in red?"

"No, because while they have some experience of war, it isn't their trade but yours. Show them you believe that matters, and they will too, even if they don't like to admit it."

She took a breath. "All right."

He flashed her a grin. "Good! Then I'll leave you to it. I have to see to the folk who don't fling fire and frost around." By that, she knew, he meant that now that both Aoth and the zulkirs were gone, he intended to shuffle the battle lines. The least reliable or ably led of the archmages' troops would stand with seasoned sellswords to steady them if need be, and also stand in less critical positions. Fortunately, the past several tendays had given him time to assess which portions of the allied army were weak, and he'd done it just as automatically as he kept track of everything else on campaign.

His mail shirt rustling, he turned and tramped away. She walked toward the waiting wizards. "Sorry to keep you waiting," she said. "But Khouryn needed to speak to me."

"What I want to know," said a Red Wizard, "is why we need to speak to you." The dagger embroidered on his cloak indicated that he was one of Lauzoril's subordinates. "Do you think it's your place to command us?"

"Someone has to lead," she replied, "if we're to cast our spells to their best effect."

"But why you?" he demanded.

She gave them Khouryn's argument. "Because I spend the better part of every year at war, and our leader needs the wisdom that only comes from such experience."

A sharp-featured woman, the collar of her blood-colored cape bearing the chain-and-manacle patch that was one of Nevron's emblems, pushed to the front of the crowd. "Every Red Wizard learns how to fight," she said.

That set them all clamoring in agreement. Jhesrhi winced at the vehemence of their rejection.

It made her want to back down, especially since she had no particular desire to command them anyway. But she'd promised Khouryn, and even more important, despite herself, she suspected he was right: she likely was the best person for the job.

So she sought for a way to maintain her composure and inner calm, and as a means to that end, observed how very alike the Red Wizards were with their hairless heads, pasty Mulan faces, and voluminous scarlet garments flapping around on their lanky arms and legs. In fact, they reminded her of a flock of agitated flamingos.

Amused by the comparison, she let them squawk, and during the course of it, an idea came to her. She bowed her head and raised a hand as if in surrender, and, expecting words as submissive as her posture, the Red Wizards gradually fell silent.

She didn't disappoint them. "All right," she said. "I can't lead if you won't follow. But we all know *someone* must command. So who among you volunteers?"

Aoth had told her Red Wizards were ambitious, and as she'd hoped, nine of them spoke up and stepped forward as one. They kept right on talking at the same time too, louder and louder until they were shouting, and their supporters were yelling along with them.

This time, Jhesrhi wasn't the focus of the rancor, and so she had to resort to stronger measures to recapture everyone's attention. She tapped her toe, and the ground beneath her amplified that tiny bump into a jolt that sent the others staggering like vermillion insects crawling on a drumhead. A couple of wizards fell on their rumps.

"Sorry," she said, making no effort to sound sincere. "But maybe now you see the problem with one of you taking charge. None of you senior Red Wizards will allow one of your peers to claim the role. You're afraid he'll parlay it into some sort of permanent ascendancy. But with me, you don't have that problem. I'm not a member of your hierarchy or even a citizen of the Wizard's Reach. I'm just a sellsword, and when the zulkirs' contract with Captain Fezim expires, I'll vanish down the road."

"You know," said a man in the back of the crowd, "Nevron does seem to think well of her. I mean, to the extent that he thinks well of anyone."

"She's got power," said another wizard. "I've seen it before, and she just demonstrated it again. And we can't take all day arguing and politicking. We have to make a choice before Szass Tam's troops show up."

"That," said Jhesrhi, "is the most sensible thing anyone's said so far. So: let me be your leader for this one battle or at least until the zulkirs and Captain Fezim return."

The assembled mages stood silent for a moment. Then the one who'd spoken first glowered at her and said, "If that's the limit of your authority, then I can tolerate it."

"And I," said someone else. The rest either grumbled their assent or at least raised no further protest.

"Thank you for your trust," Jhesrhi said. "Now, we don't have a lot of time, so let's begin. As you all know, our army took a beating seizing the Dread Ring. The army of Anhaurz is fresh, and there are a lot of them. Still, we have one important advantage: we have four archmages on our side."

Her audience looked at her in puzzlement. The sharp-featured woman in service to Nevron said, "No, we don't. As I understand it, they've abandoned us to go fight Szass Tam himself in the high mountains."

Jhesrhi smiled. "Yes, but the soldiers from Anhaurz don't know that. Apparently their autharch has no qualms about facing the likes of Lallara and Samas Kul, but I doubt that everyone who follows him is equally happy about the prospect.

"So we wizards," she continued, "are going to do everything we can to bolster the enemy's belief that the zulkirs are here and fighting to devastating effect, in the hope that it will shake their resolve. We'll accomplish that in two ways. First, coordinating our efforts, we'll strike as hard and cunningly as we can. Second, we'll employ illusion to give our foes an occasional glimpse of the archmages. I've always heard that some Thayans—in exile or otherwise—are clever at phantasms. If you're one of them, speak up."

For a heartbeat, no one did. Then an older man, also wearing Lauzoril's knife insignia, raised his hand with a seeming diffidence unexpected in a Red Wizard. "Mythrellan was the last truly great illusionist. Szass Tam killed her during the War of the Zulkirs, and the order she led dissolved not long after the Spellplague. Still, some of us have learned as many of its secrets as we could."

"Then I'm sure you can handle the job," Jhesrhi said. "So that's the general idea. Obviously, we need to make more detailed plans, and luckily, we do have a little time. The necromancers and their creatures won't attack before nightfall. But that doesn't mean *we* have to wait. Before we do anything else, I'd like to give the enemy a small taste of what we—excuse me, the great and terrible *zulkirs*—mean to do to them when the fight truly begins. A little something to think about as they march the last half mile to the battlefield."

•• •• •• •• •• •• •• •• •• •• •• •• •• ••

Aoth supposed it had been inevitable that Szass Tam would cause a stir when he emerged from the catacombs with his erstwhile enemies striding along behind him. It seemed unlikely that any of the lich's retainers had ever actually seen a member of that motley band before, but anyone who'd heard tales of gross, waddling Samas Kul in his jeweled robes and burly, sneering Nevron with his tattooed demon faces probably recognized them. From that, it would be easy enough to guess the identities of Lauzoril and Lallara, while Bareris, Mirror, Jet, and Aoth himself looked sufficiently distinctive to attract notice whether an observer knew them or not.

Still, curious as people plainly were, they were even more deferential and scrambled to clear a path for their master. So the strange procession climbed up through the Citadel quickly, with whispered speculation murmuring in its wake.

"I could have shifted—"

Startled, Aoth jerked his head around. An instant ago, or so it seemed to him, Szass Tam had been walking at the front of the parade. Now, somehow, the lich was beside him.

"—us all to the top of the keep," Szass Tam continued, "but my sense is that a *little* more time won't matter one way or the other, and walking gives you and me a chance to talk." He smiled. "It's also the only chance you'll ever have to watch Samas climb a flight of stairs. Not that it's a pleasant spectacle, especially from the back."

Aoth looked around. None of his allies appeared to notice that Szass Tam was trying to engage him in conversation. Not even Jet, despite their mental link.

"I made what's happening seem inconsequential." The necromancer looked at his left hand. The rings vanished from his shriveled fingers, and others appeared a moment later. Evidently he was arming himself for battle. "The enchantment would fail if I tried to strike someone dead or attempted some other violent action, but it should enable us to have a private chat."

Aoth took a breath. "Frankly, Your Omnipotence, I can't imagine what you think we have to 'chat' about. You want to kill *everyone,* including me. At the moment, circumstances may require us to fight on the same side, but that doesn't mean I've forgotten."

Szass Tam sighed, and Aoth smelled a hint of old decay on the lich's breath. "Plainly, Captain, something prolonged your life. Otherwise, you wouldn't be here."

"The blue fire. Turns out it did more than just sharpen my eyes."

"Ah. Well, if you live as long as Malark and I have, you may come to see what a shabby, unsatisfactory place the world truly is." Szass Tam summoned a silver wand into his hand, considered it, and made it disappear again. "Nothing here is worth preserving, and that includes your current existence and mine. They're shot through with misery, and they're going to end in a little while regardless. Would you scruple to demolish a wretched hovel if you could erect a palace where it stood?"

Aoth snorted. "You can talk all you want about creating a better world, but to me, it looks like what you really crave is to be a god."

"Well, the two goals weren't mutually exclusive." Bracers made of intricately carved bone shimmered into existence on Szass Tam's wrists. "Sadly, however, they have both become unattainable."

"How so?"

"You're a warmage, but I'm sure you know enough about other forms of sorcery to grasp the principle that one must perform great rituals on prepared and purified ground. And that if the magic fails, the wizard must rededicate the circle before trying again."

"Right. I do know that."

"Well, the Unmaking is more powerful by many orders of magnitude than any other ceremony ever conceived, and thus its requirements are even more stringent. If you begin it and something stops you from finishing—as we intend to stop Malark—then no one can ever perform it in that place. It's not possible to dedicate the site a second time."

Aoth studied the lich through narrowed eyes. "And the 'site' is

Thay itself? Because the circle defined by the Dread Rings takes in most of the realm?"

Szass Tam inclined his head. "Exactly. So you see, you no longer have to worry about me wiping you and the rest of the East from existence, and you may want to reconsider your allegiance."

Aoth opened his mouth to scorn the suggestion. But then something made him ask, "Why?" instead.

"Isn't it obvious? You deserted from the council's army and took your griffon riders with you. You were actually going to attack the Wizard's Reach at Aglarond's behest until word of my intentions persuaded you to change your plans. You then made common cause with the zulkirs and found you had to demand they treat you as an equal to have any hope of succeeding at your own objectives."

The regent replaced his blackwood staff with one that looked made of the same insubstantial shadowstuff as Mirror. Unlike the solid staff, it didn't tap or thump when the butt came in contact with the floor. "They won't stand for such 'treason' and 'insolence,' Captain. They wouldn't stand for the tenth part of it. They mean to kill you when this is over. If you ever learned to know them at all—or simply caught the look in Nevron's eyes when you dared lay hands on him—you must realize I'm speaking the truth."

From the start, Aoth had feared the zulkirs would ultimately turn on him, but he had seen no choice but to ally with them even so. "Whereas you, on the other hand, were never one to hold a grudge."

Szass Tam chuckled. "You have me there. I've taken my share of revenge. It's satisfying and one of the means by which a person gains and holds power. Yet I think you have a sense that I'm not so petty as these others. I can forgive when it serves my purposes and when a foe has won my respect. Malark is a case in point. He balked me for ten years before switching sides, and I could have punished him after I finally took southern Thay. Instead, I gave him my friendship and raised him high."

"I don't want to be a lord in Thay. I'm happy leading the Brotherhood of the Griffon."

"Then heed me now. I overheard what you whispered to Anskuld, and you're right. Assuming we all survive our clash with Malark, the council will then strike to destroy me. Stand with me, and I'll see to it that you return to your sellswords safely, with enough gold to make every one of them rich. Side with Nevron and the others, and I guarantee that even if I don't kill you, one of them eventually will."

.. ..

The wind blew out of the east, which meant it was blowing straight in the faces of the advancing soldiers. At first, it was only an annoyance, but it gained strength by the moment and in so doing, picked up stinging, blinding, choking dust.

That last proved magic had raised the gale, not that Chumed Shapret had doubted it before. Generally speaking, Thay was a dry country, but the past few tendays had seen a fair amount of rain. The ground was too muddy for even a powerful wind to strip away so much soil.

A seasoned campaigner, Chumed had long ago learned to carry a kerchief in his saddlebag for situations such as this. He knotted it around the lower half of his face, wished he had a way to keep flying grit out of his eyes as well, turned his destrier, and cantered in search of So-Kehur.

Scuttling along in the vanguard in the form of a huge steel scorpion, the autharch wasn't difficult to locate, even with the streaming brown haze in the air. "Master!" Chumed called.

So-Kehur turned to regard him with the opalescent eyes set in his mask of a face and with others that waved around on tendrils. Chumed suppressed a grimace of distaste. He never liked it when the autharch donned a body with features intended to suggest the essential humanity of what was inside. He suspected that in truth, the grotesque circumstances of So-Kehur's existence had long ago altered him into a being as alien as any devil or ghoul.

"What is it?" So-Kehur asked.

"The enemy raised this wind," Chumed answered.

"Well, obviously. But don't worry. They can't keep it up for long. Especially since I have our own wizards working to quell it."

"That's good to hear. But until they succeed, perhaps we ought to hold our position."

The metal mask didn't change expression, but Chumed could feel his master's displeasure gather like the threat of a storm in the air. Because of his psychic abilities, So-Kehur's emotions were often directly perceptible to others. "That's a bad idea," the autharch said. "The invaders may be trying to slow us down so they can slip away."

"With all respect, Milord, they have nowhere to go. Their backs are to the Lapendrar. The river's high, and they have no boats."

"But if we give them time, they might still find a way to cross. Remember, their leaders are zulkirs, with all the power that implies."

Chumed had by no means forgotten, but to him the fact suggested a need for caution, not for haste. Unfortunately, So-Kehur's ambition to prove himself a master general was coloring his judgment.

That meant it would likely be pointless to argue any further. So-Kehur might even sear Chumed's mind with a burst of psychic fire if he tried. So he simply bowed his head and said, "As you command."

The army trudged onward. The wind howled. Horses neighed in protest, soldiers coughed and complained, and their sergeants and officers bellowed at them to keep moving. When the first screams sounded, Chumed wasn't sure he'd actually heard them over the general din.

The next moment resolved his uncertainty.

Hitherto concealed by the blowing dust and the blur of tears in everyone's eyes, demons abruptly scuttled into view. Big as ogres, armored in chitin and spikes and possessed of enormous pincers, they looked vaguely like huge crabs, and they tore into the front ranks of the marching columns with appalling speed. Their claws nipped men in two. Their horns slashed and pierced.

Chumed was a soldier, not a wizard, but he'd read a book or two concerning demons in the hope of knowing what he was facing when an enemy mage conjured entities like these onto the battlefield. Thus, he recognized the attacking brutes as nashrou. "You can kill them!" he shouted. "Strike for the gaps in their armor!"

He then cast about and saw that it didn't look as though anyone had heard him. Everything was too noisy and confused.

He cursed. He was no more eager to venture within reach of one of the demons than any of the wretches they were currently tearing apart, but apparently someone needed to demonstrate how to kill them, and sooner rather than later if he hoped to avert a panic.

Off to his right, a nashrou fought a company of blood orcs. The soldiers were game. Roaring their deafening battle cries, they stood their ground and hacked savagely but to no avail. The demon was still ripping them apart.

Chumed couched his lance and spurred his mount into a charge. His steed was a pure-blood horse, not one of the unnatural hybrids many Thayan warriors preferred, but it raced at their hideous target without hesitation.

He wondered if he'd have to knock orcs aside or even trample them to reach the nashrou, but they sensed him coming and scrambled out of his way. Unfortunately, the crab-thing noticed him too, and its four legs scurrying, rushed to meet him. A set of pincers spread wide, then shot forward.

His lance, however, was a little longer than the nashrou's limb. It struck first, and punched deep into the fissure between two plates of chitin.

The claw plunged down an instant later. He shifted his shield to block, and the pincers snapped shut on the edges. The metal groaned and buckled.

But it didn't crumple completely, because at that point, the nashrou's legs gave way, and it fell. Its grip on the shield nearly yanked Chumed out of the saddle, but then the armor jerked free.

Chumed studied the motionless creature, trying to make sure it truly was dead. It looked like it to him, and judging from the cacophonous cheers of the surviving orcs, they thought so too.

He tried to pull his lance out of the carcass, but it was stuck fast. He let go of the butt and raised his hand to quiet the orcs. "Strike for the cracks in the shell!" he told them.

They did and killed another nashrou. Other people had evidently figured out how to do it too, for the crab-things were dropping one by one. Crawling and clinging, nearly burying it beneath their bodies, zombies swarmed on one of the demons like ants and stabbed it repeatedly with their blades. A Red Wizard blasted another apart with a single stroke of lightning.

It wasn't too bad, Chumed decided. They hadn't lost too many men, and only a few legionnaires had run. Winning this first skirmish might actually bolster everyone's confidence. And at least the damn wind was dying down.

Then cries rang out *behind* him.

Several dark, horned giants with batlike wings—devils called malebranches—were diving down out of the sky. Everyone had been too intent on the nashrou to see them coming.

They thumped down among the enclosed wagons. All those conveyances had guards, but they floundered back in terror. The malebranches jabbed at the wagons with their iron tridents, breaking them open as if they were made of eggshells.

It was a typical gray Thayan afternoon, the sky veiled with clouds, smoke, and ash. But enough sunlight filtered down to burn the entities riding in the wagons. One of the carriages rocked back and forth as the thing inside screamed and thrashed in its final agonies.

As soon as a malebranche finished with one wagon, it turned its attention to another. From Chumed's vantage point, it looked as if they had smashed open ten or twelve before the wizards finally took effective action. Then, one by one, the devils froze in place and vanished as magic hurled them back to their native plane of existence.

Chumed rode toward the spot where So-Kehur's steel form gleamed above the heads of his followers. When he got close, he saw that the autharch stood over the corpse of a nashrou like a self-satisfied hunter preening over the body of his kill. He'd evidently played an active part in the fighting, and not just with his sorcery and psychic talents. Spatters of ichor mottled his claws and stinger.

"Well," said So-Kehur, "that went well enough."

"I suppose you could say that," Chumed answered. "We did deal with the demons as efficiently as we had any right to expect. Considering that the dust kept us from seeing them until they were already on top of us."

Chumed regretted the words as soon as they left his mouth. But if So-Kehur even heard the implied criticism, combat had left him too exhilarated to make an issue of it. "How long to get the columns moving again?" the autharch asked.

"Not too long. The healers have to tend the wounded, and everyone needs a chance to catch his breath."

"Well, take care of it all as quickly as you can. I want to reach the battlefield by nightfall."

I don't, Chumed thought. Not especially.

It wasn't that he was afraid. He was no coward, and the army they were about to engage had all but crippled itself taking the huge fortress in the northern part of the tharch. But, So-Kehur's bloodlust aside, he still didn't see any compelling reason for this fight, and what was even worse was that the enemy had just demonstrated they could outthink the autharch. Chumed recognized it even if his master didn't.

•• •• •• •• •• •• •• •• •• •• •• •• •• •• ••

The round, flat roof of the keep provided a view of the city surrounding the Citadel and the mountains beyond. Columns of smoke rose from some of the latter, and a cold wind blew them toward the bloody sunset.

Bareris looked for some indication that Szass Tam had cast potent enchantments on this place. He didn't see any. But both Aoth and Mirror faltered when they came up the stairs. Apparently the warmage's spellscarred eyes could discern the truth, and the ghost perceived the same "unholy" malignancy to which he'd reacted before.

Szass Tam walked to the center of the rooftop, turned, and gave them all a smile that jabbed a fresh spasm of loathing into Bareris's guts. He stifled the feeling as best he could.

"Well, here we are," said the lich. "Nothing remains but to unlock the door. So if you want to enhance your defenses or anything like that, now's the time."

"So it really is going to be just us," said Samas Kul, his tone petulant. "Even though you have an entire army garrisoned here."

"He already explained," Lallara said. "Springhill is in control of the realm beyond the gate. Since he created the place, Szass

Tam can take us through even so, but we're about the limit. Any more and we'd simply lose people, much as we lost them translating ourselves into the dungeons. Now, if we could be certain of losing you—"

"I understand!" the obese transmuter snapped. "I'm just amazed that a would-be god can't do a little better."

"Perhaps the years have sapped my powers," Szass Tam said. "I suspect that the next little while will give you ample opportunity to judge."

"Before we go in," said Aoth, his fingers scratching amid the feathers on Jet's neck, "I need to be clear on one thing. Is it enough to interrupt Malark? If we knock the breath out of him in the middle of an incantation, will that stop the Unmaking?"

"Unfortunately, no," Szass Tam replied. "The ceremony involves a number of conditions and limitations, but that isn't one of them. He can pause, deal with an interruption, and then pick up where he left off."

"So we have to kill him," Nevron growled. "Fine. We all *want* to kill him. Let's get on with it."

"As you wish," Szass Tam said. He turned his back on them; Bareris shivered and clamped down on the urge to strike while the lich looked vulnerable.

Szass Tam flourished his shadowy staff and whispered words that somehow made Bareris angrier still, that seemed to feed the hate and bitterness inside him like dry wood feeding a fire. Then a square of utter blackness, big as the entry to a rich man's house, painted itself on the air.

Bareris assumed that they'd walk into it. Instead, it rushed forward, expanding as it came, first swallowing Szass Tam and then himself. And all the others too, presumably, although at that instant, he lost sight of them. He seemed to tumble through freezing darkness, then jolt down on his feet. A new world oozed into view.

It was a place of towering crags and twisting canyons, without even a sprig of brush or speck of fungus growing anywhere on the dry earth and stone. Only a handful of faint stars gleamed in the black, moonless sky.

He and his companions had arrived in one of the gorges. The others pivoted, peering around. "I assumed," Lauzoril said, "that you'd shift us into position to attack Springhill immediately."

"It wasn't possible," Szass Tam said. "He has layers of protection. I couldn't pierce them all with a single spell."

"But now that we're here?" Samas asked.

"I hope so." Turning, the lich studied the peaks and cliffs, then chuckled.

"What?" Nevron spat.

"Malark's altered the geography," Szass Tam said. "Either to disorient me if I escaped Thakorsil's Seat and came after him or simply because he finds the new skyline more conducive to focusing his thoughts."

Either way, Bareris didn't like hearing that their foe had shifted mountains like a child playing with blocks. Szass Tam had warned that Malark was a god in this realm, and that didn't seem like hyperbole anymore.

"So I take it we have to find him," Lallara said. "I can cast a divination."

"We might as well try the obvious way first," said Aoth. Jet shook out his wings, and the warmage swung himself into the saddle.

"Be careful," Szass Tam said. "I put guardians in the sky as well as on the ground."

"I under—" Aoth began, and then Jet leaped, lashed his wings, and carried the warmage aloft. Apparently, after all the time he'd spent underground, the griffon was eager to take to the sky, even the sky of a dismal place like this. Seemingly surprised by the abrupt departure, Mirror rose into the air a moment later.

Bareris watched as they soared high overhead. If something attacked them up there, he'd have a difficult time helping them.

But nothing did, and after a time, they swooped back down to earth. "Got him," Aoth said. "He's conjuring on a flat mountaintop about a mile in that direction." He pointed with his spear.

"Did he notice you?" Lallara asked.

"I didn't see any indication of it."

"Does he have a pack of guardians clustered around him?" Samas asked.

"I didn't see those, either."

"Still," said Szass Tam, "they're there. I guarantee it."

"So we hit fast and hard and kill their master before they can react," Nevron said, "just as I've been advising all along." He glowered at Szass Tam. "Captain Fezim has given you your bearings. Now can you translate us to our quarry?"

"Let's find out." The lich slipped his withered fingers into one of his many pockets, no doubt to remove a talisman or spell trigger. Then skeletal figures stalked out of the darkness ahead.

Each was half again as tall as a man, with strips of ragged, desiccated flesh dangling from its frame. Their heads were hairless, and their ears, pointed. Tiny figures writhed inside their ribs like anguished prisoners jammed behind the bars of a cage.

One of the zulkirs' surviving soldiers happened to be closest to the oncoming horrors. He wailed and raised his sword and shield to fend them off. The creature in the lead pounced. The legionnaire's blade bit into its torso, but it didn't seem to notice. It grabbed him in its jagged talons, and the man screamed, convulsed, then dangled limp as string. A new prisoner—the soldier's soul, evidently—squirmed into existence behind the skeletal entity's ribs. The creature dropped the corpse and kept coming.

"They're devourers!" Szass Tam called. Perhaps the term meant something to the zulkirs, but Bareris had never heard it before.

But if he had to fight in ignorance, so be it. He shouted, and the thunderous bellow ripped flesh from the lead devourer's frame and broke a number of its bones, even as the cry echoed down the gorge and brought pebbles showering from overhead.

Its legs shattered, the devourer fell but crawled onward. Mirror stepped up beside Bareris, brandished his sword, and light flared from the blade. The crawling devourer and the one behind it burned away to nothing in an instant.

It was encouraging to see that the things could perish, and it was good, too, that they had to come down the relatively narrow passage to reach their intended victims. It meant they couldn't spread out and surround them, and that spells like thunderbolts, blasts of fire, and Bareris's own battle cries generally hammered more than one at a time.

Offsetting that advantage, however, was the devourers' resilience and their numbers. New ones kept streaming down the defile like a rushing river, the husks of their predecessors crunching and cracking beneath their feet.

Samas pointed his quicksilver wand and turned a devourer to gold. It toppled forward. Someone else felled one of the creatures with darts of scarlet light. His tone cold and demanding, Szass Tam rattled off an incantation. It must have returned two of the devourers to his control, because they halted abruptly, turned, and lashed out at their fellows.

Bareris saw that it wasn't enough. In another moment, unless the warriors in their band prevented it, the devourers would overrun everyone, zulkirs included. And even archmages would have trouble conjuring with such creatures ripping at them.

"Wall!" Bareris yelled, and then heard Aoth and Mirror yelling the same thing. Though white-faced with fear, the last surviving bodyguard heeded the call, and Nevron sent a miscellany of demons and devils to answer it too. The one that came to stand on Bareris's right was a barbed devil, a somewhat manlike figure with a lashing tail, its body covered with spines and quills.

They just had time to form their line, and then the devourers crashed into it. Bareris cut, parried, and sang a spell to make himself a blur. The point of his spear ablaze with blue light like the fire in his eyes, Aoth thrust and thrust and thrust again. Fighting alongside him, Jet reared, slashed with his talons, and screeched when he tore off a devourer's head.

Meanwhile, flares of multicolored light and ragged blasts of shadow crackled over the defenders' heads to sear and wither the massed devourers. Bareris assumed that one or more of the wizards must have floated into the air—or simply clambered onto a rock—to evoke such magic without fear of hitting his allies. He couldn't actually look around to verify his guess, because he didn't dare take his eyes off the creatures in front of him.

A devourer's black, sunken eyes glared down at him, and for a moment, he couldn't remember where he was, what the creature was, or how he was supposed to react to it. But training made him sing the next note of his battle anthem, and his magic shattered his confusion. He cut into the devourer's torso, and its legs buckled.

"I see the end of them!" Samas called. Bareris felt a surge of renewed determination, then noticed a shiver in the ground beneath his feet.

A moment after that, someone behind him cried out, something inhuman roared, and stone rumbled and crashed. The earth heaved, and he almost lost his balance.

Now he truly wanted to turn and see what was happening at his back. His nerves sang with the fear that if he didn't, something looming there would strike him down. But it would still be suicidal to look away from the last devourers.

He hacked the leg out from under one such brute, then gutted it when it dropped. A second scrambled over the corpse of its fellow and grabbed him by the shoulder. He felt a pull through the point of contact; the devourer was leeching his spirit from his body.

He cut the devourer with all his waning strength. His sword ruined an eye and buried itself in the creature's skull, but the incorporeal pull didn't abate. He tried to yank his sword free, and it wouldn't come out of the wound.

He sang a charge of malice and loathing into his eyes, then discharged it by glaring at the devourer. The creature stiffened in pain and fumbled its grip on his shoulder. The pull abated, and he felt stronger. He jerked his blade free and drove the point into the devourer's heart, or at least the spot where a human carried such an organ. The vile thing fell.

At last, nothing else was running to attack him. Not from the front, anyway. He spun around, then faltered.

His first impression was of a corpse swarming with maggots. But in this case, the body was the ground itself and the cliffs rising on each side of the gorge, while the maggots were creatures that, except for the unrelieved blackness of their bodies, resembled the snakelike behemoths called purple worms.

It had been more than ninety years since Bareris had seen one of these monstrosities, but that occasion had been a slaughter he'd never forget. The worms were nightcrawlers. Undead fearsome enough to give even an archmage pause.

Two of the worms bursting from the ground spread their jaws wide and spewed blasts of frost. Lallara raised her staff and cried a word of forbiddance, and the pale jets split like a river streaming around a rock, spattering the sides of the cliffs instead of the people on the ground.

At the same instant, a nightcrawler that had burrowed out of a rocky wall struck straight down at her. It was huge enough to swallow her whole, and she didn't even seem to notice the threat. But Samas screamed—no incantation to it, just a noise of pure desperation and resolve—and pointed his wand at the creature's plunging head. The lead section of the nightcrawler dissolved in a puff of smoke. The rest of it convulsed, the length that still protruded from the burrow slamming repeatedly against the cliff.

Lauzoril produced illusory duplicates of himself to confuse his foes, then snapped his fingers to strike a spark that expanded into a giant made of flame. Nevron brandished his staff, and spiders fell from the ends of his voluminous sleeves. When they touched the ground, they too grew to enormous size, then scuttled to attack the nightcrawlers, spitting webs to bind them, then crawling on their ink black bodies and biting.

Szass Tam chanted in the same imperious fashion as before, and one of the nightcrawlers swiveled its head, struck, and seized a fellow worm in its jaws. Snapping and gnawing, twisting around one another, the creatures thrashed in a struggle that threatened to crush anyone within reach and sent new shocks jolting through the ground.

Bareris sang a song that made the frenzy before him appear to slow, although in reality, his own perceptions and reactions had accelerated. Then he ran at a nightcrawler that had tunneled up out of the canyon floor. The thing was twisting in Aoth's direction. The warmage was still on the ground, but at some point during the last few moments, he'd climbed onto Jet's back.

Bareris drew breath to batter the nightcrawler with a war cry, then glimpsed motion from the corner of his eye. He pivoted; a leftover devourer was lunging at him. He sidestepped its raking claws, let it blunder past, then cut at its spine. The creature toppled.

Bareris spun back around. He was too late to distract the nightcrawler from attacking Aoth, but fortunately, the sellsword commander had noticed the threat. When the worm spat frost, Jet beat his wings and bounded like a grasshopper to carry his master out of the way. Aoth hurled lightning from the point of his spear, and the nightcrawler jerked at its searing touch.

Bareris charged the snakelike undead and cut at its flank. He knew it was dangerous to fight such a colossal creature close up. Without even intending it, the nightcrawler could shift its bulk on top of him and crush him. But he trusted his heightened reflexes to protect him.

For a while, they did, and he slashed a portion of the night-crawler's body into a crosshatch of oozing gashes. Then the creature swiveled its head in his direction and hissed.

Sensing danger at his back, he whirled just in time to see a dozen shadowy figures, all but invisible in the gloom that prevailed at the bottom of the gorge, flicker into existence. Their presence chilled the air, and they charged Bareris like a pack of famished wolves.

In an instant, they were all around him, scrabbling and clutching with their freezing though insubstantial hands, and he feared they might overwhelm him with sheer numbers. Then a blaze of light withered them. It spiked pain through his body as well but didn't actually seem to injure him. He nodded to Mirror—who currently resembled Samas Kul, of all people, except that he had a sword instead of a wand—to indicate as much.

Bareris pivoted back toward the nightcrawler and thrust his sword into its body. Mirror flew into the air and cut at its head. Aoth slashed chunks of it away with a conjured wheel of spinning blades. The worm screamed, and then the top half of it plummeted to the ground like a felled tree.

Bareris watched for a moment to make sure it wouldn't start moving again, then pivoted to survey the battlefield. To his surprise, it appeared to him that he and his allies were holding their own. The last remaining bodyguard was gone, and so were a number of Nevron's demons. Severed pieces of their grotesque anatomies littered the canyon floor. But, hanging like vines from the cliffs or, in their immensity, all but blocking the defile, several nightcrawlers were dead as well, while the archmages, Aoth, Jet, and Mirror all survived.

Yet Bareris had a feeling that something was wrong, and after another moment, he realized why. The earth was quaking.

No one else appeared to notice, probably because, with the gigantic nightcrawlers tunneling and heaving themselves around, it had been shaking for a while. But this was different: more constant and growing steadily more intense.

He looked skyward just in time to see the cliffs start falling.

•• •• •• •• •• •• •• •• •• •• •• •• •• ••

Aoth's fire-infected eyes abruptly saw a new murkiness in the air. Mystical power was at work, and it was something apart from all the combat magic he and his companions were evoking to destroy the nightcrawlers.

He cast about. Chunks of stone were tumbling from the canyon walls, but that was far from the worst of it. The cliffs were lurching toward one another.

He remembered Szass Tam's claim that Malark had shifted the mountains. It stood to reason that if the traitorous whoreson could do that, he could also smash them together.

Aoth looked around for Bareris and found him too. Unfortunately, the bard stood where the stones were raining down the thickest and at the epicenter of the impending collision. If Aoth tried to retrieve him, they'd both be crushed.

Even so, left to his own devices, he might have tried or at least hesitated in dismay. But, unfurling his wings, Jet raced to carry him out of the deathtrap by the shortest possible path.

Aoth looked for someone he actually might be able to save. He spotted Lallara, tottering in an effort to keep her feet. Moving with her, a disk of crimson light floated above her head. Falling stones bounced off it.

He willed Jet to change course and felt the griffon's resulting pang of annoyance as if it were his own. Neither of them truly wanted to spend an extra instant in the danger zone. But he needed Lallara. Needed all of them, truly, but she was the one within reach.

He leaned sideways and snatched the old woman to him. At once, Jet spread his wings, lashed them, leaped, and flew.

More boulders fell. A big one shattered against the hovering disk, which then winked out of existence, subjecting Aoth, Lallara, and Jet to a shower of gravel. The converging sections of wall accelerated, springing toward one another like clapping hands. Lallara gasped as she finally perceived the true magnitude of the peril.

Aoth doubted they were going to make it, then felt Jet's savage determination. The griffon put on a final burst of speed and kept it up until the passage became so narrow that he could no longer spread his wings.

But by that time, they were close enough to safety that sheer momentum threw them clear into a wider section of canyon. Aoth automatically cast about for new threats. Everything was still.

Jet glided down to the ground. Scowling, Lallara shoved at Aoth to extricate herself from their awkward embrace.

He turned to study the cloud of dust behind him and the mass of stone sealing the passage he'd just escaped. Nothing was moving in that direction, either.

•• •• •• •• •• •• •• •• •• •• •• •• •• ••

Bareris sang a song intended to shift him to safety, and a nightcrawler turned its head in his direction. Pain and dizziness stabbed through him, and he fell to his knees. The worm had attacked him with some sort of supernatural ability. After a moment, the fierce pangs diminished, but not before he fumbled the next phrase of his spell. The power he'd raised dissipated in a useless sizzle.

He floundered to his knees, took a breath raw with rock dust, and tried to focus his thoughts for another effort even though he sensed that, his charm of acceleration notwithstanding, he wouldn't have time.

Fingers squeezed his shoulder. "Allow me," Szass Tam said. Seemingly standing without effort despite the upheavals, he touched the butt of his shadow staff to the quaking ground.

He and Bareris shot down into the earth, which parted for them as if their bodies were made of dense, sharp metal. Startled, sightless, Bareris had the mad, random thought that here at last was burial, ninety years late. Then he and Szass Tam abruptly came to rest in a bending tubular tunnel. The lich had to crouch too, or he wouldn't have fit.

"This is a nightcrawler burrow," Szass Tam said. "The way the brutes were popping up around us, I knew the ground had to be riddled with them." He crooked his fingers into a mystical sign, and sheets of dark fire crawled on the walls around them, burning away soil and rock and creating more open space. He then straightened up and stepped away from Bareris.

A nightcrawler's head burst through the ceiling, showering them with dirt. It was gouged and dented, probably battered by falling boulders. Like its foes, it must have dived into the earth to remove itself from between the converging walls.

The thing plunged into view directly above Szass Tam, and for once, even he appeared startled. The enormous jaws gaped, then snapped shut around him. Because the lich had enlarged this part of the burrow, it was high enough to admit not just the nightcrawler's head but a bit of its body. As a result, Bareris saw its throat swell as it swallowed.

For a moment, he simply stared, too addled with contradictory emotions and impulses to act on any of them. Then he rose, lifted his sword, and took a stride in the creature's direction.

Its head blew apart in a flash of scarlet light. The detonation rocked him back, even as it spattered him and the walls of the burrow with filth. Smeared with slime, Szass Tam squirmed feet-first out of what little remained of the nightcrawler's mouth.

The necromancer inclined his head to Bareris. "Obviously, I didn't actually need your help. But it's good to see you have your priorities straight."

Bareris wondered how Szass Tam knew he'd been coming to his aid. "You and I will settle our score after we deal with Malark."

Szass Tam waved a shriveled hand, and the jellied filth vanished from his person. "If you insist. If you believe your devotion to a rather ordinary girl who died a century ago requires it. But it seems to me that what you truly love is your own misery. The Maiden of Pain possessed you in the moment of your despair, and you never managed to escape."

Bareris took a steadying breath. "If you want our alliance to last until we stop Malark, then don't mention Tammith or speculate about my feelings anymore."

"As you wish. Let's turn our attention to the task at hand."

"Do we still have any hope of succeeding, even after what just happened?"

"Oh, certainly. You weren't thinking you and I are the only survivors, were you? Getting caught between two masses of rock wouldn't hurt your friend Mirror. Captain Fezim scooped up Lallara and tried to carry her out of the affected area, and I suspect he succeeded. Unless they panicked—and that's unlikely—the other zulkirs were capable of saving themselves as well."

"But we're scattered now, and we've expended a lot of our power."

"The former has its advantages. We'll all take different paths to get to Malark. Even if he realizes we survived, he and his creatures will have difficulty spotting and intercepting all of us. As for your latter point, I assume that since your odd little troupe crept into the Citadel to assassinate me, the zulkirs are carrying as many arcane weapons and talismans as I am. We have plenty of tricks left, and let's not forget that our arrival goaded Malark into squandering a good deal of his own power. It's one thing to move the mountains with proper preparation. It's another to fling them around when you weren't expecting you'd have to, essentially by sheer force of will."

Bareris scowled. "You almost sound glad that his creatures attacked us."

Szass Tam shrugged. "I try to perceive the opportunities implicit in even awkward situations."

"Have you considered that, now that they've seen just how strong and well-protected Malark is, the other zulkirs may 'perceive the opportunities implicit' in being apart from one another and free to act as they please? They may try to leave this place and flee beyond the reach of the Unmaking."

"I understand why the possibility concerns you. They are supremely selfish, and no doubt you and Captain Fezim had to coax and bully them relentlessly to get them this far. But you know, they aren't cowards. Each had to perform acts of extraordinary daring to ascend to his current eminence. And consider what finally lies within their reach: Revenge on Malark and on me. Rulership of Thay. Given the stakes, this is one time they won't play it safe."

"I hope you're right."

Szass Tam smiled. "So do I. We'll see who joins us on Malark's mountaintop."

chapter fifteen

19 Kythorn, The Year of the Dark Circle (1478 DR)

The sun had set, but the enemy seemed to be waiting for the last traces of its crimson light to fade from the western sky. After that, they'd attack.

Gaedynn used the time to work his way through the patch of woods, making sure everyone was ready, joking with the men to set them at ease. He had to be more offhand when approaching the zulkirs' soldiers. He didn't want their officers to feel he was usurping their authority. But he was willing to risk their resentment to shore up the defense.

Red Wizards and Burning Braziers evoked light in the open area beyond the trees. When the battle started, the necromancers on the other side would try to drown the illumination in darkness, so their troops could advance unseen. Patches of glow would bloom and go out unpredictably as the opposing spellcasters vied for dominance.

"They're coming!" someone shouted. Off to the right, on the

clear, slightly higher ground where Khouryn's armored spearmen stood in their lines, horns blew to convey the same message.

Gaedynn had been talking to a young, nervous-looking legionnaire. He clapped the fellow on the shoulder and dashed back to the spot from which he intended to shoot. It was centrally located enough to offer some hope of keeping track of what everyone else was doing, and the mossy oak rising there was thick enough to provide decent cover.

He'd already stuck a selection of arrows in the ground. Sadly, only two of them held spells stored inside them. He'd used most of his enchanted shafts fighting to take the Dread Ring—as it turned out, what a waste!—and while the army was on the march, Jhesrhi hadn't had the leisure to make any more.

Ah, well, at least he'd found a nice supply of the more common sort of enchanted arrow cached inside the fortress. They too would slay a vampire or wraith if he shot them straight enough.

A sort of querulous rasp sounded from the hollow in the ground where Eider lay hidden. The griffon sensed the fight beginning and was eager to take part. "Patience," Gaedynn told her. "You'll get your chance."

Then he stepped from behind the oak and started loosing arrows.

Most of the charging creatures were dread warriors, a fact that Gaedynn found annoying. It generally took several ordinary arrows to dispatch one of the yellow-eyed corpses; yet even so, it would be a mistake to use enchanted shafts. He needed to save them for foes more fearsome still.

Fortunately, the priests of Kossuth aided the efforts of the archers and crossbowmen. They chanted and whirled their chains, and the rattling links burst into flame. So did many of the arrows and quarrels arcing over the field, and when they pierced the body of a dread warrior, the zombie too burned as if it were made of paper.

Impervious to fear and constrained to obedience, the living corpses kept coming no matter how many of their fellows perished. But none made it to the tree line.

Even so, a few yards to Gaedynn's left, a sellsword lay on the ground and screamed. Someone on the other side had hit him with an arrow or a spell; the gloom prevented Gaedynn from determining which. "Help that man!" he shouted, and, keeping low, a Burning Brazier scrambled in the appropriate direction.

Then another charge exploded from the dark mass of the enemy army, this one made of howling blood orcs. Gaedynn grinned because living targets died more easily. He plucked another arrow from the ground.

At one point, pure instinct prompted him to jump back behind the oak. An arrow or crossbow bolt whizzed through the space he'd just vacated. He stepped back into the open and kept loosing arrows until the last orc dropped.

More shrieks sounded from among the trees. No doubt they'd been doing so for a while, but he rarely heard such things when fighting.

He stooped and picked up the leather waterskin he'd laid between two of the oak's gnarled roots. By the time he finished swigging down his drink, the enemy ranks were opening, clearing a corridor for something to emerge. Gaedynn suspected it would be the first truly serious threat, and in another moment, he saw how right he was.

The shadowy, long-armed giants were as tall as some of the trees, so tall that it was difficult to understand why he hadn't noticed them before, towering over the soldiers and creatures around them. Their murky forms must have blended in with the dark. "Nightwalkers!" a priest of Kossuth cried.

Seeming to move without haste, but their long strides eating up the distance, the nightwalkers strode forward, and at their approach, the patches of glow illuminating the field went out. The men in the trees stood frozen, appalled, doing nothing to stop them, and that, Gaedynn suddenly realized, included himself.

A surge of self-disgust washed away his inertia. "Kill them!" he bellowed. He nocked a shaft, drew the fletchings back to his ear, and released the string.

His arrow flew, and, to his relief, so did others. But when they pierced the nightwalkers' bodies, they looked small as slivers stuck in the flesh of a man, and the undead giants kept coming as if they didn't even feel them.

The wizards and priests of the Firelord fared somewhat better. They hurled gouts of flame and dazzling light, and nightwalkers jerked and staggered. One reeled and fell with its upper body ablaze.

But the rest continued marching forward, and as they did, they struck back. The one directly in front of Gaedynn glared; he couldn't actually see the eyes in its black smudge of a face, but he could feel the malevolence of their regard. His muscles jumped and clenched, and then relaxed again. He'd been hardy—or lucky—enough to shrug off the paralyzing effect.

Others weren't so lucky. To either side of him, men grunted or made little strangled sounds as their bodies locked in position.

Another giant shook its fist. Some of the soldiers in front of it recoiled in terror, others peered around as though dazed, and a couple even turned and discharged their crossbows into one another. A third nightwalker stretched out its hand, and men doubled over, whimpering and puking.

Fortunately, a fair number of the clerics and sorcerers weathered those first attacks. Some continued to blast the giants with their magic. Others chanted to less obvious effect. Gaedynn assumed the latter were working counterspells to free the afflicted bowmen from their various curses.

For his part, he decided it was time—past time—he used the last of his special arrows. He grabbed one, kissed the point for luck, and shot it into the chest of the nightwalker in front of him.

Strips of the giant's shadowy substance peeled away, not just where the arrow had penetrated but all over its body. It staggered a step, and then its hand lashed forward as if it were throwing a rock. Gaedynn wrenched himself behind the oak. Even so, the blast of frost chilled him to the marrow; if he hadn't taken cover, it might well have stopped his heart.

Forbidding himself to falter or his cold hands to shake, he shot Jhesrhi's last arrow. Midway to the target, it exploded into fog, and when the nightwalker strode into the corrosive vapors, its flesh sizzled and liquefied. It was a tattered, smoking vestige of its former self by the time it reached the tree line.

But it was still capable of doing harm. Agony ripped through Gaedynn's chest as though something were squeezing his heart. After a moment, the worst of the pain subsided, but by that time, the nightwalker's fist was hurtling down at him.

Spinning out of the way, he dropped his longbow and grabbed the falchion he'd stowed beneath the oak. He chopped the nightwalker across the knuckles before it could lift its fist again, then kept moving.

The giant pivoted with him, and Eider leaped up from her hollow. Gaedynn would have said she couldn't fly beneath the trees—their limbs hung too low—but she lashed her wings and managed somehow, breaking branches as she came. She slammed into the nightwalker's head and clung there, biting and clawing.

The nightwalker reached for her. Gaedynn ran in and hacked at its ankle. The giant toppled, snapping more tree limbs as it fell, and Eider sprang clear of it.

It didn't look as though the nightwalker were going to get back up again, and small wonder. The griffon had torn away a big piece of its already burned and mangled head. She spat foulness out of her beak, and Gaedynn turned to see how the rest of the battle was going.

Not well. Two other nightwalkers had fallen, but the rest—half a dozen in all—were stalking among the trees. He strained to think of a way to fight them at close range with the troops at his command. Meanwhile, sensing victory, the living men and orcs in the enemy host raised a cheer.

Then demons—hopping toad-men, slithering six-armed women whose bodies turned into serpentine tails at the waist, and a variety of others—burst from the trees behind him. They charged the nightwalkers and attacked ferociously. The sellswords and the zulkirs' troops scrambled back and left them to it.

The nightwalkers ripped a number of demons apart. If not for the damage Gaedynn and his comrades had inflicted, perhaps they would have destroyed them all. But they *were* wounded, and in time, the demons dragged the last of them down.

The giant was still struggling when Nevron—or a figure that looked exactly like him—strode past Gaedynn. Illuminated by the glimmer of his defensive enchantments, the newcomer advanced beyond the tree line, sneered at So-Kehur's army, and spat.

Then, still moving without haste, as if nothing on the battlefield posed any threat to him, he turned and tramped back the way he'd come. When he reached Gaedynn again, he stopped as though he wanted to talk, stepping behind the oak in the process.

Nevron's features dissolved into those of an older-looking man with fewer tattoos and a skinnier frame. He wore Lauzoril's dagger insignia. "I deemed it best to cut that short," he said. "I could feel the necromancers studying me, probing for weaknesses. Eventually, they might have seen through my mask."

"That would have been unfortunate," Gaedynn said. "Thanks for coming to our aid."

"It was your comrade Jhesrhi who sensed the need. You should thank her too." The Red Wizard looked deeper into the trees, where other robed figures awaited him. He'd tried to create the impression that Nevron alone had unleashed the mob of demons, but in reality, it had taken a number of lesser conjurors to command them. "And my colleagues and I should get back. You may think the enemy is pushing hard here, but it's nothing compared to what the main body of our army is facing."

"Oh, I'm sure," Gaedynn said. "I was just thinking of lying down and taking a little nap."

.. ..

Lallara seemed accustomed to winged steeds, for she rode without clutching Aoth around the waist or any other sign of anxiety. Mirror, who'd found them not long after the cliffs smashed together, flew several yards to the right of Jet. The ghost was currently a glimmering shadow of the knight he'd been in life.

They all had to fly because it turned out that Malark had enchantments in place to keep anyone from shifting through space to his mountaintop. So they used other peaks to shield their approach and kept a wary eye out as they traveled. At one point, Aoth saw a pair of the huge, batlike undead called nightwings gliding in the distance, but the creatures didn't seem to notice them. He *didn't* see Bareris, Szass Tam, or any of the other zulkirs. Not along the way, and not when he and his companions set down on a ledge thirty yards below the site of the ritual.

"Try again to find the others," he said, swinging himself off Jet's back.

Lallara extracted a luminous blue crystal cube from one of her pockets, peered into it, and muttered under her breath. "Still nothing. Perhaps they really are dead. Or perhaps they warded themselves lest Springhill locate and attack them again."

"Well, we're here," Mirror said, "and our enemy is just above us. I'm willing to go up and fight him."

"Szass Tam seemed to think it would take all of us to win," Aoth replied. "And when I remember how tough Malark was a century ago in the normal world, before the bastard even learned sorcery, I can believe it."

"I see your point," said the ghost. "But on the other hand, the Unmaking is happening right now. For all we know, Malark is only moments away from the end. How long do we wait for reinforcements that might never come?"

"I don't know. Look, I'll climb up and see what's happening. Then we'll decide what to do."

"Not a bad idea, but let me go. I can be invisible and be certain I won't make any noise."

"But we can't count on you seeing everything that I'd see." Aoth grinned. "Remember, I've done a lot of scouting. You can worry about everything else that's happening in this nightmare—the gods know, I am—but trust in my ability to sneak."

"And in my ability to shield a man," Lallara quavered. Murmuring words of power, she swirled her twisted, arthritic-looking hands in circular patterns, and a cold stinging danced over Aoth's body. "With luck, that will keep even Szass Tam's prized pupil from spotting you, and if it doesn't, I've also cast other enchantments to armor you and disperse harmful spells before they strike home. They ought to keep you alive for a few heartbeats, anyway."

"That's reassuring." Aoth stowed his spear in the harness a saddler had made for it, strapped it to his back, and started to climb.

At this point, the mountainside was steep but not so sheer that a man needed to be an expert equipped with climbing gear to scale it. That was why Aoth and his comrades had landed where they did. Yet it still seemed to take an eternity to reach the top, as he worried every moment that Malark would sense his coming despite his and Lallara's best efforts to prevent it, peer over the edge at him, and blast him from his perch with a flare of magic.

Or maybe just drop a stone on his head.

But it didn't happen, and finally, he gripped a last pair of handholds and pulled himself just high enough to peer out across the flat, rocky expanse on the summit.

Malark floated in the center of the space. He wore a jagged diadem formed of murky crystal and held a staff made of the same material over his head.

When Aoth had spotted the spymaster before, he'd been brandishing the staff and chanting, but now he didn't seem to be doing much of anything. That appearance was almost certainly deceptive. He'd simply reached a phase of the Unmaking that required pure concentration as opposed to a more conventional sort of conjuring.

At first, that was all Aoth observed. Then patches of seemingly empty space flickered and oozed in a way that made his head throb and his stomach turn. He assumed he'd located more of Szass Tam's guardians, concealed so well that even his spellscarred eyes couldn't make out what they were. But they were big and plentiful.

He decided it was time to return to his comrades. But before he could start his descent, he glimpsed something else.

Also imperceptible to normal sight, a great wheel or sphere or tangled knot of *something* hung and turned above the mountaintop. Aoth couldn't see it clearly either, or maybe his mind instinctively cringed from the attempt. He was no surer of its substance than its shape. He thought it might be akin to the blasts of shadow that necromancers hurled to kill the living.

But somehow he knew it was infinitely more poisonous than any such spell effect, as well as profoundly if indefinably hideous. He could imagine the virulence exploding out of it to shred the sky and shatter the earth. He could imagine a man gouging out his own eyes so he wouldn't have to see it anymore. Yet he found that he couldn't look away.

He whimpered, realized he'd done so, and a more practical kind of alarm cut through his trance of horror. What if Malark or one of the guardian creatures had heard him? He wrenched his gaze away from the ghastly object above him.

It didn't look as if they'd heard. He took a deep breath, then invoked the magic of one of his tattoos. The enchantment enabled him to fall slowly and harmlessly down the mountainside.

As he lit on the ledge, Jet said, "I looked through your eyes. I wish I hadn't. But I already told these two what you saw."

"So what do we do?" asked Mirror.

Why is it up to me? Aoth wondered. We have a zulkir here. But he'd insisted the archmages treat him as an equal, and, maybe because she was all out of cunning ideas, Lallara seemed content to let him take the lead.

It wasn't the first time he'd chafed under the weight of the responsibility that came with command. Although it was the first in a while and stood an excellent chance of being the last.

"I'm going back up there," he said. "Malark's intent on the ritual, and I'm invisible to him and his watchdogs. Maybe I can kill him."

"Don't count on it," Lallara said. "Hostile intent will tear the veil."

"I still might hit him before he or his creatures can react."

"The creatures, perhaps," Mirror said, "but Malark himself?"

Aoth sighed. "I admit it doesn't seem likely."

"Am I understanding you correctly?" demanded Jet. "You want to go back up there *by yourself?*"

"Yes. Let's say I take a shot at Malark and fail to put him down. If I'm alone, there are a couple of things that might happen next. He might decide to fight me by himself, without involving the guardians. His love of death always did include a fondness for killing with his own hands. If it goes that way, maybe you'll see a chance to rush in and take him unaware.

"He might even decide to exchange a few words before he strikes back at me. We were friends, once upon a time. Whatever happens, every moment he spends dealing with me is a moment when he isn't advancing the ritual. Another moment for reinforcements to turn up. And if he kills me and only me, you won't have lost all that much of your strength, at least, not if the others are still alive. You'll still have a decent chance of winning."

Mirror scowled. "I don't like it, but I follow your reasoning. And I promise, we can be on top of the mountain in an instant."

"Only if it's the right move," Aoth said. "Not just to stick by a friend, but to stop the Unmaking."

"Don't worry," Lallara said. "Everyone understands that you're expendable."

Aoth smiled crookedly. "I knew I could count on you for that, Your Omnipotence. Jet will tell you what's happening to me, so you can react accordingly." He gripped a handhold and started back up the escarpment.

.. ..

Some of the spearmen laid down their weapons and shields. Some sat on the ground. Khouryn didn't begrudge them their temporary ease, but neither did he partake of it, though a secret part of him wished he could. Instead, he prowled around the formation, overseeing the removal of the dead and wounded, the adjustments to fill the gaps they had left behind, and the distribution of water, hardtack, and dried apple. He realized he'd lost count of how many times the enemy had charged, and he absently tried to work it out.

He was still figuring when one of Samas Kul's younger officers approached him. The human wore fancy gilded armor consistent with his master's love of ostentation. It looked especially silly with the crest knocked off the helmet.

But give the lad credit. He'd actually traded blows with one of the foe, unlike some of his peers, who were careful to keep behind the frontlines.

"I was just wondering," the human said.

"Yes?" Khouryn replied.

"Are we winning?"

"Of course."

It was a lie of sorts. Khouryn's instincts told him the battle could go either way. But uncertainty would be thin gruel to offer a fellow hungry for reassurance.

Nothing could deter So-Kehur's undead troops from attacking ferociously as long as their master willed it. But Khouryn sensed a hesitance in the autharch's living retainers whenever one of the imitation zulkirs revealed himself and seemingly worked some deadly feat of sorcery. He suspected their best hope of victory lay in focusing their attacks on those who felt such qualms. The problem was that, fighting in a defensive posture, he and his comrades had limited ability to choose. They had to fight whom- and whatever So-Kehur threw at them.

But at least they had griffon riders in the sky. The aerial cavalry spent much of the time battling flyers from the opposing army but sometimes managed to shoot at prime targets on the ground.

"How many more times do you think they'll charge?" asked Samas's officer.

Khouryn glimpsed a stirring in the enemy host. "At least one. Better get back to your men. And don't worry. You're doing fine."

The human nodded and scurried away. Khouryn tramped back to his own company. No need to run. Were Samas's retainer more experienced, he'd realize the necromancers needed a little more time to organize a fresh assault.

Still, it came soon enough. At first, Khouryn only saw dread warriors, amber eyes shining in their withered faces. Then he made out the creatures—if they were creatures—in the lead. Swords, axes, and hammers whirled around with no visible hands gripping them, only a swirl of dust and a scream of wind to suggest the presence of some controlling force or entity in the middle.

"Sword spirits!" yelled someone at the back of the formation.

"Ragewinds!" cried someone else.

So now Khouryn had two names for the things. Wonderful. He wished one of the learned souls who'd recognized them had seen fit to call out something helpful, like the best way to kill them.

One thing was likely. It would take an enchanted weapon to hurt the ragewinds. He dropped his spear and shield, pulled his urgrosh off his back, and strode forth to intercept one before its spinning blades reached the formation.

The whirlwind buffeted him and made it hard to keep his footing. A broadsword streaked at him, and he ducked. A scimitar was next, and he batted it away. He stepped deeper into the storm and cut.

To what effect, it was impossible to say. When the target was invisible and more or less made of air, how could a warrior know when he'd hit it? But common sense suggested that if the entity was vulnerable anywhere, it was probably weakest at its core.

Khouryn attacked doggedly, mostly cutting with the axe head of his weapon but occasionally stabbing with the spear point at the end of it. He dodged and parried the endless barrage of weapons the sword spirit whipped at him.

Hard-pressed though he was, he occasionally caught a glimpse of other soldiers who'd emerged from the battle lines to engage a ragewind as he had. Some still fought, but a disheartening number had already fallen.

Meanwhile, the Burning Braziers and sorcerers assailed the undead with flashes of fire that momentarily lit up the night. One such blast roared close enough to Khouryn to dazzle him and make him flinch from the heat, but it didn't slow the relentless onslaught of the spinning blades.

He cut, and it seemed to him he finally felt a measure of resistance, though scarcely more than if the urgrosh had sheared through a piece of straw. He thought too that for just an instant, the stroke drew a scarlet line on the air. He wondered if it truly had, or if hope and the afterimages floating before his eyes were conspiring to trick him.

Then a falchion leaped at him. It was already close by the time he spotted it, and when he tried to parry, he was too slow. It clanged against his chest, then skipped away as the sword spirit continued to spin it around the axis of rotation.

Though the impact hurt, it wasn't the crippling shock that would have come if the weapon had pierced Khouryn's mail and the vital organs beneath. Still, it knocked him staggering, and the wind's shoving kept him from regaining his balance. He now found it impossible to attack and brutally difficult to defend.

A tumbling mace flew at him. He knocked it aside, saw the other weapons whirling right behind it, and jerked the urgrosh back into position to parry those as well. Then the wind stopped howling and mauling him, and its several blades fell to the ground. A figure made of gray vapor fumed into visibility in the center of the space the maelstrom had inhabited.

Cheers rose from the battle lines. Panting, his heart pounding, Khouryn realized that something had balked *all* the sword spirits.

It appeared to be Lallara, outlined by the golden glow of her protective enchantments, standing at the front of the formation and brandishing her staff. But something about the crone's posture told Khouryn it was actually Jhesrhi inside the illusory disguise.

That made sense. The sword spirits were undead, but they needed to manifest as whirlwinds to wield their weapons. And

Jhesrhi was adept at raising and quelling winds. In effect, she was grappling with the phantoms, gripping their wrists to keep them from using their hands.

Breezes whistled and gusted back and forth. A flail lifted partway off the ground, then dropped back. Jhesrhi had arrested the ragewinds, but even with other wizards lending covert aid, she evidently couldn't hold them for long.

Khouryn croaked a battle cry and charged the misty apparition. He struck it repeatedly, every blow gashing it with a streak of crimson light. It started to come apart, but the wind was moaning louder, blowing harder, and he couldn't tell if the phantom was dissolving because he was destroying it or because it was breaking free.

He hit it once more in the chest, and it vanished. He pivoted to find himself again at the center of a vortex of blades lifting up off the ground. He felt a pang of despair, struggled to quell it, and then the whirlwind died. The spirit's weapons dropped.

Fresh cheering sounded. He looked around and saw that Jhesrhi's intervention had likewise enabled his comrades to destroy the rest of the ragewinds in one manner or another.

In a just world, Khouryn would now have had a moment to rejoice and catch his breath. But in this one, dozens of dread warriors were still poised at the front of the enemy formation. They hadn't been able to advance with the sword spirits, or the spinning weapons would have chopped them to pieces. But now they charged, and Khouryn had to sprint back to his own battle lines to keep the undead from swarming over him. He grabbed and braced his spear just in time to spit an onrushing zombie.

•• •• •• •• •• •• •• •• •• •• •• ••

Aoth clambered onto the mountaintop. As far as he could tell, nothing had changed. It was possible—indeed, likely—that the confluence of forces overhead was even more hideous than before, but he had no intention of taking another look at it.

His mouth dry, he stalked along the edge of the high place. If he could sneak behind Malark, maybe it wouldn't matter that "hostile intent" would breach his invisibility. Maybe he could still attack by surprise.

It irked him that even close up, he couldn't see what waited in the patches of writhing distortion. He'd gotten used to seeing whatever existed to be seen, even when magic sought to conceal it. Smiling crookedly, he told himself that in this situation, he might be better off *not* seeing. Most likely, it would only be bad for his morale.

To his surprise, he reached a point directly behind Malark without anything trying to stop him. He aimed his spear and whispered the first words of a death spell. If it worked, it would grip and crush the spymaster's body like a piece of rotten fruit.

Malark dropped back to earth, whirled, and ended up in a crouch, staff cocked back behind him in one hand. A dimness, evidence of a protective enchantment, flowed over his body. Meanwhile, the guardians exploded into view.

Some were the floating spherical creatures called beholders, each with one great, orblike eye and other, smaller ones twisting around on stalks, and with mouths full of jagged fangs. Rotting, spotted with fungus, and riddled with gaping wounds, these particular specimens were plainly the undead variety called death tyrants.

The rest of the guardians were gigantic corpses with snarling, demented faces and lumps scuttling around beneath their slimy, decaying skins. Xingax, who'd invented the things, had called them plague spewers, and they were one of his foulest creations.

Aoth felt a mad impulse to laugh, for, given that he was a lone attacker, his situation was so hopeless as to be ludicrous. Instead, he rattled off the rest of his incantation. Though it seemed clear that Aoth was about to die, maybe Malark could go first.

Alas, no. A dark blaze of power leaped from the spear, but it frayed to nothingness when it touched Malark's haze of protection.

The spell Aoth had cast would enable him to make more such attacks, but unfortunately, no two at the same foe. As he scrambled sideways to make himself a moving target, he weighed whether to turn the magic on one of the guardians or try to blast Malark with something else.

His foes all pivoted with him. "Where are your allies?" the spymaster asked.

Apparently he *did* want to talk, and Aoth judged that conversation might well stall him longer than continuing a fight that would likely last only another heartbeat or two.

"As far as I know, everybody else died when the cliffs smashed together. Well, except for my griffon. He got hit by a falling boulder, but he was able to carry me this far before the wound killed him."

Malark smiled. "I'm not certain I believe you."

"The way I hear it, you're supposed to be a mighty wizard now. If anyone else were still alive, wouldn't you have found him with your scrying?"

"Perhaps, but after I shifted the mountains, I didn't try. I don't know if you can tell, but the Unmaking is close to flowering. It's possible I'm only a few breaths away. So I thought it would be a good gamble just to try to finish before any survivors reached the mountain. It still seems like a sensible strategy, once I dispose of you."

"So this is the way our friendship ends."

Malark shrugged. "It doesn't have to be. Throw your spear over the edge, submit to a binding, and you can watch the ritual unfold. You've grown into one of the finest soldiers in the East.

A master killer. A true disciple of Death, even if you don't think of it that way. I'd like to believe that if you only give yourself the chance, you'll perceive the glory of what's about to happen."

"Sorry, no."

"I understand. You'd rather go down fighting, and of course it's a proper end for a man like you." Malark lifted his hand as though to signal for the guardians to attack.

Aoth groped for something, anything, to say to keep the other man talking. "Curse it, your idiotic ceremony isn't even going to work! The zulkirs say it can't!"

"I'll wager Szass Tam didn't say it, and he's the wisest of them all, as well as the only one who's actually read Fastrin's book."

"He's also crazy, and so are you."

"It no doubt looks that way, but the reality is that he and I are idealists. We both aspire to purity and perfection, although, sadly, he doesn't understand what they truly are."

"I'm telling you, the most the magic will do is kill you and everyone else in Thay and maybe in the realms on our borders."

"I don't think so, but even if you're right, that alone will be wonderful. And now, since it's clear I can't open your eyes, I'll bid you good-bye." Malark waved his hand, and the plague spewers took a stride toward Aoth. Phosphorescence glimmered in the death tyrants' eyes.

•• •• •• •• •• •• •• •• •• •• •• •• •• ••

The last of the dread warriors dropped, and So-Kehur peered across the open ground between the two armies to see what the living corpses had accomplished prior to their destruction. Lenses shifted inside his various eyes to magnify the view.

The invaders were hauling bodies back to the rear of their formation and trying to fill the new breaches in their battle lines. That didn't work until a dwarf officer dissolved the back rank and ordered its members forward into the two lines in front of it.

So-Kehur turned toward Chumed and the other officers assembled beside him. In his eagerness, he wasn't particularly careful, and one pinch-faced old necromancer had to forfeit his dignity and scurry to keep a pair of his master's pincers from braining him. Well, no matter. The man was all right.

"Do you see that?" So-Kehur asked. "Bit by bit, we're breaking them apart."

To his annoyance, no one echoed his enthusiasm. In fact, for a moment, everyone hesitated to say anything at all.

Then Chumed drew himself up straighter. "Milord, I respectfully suggest that we consider what we're doing to our own army as well."

"I know we're taking casualties, but that's inevitable in war."

"Master, it appears to me that we might indeed annihilate the enemy, but only if we're willing to grind our own host down to nothing in the process. I ask you, is that a desirable outcome when our primary responsibility is the defense of Anhaurz? I recommend withdrawing. We've hurt the invaders badly enough that they no longer pose a threat. If they have any sense at all, they'll run for the border. If not, Thay has other armies to finish them off."

So-Kehur couldn't believe what he'd heard. Withdraw? Let some other commander steal his victory over the infamous zulkirs-in-exile themselves, and the renown that would accompany it? He felt a surge of fury, and Chumed fell, thrashed, and frothed at the mouth.

So-Kehur realized he'd lashed out at the seneschal with his psychic abilities. He hadn't consciously intended it but decided he wasn't sorry, either. Nor would he be even if the coward strangled on his own tongue.

He glared at his other officers. They cringed, either because the raw force of his anger was exerting pressure on their minds or simply because they were intimidated. "Does anyone else want to run away?" he asked.

If anybody did, he kept it to himself.

"Good," So-Kehur continued. "Now, I think we can break the enemy if we throw everything we have into one final assault, and this time, I'll lead the charge myself."

chapter sixteen

19 Kythorn, The Year of the Dark Circle (1478 DR)

Dangerous as plague spewers were, in Aoth's judgment, they were less so than beholders and far less so than Malark. So he lunged in front of one of the rotting giants with its twitching, snarling face, using the corpse as a wall to separate him from the rest of his foes.

Unfortunately, it was a wall that was just as intent on killing him as everything else on the mountaintop. It doubled over, opened its mouth impossibly wide, and puked up dozens of rats. Chittering and squealing, the rodents charged.

Aoth incinerated them with a flare of fire from his spear. Heedless of the blast, the plague spewer pounded forward right behind them. It had its enormous hands raised to grab, crush, and infect him, and its strides shook the ground.

Exerting his will, Aoth tried to seize it with the same magic that had failed to kill Malark. This time, he was more successful. Rotten hide splitting, muscles bursting and spattering slime, bones snapping, the plague spewer's body crumpled in on itself. More rats—the bulges that had scuttled ceaselessly under its skin—sprang clear of the demolition but, without the giant's will to guide them, made no move to attack.

The stink of charred rat hung in the air along with drifting flecks of ash. Aoth cast about, surveying the battlefield. Malark was circling right, so he dodged left. The maneuver brought him in front of a death tyrant. The bulbous creatures floated slowly, but they didn't need to close with an opponent to attack, only maintain a clear line of sight.

A ragged burst of shadow leaped from one of the death tyrant's eyestalks. Aoth dodged, but it washed over him anyway. He felt a stab of pain, but it faded after a moment. Most likely thanks to the wards Lallara had cast on him, the attack hadn't done him any actual harm.

He focused his will to strike back, then felt something else shaking the ground. He pivoted just in time to see the oncoming plague spewer flail at him with its fist.

He avoided the blow by lunging between the giant's legs, then drove his spear into its ankle and channeled power through the point. The joint exploded, half severing the spewer's foot and sending it reeling. It toppled into the path of another blaze of power from one of the death tyrant's eyes, and as it crashed to earth, the giant turned to stone.

The petrified corpse blocked that undead beholder, but by now, another had maneuvered into position. Two of its rotting eyestalks bowed in Aoth's direction. He reached for it with the pulverizing magic and managed to strike first. The pressure burst it like a boil, and viscera spilled from the ruptured husk.

Unfortunately, at that point, the crushing magic ran out of power, and it was questionable whether Aoth would have a chance to cast that or any spell again. Despite his best attempts to outmaneuver them, a dozen of his enemies, Malark included, had moved into positions from which they could attack him simultaneously. The only hope of avoiding the assault would be to jump over the cliff, and then Malark would either rain destruction down on him or go back to his filthy ritual.

Ah, well, Aoth had expected it would come to this. He'd needed a kiss from Lady Luck, as well as some of the best fighting of his life, to last as long as he had.

He leveled his spear at Malark for one last strike. But Szass Tam's protégé brandished his staff, and his power stabbed through Lallara's wards. Nausea twisted Aoth's guts, and his legs buckled. The strength drained out of him all at once, and the head of his spear clanked against the ground. A plague spewer lumbered forward and stretched out its hand to seize him.

Then golden light flowered at his back. The radiance didn't hurt him. In fact, it quelled his sickness and started his strength trickling back. But it seared the plague spewer, melted one of its eyes, and sent it stumbling backward.

Aoth didn't have to look around to realize that Mirror had flown up over the mountaintop and had invoked the power of his god, and at that moment, Aoth no longer cared whether the intervention was sound strategy. He was simply grateful for another chance at life.

Malark smiled as if to acknowledge an opponent's sound play in some trivial game, then aimed his staff at a target—Mirror, presumably—in the air. At that point Jet plunged down on the spymaster like a hawk killing a rabbit.

The griffon dashed Malark to earth, but his talons didn't penetrate the human's armoring enchantments, nor did his plummeting mass snap the wizard's spine or even stun him. Malark immediately hit back with a chop to the side of the familiar's feathery neck.

Perhaps because Malark was on his back, the blow didn't land hard enough to kill. But it did jolt Jet to the side, which gave the former monk of the Long Death the chance to wrench himself out from under his attacker's claws.

Run! thought Aoth. *You can't handle him by yourself!* Jet's response was a pang of frustration and disgust, but as Malark rolled to his feet, the familiar lashed his wings and vaulted back into the air.

Lallara floated down from above to alight beside Aoth. She jabbed the ferrule of her staff into his ribs, and a surge of vitality swept the last of his weakness away.

"Thanks," he said.

"Get up," she snapped. "You have work to do."

"I suppose I do." He clambered to his feet and cast a thunderbolt.

Lallara too hurled attack spells but also conjured barriers of fire, stone, and spinning blades to hold back the enemy. Sometimes she even managed to drop such a wall right on top of one of Malark's servants, imprisoning it or tearing it in two. Mirror, who currently resembled a smudged caricature of Aoth, alternated between evoking bursts of divine light and battling with sword and shield. Jet repeatedly dived, attacked, and climbed back up into the sky, circling until he saw another chance to strike by surprise.

All in all, it was a fine display of fighting prowess, and yet it wasn't good enough. No matter how many of Malark's guardians Aoth and his companions destroyed, the creatures kept coming. Aoth never actually saw new ones popping into existence, but in time he decided that somehow the supply must be inexhaustible.

What was even more discouraging was that no attack seemed to damage Malark himself. Once in a while, a barrage of ball lightning or a blast of frost rocked him back on his heels, but afterward, he quickly returned to working his own magic, methodically dissolving Lallara's barriers.

Until a flying blade made of absolute darkness streaked down at him from above. Malark sidestepped the cut, then tapped the conjured weapon with his staff. The black sword vanished.

Then he looked up, and Aoth did too. Szass Tam was hovering above the mountaintop. Malark gestured and shouted a word of command, and a dozen death tyrants floated upward like bubbles to turn their virulent gazes on the lich.

That should have helped clear a path from Aoth's position near the drop to Malark's at the center of the high place. But when Aoth looked for such a route, it seemed there were just as many guardians blocking the way as ever.

He cursed, then sensed motion on his flank. He pivoted toward the onrushing plague spewer, and a thunderous shout blasted the head from its shoulders. As it toppled, rats swarmed from the stump of its neck. Meanwhile, Bareris finished hauling himself up onto the mountaintop.

"I'm glad you made it," said Aoth. The bard responded with a nod, drew his sword, and struck up a dirge. The eerie tones had no effect on Aoth but were apt to afflict a foe with weakness and confusion.

Nevron swooped down in the midst of a throng of demons that immediately hurled themselves at Malark's minions. Lauzoril arrived in a cloud of tiny floating daggers that darted from point to point like hummingbirds. Finally even Samas Kul, whom Aoth had judged the likeliest to flee, floated up into view with his quicksilver wand in his blubbery hand.

The other council members positioned themselves near Lallara, no doubt in the hope that her wards would protect them as well. Then they attacked. Lauzoril recited an incantation in his dry, clerkish voice, and three plague spewers started mauling one another. Growling words of power, Nevron summoned a ghour, a huge, shaggy demon with bull-like horns and cloven hooves, and the thing spat poison smoke at the enemy. Samas daintily flourished his wand, and a death tyrant turned to snow, its eye-stalks and globular body crumbling into a shapeless mound when it thumped down on the ground.

Surely now, Aoth thought, hurling darts of green light at Malark, surely now, he and his allies were strong enough to win. They had to be, because no more reinforcements were coming.

Yet he could see they weren't. Their combined might sufficed to offset Malark's but nothing more, and in time that strength would fade, as even archmages ran out of magic. Whereas Malark, if he truly was a kind of god in this place, would likely remain as powerful as ever.

"None of our spells are hurting Malark," said Aoth. "Those of us who are warriors need to get over to him and see if we can do any better with our blades. And do it now, before the tide turns against us."

Lauzoril arched an eyebrow. "Are you proposing to charge straight through the middle of all these undead?"

"Yes. You zulkirs will use your sorcery to keep the guardians off our backs, both while we advance and after we engage Malark."

Samas turned an onrushing plague spewer into mist. "Even with our help, I don't see how you're going to make it to Spring-hill. But you're right, we need to try something."

"That's the plan, then." Aoth turned to Bareris and Mirror. "Ready?"

The ghost flourished his sword, and warm light pulsed from the blade. Aoth felt a rush of confidence and vitality and inferred that he'd received some sort of blessing. "Now we are," Mirror said.

•• •• •• •• •• •• •• •• •• •• •• •• ••

The enemy still had men positioned to flank the council's army. No doubt if given the opportunity, they'd make another attempt to advance into the trees. But they hadn't tried for a while, and Gaedynn had glimpsed motion behind the front ranks as their officers redirected a number of warriors elsewhere.

From that, he inferred that henceforth, his archers and skirmishers could probably hold this position without him. He set down his longbow and headed for Eider. Crouched back down in her hollow, the griffon was grooming herself, biting at the feathers she'd damaged flapping her wings among the low-hanging branches.

She jumped up when she realized her master meant to ride her. He swung himself into the saddle, strapped himself in, strung the shorter compound bow he used for aerial combat, then turned her away from the enemy, so no one would shoot her as she took off.

Picking up speed with every pace, Eider ran toward the riverbank, leaped, and soared over the black water. Gaedynn took a moment to savor the exhilaration of flight, then urged her higher. They wheeled and glided over the treetops so he could survey the battle as a whole.

Flashes of light—attack spells—leaped between the dark masses that were the opposing hosts. Then a chorus of battle cries howled from the one in the west, and the greater part of So-Kehur's army hurtled forward in what looked like an all-out effort to overwhelm the zulkirs' forces.

"Forward," Gaedynn said. He snatched arrows from one of the quivers buckled to his tack and loosed them at the charge as Eider dived into range. A skin kite flapped at him, and the griffon beat her wings, rose above the membranous undead, and ripped it to pieces with her talons.

The charge crashed into the defenders' spears and shields. As he nocked another shaft, Gaedynn peered, trying to determine if his side's formation was holding.

Some of it was. But, pincers snapping, tentacles lashing, and tail stabbing, a thing like a gigantic steel scorpion was tearing into the battle lines. Supposedly So-Kehur was a necromancer, fully capable of casting lightningbolts and the like, but Gaedynn supposed that a man didn't put on the shape of a beast unless he had a craving to kill like one.

He also supposed that it was up to him to keep the autharch from breaking the formation. It certainly didn't look as though anyone on the ground was having any luck. Touching a finger to the back of Eider's neck, he sent the griffon swooping lower.

.. ..

Bareris sang to shield Aoth, Mirror, and himself behind barriers of fear. If it worked, even the undead should hesitate for an instant before striking at them, and an instant might be all they needed to dash on by.

The magic seemed to protect them for a few strides. Or perhaps it was the zulkirs' sorcery, blasting guardians out of their way or sending snarling demons to rend them with flaming halberds or jagged claws. Or Szass Tam's wizardry. So many death tyrants had drifted upward to surround the lich that it was almost impossible to catch a glimpse of him. Power flashed and crackled as they hammered him with their malignant gazes again and again and again. Still, hard-pressed as he was, he realized what his allies on the ground were attempting and hurled lightning and beams of searing radiance to aid them.

Then another undead beholder floated out in front of Bareris. Dripping slime, the big glazed eye in the middle of its body shimmered, and suddenly he couldn't remember why he was running.

He faltered, and the death tyrant jumped at him. Its jagged fangs snapped shut on his sword arm.

If not for his brigandine and the unnatural strength of his undead flesh, the bite surely would have severed the limb. As it was, the agonizing pressure nearly paralyzed him. But the pain cut through his confusion as well, and he used his off hand to yank his dagger from its sheath and stab his foe repeatedly in the central eye. He punched holes in it, splashing himself with cold jelly in the process, but the fangs kept clamping down relentlessly.

Mirror burned away a portion of the creature's body with a flash of holy light, but unfortunately, did not affect the mouth. Aoth lunged and thrust his spear into it, sparked a blast of power from the point, and the death tyrant burst into pieces.

Bareris cast about and saw that other guardians were already right on top of them. The things would almost certainly have overwhelmed them too, except that the next moment, one plague spewer turned into an iron statue, and a second simply vanished. Hunched creatures with hairless red hides and massive upper bodies pounced on a death tyrant, pressed their mouths against it as if to kiss it, and roared. The cries blasted craters in its body, and it fell.

Mirror turned to Bareris. "Are you all right?"

Bareris flexed his perforated sword arm. It ached but seemed to work. "Yes. Keep running!"

They did. A plague spewer scrambled in front of them and opened its mouth, no doubt to vomit rats. Jet plummeted down on top of the giant and clawed its head to shreds. The griffon then sprang back into the air and flew along above them, likewise racing in Malark's direction.

Eyes glittering, two more death tyrants floated toward them. Some invisible force exerted by one of the archmages slapped the creatures out of the way as if they weighed no more than puffballs. And then—to Bareris's surprise, actually—the way to Malark was clear.

The spymaster smiled at them with what looked like genuine fondness. "Nicely done." He raised his staff in a middle guard.

∙∙ ∙∙ ∙∙ ∙∙ ∙∙ ∙∙ ∙∙ ∙∙ ∙∙ ∙∙ ∙∙ ∙∙ ∙∙ ∙∙

As Khouryn ran toward So-Kehur, a burst of fire splashed the arcing, stabbing metal stinger. One of the wizards had targeted a part he could hit without burning the soldiers trying to hold the autharch back with their jabbing spears.

Sadly, neither the magic, nor the spears, nor the arrows that griffon riders loosed from on high appeared to hurt So-Kehur. The gigantic scorpion-thing kept pressing forward, tentacles whipping to smash men's bones, pincers snipping them to pieces, stinger plunging to pierce them through. He would have broken the formation already, except that, like Khouryn, other warriors—sellswords, mostly—kept leaving their assigned positions to reinforce the point in danger of giving way, scrambling over the corpses of the men the necromancer had already killed as they rushed to take their places.

That mustn't continue, or the enemy would breach the weakened battle lines somewhere else. The defenders had to kill or at least repel So-Kehur and do it fast.

Khouryn pushed between two soldiers and charged the autharch. A tentacle whirled at his head. He ducked it and ran on underneath the scorpion body. Then he took a firm grip on his urgrosh and chopped at one of So-Kehur's eight legs.

The spindly limb wasn't as heavily armored as the massive steel body, and the axe blade dented it. Grinning, he chopped it again.

A tentacle slithered into view. But though So-Kehur had plenty of eyes, none were in his belly, and the arm had to grope for its quarry. Khouryn scurried to a different leg on the same side and bashed that one.

Then pain ripped through his skull. He gasped and fell to his knees. He told himself he had to get back up, to keep moving, but his head hurt so badly he could barely see. The tentacle found his ankle, coiled around it, jerked tight, and dragged him into the open.

·· ·· ·· ·· ·· ·· ·· ·· ·· ·· ·· ·· ·· ··

A dozen illusory Malarks sprang into being around the genuine immortal. Bareris peered in a futile attempt to determine where he should actually strike.

"Follow my lead!" Aoth shouted. "I can pick out the real one!" He lunged and stabbed with his spear.

Malark sidestepped the thrust, and his counterparts copied the motion. He whirled his staff at Aoth's head, and the war-mage caught it on the shaft of his own weapon. The impact produced a flash of dark, malignant power and knocked Aoth off balance. Malark spun the staff into position for a follow-up attack.

Flowing from a parody of Aoth to his own true image as he lunged, Mirror cut and shattered one of the phantasms into nothingness. Despite Aoth's guidance, which by rights should have pinpointed the real Malark, the illusions were maddeningly deceptive. Bareris slashed and merely burst another.

It was Jet, with his ability to look through his master's eyes, who wasn't fooled. He dived from on high, and Malark had to give up his second strike at Aoth to leap out of the way.

Jet slammed on the ground between Aoth and Malark. Beak gaping, he lunged. Malark shifted to the side and jabbed his staff at the griffon's flank. Blackness seethed around the tip.

Mirror sprang in and, despite the confusion engendered by the doubles, somehow managed to catch the stroke on his shield. Power discharged itself with a bang. The ghost swung his sword in a low cut, and Malark and his likenesses leaped above the arc of the blow. The traitor spun his staff through the center of Mirror's body. Mirror shredded into wisps of shadow. Malark poised his weapon for another strike at the tatters, which didn't even constitute a recognizable human shape anymore.

Bareris shouted to jolt everything in a certain area, the real Malark and his illusions alike. Darts of turquoise light leaped from Aoth's spear, diverging in flight to strike multiple targets. He obviously realized that even if the phantasms couldn't fool him or Jet, he needed to get rid of them so his allies could fight effectively.

The illusions vanished. It didn't look as if any of the magic had actually wounded the one remaining Malark, but he faltered for just an instant, time enough for Mirror's form to fill in and become discernibly manlike again—still faceless, but at least possessed of limbs and a head—and avoid another attack by plunging into the solid ground beneath him.

Singing a battle anthem, gripping his sword with both hands, Bareris rushed in and feinted high. Malark didn't try to parry or dodge the false attack. He simply dipped his own weapon to threaten his adversary's groin and, when Bareris tried to block, whirled and smashed a back kick into his chest.

The impact would have killed a living man. Ribs snapped, and Bareris reeled backward and fell.

As he did, he caught a glimpse of the rest of the battle. Many of the guardians were still attacking Szass Tam, the zulkirs of the council, and Nevron's familiars. But some were turning their attention to the knot of struggling figures in the center of the mountaintop.

A pair of plague spewers rushed to take Malark's assailants from behind. One collapsed into a shapeless heap of carrion, as though its bones had melted. The horns now torn from its head, Nevron's ghour lunged, tackled the other, and bore it down to the ground.

A death tyrant floated down from on high. Still all but hidden in the midst of many such creatures, Szass Tam rattled off words in some sibilant Abyssal tongue. The undead beholder twisted its eyestalks to gaze at itself, then discharged flares of virulence into its own putrid flesh.

Plainly, though surely finding it a formidable task even to protect themselves, the archmages were trying their best to do the job Aoth had given them. And Bareris had to get back to doing his. Clenching his teeth at the grinding pain of his shattered ribs, he clambered to his feet, resumed singing his battle anthem, and circled to attack Malark from behind.

The spymaster whirled, parried the cut, then spun back around and swept the staff at Jet. The griffon ducked, and the staff simply brushed across the top of his skull. Still, that was enough to make him scream and send him stumbling backward. He lashed his head back and forth as though trying to clear it.

Malark pivoted to threaten Bareris, accelerating as he moved. He was fast when he started, but lightning by the time he finished. Bareris sprang back, and the staff fell short by the length of a finger joint.

Somehow Malark had cast an enchantment of quickness on himself without the necessity of chanting or mystic passes. Perhaps he'd carried the spell stored in a talisman, or maybe it was his rulership of this place that allowed him to invoke it so easily.

He threw himself at his two remaining adversaries, and his blows hammered at them like raindrops in a downpour. Even though Aoth and Bareris tried to flank him, they still found it impossible to attack. It was all they could do to parry and retreat.

Meanwhile, Bareris sang a charm to make Aoth and himself as quick as Malark had become. But he doubted he'd have time to finish, especially after the spymaster, plainly recognizing his intent, concentrated his attacks on him.

Then a mesh like a huge piece of spiderweb shimmered into existence on top of the former monk, tangling his limbs and gluing him to the ground. Bareris suspected Szass Tam had conjured it. As Malark's wards burned the sticky strands away, Bareris sang the last note of his own spell. His muscles jumped at the infusion of power. No doubt feeling it too, Aoth bellowed a war cry, thrust his spear at the spymaster, and they all fought on.

Bareris wanted to believe he'd done more than postpone the inevitable. Surely it mattered that he'd canceled out Malark's advantage. And that Mirror was rising from the earth to reenter the fight. And that Jet, the feathers on his head soaked with blood, was bounding forward to do the same.

Surely the four of them could surround Malark and cut him down. It wasn't as if the bastard couldn't die. He'd done it once already, when Samas had buried him in molten lead.

But back in the Dread Ring, Malark hadn't been a god. In this place, he avoided nine strokes out of every ten, and the one that landed glanced harmlessly off his protections. Meanwhile, he struck back with dazzling speed and showed no signs of slowing, unlike Aoth and Jet, whose chests heaved and whose breaths rasped.

We're going to lose, Bareris decided. And he could think of only one mad ploy that might conceivably change that dismal outcome.

He raised his sword over his head, opening himself up, and charged Malark. Trailing tendrils of crackling shadow, the traitor's staff whirled to meet him, and he did nothing to parry or avoid it. It smashed into his torso, and everything disappeared.

•• •• •• •• •• •• •• •• •• •• •• •• ••

Jhesrhi dashed toward So-Kehur, never mind if it looked odd for a decrepit, hobbling hag like Lallara to sprint. At this point, stopping the steel scorpion was more important than maintaining her masquerade.

She pushed between two spearmen and obtained a clear view of all of So-Kehur, not just the part that loomed above the heads of ordinary people. At the moment, the scorpion-thing was no longer ripping into the formation, but only because he'd paused to deal with a foe who'd emerged from it to attack him. One of his tentacles was dragging Khouryn out from underneath him.

The dwarf still had his urgrosh in his hands, but he wasn't moving, and Jhesrhi couldn't tell if he was alive. If so, he wouldn't be for much longer. Not unless someone diverted So-Kehur's attention.

Drawing on her own strength and the power that other mages were lending her to aid her impersonation, she spoke to the earth, and stones thrust up out of the dirt. Then she married her mind to the wind and made it an extension of her will, like an extra pair of hands.

The wind screamed, snatched up the rocks, and hurled them at So-Kehur's various eyes. Any natural creature reflexively protected its sight, and she prayed the autharch possessed the same instincts.

One missile cracked the opalescent left eye in the mask that passed for the scorpion-thing's human face. Another snapped a writhing antenna with an optic gleaming at the end.

Still clutching and dragging Khouryn, but for the moment no longer concerned with him, So-Kehur turned to face his new attacker.

•• •• •• •• •• •• •• •• •• •• •• •• •• ••

Bareris hadn't slept since becoming undead, but violence could smash the awareness out of him, and he supposed that must be what had happened. Sprawled on his back, his torso ablaze with pain, he groggily tried to lift his head. Then, trading attacks, Aoth and Malark passed through his field of vision, the sellsword captain retreating and the immortal pushing him back.

The sight of them sparked Bareris's memory. He, Aoth, Mirror, and Jet had assailed Malark and found themselves outmatched. So, depending on his unnatural hardiness and recuperative powers to help him weather the assault, he'd allowed the former monk to land a solid blow with the staff, charged with destructive power though it was.

Remembering, he froze. His desperate gamble would fail if Malark realized he'd survived.

Although it was possible it had already failed no matter what. He'd expected injury, pain, but not agony like this. What if he could no longer move, or at least, not fast enough to make his plan succeed?

He thrust doubt out of his mind. Malark was the last obstacle on the path to Szass Tam, and after waiting a hundred years for vengeance, he'd clear the way no matter what. He just had to lie perfectly still, watch the fight through slitted eyes, and wait for Malark to set a foot in the right place.

Finally, the immortal did. Bareris snatched with both hands, grabbed Malark's ankle, and squeezed with all his might.

The bones didn't crack. Malark's mystical defenses prevented it. But Bareris had him anchored.

Its tip shrouded in writhing shadow, the staff of murky crystal stabbed down repeatedly. Still maintaining his grip, Bareris wrenched himself back and forth in an effort to keep the blows from landing squarely.

They did anyway, each jolt of torment so intense that for that moment, it was as though nothing else existed. But he managed to hold on nonetheless, and then the assault stopped. Aoth, Mirror, and Jet had rushed to surround Malark, and he lifted his staff to defend against them.

The spymaster could no longer retreat, only duck, sway from side to side, and parry. It should have made a difference, but his weapon flicked from guard to guard with impossible speed and precision, blocking one attack after another.

A death tyrant floated toward the struggle, and, sensing the threat, Jet whirled, leaped, lashed his wings, and threw himself at the creature. Malark's staff swept through Mirror's shadowy form, and the phantom flickered as though tottering on the edge of nonexistence. The staff then leaped to deflect Aoth's stabbing spear, the parry nearly knocking the shaft out of the warmage's hands.

Bareris didn't think he could squeeze any harder, but he tried anyway. Drawing on his hate and rage, he crooned a malediction.

Malark's ankle cracked, and his body jerked. The staff stopped spinning and leaping from point to point.

Already glowing, the head of Aoth's spear flared like a lightningbolt, while Mirror's blade changed from a splinter of darkness to a light as bright as the sun. The two warriors hurled themselves at Malark, and their weapons punched all the way through the immortal's torso, the spear with an audible thud and a splash of blood, the sword silently and cleanly.

The staff fell from Malark's hands to clink against the stony ground. For a moment, he looked astonished. Then he smiled, laughed, and more blood drooled from his mouth. "Thank you," he breathed. "I wish you could see it too. It's everything I . . ." His knees buckled, and he fell.

The jagged crown floated up off his head, and the staff too rose into the air. Bareris realized Szass Tam must be drawing them to him. They were likely the instruments that had given Malark control of this artificial world and had made him nearly invincible, and were apt to prove more powerful still in the possession of the archmage who'd actually created them.

Bareris sucked in a breath and bellowed with all his remaining strength. The rod and diadem shattered like the crystalline things they were.

A hurtling stone tore another eyestalk away. Jhesrhi wondered if she actually could blind So-Kehur.

Then a sort of chill stabbed into her head, and none of her wards, potent defenses against sorcery though they were, did anything to prevent it. The cold numbed her, dulled her, and the determination to fight faded into a dazed and hopeless acquiescence. She told herself she had to resist, but the thought was just babble that failed to engage her will.

The coldness in her mind commanded her to release her hold on the wind, so she did. The rocks fell and thumped on the ground. It ordered her to walk forward, and she did that too.

So-Kehur spread his pincers. At her back, soldiers shouted for her to turn around and run. She had a vague sense that it would be nice if she could.

•• •• •• •• •• •• •• •• •• •• •• •• ••

As Malark dropped, Aoth jerked his spear out of the corpse and, panting, pivoted to look for other threats. One of Bareris's thunderous shouts spun him back around, just in time to see the noise smash the spymaster's levitating staff and crown into glittering powder.

At that point, the death tyrants and plague spewers simply faded away. Evidently the talismans had maintained the endless supply of the filthy things.

Their sudden disappearance made the mountaintop seem strangely quiet and empty, although a handful of Nevron's demons—limping, mangled, and gory—remained. The zulkirs of the council now spread out along the edge of the drop. And Szass Tam hovered high over everybody else.

The lich looked down at the minute shards and dust that were all that remained of his tools. "I put a lot of work into those," he said. "But perhaps it doesn't matter anymore. Particularly if we're all willing to be sensible."

"Meaning what?" Lallara rasped. Aoth realized that despite the distances involved, no one needed to shout to make himself heard. No doubt some petty magic helped the voices carry.

"The Unmaking will never happen now," Szass Tam said. Aoth risked a glance skyward and saw that, in fact, the churning vileness was gone. "We're all tired, in some cases wounded, our magic largely exhausted. And perhaps we've had our fill of revenge, killing the man who, at one time or another, betrayed each and every one of us. So I propose we go our separate ways. I promise you and your legions safe passage out of Thay."

Bareris took hold of the sword he'd dropped when Malark had struck him, and clambered to his feet. He stood partly bent at the waist as though still in pain. But his voice was steady as he said, "Never in this world or any other."

"I'm inclined to concur," said Lauzoril, still at the center of his cloud of little darting knives. "You wouldn't suggest such a thing if you didn't recognize that we have you at a profound disadvantage."

"Don't be so sure," the necromancer replied. "In particular, don't be certain that it's all of you against the one of me." He shifted his gaze to Aoth.

Aoth took a breath. "Actually, it is."

"Even though your sellsword band and the friends who help you lead it are on the brink of destruction? I'd gladly order So-Kehur to break off the attack."

Aoth couldn't fathom how Szass Tam even knew about the battle by the Lapendrar, let alone that the invaders were in trouble, but his instincts told him the lich had spoken the truth. Still, he answered, "I trust the Brotherhood to pull through somehow. I mean to stick by the friends who need me here."

"You won't be doing them a favor. Have you forgotten they're undead, and I'm the world's preeminent necromancer? If obliged to fight, the first thing I'll do is turn them into my puppets and force them to kill you."

Bareris straightened up somewhat and smiled wolfishly. "Try."

"Yes," said Mirror, "do. I may perish in this place. A warrior runs that risk in any battle. But I have faith it won't be as your slave."

Szass Tam kept his eyes on Aoth. "Rancor is clouding their judgment," the necromancer said. "Don't let it cloud yours. Remember that your employers plan to kill you."

Aoth paused to give the zulkirs a chance to respond to the charge. None did, at least not in the moment he allowed them. It was sufficient time for an honest denial, just not enough to compose a convincing lie.

"I'll deal with that when the time comes," said Aoth. "You tried to murder the whole world. You have to answer for it."

Szass Tam sighed. "Do I? Well, if you all feel—"

Aoth abruptly saw that the undead wizard was making mystic gestures with his left hand. "Watch out!" he shouted.

Szass Tam flung out his arm, and a mass of shadow exploded into being, with vague demented faces appearing and dissolving in the murk. Growing longer and taller as it traveled, it hurtled at his foes.

Those who'd charged Malark were closest to the effect, and it was rushing at them so fast that even as Aoth leveled his spear, he felt a sick certainty that it would hit before he could cast a spell. But Mirror drew another burst of radiance from his sword, Lallara spat a word of forbiddance, and the wave shattered into nothingness as though it had smashed itself against an invisible mass of rock.

Meanwhile, Lauzoril hurled a dagger at a target too distant and high above the ground for even an expert knife thrower to hit.

Except that the blade flew like an arrow, not a dagger, and turned to crimson light an instant before piercing the lich's body.

"Fall," Lauzoril said. And Szass Tam plummeted to earth.

•• •• •• •• •• •• •• •• •• •• •• •• •• •• ••

Gaedynn often remarked that if the gods had meant for him to go within reach of his enemies' swords and axes—or in this case, tentacles, claws, and stinger—they wouldn't have made him the finest archer in the East. But his arrows weren't hurting So-Kehur, the scorpion-thing was dragging Khouryn around on the ground, and now Jhesrhi, still disguised as Lallara, was advancing entranced toward her adversary's pincers.

Gaedynn sent Eider diving toward So-Kehur, meanwhile switching out his bow for a falchion. The griffon slammed down on the autharch's head, above the human mask, and, wings extended for balance, managed to cling to the smooth, rounded steel. Up close, the scorpion-thing smelled of the gore of the men he'd slaughtered.

"Rip!" Gaedynn shouted. What he actually wanted was for Eider to break away So-Kehur's remaining eyestalks. She wouldn't have understood such a specific command, but she was in the right place for her raking talons to snag them. He leaned to the right and smashed at one himself.

Mainly, though, he watched for So-Kehur's counterattack. The arms supporting the pincers didn't look flexible enough to reach him, but after an instant, the gigantic stinger whipped up and over.

"Go!" Gaedynn touched his heels to Eider's flanks. The griffon leaped clear and lashed her wings. Behind her, metal clanged.

Gaedynn climbed, turned his mount, and grinned to see what they'd accomplished. Most of the remaining eyestalks were gone. There was even a gap between two of the curved plates comprising

So-Kehur's head. Either Eider's talons had caught in a crack and pulled them apart, or the autharch's own stinger had stabbed down and poked a hole.

Looking puny, almost vestigial, compared to the pincers, tentacles, and stinger, So-Kehur's manlike arms and hands swirled in a complex pattern. Gaedynn's momentary satisfaction soured into apprehension as he realized the necromancer was about to cast a spell. He hoped it would be something Eider could dodge.

Then So-Kehur lurched off balance, and Gaedynn saw that the tentacle that had gripped Khouryn no longer had anyone at the end of it. The dwarf had evidently come to, freed himself, scrambled back under the scorpion, and resumed chopping at the legs.

No longer mind-bound, Jhesrhi brandished her staff and cried words of power. The wind howled and threw stones. The big opal eyes in So-Kehur's mask shattered.

Spearmen shouted and advanced, weapons jabbing, and So-Kehur wheeled and scuttled away. Gaedynn started to pursue, but a zombie owl as big as Eider swooped down at him, and he had to fight it instead.

•• •• •• •• •• •• •• •• •• •• •• •• •• ••

Szass Tam smashed down on the mountaintop, then immediately tried to rise. Bareris shouted, Aoth hurled a crackling lightningbolt from the point of his spear, and Mirror drew a pulse of searing light from his sword. One of the zulkirs caught the lich in a booming blast of flame, and another—Samas Kul, presumably, although Bareris would have had to look around to be certain—turned the ground under him into sucking liquid tar.

Assailed by so much magic all at the same instant, Szass Tam nearly vanished in the flash. When it faded, his robes were charred and shredded, and so was his flesh, portions stripped entirely to reveal the bone beneath.

Yet he still moved as though his muscles and organs had merely been a mask whose loss failed to hinder him in the slightest. He planted the butt of his shadowy staff on top of the tar, heaved his feet up out of the sticky mass just as if his prop were made of solid matter, then turned the ground to rocky earth again. He pulled off a scrap of loose, blackened flesh dangling over his left eye and raised his staff above his head.

He surely meant to conjure with the staff, but a hyena-headed demon twice as tall as a man charged him and struck down at him with a greataxe, and he had to use the implement to parry. A floating thing like the shadow of a jellyfish followed just behind the brute with the axe, and then several other creatures, all of them equally grotesque, appeared. Plainly, Nevron had no intention of allowing Szass Tam to cast spells without interference.

And Bareris couldn't bear to let the familiars tear at the lich while he stood back. He sprinted toward the knot of struggling figures, and Mirror bounded after him. Aoth cursed as though he thought the two of them were doing something stupid, and maybe they were. But it was impossible to care.

Moments later, something rustled over Bareris's head. He glanced up and saw Aoth and Jet flying toward Szass Tam and the demons. The warmage evidently hoped height would give him a clear shot at their foe.

Bareris and Mirror dashed up to the circle of roaring, flailing demons. The ghost's lack of a solid form allowed him to slip through the press without so much as a pause. But Bareris had to halt mere strides away from the action.

He shivered with the mad urge to cut down one of demons just to clear a path. Then the hyena-headed giant reeled backward. Its eyes were on fire, and snakes had grown out of its chest and were biting it repeatedly. Its huge axe floated in the air, hacking at those opponents who tried to come at Szass Tam from behind.

Bareris lunged into the space the blinded demon had vacated. Singing a song of hate, he cut at Szass Tam's chest.

The blow glanced off. Szass Tam thrust his staff at his new attacker. Darkness stabbed from his eyes into Bareris's head. For a moment, Bareris couldn't see or think. But he still felt the exaltation of his rage, and when it ebbed, his battle anthem brought it surging back, and it broke the grip of the confusion.

He cut again, and again failed to pierce Szass Tam's armoring enchantments. The necromancer whispered words of power, and some of the demons pivoted to attack their fellows. He waved his hand, a ruby ring on a withered finger flashed, and a dozen wounds split the hulking body of a furry, gray-black, bat-winged creature as though invisible blades had hacked it from the inside. A flourish of the shadow staff made darkness seethe and divide into manlike silhouettes.

Bareris felt a sudden pang of fear that, though it scarcely seemed possible, he and all his formidable allies were going to lose. Then Mirror lunged and plunged his insubstantial sword through Szass Tam's body.

At first Szass Tam scarcely seemed to feel the violation. Then both the blade and Mirror himself flared, bright as the sun, and the lich cried out.

Bareris had seen his comrade channel the power of his god before, but never so much of it, because it was dangerous. No matter how worthy a champion Mirror might be, no matter how faithfully he adhered to his ancient code of chivalry, the divine light was inherently antithetical to his undead condition.

And equally poisonous to Bareris. The radiance burned him even though he wasn't the target. It might do worse if he dared step any closer.

But he didn't care about that, either. All that mattered was that Szass Tam stood transfixed and vulnerable. Singing, he hurled himself at the lich.

The light was agony, but the pain didn't balk him. Rather, it seemed to feed his fury. He cut and cut, and the strokes plunged deep into Szass Tam's body, cleaving what remained of his flesh and splintering bone.

Until the radiance died. Bareris looked and saw that Mirror had simply disappeared, like a flame that had burned out.

Bareris felt a pang of grief. Then skeletal fingers grabbed him by the neck.

"He's gone to his god," Szass Tam croaked. "You go to your woman."

The lich's fingers simultaneously cut and pulled. Bareris felt tearing pain, a nauseating whirl of vertigo as his head tumbled free of his body, and then nothing more.

•• •• •• •• •• •• •• •• •• •• •• •• •• •• ••

His tongue smarting because he'd chewed it during his seizure, Chumed put his foot in the stirrup. But before he could hoist himself onto his charger, he spotted So-Kehur scuttling toward him though the confusion of other warriors in retreat and the reserves trying to push their way forward against the tide.

From the looks of it, So-Kehur's scorpion body had taken a considerable beating. Chumed tried not to feel too pleased about it. That sort of spite could be dangerous, given that the lord he served possessed psychic sensitivities.

"Did you see?" So-Kehur cried. He spoke as if he no longer even remembered striking Chumed down.

"No, Milord. I was . . . indisposed until just a few moments ago."

"I almost killed Lallara herself! I had her in my grip!"

Almost. The boast of the weak and stupid.

"I wish I had seen it," Chumed said. "But I have tried to assess the overall progress of the battle, and it appears to me that our assault isn't breaking the stalemate. For that reason, I still advise—"

"Where are my artisans? I need new eyes, a patch, and any other repairs they can make quickly. Artisans!" So-Kehur lowered himself onto his belly, no doubt so the craftsmen could reach his upper surfaces. He had a breach between two of the plates on the back of his head.

"Do I take it that you plan to rush back into battle?" Chumed asked.

"Of course!" So-Kehur said.

"Of course." Chumed clambered onto the autharch's back.

One of So-Kehur's remaining eyestalks twisted its optic in his direction. "What in the name of the Black Hand are you doing?" the necromancer asked.

"I see a broken piece dangling. If I pull it free, that will save the artisans a moment."

"Oh. Well, in that case—"

Chumed whipped his sword from its scabbard and thrust the point into the gap between the plates. The blade punched into the silver egg housing So-Kehur's brain.

The scorpion-thing convulsed. Chumed leaped off its back. A flailing tentacle missed him by a hair, and then he landed. Awkwardly. Momentum hurled him to one knee.

He sensed the huge steel body rolling toward him. He scrambled up, ran, lunged out from under it just in time to avoid being crushed, then turned to see what it would do next.

It gave a rattling, clattering shudder, then lay inert.

Other officers had come hurrying to attend So-Kehur. Now they stood frozen, gaping at their master's body and his killer.

Chumed raked them with a glower. "I'm in command now," he said. "Does anyone dispute that?"

Apparently, no one did.

"Then pull our men back! Move!"

For a heartbeat or two, Aoth clung to hope. After all, he'd more than once seen Mirror wither to the verge of nonexistence only to reappear. And after becoming undead, Tammith had twice survived decapitation.

But this time the ghost had vanished so utterly that not even spellscarred eyes could spot a trace of him, and dark wet patches cut through the bone white flesh of Bareris's severed head and body as ninety years' worth of deferred corruption flowered in an instant.

Anguished, Aoth realized that at least his friends' deaths freed him to hurl his most potent spells at Szass Tam without fear of hitting them as well. He didn't care about Nevron's remaining demons, because they no longer posed a threat to the lich. It was all they could do to fight the fiends that had fallen under Szass Tam's control and the phantoms he'd shaped from the fabric of the night.

Aoth aimed his spear and rained gouts of fire down on the necromancer's head. The zulkirs hurled flares of their own power.

The magic tore the demons apart and seared the shadows from existence. It reduced Szass Tam to little more than a blackened skeleton, but a skeleton who kept his balance at the heart of the blast.

His rings, amulets, and other talismans glowing with crimson light, Szass Tam turned his empty orbits on Samas Kul. The lich brandished the shadow staff, and a huge pair of fanged jaws appeared in the air in front of his former ally. The apparition shot forward, caught Samas in its jagged teeth, and chewed him to bloody pieces, all so quickly that the fat transmuter only had time for a single, truncated squeal.

Aoth conjured a flying sword to hurtle down at Szass Tam, who somehow sensed it coming, parried it with his staff, and dissolved it without even bothering to glance upward. An instant later, another fiery blast cast by one of the zulkirs rocked the lich. It tore away some of his ribs, but that didn't seem to trouble him, either.

He stared at Lauzoril. *"You* fall," he said, the words clear even though his lips had burned away. "All the way to the bottom."

Lauzoril's face twisted, and he shuddered. Then he turned, ran, and hurled himself over the edge of the cliff.

Nevron finished snarling an incantation. A goristro, a demon somewhat resembling a colossal minotaur, appeared in front of him. Running on its hind feet and the knuckles of its hands, it instantly charged Szass Tam.

The lich pointed his staff and spoke a word of power. The demon turned to glass and, off balance, toppled. It shattered with a prodigious crash.

Nevron started another incantation. Szass Tam turned his fleshless hand palm up and made a clutching gesture. The demon master fell, and a second Nevron, made of insubstantial phosphorescence, appeared standing over the body. For once, he didn't look angry or contemptuous but astonished.

Szass Tam recited rhyming words, and Nevron's ghost shrank into a pudgy creature only half as tall, with grubs wriggling in its open sores. Aoth just had time to recognize it as a mane, the weakest and lowliest form of demon, slave to every other. Then it vanished, probably to the Abyss.

Lallara whispered, and a wall of rainbows shimmered into being between Szass Tam and herself. "On further consideration," she panted, "I do wish to take advantage of the truce you offered."

Szass Tam laughed. "Sorry, Your Omnipotence. But you and your allies insisted on this fight, and now I intend to finish it. There aren't going to be any more zulkirs in exile to plot against me."

He hurled a ragged burst of shadow. The rippling colors in Lallara's barrier grayed when it splashed against them, and then their brightness blazed anew.

Grimly aware that there was hardly any power left in it, or in him, for that matter, Aoth aimed his spear to hurl a lightningbolt. Lallara glanced up at him. "Come here," she said.

"My attack spells won't pass through your wall," he said.

"Now!" she snapped.

Maybe she had a plan. He sent Jet winging in her direction. Meanwhile, Szass Tam hurled another murky blast against the shield. This time, it took longer for the colors to reassert themselves, and when they did, they were softer than before.

Jet and Aoth swooped over the failing defense and landed by Lallara. Despite its sagging wrinkles, her crone's face looked taut with strain.

"What do we do?" asked Aoth.

She reached in a pocket, extracted a silver ring, and tossed it to him. As soon as he caught it, he felt the nature of the spell stored inside it. Under normal circumstances, it would enable the user to translate himself and a companion or two through space.

"Will this work now?" he asked. Maybe she'd figured out that with Malark's crystal diadem and staff broken, it would.

"We couldn't win," Lallara gritted, "even if it did. But I've spent my life afflicted with idiots and incompetents, and you were never either. Go live if you can." Szass Tam threw his power at the wall of light, staining and muting the colors, and cracks of inky darkness snaked through them. Lallara cried out as though she herself were breaking and stamped the butt of her staff against the ground.

The world seemed to fly apart, then instantly reform. Aoth and Jet found themselves still under a black sky, but one with more stars shining in it. They still perched on a high place, but a smaller one, with merlons running along the edge and other towers rising beyond. Lallara had evidently observed how to open the door between realities when Szass Tam did it, and she used the knowledge to return her surviving allies to the roof of the Citadel's central keep.

Aoth felt a clench of anger. Given the choice, he wouldn't have abandoned her.

Yet underlying the anger was a guilty relief that he had no idea how to return himself to the battlefield, for after all, she was right. They had no hope of beating Szass Tam. Maybe at the start of the fight it had been otherwise, but then the scales tipped against them.

"What now?" asked Jet.

"Fly out over the city," said Aoth. "The direction doesn't matter."

Once they passed beyond the confines of the castle and its wards, he invoked the magic of the ring.

The world shattered and reassembled itself yet again, and then he and the griffon were soaring above the gleaming black expanse of the Lapendrar. They flew west, over the ranks of their own army, and saw that the autharch's host was withdrawing.

Aoth felt some of the tension drain out of his body. This battle at least appeared to have gone about as well as anyone could have expected. Now, if only Szass Tam didn't come after him!

And in fact, when he peered around, he couldn't see any sign of such a pursuit. He supposed it made sense. He and his companions hadn't succeeded in destroying the lich, but surely they'd hurt him badly enough to make him think twice about starting a new fight with an entire army, spent and bloodied though it was. Especially considering that, as he'd made plain, it was the zulkirs he chiefly wanted to kill.

Aoth surveyed the ground and spotted Jhesrhi, Khouryn, and Gaedynn standing together. Responding to his unspoken desire, Jet furled his wings to land beside them.

Gaedynn grinned at the new arrivals. "You missed all the excitement."

Aoth dredged up a smile of his own. "Well, maybe not all of it."

epilogue

The Feast of the Moon
28 Nightal, The Year of the Dark Circle (1478 DR)

Earlier that night, processions had wound through the streets of Lyrabar, the participants singing hymns as they went to visit their dead. But when Aoth pushed open the squeaking wrought-iron gate to the dilapidated little graveyard, he saw that here at least, people had already said their prayers, cried their tears, left their offerings, and departed. Some of the votive candles were still flickering, although a chill autumn breeze was blowing them out one and two at a time.

Aoth spotted a weather-stained limestone bench and flopped on top of it. He pulled the cork from the jug he'd brought with him, took a swig, and savored the burn as the cheap brandy went down.

He'd succeeded in extricating what remained of the Brotherhood and the council's legions from Thay without the necessity of another battle, only to find that it didn't earn him an excess of gratitude back in the Wizard's Reach. He supposed he understood. If one chose to look at it uncharitably, he'd gotten all four zulkirs killed and the expeditionary force decimated. And aside from some plunder, all anyone had to show for it was his assurance that the venture had neutralized a threat many people never credited or comprehended in the first place.

In truth, he wouldn't have wanted to stay in the Reach even if the remaining Red Wizards had offered to extend his contract. With the zulkirs dead, a struggle for supremacy began, and that, combined with the damage to the legions, was likely to deliver the realm into the hands of Aglarond within a year or two. He saw little point in trying to stem the tide.

So, by dint of threat, he'd extracted as much money from the archmages' heirs as he could—about half of what Lallara and her peers had promised—and accepted an offer of employment from the Grand Council of Impiltur, where even a sadly diminished sellsword company could earn its keep by chasing brigands and covens of demon-worshippers.

And the seasons turned, and the Feast of the Moon arrived. The Brothers of the Griffon couldn't visit the resting places of their dead—the graves and pyres were scattered across the East— so they sat around their campfires trading memories of the fallen and drinking to them too.

Aoth remained with the celebration for a while. But gradually he realized he wanted to remember comrades whom, he imagined, only he mourned. Accordingly, he took his leave and, weaving a trifle, wandered in search of a place where he could be alone. The graveyard looked like it would do.

By the Black Flame, he missed Bareris and Mirror! He could only pray that true death was treating them more kindly than undeath ever had.

To his surprise, he realized he even missed the zulkirs. They'd been heartless and tyrannical, but his service to them had made him the man he was, and in the end, they'd given their lives to foil the designs of a far greater monster than themselves.

He likewise mourned the Thay of his youth, so green and rich and proud. Now, though towns and farms remained, it was in large measure a haunted wasteland, and the vilest haunters were the very lords Szass Tam had raised up to rule over the living. These masters oppressed them mercilessly and tortured and killed them merely for their sport.

A hand settled gingerly on Aoth's shoulder. Startled, he looked around. Jhesrhi had come up behind him, and Khouryn, Gaedynn, and Jet stood behind her. The griffon's crimson eyes gleamed in the dark.

Since Aoth knew how Jhesrhi hated to touch or be touched, her gesture moved him. He wanted to cover her fingers with his own but knew that would only make the contact even more unpleasant for her.

"We grieve for Bareris and Mirror too," she said.

"Yes," Khouryn said. "Undead or not, they were all right."

"They saved my life more times than I can count," said Aoth. "Who knows, at the end, maybe they saved everybody's life."

"So let's drink to them," said Gaedynn. "Unless you really would rather do it alone."

"No." Aoth raised the jug in a salute, took another swig, then handed it to Jhesrhi.

As they drained the liquor, Aoth felt his spirits lift. Surely, if there was any justice at all in the universe—an open question, but still—Bareris and Tammith were together, and Mirror sat at the right hand of his god.

Aoth himself was still alive and still possessed of staunch friends. He'd tarnished his hard-earned reputation, and the company he'd spent decades building was a shadow of its former self, but so what? He'd just have to build them again.

Khouryn tilted the jug until it was nearly upside down.

Aoth stood up. "If that one's empty, let's go find another."

•• •• •• •• •• •• •• •• •• •• •• •• •• ••

Szass Tam floated between the mountaintop and the black, all-but-starless sky and chanted. The Dread Rings fed him power of a sort, and he tried doggedly to shape it into the proper configurations. Invariably, it dissolved within his grasp, and eventually he concluded it always would.

As he drifted to the ground, he felt an urge to take his newly fashioned crystal staff and hit something. But he realized the impulse was childish and unworthy of him. Especially since he'd known before he started that Thay was no longer capable of providing the energies required for the Unmaking.

It was just that there was a difference between the knowledge derived from study and analysis and that obtained through direct experience. The former was occasionally mistaken, the latter, never, and so he'd deemed it worthwhile to conduct the experiment. Now that he had, he understood what he had to do.

He had nine hundred years left before Bane would return to enforce the terms of their bargain and carry him off into servitude. Plenty of time to strengthen his legions, conquer a neighboring realm or two, and construct a new system of Dread Rings.

Plenty of time, but that was no reason to put off getting started. His stride was brisk as he stepped from the mountain onto the apex of the Citadel.

simbarchs of aglarond

Ertrel
Seriadne

personages of thay

IN THE REGENCY

Arizima Nathandem, a rebel leader in the Citadel

Bareris Anskuld, a bard, ally to the rebels

Chumed Shapret, seneschal of Anhaurz

Malark Springhill, a zulkir

Mirror, a ghost, ally to the rebels

Muthoth, an officer in the service of Sylora Salm

So-Kehur, autharch of Anhaurz

Szass Tam, the regent

Sylora Salm, tharchion of Eltabbar

Tsagoth, a blood fiend bound to the service of Szass Tam

ZULKIRS OF THE WIZARD'S REACH

Lallara

Lauzoril

Nevron

Samas Kul

THE BROTHERHOOD OF THE GRIFFON

Aoth Fezim, captain of the Brotherhood of the Griffon

Gaedynn Ulraes, Aoth's master of bowmen, scouts, and
   skirmishers

Jhesrhi Coldcreek, Aoth's chief wizard

Khouryn Skulldark, Aoth's aide-de-camp and master of
   heavy infantry, artillery, and siege craft

FORGOTTEN REALMS®

Ed Greenwood Presents

Waterdeep

BLACKSTAFF TOWER
STEVEN SCHEND

MISTSHORE
JALEIGH JOHNSON

DOWNSHADOW
ERIK SCOTT DE BIE
APRIL 2009

CITY OF THE DEAD
ROSEMARY JONES
JUNE 2009

THE GOD CATCHER
ERIN EVANS
FEBRUARY 2010

CIRCLE OF SKULLS
JAMES P. DAVIS
JUNE 2010

Explore the City of Splendors through the eyes of authors
hand-picked by FORGOTTEN REALMS world creator Ed Greenwood.

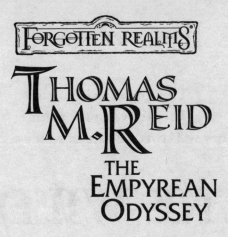

FORGOTTEN REALMS

THOMAS M. REID

THE EMPYREAN ODYSSEY

What could bring a demon to the gates of heaven?

Book I
The Gossamer Plain

Book II
The Fractured Sky

Book III
The Crystal Mountain
July 2009

What could bring heaven to the depths of hell?

"Reid is proving himself to be one of the best up and coming authors in the FORGOTTEN REALMS universe."
—fantasy-fan.org

They engulf civilizations.
They thrive on the fallen.
They will cover all trace of your passing.

THE WILDS

THE FANGED CROWN
Jenna Helland

THE RESTLESS SHORE
James P. Davis
May 2009

THE EDGE OF CHAOS
Jak Koke
August 2009

WRATH OF THE BLUE LADY
Mel Odom
December 2009